Books by Terri Lynn Wilhelm

Storm Prince
A Hidden Magic
Fool of Hearts
Shadow Prince

Published by HarperPaperbacks

Storm Prince

TERRI LYNN WILHELM

HarperPaperbacks
A Division of HarperCollinsPublishers

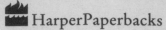

HarperPaperbacks

A Division of HarperCollins*Publishers*
10 East 53rd Street, New York, N.Y. 10022-5299

This is a work of fiction. The characters, incidents, and dialogues are products of the author's imagination and are not to be construed as real. Any resemblance to actual events or persons, living or dead, is entirely coincidental.

ISBN 0-06-108384-4

HarperCollins®, ██®, HarperMonogram®, and HarperPaperbacks™, are trademarks of HarperCollins*Publishers,* Inc.

HarperPaperbacks may be purchased for educational, business, or sales promotional use. For information, please write:
Special Markets Department, HarperCollins*Publishers,*
10 East 53rd Street, New York, N.Y. 10022-5299.

Cover illustration by Jon Paul

First printing: July 1997

Printed in the United States of America

Visit HarperPaperbacks on the World Wide Web at
http://www.harpercollins.com

❖ 10 9 8 7 6 5 4 3 2 1

For Gregory Lynn Wilhelm,
my own personal hero,
with all my heart.

*Love is the joy of the good,
the wonder of the wise,
the amazement of the gods.*

—Plato

Prologue

Nature's mighty law is change.
—Robert Burns

1810

He shot through the deep water, sending a glittering shoal of tiny fish veering away. Violet sponge towers clung to rocky outcrops in the canyon walls that rose on either side of him. Flowery anemones dotted the seascape with vivid color. High on the plains above, tall grass undulated in the gentle current.

As he sped by, the firm pressure of cool seawater coursing over his sleek sides, he noticed few of the things that normally delighted him. He had been summoned. His father lay dying.

He spied the entrance to The Citadel ahead of him, its majestic entrance jagged with shimmering crystal. Minutes later, he broke the surface of the water inside the gathering place of his people. Within this enormous, air-filled cavern, and the countless smaller ones connecting to it, the young of his clan received many of their lessons. Here was stored the eons of learning his clan had accumulated. Here the sacred ceremonies were performed. Here his father lay, surrounded by the members of the clan he led. They raised their voices in a raucous cacophony of grief.

Torcuil went directly to his father's side, where the chief lay on the stone worn smooth by eons of use. The sight rattled Torcuil. He'd never seen Uisdean of Clan MacCodrum looking so ill. His black eyes were glassy. His usually glossy coat was dull.

Anxiously, Torcuil searched his father's large, stream-lined body for blood or a gaping wound. He found only a recently healed gash that had come of an encounter with a killer whale.

His father's voice whispered weakly in Torcuil's head. *You've come.*

Of course, Father.

Your brother Anndra is here also, came the voice of Torcuil's mother. Torcuil turned his head to see his younger brother. Little more than a pup, Anndra pressed close to their mother.

Emotion churned in Torcuil's chest. He'd never seen his father like this. It frightened him.

I wish I could see Eideard one last time before I pass to the Other World, came his father's faint voice.

Eideard, the eldest son. Eideard, the heir. Eideard, their father's favorite.

Torcuil bowed his head, filled with secret, covetous yearning. Always it had been Eideard. Or Anndra. Never Torcuil.

I will find him for you, Father, he promised impulsively, and he felt that the flicker of hope he saw in his father's dark eyes was worth any danger. *I will find him and bring him back to you.*

You are a good son.

The rare words sent Torcuil's spirits soaring. He would seek his brother, and when Eideard heard the tidings of their father's health, he would hurry home. And Torcuil would hear those words again.

The clan rejoiced, and all proclaimed Torcuil a hero. The auguries were consulted. Solemnly, his father and the elders of the clan invested Torcuil with the three necessities for his undertaking. The companions of his youth swam with him through the canyons and across the abysmal plain. As they approached the shore, he bid them farewell and continued on by himself until he reached a familiar point. He swallowed hard.

He didn't want this. The sea was his true home. The blue-green shades of water, the distant glow of volcanoes, the laughter of dolphins. The lives of silkies were irrevocably intertwined with these things.

But he'd made a promise to his father.

Torcuil closed his eyes and concentrated. As he'd been taught to do since childhood, he drew on the power of the wind and the sea. Deep within him, energy hummed, warm and magical.

The Change began.

1

*The longest part of the journey is said to be
the passing of the gate.*
—Marcus Terentius Varro

A naked man rose from the storm-churned sea along the Scottish coast. Tall, broad-shouldered and lean, Torcuil moved with a sure, unconscious grace. His long hair clung to his neck, to his smooth shoulders and back. A pouch slapped against one slim hip, suspended from a sharkskin belt around his waist. At the other hip rode a sheathed long knife.

Lightning slashed across the black sky, dazzling the dark water with shots of silver. Seconds later the deep bass of thunder rumbled out over the Atlantic Ocean.

Squinting against the violent rain, he deftly avoided being crushed against the jagged rocks as murderous waves hammered the cliffs. Seething foam and inky water submerged the swath of flinty beach in this isolated cove where, for years, he had practiced the use of knives, pistols, and swords with his father and uncles. He no longer noticed the sharp stones beneath the toughened soles of his feet.

Torcuil easily found the steep, narrow path from the beach that he'd seen fishermen use on rare occasions. It was a path he had never before taken.

As he climbed the slippery rock, he felt a grudging admiration for the fine dexterity of his arms and hands, for the mobility his legs and feet gave him. They were near-useless in the ocean. The ocean he'd never wanted to leave. The ocean that now dropped farther below him with each step.

When he neared the top and saw how far he'd come from the sea, an unexpected wave of dizziness sent him clawing for a grip on the tufts of grass that lined the rim of the cliff. For long minutes he stayed there, panting, fighting down a surge of panic as the rain poured off his nose and chin. He had to do this, he told himself, appalled at his craven behavior. He *had* to.

Gritting his teeth, he scrambled to safety. He crushed the urge to look back and swung in the direction given him by Uncle Coinneach—and abruptly halted, stunned by the sight before him.

Land, as far as the eye could see. Land stretching out in every direction but the one behind him. Not merely a stretch of beach, a small island, or a hillock of stone jutting from the sea, favorite basking places of terns and seals. No, here was a vista of rolling, stone-studded, solid land.

Torcuil's heart hammered as he faced this storm-cursed scape of the unknown. His eyes took in unfamiliar details that seemed to have been drawn by a sparing hand. Rain-beaten grass, stunted shrubs, and wind-gnarled trees, broken only by the ribbon of dirt he recognized from his father's description as a road. All he had to guide him in his quest was a clue several gale seasons old and the youthful memories of his elderly kinsmen. The folk that walked this land were violent and lacked the strong sense of justice his own people possessed. Even the golden glow of time since his father and many of his uncles had come here had not succeeded in mellowing some recollections. Grim recollections of betrayal and murder bobbed like thorny blowfish on a current of pleasant memories, released for his protection.

But memories were not all he'd been given for his safety. Automatically, his hand went to the hilt of his long knife. From childhood, he'd been taught by the most skilled warriors of his clan. With caution and perhaps a bit of luck, he'd survive this alien world and find Eideard.

Squaring his shoulders, Torcuil strode over the uneven ground to the road, then headed south. He squinted against the rain as he searched for the cottage belonging to the woman who would give him clothes for a service rendered.

Clothes, he knew, were a requirement here. Several of his uncles had told him of this female who would see him clothed. She had a particular fondness for the men of Clan MacCodrum. Always the telling of this fact had been accompanied by a sly wink and a chuckle, leaving him to draw his own conclusions as to the particular service she might require of him.

He walked on determinedly. With the moon hidden behind a thick layer of clouds, it was difficult to tell the passing of the time. Rain continued unabated, and the road turned to slippery mud that sucked at his bare feet until he decided to walk along the side, which was paved with clumps of wild grass, weeds, and stones. Across the dreary landscape, no beast or man stirred.

When he caught sight of a low building set some small distance from the road, Torcuil's heart began to pound again. The first step in his quest.

He approached cautiously. The animal pens were empty and neglected. He frowned as he realized there was no light in the cottage and that a portion of the thatched roof had caved in. The wind banged open the sagging door, and he jumped nervously. Sliding his knife from its sheath, he circled closer. After several seconds he picked up a small rock and tossed it inside. It rattled against the wall. Nothing else stirred.

Where was she? Was this the right cottage? It certainly didn't fit the descriptions of the snug, well-kept hut he'd been given. Yet no one had mentioned any other building between the woman's place and the strand he'd left behind. Fervently hoping this shambles belonged to some other land creeper, Torcuil drew closer. Unable to resist his curiosity, he ran his palm over the stacked stones that formed a wall. It was rough to the touch.

With mounting apprehension, he studied the moldering roof and the collapsing fireplace. Then his eyes caught the crudely carved shapes of seals set in a row whittled into the lintel over the door. Anxiety twisted in his belly. There could be no doubt.

This was her cottage.

From the condition of things, no one had lived here for a long time. It seemed those lusty memories so treasured by his elder kinsmen were older than they realized.

Which left Torcuil naked among the land folk. Naked, and therefore conspicuous.

The last thing he wanted to be among a people known for their unreasoning violence was conspicuous. Actually, he didn't wish to be among them at all. All silkies knew land creepers were treacherous barbarians who enjoyed murdering the magic in the world. They could be cunning, even intelligent at times. That's what made them so dangerous.

He looked around inside as he considered his predicament. His father and uncles certainly couldn't have known she would be gone. These were grim times for his people, and only one MacCodrum had ventured away from the clan in many years. He had not returned.

Torcuil sheltered under the remaining roof as he tried to formulate a plan on how to proceed. There were no clothes for him here. No food. Only a leaking cover. He wrinkled his nose against the stale, mildewed stink. Then a strange, prickling glimmer flowed under his skin.

" 'Tis a night to stay home," said a gravelly voice next to him.

Torcuil whipped around to find a small, thin, elderly man with a long white beard sitting cross-legged next to him. In front of the intruder lay a pile of dried twigs surrounded by stones fallen from the fireplace.

Torcuil's hand edged toward his knife. "How did you get here? My hearing is good, but I heard nothing."

The little man waved his hand dismissively. "Och, be at ease. I mean ye no harm. Besides"—his blue eyes twinkled—"what could a wee fellow such as myself do to a strapping lad like you?"

Torcuil scowled. "Poison comes in wee packages."

The white-beard flicked his fingers and a fire sprang up in the twigs. Torcuil drew back. He'd heard of the stuff, but before this moment had never seen it. Warmth touched his skin where it faced the flames. Fascinated, he eased a little closer. It felt good on this cold night.

"And what's a young silkie doin' this far on land?"

Alarm rushed up in Torcuil. "How did ye know?"

The man smiled. "That ye're a silkie?" His smile widened. "I'm the broonie, and a fine broonie I'd be if I couldna spot a silkie or a faery. I sense the glamour about ye that ordinary men or women lack. Can ye no feel that thrummin' under your skin?"

The broonie! Torcuil had heard of "the wee fellow" who could take any form, but usually chose that of a beggar. People who were kind to a beggar were likely to be kind to anyone. But those who were stingy and turned him away— well, they were not good at heart. For their own sakes, the broonie taught them a lesson. Torcuil nodded.

"That's my glamour," the broonie said. "It surrounds each of us descended from the ancient ones, the ones about whom the legends were told and glorious songs sung. The first fair folk. Och, but all that seems to be forgotten now. Land folk think they know all there is to know. 'Tis arrogant they are." He cocked his head as he studied Torcuil. "I've no seen a silkie for many a year. I'd wondered if there were any left."

"Aye, but one clan only."

"Dinna tell me, let me guess." The broonie's eyes crinkled at their corners. "That clan would be the MacCodrums, am I right?"

Torcuil grinned, pleased. "Ye are indeed. How did ye guess?"

The broonie chuckled. "Even when I was a lad, a hundred summers ago, Clan MacCodrum were the most powerful of all the silkie clans. A stubborn lot they were. Stubborn and fierce and loyal. If anyone could survive this miserable age of man, it would be the MacCodrums. They always had a strange affection for 'em. The men and women, and especially the children, who dwelled along the coast of MacCodrum territory ever prospered, more than other folk. I never knew one to harm a seal, either. Never knew when one might be a silkie. So"—the broonie held his thin hands out to the warmth of the small fire— "what happened to the other silkie clans?"

Torcuil pushed away the rage that came with memories. "The MacNasligeans were murdered by a mob o' fishermen down the coast, who slaughtered every seal they could find, believin' they stole fish from the nets. The survivors—a few females and their bairns—went to the MacTuinns, who later chose to move far away from the land creepers. Their chief came to bid my father good-bye. They went to find a new place. Other clans perished by harpoon and poison. The MacCodrums are the only clan left here. Even we are no so numerous as once we were. My father, my uncles, and their mates, they miss goin' among the land creepers. They have a kind of love for them, I think. Perhaps there was once more of a respect between men and other creatures than there is now. I canna say. All I know is that I dinna wish to take my man shape. I would have been happy to remain as I was. But I must find my brother, Eideard. He came here two years ago, and now he must return."

"He is yer father's heir?"

"Aye. He thought it fitting that he learn more about land folk, that our clan's growin' ignorance of men, of their ways, which have changed, was a danger to us all." Torcuil cautiously extended his finger toward the dancing golden light. He'd never seen fire this close up, never felt its heat.

"Mayhap he's right. Two years, ye say?"

"Aye." A flame danced up to lick his finger, startling a grunt of pain from him. He snatched back his hand and glared at the fire.

"I take it ye've no experience with fire," the broonie said as he fed in another dry twig, which seemed to have appeared from nowhere.

"Before now, I've had no use for it," Torcuil replied peevishly. He wished he still had no use for the stuff, but despite his throbbing finger, he had to admit the warmth the fire brought was welcome. Curse men and their paltry weaknesses!

"Where is yer brother now?" the broonie asked.

"I canna say. The last we heard, he had made his way

to a place called London, but that was over a year ago. Still, I've no other clues, so to London I must go."

"Och, I've heard London is a terrible place. Full of greed and lechery. A foul-smellin' hole no self-respectin' silkie would stay in for long. Be watchful, lad." The broonie eyed Torcuil. "And be clothed. Where are yer breeches? Yer shirt and coat? A fine thing when a father sends his son out amongst mankind wi' no more than a belt, a knife, and his hood."

Torcuil noted the texture of the smooth blue cloth that covered the broonie's hips and thighs. "These are breeches, then?"

"They are."

"I thought ye went among men as a beggar."

The broonie sat up straight. "I do. But I'm not among men now, am I?"

"I dinna mean to insult ye," Torcuil said hastily, unwilling to offend the only friendly face, indeed the only face he'd seen at all, in this strange new world. "'Tis only that it looks so smooth. Do beggars wear such breeches?"

"Nay. Beggars wear rags. They suffer hunger, cold, and sickness."

"Oh." Torcuil frowned in puzzlement. Why did men allow their kin to go hungry? Perhaps he would never understand land creepers. It seemed they were a breed gone berserk.

"Dinna try to comprehend them, lad, when ye know so little of them. They have good ways as well as the bad."

Torcuil sent the broonie a skeptical glance, but decided his experience with land folk was too limited to debate his companion's statement. Watching and listening to fishermen while unnoticed had helped him to learn to speak their language—one of the several languages he'd mastered—and a few of their customs, but little else. Yet it had seemed to him that the men he'd observed had cared about their families. They'd spoken of their mates and young with a kind of rough affection. Still, it was fishermen like them who had joined to slaughter the MacNasligeans, a clan who'd been ever generous to land folk in the silkie way. Clearly men were dangerous, not to be trusted.

"If ye're determined to hate them, have a care with their women," the broonie said, producing a white clay pipe. "While there are those who are devious and cruel, many are kind and generous." He cocked an eyebrow and poked the air with his unlit pipe. "They're the ones to beware, and no mistake. Such a woman will find a place in yer heart, and ye'll ne'er be free of her. Certain misery for a silkie. Ye'd pine for the sea, but she could no follow ye there."

Torcuil tried to keep his expression solemn, he truly did. He knew it was unspeakably rude not to take the advice of an elder seriously. Or to at least act as if you did. But this—*this* was ludicrous! Mirth rolled up his throat and burst from his lips despite his efforts. Finally, he just threw back his head and gave himself over to laughter. "I do earnestly beg yer pardon, sir. There's *no* possibility of me losin' my heart to a land creeper! Ha!" He shook his head, struggling to bring his hilarity under control. "Who'd be fool enough to have feelin's for any of that low, violent, connivin' breed?" He remembered the bodies of murdered silkies drifting in the water, small fish picking at them. Abruptly his amusement fled. "I hate them," he said, his voice low and raw. "I hate them all."

"Now ye speak as a child, no a man. What experience have ye with 'em?"

"I've seen their handiwork."

The broonie studied Torcuil's set expression for a moment, then shook his head. White locks swayed upon his shoulders. "Ye've much to learn."

There was no use discussing the subject further,

Torcuil thought. They'd never agree. He wanted as little to do with the land creepers as possible.

"Look at ye, lad," the broonie said. "Ye have no clothes. And yer hair. Too long."

"It's caused no difficulties that I've been told of."

"In the country, mayhap, but ye're goin' to London town. Silkies there are as rare as hen's teeth. Indeed, save for yer brother, I've never heard of a silkie leavin' their coastal areas. And ye can be certain that before ye even get to that wicked place ye'll have drawn attention to yerself with yer nakedness and the length of yer hair." The broonie stirred the fire with a twig. "Men now cut their hair so short it barcly touches their ears."

Torcuil's hand went to his hair. "So short?" He tried to envision how that would look. Revulsion sent his fingers curling tightly into the wet mass. "I'll no chop off my hair. A warrior wears his hear long—'tis his pride!"

The broonie sighed. "Aye. Once that was so, in the golden days past."

"I'm no cuttin' my hair," Torcuil repeated. Even Eideard had worn his dark locks long when he'd assumed his man form. A silkie's heritage stretched back into the mists of time, when enchanted warriors had gone into battle with their shining hair streaming down over their shoulders. Only weans had short hair.

The broonie waved a hand. "Then do something with it. Pull it back. Make it less noticeable. Ye're noticeable enough as it is."

"I've been told the woman who lives here—lived here," he corrected, "would give me clothes."

The broonie wrinkled his forehead as he peered into the gloom-filled corners of the half-tumbled-down hovel. "Looks to me as if she's been gone a long time."

"Aye." Which brought Torcuil back to his present dilemma. Nothing would be accomplished while he stayed here. Sitting here, warmed by the fire, talking with the broonie brought him no closer to Eideard. There was no choice to be made. He must go to London, the last place Eideard had been seen.

Reluctant to leave, he turned to the broonie. "Though 'tis pleasant sittin' here, chattin' with ye, sir, I must be on my way."

"So ye're determined to go to London, are ye?"

"I am."

"Och, weel." The broonie's lined, pink-cheeked face broke into a merry smile. "Perhaps we shall meet again some day. If we do, ye may call me Seumus."

"And I am Torcuil MacCodrum of Clan MacCodrum."

"I wish ye well, lad. Have a care."

"Thank ye, sir, I shall."

Torcuil rose to his feet and picked his way across the room. Then he ducked his head and stepped out through the open doorway, into the rain. He strode back to the road, continuing in his original direction. The broonie's words concerning Torcuil's appearance gnawed at him. He'd have to be extremely careful until he could get clothing.

He'd gone only a short way when he heard two loud cracks, like the reports of pistols. Ahead of him in the road, a light shone. Silently, he moved toward it, slanting out into the field to take cover behind a pair of gnarled trees. Though storm clouds concealed the moon and stars, Torcuil had no difficulty in seeing clearly. But land folk, he knew, did not see well in the dark.

His eyes were first drawn to the great, hollow, shell-like object resting on four wheels, and he searched his memory for the word his father had used. Carriage. And just as his father had described, horses, four of them, had been attached to the thing to drag it along. The carriage stood motionless now, its lanterns casting out a hazy net of wan light.

Two men, wearing black masks, sat on horses. They pointed their pistols at an older man and a young female standing near the carriage. Two other men lay sprawled in the mud, unnaturally still.

One of the armed men released the horses from the carriage, gathering their reins in his hand. "Fine beasts," he declared. "Only the best for our marquess."

The other masked man guided his mount closer to the young woman. "Aye," he said. "Only the best. But we'll not leave behind the best mount of all." He leaned down and grabbed her arm. "Climb up in front of me," he ordered.

"No!" she cried as she struggled to free herself from his grip.

"Release her this minute," the older man commanded.

Stealing females was not uncommon among his folk, but always there was at least a tacit agreement between the female and her abductor. He saw no sign of that here. Her frantic resistance and that sharp note of fear in her voice testified that she had no wish to be the masked man's mate. And such cowardly odds. Two men with weapons against an unarmed elder and a girl. It was *wrong*. Torcuil eased his knife from its sheath. Crouched, he quietly moved closer to the group. No one glanced in his direction as they stood in the ring of lantern light.

Grinning, the masked man roughly hauled her up over his horse.

As Torcuil glided forward, the older man rushed toward her assailant. "Unhand her, you—"

The rider's pistol roared, and the elderly man crumpled to the ground.

"Not a bad deal," the rider declared. He slapped the young woman's thigh. "We get you an' the horses, and the toff gets Coristock."

Torcuil sprang at the masked man, dragging him from the saddle. Out of the corner of his eye, he saw the female land with a splash in the mire. He slammed his heel into the back of the masked rider's hand. The man cried out, his fingers jerked in pain. Torcuil shoved the weapon away with the side of his foot. When the masked man dragged a knife from inside his coat with his other hand and lunged it at Torcuil's chest, Torcuil dodged to one side and regretfully split the fellow's throat.

Before he could turn around, he heard another crack of pistol fire, and a bullet hissed by his ear. Torcuil cursed his inattention to the other rider, who now charged directly at him, the mighty hooves of his horse throwing up gobs of mud. The man aimed a second pistol. Torcuil launched himself at the man's unguarded left side, driving his knife up under his attacker's sternum. They tumbled off the horse and struck the sloppy road with bone-jarring force. Brown ooze fountained in all directions.

Through the slits in the black cloth, Torcuil read surprise in the man's eyes. Gradually, the face around them went slack.

The only sounds were Torcuil's heavy breathing and the hammering of the rain. It seemed to echo the hammering of Torcuil's heart as the hot battle blood pounded through his veins. He prized his blade from the man's chest, wiped it on the torn shirt, and slipped the knife back into its sharkskin sheath. Then he walked over to where the girl struggled to wrap her companion's blood-soaked shoulder with a ragged strip of white cloth.

He knelt beside her and, without asking, eased the burden of the man's upper body from her arms so that she could more easily dress his wound. She stared at him, and for the first time, he got a close look at her.

He guessed she was tall for her kind, as she equaled in height the elderly male who had tried to protect her. She

was slim and fine-boned. The hair that peeped from the
sodden head covering was wet, its true color indeter-
minable. Shadows made it impossible to tell the hue of the
wide eyes that regarded him. Her nose was short but
nicely shaped. Her lips were full and soft-looking. Torcuil
supposed that among land folk she would be considered
pretty. Did she stare because she feared him? He smiled,
hoping to put her at ease.

Then he remembered he was naked.

Quickly he snatched the cloak off a dead man and
donned it, tying it by the ribbon at his throat. He took off
his belt, then refastened it over the closed garment.
Immediately, she seemed to lose a little of her tension.

Verity Alford stared at the tall, naked savage who had
burst from the thick darkness of this deluged night to
come to her aid. She had heard the Scots were often
casual in their mode of dress, but she'd never suspected
they might roam about wearing nothing save a belt! And
here he knelt, helping her again.

His long, dripping hair was dark, and there was a
small dip, a perfectly centered V in his forehead hairline.
Arched eyebrows curved over eyes so dark in color as to
appear black. A wide, elegantly cut mouth suddenly
curved up in a smile. If the clouds had suddenly parted
to reveal a host of angels, Verity doubted she would be
more affected.

Abruptly he stood to dress in the cloak of one of the
fallen men, covering all but his head and neck, his bare
arms and legs and feet, removing the temptation to further
sate her unmaidenly curiosity. Not that there was much
she hadn't seen, what with him leaping and lunging and
rolling, bare as the day he'd been born. Well, almost. Few
babes entered the world wearing a belt and sword. But she

couldn't think of what she'd seen now. Her father needed her attention.

Quickly she bent to finish wrapping his wound, hoping the applied pressure would stem the flow of blood. "The bullet went through his shoulder," she told the stranger. "He must see a surgeon very soon or I fear"—her voice broke—"the worst." She cleared her throat, delaying while she composed herself. "He's losing so much blood."

"Och, well, lyin' here in the mud can no be doin' him any good," he said in a deep, lilting baritone. Gently, he scooped her unconscious father into his arms, carried him over to the carriage, and laid him inside on the squabs. "Is there a healer nearby, then?"

A peculiar numbness rolled through her like a heavy fog. "We passed a village a few miles back." Verity looked around blankly. This wasn't like her. She was efficient. Reliable. Her . . . her father needed her. With shaking fingers she tried to retie the mud-soaked ribbons that dangled from her bonnet. Her gaze darted from body to body. Two of the four were men she'd known, servants who had been in her father's employ for a few years.

Suddenly, the enormity of what had just taken place struck her like a blow.

Four men had been killed. Her father had been shot. She'd been assaulted.

Standing there in the sullen rain, Verity began to shake. Her teeth began to chatter.

She felt a coat being wrapped around her. No matter how she tried, she could not stop shaking. The stranger lifted her in his arms and laid her down on the squabs across from her father, his hands arranging her feet so that they were propped up on a leather traveling case, which placed them slightly higher than her head, leaving her in a vastly immodest position. She felt the hem of her muslin gown slip toward her knees, and she struggled to sit up.

"Lie ye still a bit," he said in a low, comforting croon. " 'Tis a terrible thing that's happened here, and no mistake, but ye've been a fine, brave lassie through it all." He sat down on the floor of the carriage, wedged between the two seats, so that their faces were almost level. His long legs hung out of the carriage.

"I-I don't know what's come over me," she stammered. A shudder ran through her body. "I'm u-usually m-much calmer."

His mouth curved in a reassuring smile. "It's shock, ye see. There's no shame in it. I've seen it in some males after a close battle." His long fingers softly stroked a wet curl of her hair back from her cheek.

"But my father—"

"Is sleepin'. The bleedin' has slowed."

"It has?"

He nodded. "Aye."

The bone-deep shudders eased to periodic shivers. "I didn't thank you for saving me."

Color tinged his high, broad cheekbones. "No thanks are needed."

He was blushing! Verity found his modesty charming. "We'll discuss that later. Allow me to introduce myself. I am Lady Verity Alford, and my father is Philip Alford, marquess of Ravenshaw."

"I'm honored to make yer acquaintance, Lady Verity." He inclined his wet head with a regal air that defied his mud-caked appearance. "I am Torcuil MacCodrum, second son of Uisdean, the MacCodrum of Clan MacCodrum."

He spoke as solemnly as if he were announcing royal lineage, and Verity thought she should feel uneasy in the face of such obvious madness. But as she studied his exquisitely formed features and the grace with which he moved, she was struck by the crazy notion that he just might be, if not royal, at least highborn. Why, then, was he cavorting about a storm-driven countryside wearing only a belt?

Was he a disgraced minor son of a noble household?

Or was he an escaped lunatic?

A tiny frisson of anxiety went through her. He was dangerous. She had witnessed for herself his skill with pistol and knife. Perhaps that very boldness with which he fought—as if death did not matter to him—was even a more telling testimony to dementia than his lack of clothing.

Mad or not, he was her father's only hope of survival.

"Enchanté," she murmured, wondering why she didn't feel more worried than she did.

He frowned over her father, who lay so pale and still on the wine-colored velvet squabs. The Scotsman examined the ragged bandage. "I dinna like to move him," he said consideringly, "but the bleedin' hasna fully stopped."

"The horses are gone. Will you go to the village to get help?"

Slowly he shook his head, and her heart sank. It seemed she must make the journey herself, which would mean leaving her father alone, for surely this princely madman did not plan to stay here.

"Nay," Torcuil said, apparently unaware of the direction her thoughts had taken as he carefully wrapped her father in the redingote lying on the cushions. "'Twould take too long. By the time I walked there and returned with help, yer father might well be dead. There's no help for it. I'll have to carry him."

Verity stared at him. "Carry him? Impossible. It's at least three miles to the village." That settled the matter. The fellow was obviously insane.

"Och, he's as light as a scale off a fish," Torcuil announced, despite the fact that anyone could see her father weighed several stones more than a fish's scale.

" 'Tis only that movin' him may hasten the bleedin' a bit. I'll do my best no to jiggle him."

Panicked, she sat up abruptly. Her mind groped for an alternative to Torcuil's proposal. "A tourniquet! We must try a tourniquet."

He gave her an uncertain glance. "Have ye used one before?"

"Well . . . no."

"Nor have I. I've heard ye must judge when to loose and tighten the thing to a fine degree or the result is gangrene. A painful way to die, I'm sure ye'll agree. I dinna think we're so desperate yet. But even as we speak, we could be moving closer to the village and its healer."

Verity had to admit to the truth of what he said. She'd heard the same thing about the use of tourniquets. Besides, assuming she managed not to inflict gangrene on her father, there was still no guarantee the device would stop the bleeding. As little as she liked taking her father out in this awful weather, and as small as her hope was that Torcuil could carry him the miles back to the village, at least Torcuil's way her father stood a chance of survival. The alternative was to let him slowly, surely, bleed to death, for she had seen no other traffic on this isolated road tonight. No other traffic except, of course, two masked men.

She placed her feet on the floor and pulled on her fur-lined cloak. "I'm ready."

With a nod of approval, Torcuil helped her out of the carriage, then stepped back inside to lift her father into his arms. The carriage swayed as he trod down the steps, and as she tucked the collar of the redingote around her unconscious father's throat, she knew that time was their enemy.

She felt certain Torcuil would be unable to carry the

weight of another man all the way to the village. What man could? When he could go no farther, she would finish the distance to the village and bring back help. As far as she could see, it was the only solution.

Rain battered them. Slogging through mud that tugged at her ruined slippers, she removed the carriage's lanterns from their holders, praying the candles would, by some miracle, last until she could reach the village. The light they provided was pitifully little and of no practical use, but even that bit would help to keep their spirits up. If they were lucky, it would be a signal to anyone who might happen along. Unfortunately, the lanterns lacked any handles, which made them awkward to carry.

Torcuil set a brisk pace she found difficult to maintain. How could he move so quickly, so surely in this dreadful darkness, burdened as he was with the weight of a full-grown man? Determined not to slow him down, she kept her head lowered against the downpour and forged ahead.

As she marched beneath the moonless sky, time lost meaning, flowing out beyond her comprehension like an endless river. There was only the driving urgency and the sound of the rain, the ache in her arms as she held up the lanterns, and the increasingly sharp catch in her side.

After what seemed like hours, she was barely managing to keep up with Torcuil, who revealed no signs of fatigue. The wet ground clutched at her feet with each step, succeeding finally in pulling off one of her useless satin shoes. Unwilling to take time to search for it, she trudged on, clenching her teeth at the stab of twigs and pebbles. Now and then Torcuil warned her of a large stone or rabbit hole. At first it amazed her, but as the struggle to keep up continued, and the chill downpour soaked her, she accepted each evidence of his astonishing strength and vision in mute misery.

"Aren't you tired?" she finally gasped out. Surely they had gone at least three miles by now. They must be close to the village.

"A wee bit, perhaps."

"How—" She broke off to drag in sufficient breath. Her bare foot ached. "How do you manage to carry my father so far?"

"I told ye. He's as light as a fish's scale. Did ye no believe me, then?"

"I thought you were making"—she panted for oxygen—"light of the task." He wasn't breathing hard; he wasn't staggering under her father's weight. The man was unnaturally strong. Thank God.

She let the conversation drop, unable to keep it up and breathe, too.

Gradually, the rain eased and slowly drizzled to nothing. She fretted that she had underestimated the miles she and her father had come from the village.

"Let me check him again," she said, wheezing.

Torcuil stopped, and she checked her father's breathing. Though growing shallower, it at least remained even. She couldn't see well enough to check the bleeding. The candles in the cumbersome lanterns had burned away an eternity ago, and she'd abandoned them.

"He's bleedin' a bit heavier," Torcuil admitted, as if he guessed what she looked for. He shifted from one bare foot to the other, gently resettling her father in his arms. "Dinna fear, Lady Verity. He'll make it."

"How do you know?" she asked breathlessly, her voice catching on the sob she'd been trying hard to suppress. "How can you be certain?" She wanted so badly to believe him.

"I can see the village."

She squinted, trying to catch a glimpse, but all she saw was the terrible black night that seemed to have absorbed every trace of light in the universe. "Where?"

" 'Tis no too far now. We'll be there soon."

It seemed much farther than he made it out to be, but before long they walked into the sleeping hamlet. Save for the occasional lantern in a window, it was as dark and as wet as the countryside.

"Where is the healer?" Torcuil asked as he stared around at the black-on-black shadow-buildings. Silence lay over the village.

"I saw an apothecary's shop when we came through here," she said, straining to distinguish the details of the structures she felt sure must be the shops she'd seen earlier. "There was a light in a window. . . ." Urgency and frustration tangled inside her chest. Where was the shop now?

As if by divine signal, a dark cloud drifted away from the moon, spilling pale, silvery light around them.

"There!" She pointed to a window filled with the shadowy figures of jars, bottles, and a large mortar and pestle. Praying that the apothecary lived above his pharmacy, she dredged up her last grains of energy and splashed through puddles and mire to the shop. Hope surged through her, and she pounded on the door. She kept beating on it as Torcuil came to stand beside her, her father gently draped over his arms, cradled against his cloak-covered chest.

Light appeared in a window several feet above their heads. Curtains parted to reveal a man in a skewed nightcap and a plain white nightshirt. He opened the window.

"The shop is closed now, as anyone can plainly see," he informed them querulously, his voice rusty with sleep. "Come back in the morn at a respectable hour."

Verity and Torcuil backed away from the door in order to get a better look at the speaker. "My father has been injured," Verity called up to the man whose sleep she'd disturbed. "We need a physician."

"What?" The thin man peered down. "Och." He sighed. "I'll be down directly."

No more than a minute later, the man, who was of medium height and looked to be in his fifties, opened the shop door to them, setting off a gaily tinkling bell. He wore a dressing gown over his nightshirt now. His feet had been thrust into worn embroidered mules. He held a lamp to light his way.

"Haste, haste, bring him in here," he urged, leading them through the shop to a small, Spartan room with a long, tall table, a desk and chair, and a cabinet filled with myriad small drawers, each neatly labeled with Latin inscriptions. "Lay him on the table. Och, and to be out in a night such as this." He shook his head, clucking his tongue in disapproval. A fringe of carrot-colored hair stuck out under the edge of his tasseled nightcap.

Water poured onto the polished, wood-planked floor as Torcuil eased the marquess onto the table and opened the redingote. The apothecary's eyes widened when he saw the dark stain of blood on the front of the injured man's shoulder.

"The ball passed through," Verity informed him. "We didn't know who to bring him to. Is there a physician in this town?"

"A surgeon-apothecary, and ye've come to him," the man said without looking up. He thrust the lamp at Torcuil, who held it to light the wound.

After a few minutes of examination, the surgeon-apothecary straightened. "Well, the ball made an amazingly clean exit, but I must swab it out so I can fully evaluate the damage." He turned away and moved about the room, going from one drawer to another, scooping dried bits of various substances into a white porcelain mortar. He hurried out the door and was gone but a moment before he returned with a blue-banded earthenware bottle. He set this aside and proceeded to cut away her father's coat, waistcoat, and shirt, until the wound was bared. Without a word, he directed Torcuil's lamp lower, and he bent over, peering into the damage, touching it delicately here and there. Then he pulled the cork stopper from the bottle, releasing into the small room a pungent herbal scent. He moistened a square of muslin cloth with dark greenish brown liquid from the bottle and then swabbed the pale skin surrounding the injury, washing away the gummy buildup of blood. With a fresh piece of cloth, he applied more of the liquid to the wound itself, lacking the gentleness Verity would have preferred.

Her father stirred sharply to consciousness, his breath hissing between clenched teeth. A sound of protest grated in his throat.

Torn between relief at finding him able to respond and the pain of seeing him suffer, Verity leaned close to his ear as she gently stroked his thinning silver-white hair. "You've been shot, Papa," she explained softly, "but your wound is being tended. Rest now, Papa. Sleep." She would worry enough for both of them.

His eyes remained closed, but he tensed at the surgeon-apothecary's probing, and Verity was certain her father must be in agony.

She drew herself up to her full height, trying to ignore the sodden bonnet that lay on her head like a stewed plum. Despite the saturated gown and cloak that dragged at her, she faced the apothecary squarely. "You will not allow him to suffer," she informed him imperiously.

The surgeon-apothecary did not pause in his work. "I dinna like to use laudanum as a first resort. He's better off without it, if he can manage with clove tea. But dinna worrit; I'll no allow him to suffer needlessly."

It occurred to her that she didn't even know his name. "I am Lady Verity Alford, and this is my father, the marquess of Ravenshaw, and Mr. Torcuil MacCodrum," she said. "And you are Mr. . . . ?"

With an evil-looking instrument, he removed a bit of fabric embedded inside her father's shoulder. "MacDougall," he supplied, without moving his gaze from his task. "Walter MacDougall, at yer service. The ball severed a wee vessel."

"Mr. MacDougall, I thank you for your aid."

She stroked her cold fingers over her father's mussed hair, smoothing the white locks back off his lined forehead. A knot of fear tightened in her chest. "He will get well, won't he, Mr. MacDougall?" Her voice rasped through her tight throat.

Torcuil placed his hand on her shoulder, and she looked up into his face and found concern in his dark eyes. His long, tapered fingers and his palm warmed her through her clammy clothes. "'Tis no so terrible a wound, for all the fright it's given ye," he said, his deep voice lilting.

"Listen to the lad," Mr. MacDougall said kindly. "If there's no festerin', yer father will be up like a lark in no time at all."

Verity suddenly felt dizzy with weariness. "Festering?"

"'Tis always a danger, Lady Verity," Mr. MacDougall admitted as he wrapped the cleaned and swabbed area with fresh linen strips. "I'd be remiss if I dinna warn ye."

She waved a dismissive hand, and the effort it cost her surprised her. "I understand about festering, Mr. MacDougall. I've sewn up enough cuts to understand the risk. That's what concerns me."

Mr. MacDougall's bushy, copper-colored eyebrows drew down a little, and his hands paused in their task as he studied Verity more closely.

"She's exhausted," Torcuil said, easing his arm around

her shoulders to provide her a much-needed support. "She's been through much this night, not the least of which was walkin' here."

"Do ye have a place to sleep?" Mr. MacDougall asked.

Verity found herself leaning back into the haven of Torcuil's strong arm and shoulder. The man should be even more weary than she. He'd leaped out of the night, fought two mounted men, then carried her father for miles. . . .

"We've nowhere."

"Is she yer wife, then?"

"No." Verity sighed.

"She's no my mate. I just happened across them," Torcuil said, his arm curling more securely around her. "Set upon by robbers, they were. Their men were murdered."

"And ye? How do ye figure into all this?"

"He saved us," Verity mumbled.

Mr. MacDougall chuckled as he guided Torcuil and Verity out the door. "Och, a hero, are ye?"

"The lass is asleep on her feet." She felt him move, and then she was being lifted into his arms.

"No," she protested feebly. "You've already carried Papa—"

"Whist, now," he murmured to her, and she thought a woman could curl up and feel protected by such a voice. Though the words were quietly spoken, the voice held a power that was as deep, as timeless as the sea.

She forced herself to pay lip service to what she knew was proper. "Please put me down." Even to her ears her request lacked conviction. But she didn't possess the strength to do better.

"Come," Mr. MacDougall said. "My sons are in Portugal with the Seventy-first Highlanders, so I've a couple of spare rooms."

Through the gathering haze of her exhaustion, Verity heard the wistful note in his voice. "I'll pray they return safe to you," she assured him as she rested her cheek against a warm, wall-like chest swathed in a wet wool cloak, and her eyes drifted closed. She sank into sleep listening to the steady beat of Torcuil's heart.

2

I begin to smell a rat.
—Miguel de Cervantes

Torcuil followed the apothecary up a flight of stairs. He wished he had time to examine the steps. He'd only seen them carved into stone before, on the side of the cliff, but here they were constructed of the same stuff used for skiffs and ships.

As they reached the floor above the shop, they were greeted by a woman swathed in billowing white cloth with a cap on her head that brought to Torcuil's mind an image of a beribboned white jellyfish. It was clear to him this woman got her share of prawns and mullet. She was plump and her brown eyes were bright with health.

"My dear!" she whispered loudly as she rushed to hover over Lady Verity Alford, who slept in his arms. "Och, the poor lassie. What happened, Walter?"

"Dinna fret, Emily. She's no been harmed, thanks to the lad, here. He fought off two highwaymen. But her father is downstairs. I just cleaned his bullet wound. He's lost a deal of blood." Quickly he introduced Torcuil to his wife, Emily MacDougall, and went on to ask her to settle their guests for the night while he made arrangements to have the bodies of the slain men and the marquess's carriage brought to the village.

Walter MacDougall hurried away, and his mate led Torcuil to a chamber down the corridor. As he looked about the room, he was glad for the lessons his aunties had given him, starting when he was a pup. The contents of wrecked ships through the ages had been collected by generations of MacCodrums in The Citadel. He recognized the pieces of furniture he saw now in this chamber, though they differed in style, being somewhat less ornamental than most of the beds, chests, and wardrobes in The Citadel.

As Mrs. MacDougall fussed over the bed and its linens and quilts, Torcuil felt oddly aware of the woman he held in his arms. She nestled so trustingly against his chest. Her slim body warmed him through the wet, night-chilled cloth of the cloak that covered him. The lashes of her closed eyes curved against her cheeks. Through her parted lips, her soft breath sighed.

"Lay her down here," Mrs. MacDougall said in a low voice as she patted the bed where she had folded back the covers.

Torcuil shouldered aside blue woolen tester draperies and gently eased her down on the soft mattress. A small frown creased her brow and her lips moved as he slipped his arms away from her, and, for some reason unknown to him, he felt a slight pang of regret. Then Mrs. MacDougall began to unbutton the wet dress. Her fingers stopped on the second button.

"Mr. MacDougall dinna say, but I assumed ye're the lass's man." She raised her eyebrows in question.

Torcuil shook his head. "I came across her and her father only this night."

"Oh! Well, then, I'll just show ye to yer room before I remove the poor thing's wet gown." She quickly lit the bedside candle, lifted hers and hustled him down the hall to a closet, from which she retrieved a rectangle of absorbent cloth, which she handed to him with the simple command, "Dry off." Then she led the way to another chamber, where she lit another candle in a brass holder on the simple bedside table. That done, she pulled back the quilts on a bed that looked much like the one in the other room. She smoothed the linens and lifted what he felt certain must be pillows to beat them. "I have a son about yer age, Mr. MacCodrum."

Torcuil watched with interest as she pummeled the pillow. "Why do ye do that?" he inquired.

His hostess looked at him in surprise. "Why, to shift the feathers, and plump some air into the pillows." She smiled and laid the pillow back in place. "Have ye no e'er seen yer mother or wife plumpin' the pillows, then?"

He'd seen pillows before, in The Citadel, but they hadn't been so light as this. Seawater, it would seem, did not agree with them. "We dinna sleep with pillows."

"No pillows! Och, ye poor lad." She reached up to pat his upper arm, coming, as she did in height, only to the middle of his chest. "Well, ye'll sleep on pillows while ye stay in our house, that ye will," she said, a determined light in her eyes. "Now get ye to sleep and have sweet dreams." She closed the door quietly behind her.

Torcuil went to the bed and inspected it, slipping his fingers over the linens and quilts, and breathing in the unfamiliar scent that struck him as fresh and yet, at the same time, as a sort of warm, if temperature could be a smell. He leaned closer and lightly slapped the pillow, as he had seen Mrs. MacDougall do earlier. It made a soft, satisfying thud as it gave way before his hand, rising up to surround it up to his wrist. He knew land folk laid their heads on pillows as they slept. How did they breathe? Och, he supposed he'd learn soon enough.

By the golden light of the tiny candle flame, Torcuil unbuckled his belt and shucked off the wet cloak. He shivered slightly in the chill of the unheated room, trying to determine what he was expected to do with the garment. Finally, he laid it on the stone hearth of the dark, cold fireplace.

A knock sounded at his door, and he went still, uncertain what was expected of him. Mrs. MacDougall spoke to him from the other side of the barrier.

"Mr. MacCodrum, I've a nightshirt belongin' to my son. He's no so tall or strappin' as yerself, but I thought it might serve ye for the night. I'll just open the door a wee bit and slip it to ye, if ye dinna mind."

Obediently, he took the white cloth shirt from her hand, careful to stand behind the door to protect her eyes from his nakedness. He searched for the correct response to her offering. "Eh . . . thank ye, Mrs. MacDougall."

"I've seen to the lassie. She's warm and dry now, and sleepin' like a bairn."

"Thank ye, Mrs. MacDougall."

"Aye, I thought ye'd like to know. Pleasant dreams." The door closed and the scuffing sound of her slippers on the wood floor gradually faded from hearing.

"Thank ye, Mrs. MacDougall," Torcuil muttered as he held up the shapeless garment for inspection. Did land folk sleep in these things? And if so, why? He frowned in rebellion, resenting the need to smother himself in the useless fathoms of fabric. He wasn't *that* cold. But she had definitely called the thing a "nightshirt," and a shirt, as he knew from stories and lessons, was something a man always wore. This particular shirt was obviously intended to be worn at night.

Grumbling to himself, Torcuil struggled into the treacherous, flapping garment, certain he now knew how a clam must feel when enveloped by a voracious starfish.

It didn't fit. It *couldn't* fit. Surely not even a land creeper would torture himself with this. The tubes for his arms were not long enough. It squeezed his throat, and the bottom edge didn't quite cover his buttocks, and he distinctly remembered warnings from his kinsmen on the etiquette of covering one's backside. And frontside, for that matter. Who could sleep in such a tangle?

With a low growl, he fought his way back out of the nightshirt and cast the offending garment away from him, onto a straight-backed chair near the washstand.

As he stood there, naked in the strange room, fatigue suddenly weighed down on him. His gaze slid slowly over his alien surroundings and he was suddenly seized by a desire to jerk open that door and run, *run* all the way back to the cove, back to his kinsmen and the world he knew.

He called up the memory of moving through the path the crowd of clansmen made for him as he answered their chief's summons. His young brother, Anndra, had lifted his frightened face to Torcuil, dark eyes imploring him to restore order to their universe. And their father, ever so robust and vital, lying so uncharacteristically still and weak.

Instantly, Torcuil's words sprang again to his lips.

I will find him for you, Father. I will find him and bring him back.

He'd found his reward in that easing of the worry he'd seen etched in his father's face. But with every step he'd taken away from the cove, Torcuil had been assailed by second thoughts about his rash pledge. He'd never ventured so far upon land. He had no idea where to find London. If he hadn't been so caught up in the emotional turmoil of the moment, he might have thought to find it on one of the myriad maps preserved in The Citadel.

Very well, he had forgotten one minor detail. He would find London somehow. He would ask the way. Then he would go to London and search for his older brother.

What if . . . what if there was no Eideard left to bring back? Torcuil shook his head in angry denial. Impossible! If Eideard's life had been extinguished, he would have known it immediately. Every silkie related to Eideard would have known it.

A poisonous doubt crept in. What if the land folk possessed the power to conceal a broken blood bond?

Abruptly, Torcuil thrust that thought away. Ridiculous. What did men care of silkie blood bonds? No, Eideard was alive. When he learned their father's condition, he would hasten home.

Torcuil walked heavily to the bed and tentatively sat down on it. It gave slightly under his weight. Burdened with weariness, he swung his legs up and stretched out, allowing his head to sink into the pillow. Cold cloth chilled his cheek and the length of his bare body, yet gradually it warmed. When nothing happened, his muscles eased. The bed's give beneath his weight felt . . . well, strange. Comfortable, but strange. He dragged the thick quilts over him. With a sigh, he surrendered to the land creeper's sleeping place.

As much as he wanted sleep, it eluded Torcuil, lulling him for a short while, then slipping away to leave him staring at the canopy. He missed the sounds of the sea. Here, there were different noises—an occasional creak, a distant barking, the hollow *tock* of the great clock near the front door downstairs. A glance at the window told him the rain had stopped. The full moon shone brightly, shedding silver on dark banks of receding clouds.

He found himself wondering how the marquess and his daughter fared. Was the girl sleepless, too? Did the marquess thrash about from fever? A wound such as that bullet hole could go bad as easily as it could heal.

Kicking back the covers, Torcuil rolled out of the bed, pulled free a quilt, and wrapped it around his hips. Then he eased the door of his chamber open and stepped into the hall. Nothing stirred.

Quietly, he eased into Verity's room. His bare feet moved silently across the floor to the bed where she lay. Beneath the coverlet, her chest rose and fell with the slow regularity of deep sleep. One hand peeked out from the covers, resting on the pillow beside her cheek. Her slender fingers were slightly curled, her slim palm exposed, endowing her with a curiously vulnerable air.

Moonlight gilded her face with strokes of silver satin, touching her forehead, a delicate cheekbone, her full, faintly pouting bottom lip. Short, damp curls framed her face. Torcuil moved closer, feeling strangely drawn to her. With only the moon to light the room, color melted into shades of gray. He resisted the urge to touch her hair. It looked lighter than it had when it had been dripping wet. He took a lock of his own hair between his fingers and found it considerably drier than when he had arrived at the MacDougall house. It didn't curl like hers.

Abruptly, he straightened and turned on his heel. He had no interest in land folk. They were far too unreliable a breed, he told himself as he moved soundlessly down the tenebrous hall, toward the stairs. Devoid of inner magic.

He found the room where the surgeon-apothecary had cleaned the marquess's wound. The marquess still lay upon the high table, though straps bound him in place.

Torcuil leaned over the older man, listening for any irregularity in breathing. The soft, steady sound of normal respiration satisfied him. He checked the bandaging and was relieved to see no sign of further bleeding. But why had he been left here, on this hard wooden table, when there were such comfortable beds in the house? Torcuil frowned at the straps. The sight of them struck an uneasy chord in him. No one, not even a land creeper, should be bound like a netted fish.

He wondered why Mr. MacDougall hadn't removed his patient to one of the beds. As Torcuil frowned down at the straps, he remembered what his host had said. That there were a couple of empty rooms. Not three. Two.

This white-haired elder had been strapped to a hard table while Torcuil had been offered the luxury of a soft bed. It wasn't proper. Quickly, he unfastened the buckles and pushed aside the leather bonds. Carefully scooping the marquess into his arms, Torcuil took him upstairs, where he placed him on the bed he'd earlier vacated. The marquess made a harsh sound in his throat, then turned on his good side and slid back into sound sleep.

Torcuil moved the chair near the washstand closer to the bed, where he could keep an eye on the patient. The marquess might be more comfortable here, but the bed had no straps to keep him from falling if he grew restless. These next several hours would determine whether the wound healed or festered.

Bundling up in his quilt, Torcuil sprawled in the chair and began his vigil, his thoughts returning to his home and his own ailing father.

Upon waking, the first thought in Verity's mind was for her father. The second was that she was wearing an unfamiliar night shift.

In the dark room, she fumbled with the tinderbox her fingers located on the bedside table until she got a flame to take hold on the candle wick. She shivered in the cold.

It had been so late last night when they had arrived, she didn't wonder no servant in this household had been called to lay a fire in the fireplace.

Slipping from the warmth of her covers, she took up the candlestick and quietly left the chamber. As much as it went against her sense of propriety to prowl another's house, she wanted to check on her father. Now, where would he be? The living area above the shop involved this hall and four rooms. One was her chamber. Another would likely belong to Mr. MacDougall and his wife. There was only one open door. She stepped over the threshold. The light from her candle revealed a small sitting room. She worried her bottom lip between the edges of her teeth as she considered what to do next. Her bare toes burrowed into the pile of the Turkey carpet. Coming to a decision, she went back into the hall and padded down the steps.

She found the room where she'd last seen her father. The table where Mr. MacCodrum had lain him and Mr. MacDougall had treated him stood empty now, except for the ends of what she assumed must be restraining straps. Why—?

Instantly, images of her father wild with fever rose up in her mind. Infection! Dear God! Fear for him sent her racing through the rest of the ground-floor rooms, even the kitchen in the back of the house. When she found nothing but a few snoring servants curled deep beneath the blankets in their tiny, Spartan cells, she hurried back upstairs. She opened the first door she came to.

Mr. MacDougall and his wife slept, undisturbed by her visit. She closed the door, then hastened to the last, unexplored chamber.

Inside, the soft glow of her candle illuminated the two still figures. Her father, still wearing the shirt in which he'd left Ramberly, lay on the bed, a quilt and coverlet neatly tucked around him.

Verity tiptoed over to his side. Unlike the fearful specter that had frightened her, he did not perspire, nor did he thrash or moan. She pressed her palm to his forehead, then, content with his temperature, she bent to listen to his breathing. His bandage bore no fresh blood. She breathed a deep sigh of relief. Then she turned her attention to the other sleeping figure.

Torcuil MacCodrum sprawled in his chair, his impressive height and breadth of shoulders dwarfing that piece of furniture. The glow from her candle revealed that his tangled dark hair came almost to his waist. The evident depth of his slumber encouraged her to move closer to him.

Her gaze went to his dark eyebrows and to his thick, dark lashes. And to his exquisitely formed, slightly sulky mouth. Who was this towering man with the uncanny strength who had leaped out of the stormy night to save her and her father? The memory of how he had looked at that moment was emblazoned in her mind forever. The way his wild, wet mane had fanned out behind him. The way the carriage lamps had reflected on wet skin, rippling smoothly over long, powerful muscles. The sword flashing in his hand. His flat belly. His . . . manly endowments.

Heat rushed to Verity's face as she remembered how, after the battle was over, she had looked her fill. She'd never seen a full-grown male thus . . . er, revealed . . . extended . . . Oh, dear, so very close up! She had not forgotten Cousin Fanny's confidential, if shockingly frank, pronouncement concerning just that matter. Verity had taken it as truth, for who would know better than a happily wed woman with three beautiful, healthy children and another on the way?

Automatically her gaze dropped to his lap, now covered with a quilt. Long legs spread wide, entangled in the covering. His bare feet, she noticed appreciatively, were well-formed. As she stood there staring at him, he stirred in his sleep, startling her enough to recall herself. A lady did not invade a gentleman's bedchamber to gape at him! She hurried out of the room, closed the door, and then quickly returned to her bed. As she slid beneath the covers, another tidbit of her cousin's sagacity came back to her. A lady might not invade a gentleman's bedchamber to gape at him, but she might very well invade for other reasons.

As Verity drifted back to sleep, a smile curved her lips. Fanny would most definitely approve of Torcuil MacCodrum.

Shortly after dawn, she broke her fast with Mr. and Mrs. MacDougall. Mr. MacDougall had arranged for one of her trunks to be brought from the carriage, and out of it Verity had pulled a suitable gown and accessories. The garment had been brushed out and looked good enough to wear here, where standards were more casual than in Town. Verity expressed her sincere thanks to the MacDougalls for their generosity in taking them all in, strangers in the dead of night.

A new fire crackled in the dining room fireplace. Pewter serving dishes almost obscured the polished mahogany surface of the sideboard, which had been set with bread, ham and cod, porridge, and tea.

"When did ye have MacCodrum move yer father upstairs?" Mr. MacDougall asked as he and the two women sat at the table.

Verity looked at him in surprise and lowered the teacup back to its saucer without taking a sip. "I had Mr. MacCodrum do nothing." She'd thought the apothecary had been responsible for moving her father! To say as much, however, would reveal to all that she had roamed the house earlier that morning.

Walter MacDougall seemed to consider his porridge for a moment. Then he smiled. "Then it seems our Mr. MacCodrum must have put yer father in the bed upstairs on his own."

"Where was my father before, that Mr. MacCodrum would feel the need to move him?"

"On the table in my examining room."

Verity's eyes widened. "You left my father on that hard table?"

"We have only the two spare bedchambers." MacDougall shrugged. "By the time I'd sent the men to retrieve the bodies and yer belongings, I discovered that Mr. MacCodrum had already been given the only spare bed other than the one in which ye slept. Lord Ravenshaw was sleepin' soundly on the table. I'm no a weak man, ye understand, but yer father is at least as heavy as I am. I'd fear to damage him further if I tried to move him m'self."

"So . . . Mr. MacCodrum came down to get my father later in the night?"

"So 'twould seem. I went to examine Lord Ravenshaw a while ago, but he was no where I'd left him. So I sneaked a peek into Mr. MacCodrum's room and there was yer father, snoring loud as ye please, and our young hero asleep in the chair." He slowly shook his head. "He's a rare strong lad, to have carried Lord Ravenshaw so far. Not many men could do it."

"And that was after he fought off two men with pistols. He had only that sword of his." And then, Verity thought, he had given up his bed to her father and spent the night in an uncomfortable wooden chair.

"'Tis amazin'," Mrs. MacDougall said, admiration warm in her voice.

"What happened to his clothes?" Mr. MacDougall asked casually. His blue eyes twinkled over the rim of his cup.

Verity refused to have anyone think ill of Torcuil MacCodrum, and she felt certain there must be a perfectly logical explanation for his nakedness. She would get that explanation later, in private. A believable reason was required now, so she made one up.

"The highwaymen attacked him before getting to us. Drove off his horse, stole his clothes, and . . . and left him for dead." She decided that wasn't so bad a lie, considering how little time she'd had to come up with it and how poor she was at lying. Not bad at all.

"Och, poor man!" Mrs. MacDougall exclaimed.

"Indeed," Mr. MacDougall agreed. "It seems particularly careless of them, though, to have left him with his long knife."

"They thought he was dead."

"Ah. So ye said." He nodded. "Must've been wearin' fine clothes to have occasioned the thieves takin' them and leavin' the lad bare."

"I believe you've said it yourself, Mr. MacDougall—they were thieves. And judging from what I've seen of this area, pickings are thin for highwaymen."

"Aye. That they are. Especially on such a foul poor night as last night." He cocked his head. "Now, I wonder why a man would be out alone, on that road, in a storm."

Verity was becoming impatient with the interrogation. "Mr. MacCodrum is the son of a Highland chief, and he was venturing away from his home for the first time in his life. He got caught in the storm, 'tis all. A fine thing when a man leaves out of the mountains and straightaway is set upon by bandits."

"From the mountains, is he?"

Mrs. MacDougall broke off a bit of bannock. "I've heard that some of the clans have managed to elude the English grasp, and live as they did centuries ago. Wild, they are. Savages." She slipped the piece of bannock into her mouth.

"Many of them are," her husband said. He gave Verity a solemn nod. "Best ye remember that, my lady. He's a fine-lookin' lad, and strong in the bargain, but he's a stranger to ye. English ladies are best to stay clear of anyone from the Highlands. Yer soldiers have torn their lives asunder. Yer Parliament has robbed them of their heritage. He may be out for a bit of revenge."

Verity stiffened. "The Jacobites were rebels, sir. Traitors."

MacDougall's mouth flattened. "All I'm sayin' is that he might be out for a bit of revenge. Have a care."

She searched her host's face and realized he was serious. "I'll be careful."

A few minutes later, Verity excused herself to attend to the matters that required her attention. After digging out a few gold coins from her stash concealed in the false bottom of her trunk and plunking them into her reticule, she donned her creased spencer of mauve taffeta over her wrinkled pink gown and set out to attend to necessary matters while Torcuil and her father slept.

First she went to the smithy, where the carriage had been taken. Just before she'd arrived, a farmer had brought in two of the grays that had been freed from the traces by the second masked man. From the blacksmith, she obtained the farmer's name and the directions to his farm. After engaging one of the blacksmith's many young sons as her messenger for the duration of her stay in the village of Dundail, she sent the lad off to tell the farmer that when he was in the village again, to stop at the apothecary's shop to collect his reward of five guineas. Next she made arrangements for the bodies of her father's men to be taken back to London, where their families and her father's steward would attend to the details of the funerals, since she would not be back in London until her father was well enough to travel.

On Mrs. MacDougall's advice, Verity went to the small inn not too far from the apothecary. When she left there, the innkeeper and his family were already bustling about, scrubbing and airing out their four rooms. She left with them a stack of the fresh linens she always packed when she and her father traveled, pleased that she had brought more than enough extra for Torcuil's bed.

As usual, she had gone over with the proprietors every detail of what she expected from them. Experience had taught her that one was less likely to encounter dissatisfaction if one made one's requirements absolutely clear from the beginning. Her father's comfort rested entirely in her hands, as it had done since she had turned fourteen and her mother had run off to Italy with the dance master.

As she crossed the muddy street in her pattens, memories of those dismal days flooded back to Verity. She had sensed, rather than seen, her father's deep embarrassment over his wife's desertion. Her mother's action had left Verity stunned. She'd felt abandoned and utterly rejected. Heaped upon that had been the poisonous sting of society's pity.

Gradually, Verity had stepped in to assume the reins of the household. She'd organized. She'd listened. She'd instructed and interceded. Verity had made certain that each servant, tradesman, and merchant who dealt with Ravenshaw House knew what she, as de facto chatelaine of that large stone mansion in Grosvenor Square or one of her father's sprawling country palaces, expected of them. Gradually, a harmony that had never existed there before settled over each place.

It gave one a good feeling to be needed.

Verity adjusted the wilting satin ribbon of her bonnet, then gave up and retied it under her chin, creating with firm fingers her usual saucy bow. That done, she waded back through the mire that passed as the high street of this small town, holding up her skirts and nodding pleasantly to a passing gentleman who tipped his hat.

She found the shop she sought, and a small bell over the door announced her entry. A short, thin man passed between the curtains that hung over the passage to the back. Around his shoulders, shawl-fashion, rode a well-worn measuring tape. His gaze quickly took in her fashionable mauve taffeta bonnet trimmed with cream-colored silk roses and the excellent quality of her wrinkled pelisse.

"How may I assist ye?" he asked.

"I am Lady Verity Alford," she informed him. "I have it on good authority that you are the finest tailor in Dundail."

The tailor beamed. "I am Robert Graham, at yer service. Ye havena heard wrong, my lady."

"Excellent. I require a suit of clothes for a man."

"May I inquire of his measurements?"

"He is tall. Quite tall. Well over six feet in height, I should say. And he has broad . . . strong . . . shoulders. He is . . ." She recalled Torcuil in all his naked, manly glory. "He is enormous. Er, that is to say . . . He is quite fit." She cleared her throat. She could almost hear Cousin Fanny laughing at her unmaidenlike faux pas. "I thought you might have something he could wear while you make the suit." But she had noticed more than Torcuil's manly endowments. She remembered with clarity the oddest details. In her mind's eye she could still see his wet skin gleaming in the light of the carriage lamp. His streaming hair clinging to his shoulders and back. His fierce, dark eyes. Strange that she should have noticed their intensity when, in the dim light, she could not see their true color.

"Alas, my lady," the tailor said, his thin face creasing with disappointment, "I have nothing ready for so sizable a gentleman."

"Do you have anything you might quickly make ready?

Something that can be altered to make do for a few days, perhaps?"

He thought a moment. "Only a silk dressing gown. 'Twas made for a fellow who had the ill fortune to be caught cheatin' at cards. He fled the country before I could deliver it. He was no so large as yer gentleman, though, bein' only six feet tall himself, but 'tis the best I can offer at this moment."

Verity purchased the dressing gown and agreed upon a time for Mr. Graham to go to the inn to take Torcuil's measurements. Tucking her parcel under her arm, she hurried back to the apothecary, where Mrs. MacDougall led the way into the upstairs chamber where her father lay.

Anxiously Verity studied his drawn face. "Good morning, Papa." She leaned over to kiss his cheek. "You gave me quite a scare."

"You worry overmuch about me, my dear." He accepted her hand and patted it.

She smiled. "And you adore every minute of it."

"Yes, I do, you saucy chit. Where have you been this morning?"

Before Verity could answer, Mrs. MacDougall picked up the tray with its single setting of empty dishes rattling together. With a nod to her guests, she left the room.

"Has anyone told you what happened last night, after you were shot?" Verity asked as she took the chair Torcuil had slept in.

"The lad related the whole terrible tale."

"Lad?"

"Mr. MacCodrum." The marquess weakly waved one hand. "For all his size and courage, he's naught but five and twenty."

She tucked a corner of the quilt more securely around him. "At such an age, Papa, he is a man."

"When one is my age, child, five and twenty years seems little more than infancy."

"Oh, pooh. To hear you talk one would think you were Methuselah. You are a vital man with many years left."

He shifted restlessly and winced. "I pray I may live long enough to have grandchildren to dandle."

Verity smiled lovingly as she smoothed a stray silver lock back from his forehead. "You shall."

"Since your Aunt Judith brought you out, you've had countless proposals of marriage, but you've turned down every blasted one of them. What are you waiting for?"

"The right man, Papa." They'd had this conversation before.

"Twaddle! The right man indeed! This is what comes of allowing you to read novels. I've indulged you entirely too long," he ended sternly.

"Now, Papa, you're upsetting yourself."

"Sheldrake has asked me if he may call on you. He's only a baron, but he *is* one of the partners, and you've already refused every other, more eligible man who has asked for your hand."

"They've all been admirable enough, Papa, but—"

"Is it a bounder you want?" he demanded.

"Of course not. But the gentlemen who wished to wed me . . ."

Her father glowered at her. "Yes?"

"None of them needed me."

The marquess's busy eyebrows climbed. "Needed? Of course they needed you. Every gentleman needs a wife."

Verity implored him with her eyes. "A wife. For that, any young woman of respectable family who has a comfortable dowry will do." Slipping from the chair, she knelt by his bedside. "Oh, Papa, I don't want to be an ornament. I want a husband who truly needs *me*."

Her father stroked her cheek. "This brush with

highwaymen has made me realize how remiss I've been in my fatherly duties. I would see you settled with a husband. I want only what is best for you, my dear." He paused. "How would you know when a man needed you beyond the usual measure?"

"I'll know," she assured him fervently.

"I wish I could feel as certain as you do. I've already placed too heavy a burden on your young shoulders. Seeing to a houseful of servants, catering to a sour old man—"

"You are not sour!"

"I should not have allowed you to assume such responsibilities." A corner of his mouth lifted. "In truth, home was never so pleasant a place when your mother was mistress of it. I fear efficiency was not her strength." He sighed. "You know I abhor the thought of forcing you to wed a man you do not want."

"Yes, Papa."

"'Tis only that I fear you are being over-selective, and that the older you grow the fewer choices you shall have, until you have no choice at all." He frowned slightly, as if an unsettling thought had only just occurred to him, and he wondered why it had not occurred before. "You do wish to wed, do you not?"

His consternation caused her to reassure him with a smile. "Yes, Papa."

This, also, was a subject on which they'd spoken before. The marriage between her father and her mother, who had died in Italy two years ago, had been arranged by their parents. It seemed to Verity that the two had been ill suited from the start. Her father was passionate and impatient. Her mother had been timid and absentminded. Tempers and tears had flowed continually, no matter in which of the marquess's mansions they were living. Household turmoil had surrounded them in Town and country. As a result, her father was loath to push Verity to wed a man she did not want.

He looked relieved. "There's a good girl."

"Never fear, Papa. I'm ready to manage a husband. But not just any man will do."

He shook his head—and winced. "I tremble for the man who takes you to wife, my dear. His house will be a haven of comfort, his investments skillfully increased, and other men shall envy him the beauty and deportment of his wife. Poor chap will never even realize he's not truly in charge."

She laughed as she rose to her feet. "I'm not as bad as all that," she protested.

"About that we shall see. Now, as to the young man who snatched us from the jaws of disaster, I still don't understand why young MacCodrum should have been . . . er, unclothed when he came to our rescue. Surely he wasn't roaming the countryside that way?"

"I cannot say. But I told Mr. and Mrs. MacDougall that he had been set upon by the very men who accosted us, and his clothes stolen."

"Hmm. Possible. In fact, I would not be at all surprised to find that's what actually occurred."

Verity inspected her fingernails. "I think we should persuade Mr. MacCodrum to travel with us."

"Eh? Travel with us?"

Verity caught a movement out of the corner of her eye and turned to find Torcuil MacCodrum filling the doorway, wrapped only in a quilt secured by his sharkskin belt.

His gaze met Verity, then traveled on to her father. "I came to see how ye were feelin'. Mrs. MacDougall told me ye were awake."

"Come in, Mr. MacCodrum," the marquess invited, clearly pleased to see the tall Scot. "I'm feeling well"— he caught the skeptical lift of Verity's eyebrow—"or at least as well as a man can feel with a hole through his shoulder."

Torcuil advanced into the room, his beautiful mouth curving in a faint smile. "Och, ye appear more lively than I expected ye would today, but yer color is yet a wee pale." He stopped by the side of the bed. "Have ye broken yer fast yet?"

"Yes. The good Mrs. MacDougall saw to that. And you, sir? Have you had your meal?"

Torcuil shook his head. "Nay. I think Mrs. MacDougall doesna like me much. She ducks her head and skitters away like a crab from a starfish every time I come near."

Verity swallowed a chirrup of laughter. "I think Mrs. MacDougall's aversion might stem more from beleaguered modesty than dislike. I doubt she often entertains gentlemen clothed only in quilts. But I have undertaken to put that to rights."

She went to her room and retrieved the parcel-wrapped dressing gown.

"I owe you a great debt," her father was saying as she reentered his chamber. "You saved our lives."

Crimson crept up Torcuil's neck. "Ye owe me nothing. I did only what I should have done. 'Twas no a fair fight, two armed men on beasts against an elder and a female. It wasna *right*."

"Right or not, few men would have risked themselves as you did."

Torcuil made a rude noise in his throat. "That I dinna argue. But my people feel strongly about such things."

"Your family?" Verity asked, charmed by his refusal to bask in the glory he justly deserved.

Torcuil frowned down at his bare feet. "Aye. My clan."

"They would have been proud to have seen the way you came to our rescue."

Dark eyes regarded her. He offered no comment.

Sensing his discomfort, she changed the subject. Holding the parcel out to him, she said, "I have taken steps to remedy your problem with clothes." Or rather, she thought, the lack of them.

He hesitated in accepting the package.

"Please, take it. Open it." She smiled. "Perhaps now you will get breakfast."

Torcuil took it then, and slowly unwrapped it, fingering the twine. To her surprise, he seemed fascinated with the common brown paper. He examined both sides of it. To her amazement, he lifted the paper to his nose to sniff at it. Carefully, he crumpled it in his hand and seemed to take note of the result.

"Don't they use such paper in the town from which you come?" she asked, refusing to comment on his rather basic techniques of inspection.

For the first time, he noticed the blue-green silk of the dressing gown that lay in the paper like an exotic egg in an ordinary nest. "I dinna come from a town," he murmured absently, his eyes only for the glorious colored silk.

Which explained his reaction to the twine, the paper, and now the robe. Evidently he lived remote from civilization. She'd heard that of Highlanders. To be fair, though, there were those even in England who never went farther than a few miles from home in their entire lives.

As he sifted the luxurious fabric through his hands, his handsome face lighted. " 'Tis like water," he said. "Cool water."

His obvious pleasure in the robe sent a warm thrill of delight fluttering through Verity. She'd not have thought to liken the sensual glide of silk against one's skin to the feel of bath water, but since he mentioned it . . . "Yes. Yes, I suppose it is." How clever of him to notice the similarity. Was he a poet? She asked him as much.

Torcuil's hands ceased their motion. "Poet?" The

careful way he mouthed the word told her it was unfamiliar to him.

"A man who composes poems." She searched for an adequate description. "A type of storyteller. He uses words with grace."

"*Bàrd?*"

"Bard. Yes. Are you a bard?"

He grinned, and through his beauty shone a ferocity that shook her to her core. Why this man should have such a strong effect on her she did not know.

"Nay, madam," he said, his glittering dark eyes meeting hers. "I'm no a bard."

"Then what are you?" she asked, surprised at the thread of breathlessness that seized her, surprised even more that she should ask this near stranger such a tactless question. "I mean—"

"I am a warrior."

She'd not heard that term used in everyday conversation before. "A soldier?"

"A warrior," he said flatly.

"Oh." Clearly he made some distinction between the two, but now was not the time to pursue the subject. She had something important to discuss with him. First, however, she must speak with her father.

"There are no clothes to be got for you that will fit, Mr. MacCodrum. I've therefore arranged for Mr. Graham, a tailor, to meet us in our rooms at the inn to take your measurements. He has assured me that he will have a suit of clothes finished for you by day after tomorrow."

"I must leave today," Torcuil said. "I—"

"Won't you please try your new robe on now?" she cajoled. "I'm sure you'd like to be clothed again." She placed her palm on his bare elbow and ushered him to the door. "It won't take a minute. Just go right into that chamber." She smiled up into his glowering face and indicated the room where she'd slept. "Please don't dally."

He stalked into her room and closed the door with a thump. Verity hurried back to her father.

"What was all that about?" he asked.

His face had been growing steadily paler. She disliked broaching this subject now, but she feared the consequences of delay.

"I think you should hire Mr. MacCodrum as your personal guard," she said.

He stared at her. "Whatever for?"

She leaned closer to her father, clasping his hand between both of hers. "Papa, I don't believe those men who shot you were highwaymen."

"Of course they were highwaymen. What else could they have been?"

She met his eyes. "I think they were assassins."

3

The tongue of man is a twisty thing.
—Homer

"Assassins?" he croaked. "Good God, Verity, what put that maggot in your brain?"

"I'm sorry, Papa. I would not have spoken of the matter now if I did not believe we need Torcuil MacCodrum."

The marquess waved his fingers with weak impatience. "Another extraordinary idea. First tell me why you believe those scoundrels were not ordinary highwaymen."

"After you were shot, they mentioned Coristock. They said, 'and the toff gets Coristock.'"

His eyes widened.

"Precisely," she said, concurring with his silent astonishment. "How would two brigands in Scotland come to know of a Devonshire tin mine? Unless—"

"—they were in the pay of someone interested in closing the mine." As if this last shock were too much for him, he closed his eyes and released a long sigh.

She rested her temple against his pillow. "Please offer Mr. MacCodrum a position as your bodyguard."

"No."

"Papa, *please*. Someone means you harm. Simon and Tom are dead. You've been shot and would have been left for dead. I would have been dishonored and most probably murdered. Mr. MacCodrum saved us. Do you know he had only a long sort of knife? *They* had pistols. And horses. He was magnificent. A true hero. We need him, Papa. You have enemies, and I know as surely as the sun rises in the morning that they will strike at you again."

"We know nothing of him." His voice was getting fainter.

"He told me that his father is a clan chief. If his father is chief of one of those Highland clans, wouldn't that make him a kind of prince?"

"He came out of nowhere. What if he's part of this alleged plot?"

"He killed those men, he didn't just chase them away. He's been so kind. And so very gentle with you. Papa, he carried you for *miles*. I cannot believe he is our enemy."

The marquess didn't reply for a few moments. "Very well. To satisfy you, make him the offer. I will speak with him later."

Verity pressed a kiss to his cheek. "Thank you, Papa."

She remained beside him until he settled into slumber a minute later. Quietly she left the chamber.

Across the hall, she knocked lightly on the door of the room to which she'd directed Torcuil. He'd had plenty of time to don the robe. When there was no answer, she hesitated. Perhaps he'd gone into the parlor. A quick check revealed he wasn't there. Silently, hesitantly, she entered the bedchamber—and stifled her laughter.

He stood across the room, absorbed by his image in the long looking glass. He wore the dressing gown backward, over the quilt still belted around his waist. The garment was hopelessly tight across his shoulders, and much too short in the sleeves and through the body.

As she watched, he raised his hand to his face, never taking his gaze from the matching movement in the looking glass. With his other hand he reached out to tentatively touch the mirror. He took his hand away from his face and watched as his reflection mimicked the motion.

Dear God, she thought. He's never seen his own reflection.

Suddenly, as he sensed her presence, he stiffened and slowly turned to face her.

"I knocked," she offered lamely.

"Aye. I heard." He glanced back at the mirror, then resolutely away. "Why?"

"I wanted to talk to you."

"No, I mean why do ye knock?"

She blinked, surprised. "On the door?"

He nodded. His tangled mane rippled against his shoulders.

She searched for a clear, honest answer to give him. "Well . . . it's a manner of asking permission to enter. And sometimes," she added hastily, "it's a way of announcing someone is coming in."

"And when ye knock, is anything required of me?"

"If you wish me to enter, you say 'Come' loud enough for me to hear. If you do not wish me to enter, you tell me so."

"Would 'aye?' no do?"

"It does quite well."

He lifted one of his eyebrows. "How shall I know if yer knock means ye're askin' permission or announcin' yer entry?"

She folded her hands in front of her. "Much has to do with the relationship. That determines what is implied."

"And what if there is no relationship?" He drew out the last word, imbuing his exaggerated articulation with a faint note of impatience.

She walked farther into the room and circled him slowly as she studied the backward dressing gown. The wide sleeves ended high on his forearms. His broad, smooth back with its columnar indentation, was revealed where the dressing gown flapped open. Over his shoulder was draped the tasseled sash.

"There is always a relationship," she said firmly as her gaze took him in. "Even strangers have a relationship to each other. You see"—her gaze met his—"everything is relative."

He continued to watch her, but he made no reply.

Reaching up, she eased the gown forward, off his shoulders. For a moment, he stood straight and still. Then he leaned forward, accommodating her. As careful as she was, the backs of her fingers brushed against his bare arm. He felt warm and solid to her touch. An unfamiliar chord resonated in her breast.

Startled, Verity dropped her gaze to the robe and busily, yet carefully, slipped the garment the rest of the way off him. "It goes on thusly," she murmured, sliding the correct sleeve on the correct arm without looking at Torcuil, then walking around behind him to hold out the other sleeve.

She could feel his gaze on her as he inserted his long, muscular arm into the garment. Without a word, she closed the opening of the dressing gown. Which left her in the position of having to loop the sash around Torcuil's middle.

A strange, nervous vibration hummed through her body as she stepped improperly close to him. The heat from his deep, naked chest warmed her cheek and throat as she stretched her arms to reach around him without coming into contact. She took a breath, which brought with it the faint scent of the sea. How singularly odd. She took another breath. There it was again—the faraway fresh tang of sea air. But they were nowhere near the sea now.

Her brow drew down in puzzlement as she turned her face into his chest, nearly burying the tip of her nose in the springy, dark curls. She sniffed. Yes, there it was again. Had he swum in the ocean before coming to their rescue? But that was ridiculous! It had stormed all day. Waves would have crushed him against the rocks. Hours of heavy rain since then would have washed any vestige of seawater from skin and hair. She peered up toward his hair.

And met his dark eyes. "Is this a ritual of yer people?" he asked. His tone held nothing but curiosity.

Realization of what she was doing slammed into her. "I do beg your pardon," she mumbled, shocked at her own behavior. Hurriedly she finished wrapping the sash around him, tied it, then took two steps back. She waved a hand toward the silken garment. "That's how a dressing gown is worn."

He looked down at his attire, which bulged out over the quilt still belted around his waist, then his eyes went to her. "What ye just did, that was no a custom of yer people?"

"Uh, no." She smoothed her palms down the skirt of her gown, blushing hotly. "No, definitely not. In fact, it was . . . it was quite improper. I-I don't know what got into me. I do apologize."

To her astonishment, he took her hand and pulled her gently back to him. "Smells are important," he told her, catching and holding her gaze. His deep, lilting voice surrounded her senses, lulling her, luring her. "The nose brings us essential information. What did you learn?"

She shook her head bemusedly. "Only that you smell like the sea."

"Like the sea," he echoed softly. Slowly he lowered his head. "Now 'tis my turn."

She'd already apologized for her unseemly behavior, and now she knew she should refuse. She should simply enforce that proper, unspoken distance. Instead, she found herself standing very still for him as he brought his face close to hers.

His thick lashes lowered, and she heard him gradually inhale, the sound as soft as a sigh. He moved his head, an inch at a time. His straight, elegant nose, his marvelously sculpted lips skimmed but a fraction of an inch from her own. The tip of his nose brushed her eyelashes.

Verity discovered that she was holding her breath. That her heart was beating more quickly. Torcuil moved his face to the side of her head. For a fraction of a second, his lips touched the edge of her ear, and she shivered. Oddly, she knew he had not meant to take improper advantage of her. And, for a fraction of a second, she wished that he had.

He opened his eyes, and she saw for the first time how very dark they were. Before she had thought they must be a very dark brown. Perhaps they were—but they *looked* black to her. A bright, intelligent jet that spoke to the fancy she'd never known dwelt inside her.

These were eyes, she thought, that knew things foreign to her life.

"Ye smell different," he said.

"Oh." She wasn't sure how to take his pronouncement.

"I like it."

She smiled, ridiculously pleased.

"Yer eyes are green," Torcuil said. "Green as the moss on the shore rocks."

His observation lacked the schooled tones of polished flattery usually employed by men of her acquaintance. Instead, she heard only honest surprise in his lilting baritone.

"And yer hair." He raised his free hand to trace a forefinger over the curl that dangled in front of her ear. " 'Tis the color of pirates' gold." Again, she heard his astonishment.

"You are a poet, sir," she said, forcing a lightness into her voice to counter the embarrassed modesty that made her feel awkward. Compliments were easier to bear when they were delivered regularly and ritually. She sensed Torcuil's words weren't calculated flattery. They sounded more like . . . discovery.

"Warrior," he corrected absently.

"Aren't any of your, uh, clan blond? Do none have green eyes?" she asked.

He shook his head, and the weight of his hair shifted across her back. "We all have dark hair. Dark eyes as well."

Remembering that the chamber door stood open, too conscious of his nearness for comfort, Verity eased a step back from him. Then another step.

He released her hand and straightened.

She searched for something to break the ungainly silence. "What do you think of your dressing gown?"

He looked down at the expanse of blue-green silk. He ran a hand over cloth, which covered the bulging quilt beneath. "It doesna look like the clothes yer father or Mr. MacDougall wear."

"I wanted a suit of clothes for you, but Mr. Graham—the tailor—had nothing ready that would fit you. This, I fear, was all that was available."

"Aye, well, it's comfortable enough. It will do. Now, there is a service ye require of me before I go, is there not?" He waited, his gaze trained on her.

She thought she caught his eyes sliding toward the tops of her breasts, but in the next second they were focused back on her face, so she supposed it must have been her imagination. After all, Torcuil had thus far displayed no improper interest in her at all. His had been an innocent curiosity.

"Service?" she asked, frowning over her foolish disappointment.

"Ye know." He cleared his throat. "In exchange for clothes." He lifted his eyebrows in a way that seemed to say she should know what he was talking about.

"After what you've already done for me? For my father? Truly, what an ungrateful person I would be to require anything of you for this dressing gown."

Incredibly, he looked disappointed. "Oh."

Puzzled by his peculiar reaction, she offered a bit of encouragement. "Now that you're covered, I think we can find some breakfast for you."

"Och, a meal would go well before I leave."

On her way to the door, she stopped abruptly. "Leave? Oh, no! You mustn't."

"But ye said—"

"Yes, I know—"

"—I've an important matter to attend—"

"Important matter?"

"Aye, a verra important matter."

"We'll discuss everything while you dine," she said brightly, resolved not to show her panic. He couldn't leave! He was the only man she knew who might be capable of protecting her father from an unidentified enemy.

His jaw took on a stubborn thrust, and she brazenly seized his arm and steered him out of the bedchamber, toward the stairs. "A good meal is just what you need. I never inquired how you came to be out on such a terrible night. And without clothes. It must be quite a story, and you can tell it to me as you break your fast."

She maneuvered him into the dining room and to a seat, becoming the room's only occupants. Mrs. MacDougall had kept the food warming on the sideboard for Torcuil.

Verity dished onto a platter several dried-up slices of ham, eggs swimming in butter, oversimmered kidneys, and wilted wedges of toasted bread. She filled a bowl with oat porridge. She set the dishes in front of him, careful not to meet his eyes. "There now, doesn't that smell delicious?" Everyone else had eaten hours ago. The poor man must be starving.

Turning quickly, she swept back to the sideboard, where she poured him a cup of steaming tea from a heated teapot, which she brought to him. He had not tucked into the meal, as she had expected, but rather he ate . . . well, *cautiously* was the only way she could describe it.

He eyed the kidneys, then took a small bite. He tensed as he tasted it, then choked it down. "What is this?" he asked, touching the greasy fried eggs.

She took the chair across from his. "Eggs. I fear they might have been a trifle better about two hours ago."

"Eggs." He studied the brown and white mass on his plate. He turned a skeptical eye toward her. "Eggs from what?"

She regarded the stuff doubtfully. They *had* turned rather unappetizing-looking. Actually, they'd ceased to look egglike. "Try the ham."

He sawed off a bite. Carefully, he chewed. "Salt," he announced.

"That's the way it was cured."

Torcuil frowned down at the remainder of the slice. "Was it sick?"

She smiled. "No. Perhaps your people have another name for it. It's the method used to keep the meat from spoiling. How do your clan treat their ham to keep it edible?"

He took another bite, finishing it more quickly. "What is ham?"

"What language do you speak in your home? The old Highland language? Gaelic, I believe it is called."

"Gaelic, aye," he said promptly.

"Does no one speak English there?"

"There are those who speak English." He paused. "Visitors."

"Try the toast and the porridge," she suggested when he'd finished the last of the ham. "Your English is extraordinarily good, especially if you only had visitors to teach you."

"Nay. We are taught a few languages." He tried the toast. Apparently not finding it objectionable, he took another bite.

"Such as?"

He swallowed. "Gaelic. English. Latin. Greek."

She watched him take a taste of the tea. He made a face and set down the cup. "Is there no water for drinkin'?" he asked.

"Water? I wouldn't recommend it." It was plain he'd never tasted tea before. Just how far up in the wilds of Scotland did his clan live? "How about some chocolate?"

He tested the word in his mouth, pronouncing it one syllable at a time. He cast an uncertain glance at the sideboard. "Is it like this?" he asked, nodding his head at the teacup.

"No. It's sweet."

She rose and poured two cups of the luscious-smelling liquid. The chocolate seemed fresher than the rest of the offerings. Perhaps Mr. or Mrs. MacDougall liked it and so kept it available. Verity set his cup at his place and carried her own to her chair.

"Try it," she coaxed.

With a sigh and a lift and drop of his eyebrows, Torcuil brought the cup to his lips and took a swallow. His face lighted. "I like this cho-co-lat."

She found herself smiling back at him. That tumbled mane of his needed brushing, she thought.

"What other kinds of things were you taught?" she asked.

He shrugged a shoulder. "Mathematics. Science. The classics."

"Can you read and write?"

"Aye. I can."

"In English?"

"Aye, in English. And Gaelic and Latin and Greek." He regarded her from beneath hooded eyes. "Why are ye askin' me all these questions?"

"Your Highland schools sound quite excellent."

"Highland?"

"That's where your clan lives, does it not? The Highlands?"

"Yes. The Highlands," he said quickly. "That's where they live. Why are ye askin' me these questions?"

"Bear with me, Mr. MacCodrum." She leaned forward in her chair. "You asked me if I wished a service of you."

He went very still. "Aye."

His caution made her feel awkward, and she dropped her gaze to her hands folded neatly on the edge of the table. She had employed men before. Tradesmen. Servants. Torcuil MacCodrum was neither. For all his peculiar innocence, she had seen that he was a capable, deadly man who did not seem to consider anyone his better, as if he were indeed the clan chief's son he claimed to be. As peculiar as it seemed, this man, who had not a scrap of his own clothing with him, treated a marquess and his daughter as equals.

Thus, Verity was not now in the position of hiring an underling. She must negotiate with this intimidating prince to save her father's life.

She raised her eyes to Torcuil. His expression offered no clue to his thoughts. Carefully, Verity weighed how best to approach him for what she wanted.

"Mr. MacCodrum," she said finally, "you are the most bold and fearless gentleman of my acquaintance. It is for this reason alone that I come to you with this proposal—not because you owe me a service of any kind. Indeed, my father and I are in your debt, a subject he shall discuss further with you when he is better recovered. What I wish to put before you now is another matter."

Apparently prepared to listen, he sat quietly, as at ease in the straight-backed chair as if it were his throne.

She drew in a long breath and sat quite erect. "I believe that the two highwaymen you dispatched were not acting on their own. I believe they were, in fact, assassins sent to murder my father." Pausing a moment to allow the full meaning of her words to impress itself on Torcuil, she saw no change in his guarded expression. "Whomever sent them will certainly try again. I wish to offer you the position of my father's bodyguard."

Torcuil frowned down at the plate of revolting offal that passed for food among the benighted land folk. As intriguing as he found this female, he must find Eideard. *That,* and that alone, was his task.

It was Eideard their father had yearned to see at his bedside. Not Torcuil. Never Torcuil. The second-born of three sons, Torcuil knew he must make his own place. He was neither the pride of his father, the heir, nor the adored, eternal babe of their mother, the youngest offspring. While Anndra was actually no longer a pup, he was still quite young. And, Torcuil admitted fondly, sweet-natured and generous. But passing years would never diminish the stripling's place in his doting parents' affections.

Torcuil wanted his own place in the regard of his

mother and father. The return of Eideard to their people would be an accomplishment that could not be ignored.

To be fair, Eideard had always been aware of his responsibilities. Only his desire to learn more about land folk for the better protection of the clan had taken him away. There was no doubt he would return immediately to the sea when he heard the news Torcuil carried. An ailing clan chief, to say nothing of an ill father, was no light matter.

But first Torcuil had to *find* Eideard in this strange world, and the only clue to his whereabouts was two years old.

Finally, Torcuil looked up. The anxiety he found in Verity's face struck at him with the sharpness of a shark's tooth. He chided himself for being foolish. Would Eideard have felt any sympathy for a member of such a treacherous breed? Ha! Still, it bothered Torcuil. Determinedly, he hardened his heart. "I am searching for my brother. 'Tis a matter of urgency."

"Where is he?" she asked politely. Apparently his answer was sufficient to silence her further on the subject of becoming her father's bodyguard.

Relieved at not having to contend with her regret—or, worse, her importuning—Torcuil answered her without his usual caution. "London." He hoped.

"How vastly interesting. May I inquire where in Town?"

He eyed the bottom of his empty cup. A marvelous substance, this cho-co-late. "I'll find him."

With a smile, she took his cup and went to the side-board to fill it. "London is a large city." She replaced it in front of him and gracefully took her own chair. "Have you been there before?"

He curled his hand around the cup, cataloging the smooth, warm sensation against his fingers and palm. "I'll find him."

"So you said. My father and I live in London several months of the year, you see, so I am more than passing familiar with the city. I do not wish to alarm you, Mr. MacCodrum, but if you don't know where your brother is, I fear you shall have a most difficult time locating him. There are countless streets, lanes, and alleys there. Building upon building. People everywhere. Some areas are lovely and pleasant. My father's house is in such a place. Many other areas, however, are squalid. Violence abounds." Her gaze wandered off into the distance, as if she could see London laid out before her. She shook her head. "Unless you have a friend there, mayhap even a powerful friend, I cannot believe you will ever locate your brother."

Torcuil took a gulp of his drink. It rolled down his throat almost unnoticed as he pictured a larger, compressed Dundail. The thought of being so closely surrounded by land folk, many violent, according to Verity, made him feel slightly sick. Silkies did not live on top of one another as land folk did in Dundail, and certainly not as they must in London, if the broonie and this female were to be believed. And the broonie had no reason to lie to Torcuil. They were kindred with separate interests.

"How will you get to London?" she asked.

"I'll walk."

"Slow and full of dangers."

She tilted her head to one side and seemed to study him. Levelly, he met her stare.

"You never said what you were doing before you happened so fortuitously onto our moment of need," she said softly.

The story his uncles had given him suddenly seemed inadequate. Being washed off a pleasure barge did not seem as if it fully explained his lack of clothing—clearly an important lack to land folk. His mind raced. If only he were more familiar with their peculiar customs! "Eh . . . I was attacked." She herself had spoken of the many dangers abounding on the land. At least in the sea, the dangers rarely came from one's own kind. "By the men who attacked you." Such brilliance! "They stole my clothes."

She smiled. "I thought as much. It's strange that they left you with your weapon."

"It fell some distance away. Perhaps it was lost in the struggle."

"And they just left you?"

"They . . . made me unconscious." Suddenly he realized that the direction in which he was headed was closed to him. Land folk possessed no spells or charms. Gradually they'd stopped believing in magic until it had faded from the land. The highwaymen could not have cast a sleeping glamour on him. "They, uh, struck me a blow." Pleased with his own nimble thinking, he elaborated. "When I came awake, they were gone and so were my clothes. Grand clothes they were, too."

Her pretty green eyes flooded with sympathy. "You poor man! And after all that, you so gallantly undertook to save us from an even worse fate."

Torcuil gave her a long-suffering smile, even as a tiny, niggling guilt refused to let him fully enjoy his triumph. A triumph that vanished as he realized that his story contained three important flaws that could prove him lying.

Why had the highwaymen not taken his long knife? It was a weapon the most particular warrior must covet, having been forged by a patient master sword maker in Nippon a century ago. Swords, like pistols and muskets, were cumbersome, nearly useless to silkies. While Torcuil had learned to use them all, long knives sliced through the water and the enemy more efficiently.

Why had the masked men not stolen the supple hood of gleaming seal fur neatly folded in the pouch that hung at his waist? Every silkie knew the barbaric land folk valued sealskin, with its luxurious fur.

Why had the thieves made off with his clothing, yet left behind the solid gold, gem-encrusted collar and cuff also nestled in his belt pouch?

All would be questions impossible to answer without revealing his lie. If land folk believed him capable of one lie, wouldn't they question everything else about him? Question him more . . . strenuously? Perhaps even seek to keep him from Eideard? Beneath the table, Torcuil's hand closed protectively over the small-buckled closure of the sharkskin pouch. No one must learn what he carried on his hip.

"Your wife will soon miss you, will she not?" she asked gently.

That seemed an innocent-enough question. "I have no wife."

"One who is promised? Betrothed?"

He shook his head, beginning to worry. Was this a trap? Her kindness could be a ruse—but he did not believe that was so. She had been too brave, too caring. She possessed a certain *honor* that shone about her like a glamour.

He studied her face framed by bright tendril curls. She was a daughter of the land folk, he reminded himself. Land folk had rejected the old ways. He could imagine her reaction to being told that he was a silkie come to seek another silkie. That he would then return to a life she would consider not only extraordinary but impossible.

She smiled. "You must feel as if you're a long way from home."

"Aye." He had been farther from his clan in actual distance before, but never had he felt so separated from them.

She glanced down at the white cloth over the table,

then up at him. "It is important to you, finding your brother?"

"It is."

"Then please consider my proposal. Take the position as my father's personal guard. As soon as my father recovers sufficiently to travel, we shall return to London. There, I will inquire after your brother among my acquaintances, and Papa will employ a Bow Street Runner to search for him. Who better than a Runner to find a man in London, indeed, in all of England? You will be well compensated for keeping my father safe." She named an amount. The figure meant naught to Torcuil, who had nothing by which to judge the numbers.

"I have no been a personal guard before," he admitted cautiously. "I'd no ken what is fair."

She laughed. The sound distracted him, hooking his full attention with its infectious golden notes.

"To own the truth, neither would I," she said, her eyes reflecting genuine mirth. "I took what I know is the salary of my father's steward and added a sum to it—for the danger to you." Her smile faded. "There will be danger, you know. I would not have you accept this position if you did not understand that. You've already had a taste of the danger, but perhaps it will increase, I cannot say."

Torcuil brightened. *This* was something with which he could cope. This was what he'd been trained for. Danger.

"If what I have offered is not an equitable amount, I know my father will adjust it. In any case, he will wish to speak with you." She leaned forward a little more as if to confide a secret. Torcuil found himself leaning closer to her. "He's not pleased with the idea of having a bodyguard," she said softly. "He does so for my sake." Her bright smile returned. "I can be quite persistent when I need to be."

"I shall bear that in mind," he vowed solemnly.

"Will you take the position?"

He weighed the advantages of her proposal. Locating his brother was clearly going to be a more complicated undertaking than he'd anticipated. He found himself unwilling to turn down possible aid. "Aye," he said slowly, reluctantly. "I suppose the arrangement would benefit us all. I'll speak with yer father when he is able."

Her lovely face lighted like sunshine. "Excellent." She rose to her feet. "Now, if you'll be so kind as to excuse me, I must make arrangements for the move to the inn." She scrutinized his attire. "I do hope the cloak you wore last night is dry."

"Why? I've got this new . . . this new . . ." At a loss for its proper name, he plucked at the cloth-like-water.

"Dressing gown. It's not appropriate for you to wear it in the street. Especially when you take off that quilt."

"Why?"

"Why?" she echoed blankly. "Well . . . because . . . too much of your manly physique would be revealed."

He watched with interest as her cheeks turned pink. She made a small gesture toward his plate. "Please, finish your breakfast. I'll return for you when we are ready to depart for the inn."

Verity discovered that Mrs. MacDougall had kindly hung Torcuil's cloak, her father's redingote, and the pelisse she'd worn on that rain-battered trek to the village in front of the low-burning kitchen fire last night, so by the time she and Torcuil walked to the inn beside the litter that conveyed her father, the garments were almost dry.

She was painfully aware of Torcuil's bare legs and feet as the small party negotiated the mire in the high street. Out of the corner of her eye she saw heads turn and knew others had noticed his lack of breeches, stockings, or shoes. The rest of him was cocooned in the cloak, just as she'd arranged it around him. It simply was not large enough to cover him as a cloak should.

She had suggested that Torcuil ride in the coach when it was moved from the livery to the carriage house at the inn, but he had insisted on staying with her father. The mode of travel for her father had been chosen by Mr. MacDougall—four men and a litter, which he pronounced would be easier on his patient than a jostling, jolting ride in a carriage.

Torcuil seemed unaware of the glances he drew. From the way he gazed around him at the buildings, wagons, livestock, and people, she might have supposed he'd never been in even so small a town before. A silly idea, of course. The Highlands possessed such places. Didn't they?

In no time, they had entered the common room of the Crown and Thistle, where Mr. and Mrs. Candlish themselves hurried out to welcome her and her father, and, more hesitatingly, Torcuil, to their home and establishment. The innkeepers' pretty fifteen-year-old daughter, Susan, knelt to remove Verity's pattens as Verity instructed the litter bearers to have a care when conveying her pale father upstairs to the room she'd arranged for him.

Two of the blacksmith's brawny sons stamped into the common room, inquiring in their heavy Scottish burr where she wanted the supplies she'd ordered. To add to the commotion, a handful of taproom patrons gathered around, cups in hand, to observe and comment on the newcomers.

As Verity issued orders, she saw Torcuil standing calmly by her father's litter, head and shoulders above the other men in the room. His eyes seemed to miss nothing. No one other than Torcuil and the litter bearers moved close to her father.

The instant the pattens were off her slippers, she rose and directed the bearers to the rooms she'd retained, striding ahead of them up the narrow staircase. Behind her, she sensed the solid presence of Torcuil and was thankful he'd agreed to stay. It seemed odd to place so much trust in a stranger, but something about him drew it from her. Perhaps it was his peculiar blend of competence, masculine confidence, and ingenuous honesty. He seemed completely unaware of his astonishing beauty.

Mrs. Candlish and her daughter, however, did not miss it. Each sneaked frequent awestruck glances at him as they followed the marquess's party up the stairs to their rooms. The blacksmith's sons covertly sized up Torcuil, then appeared to accept him without challenge, as one male sometimes accepted the unspoken superiority of another male despite rank, wealth, or, in Torcuil's instance, appropriate attire. The young men carried the parcels upstairs and placed them in the chamber that would serve as the parlor. When their task was completed, they bowed to Verity, then to her father, who was being attended by Mr. MacDougall. To Torcuil they accorded the same respectful bow. He acknowledged them with a solemn nod, looking, for all his wild, long hair and his bare, mud-spattered legs and feet, like a prince of the blood.

Finally, under Verity's supervision, the marquess was settled into his room to Mr. MacDougall's approval. After her father fell asleep, the surgeon-apothecary went home. Verity ordered the simple, hearty luncheon the inn offered, as well as a pot of tea and a pot of hot chocolate, which sent the Candlish females whisking out of the rooms. After the departure of the litter bearers, she showed Torcuil his chamber. She checked on her father again, then went to her own room to freshen up.

Alone and glad of the quiet, she removed her bonnet and gloves. As she peeled out of her pelisse, she missed the assistance of a lady's maid. When they returned to London, she must engage one to replace the girl who'd recently married and moved to Birmingham with her husband.

When she'd left Town without a maid, she hadn't expected to be stranded here, worried for her father and left by herself to attend not only to her own needs but to those of her father, and now Torcuil. As she warmed herself by the cheerful fire in the rustic stone fireplace, a smile nudged at the corners of her lips. Torcuil most assuredly needed every bit of help she could give him, poor fellow. Those Highlands of his must indeed be a very isolated world. Differences seemed to abound. And, of course, she reminded herself as she went to the washstand and poured water into the basin, English was not the language to which he'd been born. She scooped icy water into her cupped hands. Odd. She'd always thought the government had insisted upon building English schools in those Scottish hinterlands, the better to bring the residents into the present.

Minutes later, she went looking for Torcuil. She found him in the makeshift parlor, minus the mud that had caked his feet and legs. He remained bundled in his cloak.

"Do you still wear your dressing gown?" she asked, unable to glimpse the blue-green silk.

"Aye, I do."

"If our food is brought soon, we shall finish before the arrival of Mr. Graham and the shoemaker." She searched through the baskets and parcels of purchases she'd made that morning. "Your hair must be dressed, Mr. MacCodrum. I shall do that while we wait." She found what she was looking for. "Ah! Here it is." She stood and held up the hairbrush and comb she had bought for Torcuil.

Torcuil's eyes widened. "Touch my hair?" he asked in a scandalized voice as he took a step back.

"Someone must," she said firmly. "It's a tangled disgrace. Add that to the fact that you are not wearing what a proper gentleman wears to receive his tailor and bootmaker and you will certainly cause talk."

He directed a suspicious look toward her. "Talk?"

"Gossip. Unpleasant speculation. And any such speculation you excite will attach itself to my father."

"And to ye?"

"Assuredly. Gossips delight most in shredding the reputations of marriageable young women."

"Why?"

She balanced the boar's-bristle brush in one hand. "Because the good name of an unmarried young woman is everything to her. Once gone, it is irretrievable, along with her hopes of making an acceptable marriage—or any marriage at all."

"If I allow ye to brush my hair, this will give ye a better chance to wed?"

"Perhaps." She smiled, sensing victory. "You could sit here on this chair. We'll move it in front of this lovely warm fire."

With reluctance stamped clearly in every movement, Torcuil picked up the wing-back chair she'd indicated and set it on the hand-knotted carpet in front of the hearth. He folded down into it, the knees of his long legs and the elbows of his arms overlapping those places designed for them.

"Lean back a bit," she coaxed.

He made a disgruntled noise in his throat, but accommodated her.

The heavy, tousled drapery of his hair flowed over the top of the upholstered chair back to drop like a sable waterfall.

Patiently, she worked through one small tangle after another. She found no matting or any other sign of long-term neglect. Just shining, healthy hair that tempted her to slip her fingers into it. Instead, Verity restricted herself to stroking it with the brush, enjoying that slight, satisfying resistance against the tug of the bristles.

Outside, in the street, the rumble of wagons and the thud of hooves filled the damp spring air. Voices hummed, punctuated by a costermonger's cry to buy his apples. Inside the room, the only sounds were the occasional snap of the fire as it consumed the air-dried bricks of peat and the soft hiss of the brush as Verity drew it through the length of Torcuil's hair that slipped over her palm, again and again. Gradually he relaxed, his broad shoulders curving more fully into the back of the chair. His lashes drifted lower and lower. The grip of his fingers eased on the armrest. The relative quiet seemed to bind them together in a separate world.

At last she knew she could no longer justify further handling his hair. It was as brushed as it could ever be.

"There," she murmured, reluctantly finishing the last stroke.

She stood behind him, gazing at him stretched out in the too-small wing-back chair. For minutes, neither moved.

"Ye dinna make the braids," he said softly.

"Braids?"

"Aye. A warrior's braids."

Verity moved closer to him, to his side. "Tell me how I should make them."

He reached back, and his long-fingered hand closed gently over hers, guiding her to his temple. "Here first. A narrow one down the side." He held her for seconds longer than needed. By the time he released her, her heart was beating rapidly.

She took a deep, steadying breath, surprised to find how quivery she felt inside. "Don't move," she said to him, then hurried into her bedchamber, where she wrestled with unopened trunks from the carriage, until she found the one she wanted. Inside, she found the box she sought. She took it to her bed and dumped out the contents, a riotous rainbow of ribbons and combs and pins.

She carefully selected several narrow black ribbons, stuffed them in the cuff of her sleeve and then returned to the parlor, her quick steps slowing as she approached him. He asked her no questions, and she offered no explanation for her abrupt departure and return.

Reminding herself that she was the soul of practicality and efficiency, Verity schooled her fingers to a slower, more sure pace, until a natural, unhurried rhythm took over. Torcuil looked perfectly at ease—until she noticed his pulse beating rapidly on the side of his neck.

At the end of the narrow plait, she tied off the ribbon, leaving a couple of inches of hair unbraided. Her fingers brushed against his jaw.

"What have ye done?" He lifted the end of the plait to examine the dark plait and the black ribbon she'd woven through it. His gaze moved up to hold hers. " 'Tis a verra fine braid," he said, his deep voice low and lilting. "One any warrior would be proud to wear."

He released the braid and took her hand again. He led her around in front of him, to his other side. His skin was warm, and she could feel calluses on his palm. Guiding her fingers to his temple, he said, "Another braid, the same as the first, must be woven here."

Pleased that he liked her first effort, she went to work again, winding the second ribbon through the long, slim locks of hair.

"You said you were the son of a clan chief," she said.

"Aye, so I did."

"What is it that a chief's son does to make calluses on his hands?" she asked lightly.

He continued to look at the fireplace. "He practices."

She smoothed an errant strand of hair and lay the ribbon into place. "And what does he practice?"

"What would ye have a warrior practice?"

"Peace?"

He sliced a sharp glance up at her. "Peace is bought with sweat and blood and hours and years of . . . practice."

"With knives? Such as the one you wear?"

"And swords, pistols, muskets, bows, and bare hands. I can make a weapon from a reed."

"Who would you fight?"

A muscle jumped in his jaw. "The enemies of my people."

She finished tying off the plait. "Yes, but who—"

He launched himself from the chair. "Ye ask too many questions, woman," he said as he stalked to the window.

A knock sounded at the sitting room door before she could continue. She opened it to find Mrs. Candlish and her daughter bearing trays of steaming bowls of meaty stew, loaves of fragrant bread, a small block of butter, spoons, knives, cups, and two covered pots.

Immediately, Verity stepped back to allow them in. They went to the table and laid everything out. Or rather, Mrs. Candlish did. Susan spent most of her time staring at Torcuil, who still stood rigidly at the window, his back to the room.

"Susan, ye silly lass," her mother scolded in a terse whisper. "Ye forgot the napkins."

Susan pulled a wad of them from her apron pocket. The high color that lit in her mother's face did not bode well for her. As soon as the napkins were properly placed, Mrs. Candlish herded Susan out the door. Verity heard the woman's exasperated voice carry down the hall. "What's got into ye, child? I've never seen ye act so cork-headed!"

Verity turned away from the door to find Torcuil facing her, still across the room at the window. With his hair brushed, wearing those barbaric braids, he looked more magnificent than ever. Was it any wonder he had Susan Candlish gawking like a ninnyhammer?

She picked up the tray Susan had left behind and began to put her own dishes and those of her father back onto it. "You quite unsettled Miss Candlish."

"And just how could I have done that? I dina even look at the female."

"I believe she was struck by your fine looks," Verity replied, arranging each cup and bowl on the tray more perfectly than strictly necessary.

"Och, aye. And I'm Aonghus Óg."

Verity paused in what she was doing. "What is oo . . . ee—"

His eyebrows rose in surprise, and his lips parted as if to say something. In the next instant his surprised expression vanished. "Aonghus Óg is the god of love," he said flatly.

"Whose god of love?"

Though he only stood across the room, it was as if a veil of great distance fell over him in that moment. "Not yours, it seems."

Before Verity could reply, her father's call came through the partially opened door to his room. She picked up the tray. "My father cannot join us at table, so I will eat in his room with him. You may join us if you like, but I fear you must carry your dishes, for I cannot fit more onto this tray."

"Thank ye, I'll take my meal in here."

"We would enjoy your company," she persisted, not wanting to leave him before dealing with this change in his mood.

"Ye need some time alone with yer father, and I have much to think on." When still she hesitated, some of that ice around him seemed to melt. "Ge' on with ye, now. He's waitin'."

Still puzzled and reluctant, she nodded, then swept in to her father's bedchamber, a bright smile fixed on her face as she greeted him. But thoughts of Torcuil continued to send disturbing ripples through her.

4

The superfluous is very necessary.
—Voltaire

The marquess's snowy hair was so mussed it stood out in all directions, reminding Verity of those white Australian crested parrots she'd seen in Fanny's aviary. To her relief, his steel gray eyes were bright and clear, and a palm to his forehead revealed only a little fever. Please God it continued so.

"You appear to have weathered the move well," she informed him as she drew a straight-backed chair to the side of the bed. She set the plain wooden tray on it, then fetched a three-legged stool and sat down.

"I feel as if I've been kicked by a particularly foul-tempered mule," he grumbled.

"Poor Papa," she soothed as she poured their tea. She brought his cup to his lips. He drew back. As ever, an impatient patient, she thought.

"I'm quite capable of taking my own tea," he told her indignantly. "Thank you very much."

Reluctantly, she released the cup into his hand. "It sounds to me as if that mule is not the only foul-tempered beast around."

Her father took a swallow. Verity noticed the tremor in his hand and gently reclaimed the cup.

"You will not use your wounded arm," she told him firmly. Filling a spoon with beef, vegetables, and broth, she held it out toward him. He tried to take the spoon from her, but she eluded his grasp. "It is too awkward for you. You'll spill it. Then you will have no stew, and I shall have a mess to clean up."

"Oh, very well. But only because I'm so blasted hungry." He opened his mouth, and she neatly tipped in the stew.

He chewed with relish. "It's cold."

She took some of her own stew. "No, it isn't. Merely tepid. As it is when you eat it most places."

His eyes twinkled. "Not in my house."

Verity served him another spoonful. "Ah, well, there you are. I've spoilt you, you see. You've become far too used to having your meals still hot when they are set before you."

The marquess swallowed. "You have indeed spoilt me, my dear. You shall make some fortunate man an excellent wife. Hot meals are rarer than rubies. I'll not scruple to say that if I had leaked the news of your ability to furnish a man a hot meal in the comfort of his dining room years ago, you'd have been carried off by some eager man jack the minute you'd come out."

She filled his mouth with stew again. "I haven't wanted for offers," she reminded him. "I've only wanted for an offer from the right man."

Taking a bit of her own stew, she wondered how Torcuil was faring out in the parlor. The foods he'd been served for breakfast had seemed strangely alien to him, and he'd eaten little. He really should eat all of his stew. Was it enough stew? A man his size would likely need at least two bowls.

"Mr. MacCodrum is searching for his brother," she said, shifting the subject away from her marital status. She handed her father his cup, and he stubbornly took it with his right hand. She held her breath when he nearly tipped his tea down the front of him.

She removed the cup from his fingers as soon as he'd taken a healthy swallow. "He has agreed to accept the position as your personal guard. He's searching for his brother, and the only clue he has to his whereabouts is the fact that he is in London. I told him we would help."

"Has he any idea where in London his brother is?"

"No. He knows nothing about London at all." She leaned closer to her father. "Papa, so many things are new to him. I suspect that he has never been in a town before."

"Oh, excellent. My daughter has engaged a bumpkin to guard my person."

She picked up the tray of empty dishes, pleased that her father had eaten so well. "Not a bumpkin, Papa. A rustic, perhaps, but never a bumpkin. He has about him . . ." She searched for the words to describe Torcuil's regal grace, his quiet, confident bearing and insatiable curiosity. "He has a dignity, but it is not a false dignity at all. He's not embarrassed to ask questions, and he learns rapidly. I cannot think he'll be anything but an asset to you. And you saw how he watched over you when we moved to these rooms. He never left your side, and no one wished to risk coming close to you." She cocked her head. "Why that should be, I cannot conceive, for he doesn't threaten, nor even appear overthreatening, save for his height. And the broadness of his shoulders. Oh, and his fine muscles."

The marquess regarded her from where he lay. "Daughter, it sounds to me as if you've been spending altogether too much time noticing this man. I'm not acquainted with his family."

She leaned over to kiss his forehead. "You worry overmuch, Papa. I'm simply trying to provide my father's savior and bodyguard with the things he'll need to perform his duties."

Her father sighed. "True, he was my savior." He took her hand. "More importantly, he was yours. I will not forget that." His mouth moved in a weak smile. " 'Tis only that there is another male near my daughter, and I am unable to act the proper master. Damnably frustrating."

Verity gave his hand a little squeeze. "Do not worry, Papa." She heard a knock on the outside of the parlor door. "I believe the tailor is come."

"You will not be present while Mr. MacCodrum is being measured and . . . er . . . scrutinized." His words hovered between question and statement.

"I must. In this matter, he is an innocent, Papa. He needs my help." She laughed. "I have already seen all there is to see of Mr. MacCodrum."

"*That* offers me no reassurance at all."

"Papa, I am a full eighteen years. For the past four years I have been mistress of your several large households. You must admit I am a very capable sort of female."

"Yes, yes, but my worries have little to do with your housekeeping abilities," he fretted.

She lifted a reproving brow.

"Very well, very well. Go. See to our Mr. MacCodrum's sartorial respectability. But do at least *try* not to see anything more than you must?"

She laughed again, wondering if she could keep such a promise, and decided likely she could not. She found the chief's son entirely too fascinating. "Go to sleep, Papa."

"Send him to me when the tailor and whoever else you have employed to spend my money has departed."

She pressed a kiss to his pale cheek, unable to keep from smiling at what she knew to be an empty complaint. "Yes, Papa." He nodded and closed his eyes. As she set the tray and dishes on the dining table in the parlor, she noticed Torcuil's empty dishes and made a mental note to make certain that the stew had been to his liking and to have the innkeeper provide him with larger portions in future.

Torcuil himself stood by the door into the hall. His cloak was fastened about his throat as it ought to be and tossed back over his shoulders, clearing his access to his long knife, which was belted around the dressing gown.

She opened the door and welcomed Mr. Graham. His young assistant was introduced as his second youngest son, Jamie. The lad looked to be about ten years old.

"Mr. Young is the bootmaker I spoke to for you. He shall join us shortly," the tailor told her as he began laying out his bolts of cloth and arranging his measuring tape, pen, ink pot, and paper.

She thanked him, and he glanced significantly at Torcuil, who still stood near the door, then back to Verity.

"Mr. MacCodrum, if you please," she said, holding out her arm in a beckoning gesture. He sauntered over to her, dividing his unsmiling attention between Mr. Graham and Jamie, and she made the introductions, hoping to put him more at ease. She doubted the village tailor was an assassin. "He has been so kind as to call upon us that your measurements might be taken and cloth selected for a suit of clothes and the other things you need."

Torcuil gave Mr. Graham a curt nod of acknowledgment.

Verity saw the tailor take in Torcuil's long hair and narrow braids. Mr. Graham's fingers drifted to his own bushy jaw-whiskers and his cropped hair. Abruptly, he removed his hand from his hair, as if catching himself in a daydream. With a stiff smile, he reached up toward the fastening on Torcuil's cloak.

Without a change of expression, Torcuil took one step back.

"Yer cloak must come off, if I'm to take yer measurements," Mr. Graham said. His words were spoken politely, but Verity did not miss the nervous swallow that made his Adam's apple bob in his throat.

She came around behind Torcuil and lightly tugged on the cloak. "Please take it off," she told him in a voice pitched for his ears only. He hesitated, then unfastened the frogs. She gathered the voluminous garment in her arms. "Now stop frightening the poor man." He turned his head, but said nothing.

She draped the cloak over the wing-back chair where he could see it. Then, noting the enormous disparity in height between the men, she went to her room and came back with a stool, which she placed next to Torcuil. His mouth curved in a faint smile.

Mr. Graham commenced taking measurements, calling them out to Jamie, who scrupulously wrote them down on the foolscap his father had given him. The tailor was forced to climb onto the stool to take the measurements for Torcuil's upper body.

With stoic aloofness, Torcuil bore the tailor's brief, nervous touches, holding each arm out when asked. Bending it at the elbow. Putting it back down to his side.

"Please, remove yer belt, Mr. MacCodrum," Mr. Graham said, holding out the cloth tape with inches marked on it, clearly ready to measure Torcuil's waist.

Torcuil ignored his request.

"I canna obtain an accurate measurement of yer waist if ye dinna take off yer belt, sir."

Torcuil did not even glance at the tailor.

Mr. Graham turned to Verity, indignant color bright in

his cheeks. "Really, madam, I canna be expected to make well-fittin' clothes if I dinna have accurate measurements."

"I comprehend perfectly," she said soothingly as she moved back to Torcuil's side. His only movement to acknowledge her presence was the lowering of his eyelids as he looked down without so much as moving his head.

"Why are you being so difficult?" she demanded in a low whisper. "You must have clothes. Proper clothes. In order to *get* those proper clothes, you vexing man, Mr. Graham must know *how* to sew them. Which means he must take all of your measurements, not just the ones you feel inclined to tolerate."

"He wants me to take off my belt."

Suddenly she realized what Torcuil's objection really was. "Your sword."

"Knife."

She frowned. "Sword. Knife. It's big and it's sharp, and that's all that matters." She drew in a breath to continue, and leaned slightly closer to make her point.

And discovered that his dressing gown had parted in the front, revealing his deep chest, with its sprinkling of crisp dark hair, and part of his hard, flat belly. She'd never expected to get so close to this much uncovered man before her wedding night.

And *such* a man was Torcuil MacCodrum, she thought. So tall and commanding, with his long, dark hair and wild, exotic beauty. Heat from his body rolled out over her, and the heady scent of warm male skin, accompanied by that peculiar undernote of fresh sea air, swirled around her.

She remembered all the things Fanny had confided shortly after her wedding. All those astounding, wondrous, intriguing disclosures about the physical side of marriage. Fanny knew Verity had no mother to prepare her for what to expect the night of the wedding, and so Fanny had sought to put her at ease over what many women dreaded, or worse, feared.

Now, recalling her cousin's words, Verity wanted to nuzzle her nose into that crisp, curled hair less than an inch away. Temptation urged her to swirl the tip of her tongue around that flat brown nipple so unlike her own.

The silence that throbbed throughout the room bored its way into her awareness. "Uh." As a stalling tactic, that single, inarticulate syllable lacked inventiveness, but it was the best she could manage. Never before had she all but buried her face in a man's naked chest. She could only pray that no one had noticed. She frantically scoured her memory for her thread of thought that had snapped at the sight of Torcuil's chest.

"Take off your belt," she said, cringing against that inelegant breathlessness in her voice. "You must learn to protect my father without seeming obvious about it. 'Tis highly desirable that no one knows you are even guarding him."

"Ye're hopin' the culprit will come out o' hidin', then? That he'll expose himself in another attempt to murder yer father?"

"Well . . . no." Nothing so bold, risky, or even so well thought out as that. "Papa won't tolerate someone hovering over him, sporting a sword—"

"Long knife."

"—and generally proclaiming for all the world that he must depend upon someone else for his safety."

Torcuil made no reply.

"How would you feel if your positions were reversed?" she prodded.

"Our positions would no be reversed."

"Oh? Will you always be young and strong? What if you were his age, and . . . and chief? Would you not consider your responsibilities to your people above your own desires?"

"Och, aye, were I chief, but—"

"My father is chief of *my* clan, and the welfare of many people rests on his shoulders. Especially now. The miners have no one else to fight this battle for them. Their very lives may depend on his success—and his enemy's failure."

Torcuil's mouth tightened briefly. "What is that ye would have me do?"

"Be his bodyguard without letting others know. Without letting them know we're aware there is any danger at all. Which means you must take your belt off so Mr. Graham may measure your warriorlike waist." She batted her lashes at him.

A ghost of a smile flickered across his lips. His fingers unfastened the silver buckle of his unusual belt.

"I knew I could count on you," she said, pleased with herself.

"Aye, well. If he makes a wrong move, I'll break his wee neck."

Because she wasn't certain if he was jesting, Verity cautioned Mr. Graham to swift efficiency, which he heeded admirably. Silently, she breathed a sigh of relief.

Mrs. Candlish came to collect the tray and dishes. As she gathered them up she inquired if anything else was needed. Verity requested tea be brought, and she was in the middle of instructing Mrs. Candlish regarding larger portions for Torcuil when she heard a frightened yelp.

"What d'ye think ye're doin', ye wicked birkie?" Torcuil roared, lifting Mr. Graham by the back of his coat until the tailor dangled at eye level with him. Torcuil shook the wide-eyed Mr. Graham with the ease of a wolfhound shaking a hare. "I'll no have any man touchin' me so! Ye pervert!"

Jamie dropped his quill, spattering ink on the white cloth Verity had spread over the table. The boy leaped up and raced over to Torcuil.

"Let him go!" the boy cried. "Let him go!" He raised his well-shod foot over Torcuil's bare one.

Verity grabbed the lad by his shoulders, pulling him away. He stumbled, and slammed into her, sending her staggering backward, dragging him along. The back of her leg collided with something solid, and she sprawled abruptly into a wing-back chair. Jamie landed spread-eagle half across her lap.

"Torcuil, stop!" she shouted. "Stop!" She slid the boy off her, onto the carpet. Launching herself out of the chair, she flew across the room to the two men.

"I was only measurin' for yer breeches and pantaloons!" Mr. Graham wailed.

Verity drew herself up to her full height, which placed the top of her head well below Torcuil's impressive shoulders. "Torcuil, please put Mr. Graham down at once. He was not being improper. He was being conscientious."

Torcuil glared at her. "Conscientious, is it? When a man fingers the inside of another man's thigh? Where I come from, we have another word for it."

"A-and what would that word be, sir?" Mr. Graham squeaked, his face bright crimson.

Torcuil's eyes narrowed. "Dead."

"Put him down at once!" Verity bellowed in her best commander's voice, which had never failed to obtain immediate obedience from the few persons who'd ever heard it. "At once, Torcuil, *do you hear me?*"

All three males stopped what they were doing. They and Mrs. Candlish, who stood stock-still at the door, stared at her. The only sound in the room was the heavy thud as Torcuil released his grip and Mr. Graham dropped to the carpet. Jamie ran to his father.

"Mrs. Candlish, I will thank you for that tea now," Verity said over her shoulder as she helped Mr. Graham to his feet.

"Aye, m'lady." Mrs. Candlish hastily fled.

"Are you bruised, Mr. Graham?" Verity asked, examining him for damage.

The tailor jerked at his waistcoat. "Only my pride, Lady Verity." He shot a glare at Torcuil, who glowered back at him.

"Please accept my most sincere apologies," she said, embarrassed that he should have suffered such a humiliating experience—and in front of his son. "It is only that Mr. MacCodrum's unused to having his measurements taken."

"So I gathered," Mr. Graham said dryly, smoothing his hand over his clinging son's back.

"Please, be seated and compose yourself. I've ordered tea, which will be up shortly. Will you excuse me a moment?" Before he could answer, she rushed to the partially open door of her father's chamber, and poked her head in.

"What's going on out there?" her father demanded.

"Nothing. Nothing at all, Papa," she answered brightly. "Mr. Graham is merely taking Mr. MacCodrum's measurements for clothes."

"Hmph. Sounds more as if Mr. MacCodrum is taking Mr. Graham's blood."

She kept her brilliant, false smile pasted to her face. "I do hope we didn't awaken you."

"I imagine you've awakened even those persons buried in the churchyard," he said sourly. "The first mate on a frigate would envy your lung capacity, my dear."

"Yes, Papa."

"Are you finished yet?"

"No, Papa."

"Don't forget to send Mr. MacCodrum to me when you are."

"I won't, Papa." She saw the suspicion growing in his eyes, and quickly closed the door. Leaning back against it, she turned toward the tailor, who sat in a chair by the table.

"Mr. Graham, do you have all the measurements you need to make Mr. MacCodrum the suit of clothes and other items that he will be needing?" She prayed that he'd obtained those last figures before Torcuil had snatched him up into the air.

"I do," he said stiffly.

She walked to the table and took a chair next to his, in front of the bolts of cloth that he'd piled there. "Excellent. Then perhaps, while we await our refreshment, we should look at fabric and these sketches you brought." Out of the corner of her eyes, Verity saw Torcuil strap his belt back around his waist.

Slightly mollified, Mr. Graham adeptly spun out the cloth before her, draping it over his arm with a salesman's skill that tempted her to touch and stroke. It was all of good quality for the suits of the local gentry. Sturdy, fine-woven wools and linens and a few silks. Instead of dolls, he offered sketches, which had all been carefully tinted with aqua colors.

"Pray, come look at these materials, Mr. MacCodrum. Do you care for this style?"

Torcuil remained where he was, standing across the room. "Ye're the expert. Ye'll do what ye please in any case."

Color heated her cheeks at his blunt reply. "If you show no preference, I certainly shall."

Stubbornly silent, he raised one shoulder and let it fall.

As she turned back to the table, her annoyance at Torcuil was mingled with relief. Now she would have a free hand in selecting his attire, and the less contact there was between Mr. Graham and Torcuil the better.

The styles the sketches offered were suitable for the country, but not modish enough for London, which would not work for the plan she was forming in her head. So, after conferring with Mr. Graham on the changes she wanted made, she scratched out a couple of simple drawings to illustrate the small differences between what he offered and what she required. He studied her handiwork, nodding to himself.

"But this would be quite simple to change, Lady Verity," he assured her, delighted to have illustrations of current London styles in his possession.

She handed him the list of items she required for Torcuil, then selected the fabrics.

The size of the order pleased Mr. Graham, which pacified her conscience somewhat over the indignity he had suffered. The rest of Torcuil's wardrobe would be got in London, where the selection of cloth was infinitely larger and where there would be more time.

Mr. Young, the bootmaker, arrived with Mrs. Candlish, who carried the tray of tea and cakes Verity had ordered. As everyone sipped tea, Mr. Young decided that the boots he'd brought with him were drastically too small for Mr. MacCodrum. Everyone watched as he took plaster of paris impressions of an impatient Torcuil's bare feet.

"I've never seen this done," Verity admitted. "I've seen only the wooden lasts."

Mr. Young carefully removed the plaster from Torcuil's feet. "I believe this to be faster and more accurate."

But the making of the boots and shoes would not be faster. "I will have the shoes ready in two days, and boots in four."

Their business concluded, Mr. Young, Mr. Graham, and Jamie took their leave.

Verity nibbled on a seedcake. To her mild surprise,

Torcuil approached and looked over the refreshments. "There's no a pot o' cho-co-late."

"It appears that you must accustom yourself to drinking tea until we get home, Mr. MacCodrum. Mrs. Candlish has no more chocolate." She removed the quilted cover from the teapot, then poured him a cup. She added two spoonfuls of sugar and stirred. "Take a seat, please." When he did, she handed him the cup and saucer. "Perhaps this will be more to your taste than that you tried this morning."

He took the cup from her and sniffed its contents. His nose wrinkled.

"Let's try a bit of cream." She added a smooth white dollop to his tea. "Better?"

He sniffed again, then cautiously took a sip. "'Tis no so bad."

"I am all delight to hear that."

He took a cake from the plate and sniffed that, too, then broke it in half. One of the halves he popped into his mouth. His eyes lighted with pleasure as he chewed.

"Mr. MacCodrum, it would be well to refrain from sniffing your food or drink before consuming it."

Torcuil looked surprised. "Why?"

"Well . . ." She searched for a kind explanation. There wasn't one. "It's usually associated with . . . animals."

The enjoyment he'd been taking in the treat faded. He regarded her from under lowered lashes, the other half of the small cake still held in his fingers. "Do ye no find it curious? Because beasts sniff their food, men do not. Yet beasts have less to fear from each other's treachery than men."

She looked away, toward the door to her father's chamber. "Often that is true."

"Verra often."

"My father asked if you would be so good as to speak

with him when we concluded the ordeal of obtaining you clothes."

"He did, did he?"

Verity nodded. "Please knock softly before you enter his chamber."

Torcuil rose from his chair and walked to the door. He rapped lightly on her father's door. She heard her father's voice, and Torcuil went in, quietly closing the door behind him.

With a sigh, Verity poured herself the last of the tea. There for a moment she had feared for Mr. Graham. When the danger had passed, she'd worried that he might refuse to have anything more to do with Mr. MacCodrum or, for that matter, with her. Apparently Mr. Graham was made of heartier stuff than he appeared.

She took a swallow of comfortingly warm tea. It was clear that Mr. MacCodrum had never worn tailored clothes before, which she thought odd, even considering his origins. Perhaps when the ban on wearing Highland garb had been lifted, back in the1780s, his family had returned to wearing their skirts. It seemed that the man had lived in an even more remote place than she'd expected.

Torcuil took the chair Lord Ravenshaw waved him to and impatiently composed himself. He hoped he was being wise in allying himself with this elder and his daughter. He chaffed against the delay, yet he had already discovered how terrifyingly great was his ignorance about land folk and their ways. Doubtless he would have fared well enough if all he'd had to do was come ashore and make merry with some female, as it now seemed was all his uncles had done. But living among this alien breed, trying to travel their confusing land to a certain place, was a squid of a different color. If London was larger than Dundail, then he was in shark-infested waters indeed.

The swiftest, surest way of finding Eideard was with Philip and Verity Alford.

If only he could endure the tailors and bootmakers and any other helpful tortures they planned for him.

"Do you mind explaining the small riot I heard taking place a while ago?" the marquess asked.

Torcuil frowned down at his bare knees. "The wee tailor took liberties."

Ravenshaw's eyebrows lifted. "With my daughter?"

"With me."

The marquess stared at him. *"You?"*

Torcuil suddenly felt foolish over the disparity in size between himself and that krill, Graham. "Aye. He claims he was measurin' for a seam on the inside of my . . . leg."

"Oh." The marquess tried valiantly to smother his smile, but to Torcuil's chagrin, the man did not succeed. To cover his indiscretion, Ravenshaw noisily cleared his throat. "Never liked being measured for a suit, myself. Damnably embarrassing, having those fellows grope about. Never have been entirely certain some of it wasn't gratuitous."

Torcuil's embarrassment eased. "Ye've had a similar experience, then?"

"What gentleman has not? Once I could have sworn the fellow fondled my bum."

"Bum?"

"Er, buttocks."

"And did ye kill him?"

"Good God, no, man!"

"But yer honor—"

"Did not demand I murder that miserable wretch. That's not the way a gentleman handles things."

What was a gentleman that made him different from

other land folk? According to everything Torcuil had learned about the breed, murder was common among them and often took place with little or no instigation. Their society teetered on the brink of chaos. They were blind to the magic around them, denying its existence. Torcuil pitied them.

"What does a gentleman do?" he inquired.

"Why, I just turned around and looked him straight in the eye. I told him if he ever did that again—or anything like that—I would take my business elsewhere."

"What did he do?"

The marquess flipped his hand where it lay on the quilt at his waist. "Oh, he denied having fondled me. And perhaps he was telling the truth. One can never tell what a tailor *needs* to do, really. At any rate, he never repeated the performance, and my suits have always turned out excellently. You'll see soon enough."

"I will?" Torcuil hoped not.

"If I know my daughter, she will have you to Mr. Wrighton in a trice, for you will need more fashionable clothes than can be got outside of Town. Just remember to look him sternly in the eye before ever he comes near you."

"I will, and no mistake." The bootmaker had taken no unseemly liberties. Torcuil wondered if perhaps all tailors were perverted.

The marquess shifted his position, working his way to sit up. He winced, but persevered, his attitude seeming to welcome no assistance. Finally he managed. "Now, I expect you wish to know the circumstances for my daughter insisting I have a personal guard."

"Aye. Otherwise I'll no make an effective protector for ye."

"Yes. Well. I mislike resorting to hiring another man to look out for my worthless skin, but Verity is quite adamant, and she is not a silly girl. Not given to romantic imaginings, you understand."

Torcuil couldn't envision any of these magic-lost land folk being given to romantic imaginings. But he thought if he could, it would be Verity. Something about her . . .

"I am one of six partners in a Devonshire tin mine called Coristock. The ore production has declined over the past year, and now one of the owners is pressing to close the mine, since it is no longer profitable. Most of my fellow partners are ambivalent. I am the only one who strongly objects to the closing of the mine. You see, if the decision is made to close Coristock, over a hundred miners will be thrown out of work. Men, women, and children will starve. Their town will wither and die."

Childhood lessons had taught Torcuil something about mines and what it took to bring the ore out of them, but what he remembered most was the backbreaking labor and dangerous conditions. That men would do this to feed their mates and young had served as a point in their favor in Torcuil's eyes.

"Word has leaked that the mine may be closed, though none of the partners has confirmed it. After all, no vote yet has been taken. That won't be done until the general partners' meeting in six weeks. But the miners are up in arms. Oliver Underhill, the mine manager, is furious in his appeals, and rightly so. Closing that mine will ultimately affect some two hundred families."

The marquess shifted again and swore under his breath. Torcuil rose and adjusted the pillows at the elder's back.

"Thank you, my boy." Ravenshaw eased back with a huff of relief. "On my own, I've had some tests run on samples from Coristock. Two tests, actually. Both have turned up first-rate copper. It could give new life to the mine, and preserve the jobs, but it will require an investment, and there is risk to the partners. The pumps and some of the other equipment need to be replaced, as well as many of the timbers. And there is no way of knowing how much copper could be got from the mine in return for what would amount to a substantial investment of funds."

Torcuil sat quietly, digesting what the marquess had told him. A few men controlled the lives of many. They balanced the cost of machinery against the welfare of hundreds of land folk, with the greater interest in their purses. "These partners of yers, are they gentlemen?"

"Yes. Yes, they are."

Torcuil decided that gentlemen had a peculiar code of behavior. They were gentle with licentious tailors yet uncaring of the welfare of those who toiled for them, depended on them. "Are tailors the blood kin of gentlemen?"

The marquess's brows drew down in puzzlement. "Eh . . . no. That is to say, it is conceivable, but I know of none. My tailor is certainly not related to me."

"Are the miners clansmen of the gentlemen partners?"

"Again, not that I know."

Very curious indeed.

"Ye're the only partner interested in keeping open this mine?" Torcuil asked.

"No, I have just persuaded James Cowen, the earl of Mifflin, to support me in the vote. We hope to convince enough of the other partners to carry the vote in favor of converting Coristock to copper. By the time of the general partners' meeting, I plan to have called on every other partner to try to sway them to reinvesting in the mine. Every partner, that is, except Isted. He's made his opposition abundantly clear."

"Has he attempted to harm ye?"

"No. At least, not that I'm aware of."

"But it is possible."

"Yes, I suppose."

"He wants the mine closed, does he not?"

"Very much so."

"Is there anyone else ye know who might want the mine closed?"

"No."

"One of the undecided partners may be not so undecided as he'd have ye to believe."

The marquess frowned. "I shouldn't like to think one of my own partners would try to have me killed." His jaw tightened. "Verity is my primary concern. She has already been accosted, and she would have been ravished if you had not intervened. My daughter is precious to me, Mr. MacCodrum. She must be kept safe."

Torcuil asked a few more questions, then the marquess opened the subject of money and terms for a bodyguard's services. Having nothing with which to compare such terms and figures, Torcuil accepted the marquess's offer. After some further discussion, he left so his employer might rest.

Tailors, gentlemen, and assassins. As he eased the chamber door closed behind him, Torcuil wondered how he would ever find his way through the maze of land folk intrigue to find his brother.

5

There is no fire without some smoke.
—John Heywood

Verity led two of her father's carriage horses, a set of reins in each of her leather-gloved hands. Hooves thudded rhythmically against the moist turf. All around them rolled lonely green hills. Although Dundail was less than a mile behind them, it had fallen completely out of sight. They ought to be isolated enough here for her to teach Torcuil to sit a horse without observers.

"I dinna see why I must learn t' ride this sorry beast," Torcuil grumbled for the fourth time as he matched his stride to her shorter legs. " 'Tis enough that ye've got me all trussed up like one o' Mr. Candlish's chickens with these breeches 'n neckcloths"—he tugged at the linen swathing his throat—" 'n boots and the like."

She turned her head to look at the tall Highlander. His long hair unfurled upon the wind like a dark flag. As of yesterday he was properly clothed, and as they walked she thought how fine he looked in his gleaming top boots, buff-colored breeches, green silk waistcoat, and a dark gray riding coat.

"You look magnificent, Mr. MacCodrum." Oh, and he did. More magnificent than any man she'd ever seen before. Looking on him was enough to take a woman's breath away. "I believe you've been told so already."

He smiled, and his eyes twinkled with a lightness of spirit she'd not seen in him before. It reached out and lifted her heart as well as the corners of her mouth.

"That's so, but I like to hear ye say it."

She laughed. "You're incorrigible. You near terrify poor Mr. Graham to death. You complain and chafe against your finery, yet you're only too willing to accept compliments."

His exquisite mouth curved slightly higher, revealing an unexpected dimple. "Aye."

She wondered that his beauty had not prompted others to spoil him. Indeed, he had seemed unaware of his incredible good looks until she had pointed them out the first time he'd stalked, glowering and impatient, into the parlor wearing his new clothes. Seeing him properly dressed had given her almost—but definitely not quite—as thrilling a shock as she'd received when he'd leaped out of the dark night to rescue her, clad only in his wild mane and a sharkskin belt. A bright echo of that impact caught in her chest whenever she looked at him.

The toe of her half-boot sank into a dip in the turf, and she stumbled. Torcuil's hand flashed to her arm, supporting her like a granite balustrade. His palm cupped her elbow in an embrace that warmed her through the wool broadcloth of her daffodil spencer. The faint pressure of each of his fingers sent a rush of awareness through her. Though the air was brisk with budding spring, warmth surged through her body and she found herself staring up at him. Quickly she looked away.

With the tip of a gloved forefinger, he persuaded her chin back toward him, and, surprised, she didn't resist, meeting his compelling gaze.

"Ye're as bonny as an anemone," he told her solemnly.

To her surprise, she blushed. "What's an anemone?"

"Ye've no seen an anemone? Och, they're the flowers o' the sea."

"Oh." She smiled, ridiculously flattered. "You're too kind."

"Well, they're no actually flowers," he admitted, apparently unwilling to utter even the smallest untruth.

The power of his touch grew each second. "No?" Gently, she extricated her elbow from his clasp, and continued in the direction they'd been heading before her stumble.

Effortlessly, he kept apace of her. "Nay. They're tiny wee beasties."

"Beasties?" The compliment began to wilt.

He nodded enthusiastically. "Aye, with bright-colored tentacles."

"Tentacles. How . . . attractive."

"They sway in the water, like petals in the breeze."

Oh, well, that didn't sound so bad, really. Brightly colored, swaying petals, like a blossom in May.

"Ye dinna wish to brush against one, though. Its tentacles will sting ye with venom."

The image of May blooms evaporated. "You certainly know how to turn a lady's head," she said dryly.

"O' course I do. With my finger. Why wouldna I know how to do that?"

Verity looked into his face and saw only honest curiosity, and her small pique faded. For her, his honesty was what set him apart from other people. Most men of her acquaintance would rather remain in ignorance than ask such questions, particularly of a female. But then, most men of her acquaintance already knew most of the answers to the questions Torcuil asked.

In a world where wives betrayed their husbands and mothers abandoned their children, where lies were spoken with polite smiles and accepted as social acumen, his clean honesty felt like a fresh sea zephyr wafting across her too-old soul. His honesty and that strange innocence of his regarding the most unexpected, everyday objects and customs.

"To turn a person's head, Mr. MacCodrum, is a saying. It means to dazzle with your flattery."

He grinned, revealing strong white teeth. "I dazzled ye, did I?"

"Well . . ."

"I'll have to tell ye I think ye're beautiful more often."

She almost stumbled again. "Is that what you meant when you called me an anemone?"

"Of course." He allowed the green veil fluttering on her yellow top hat to mold itself around his finger, urged by the spring wind. "'Tis only that ye've naught seen an anemone before, or ye'd no have a question about it."

Realizing she'd all but begged him to elaborate on his unexpected compliment, Verity stopped abruptly and fussed over checking the stirrups on each saddle, waiting for her cheeks to cool. "This is far enough for privacy's sake. No one will see any mistake you might make while you learn."

Torcuil gazed around them. "So much land," he murmured.

She handed the reins of the gelding to him. "Yes. So much land. And both of us are so very far from home."

"Aye. Verra far."

"Come. Feeling sorry for ourselves accomplishes nothing. We must occupy ourselves in a constructive manner."

"An' climbin' on the back of this beast is constructive?"

"Yes," she said crisply, trying to cover her urge to laugh.

"I should be guardin' yer father from assassins."

"Daniel and Mr. Teak are with him," she said, referring to the senior footman and the coachman who had been sent to them from London directly upon their butler's receipt of her courier. "There will be much greater risk on our journey back to Town, so for both your sake and Papa's, you must know how to at least sit a horse and hang on."

Torcuil looked at the animal and heaved a sigh of resignation. "What must I do first?"

"Well, you shouldn't be afraid of him."

He looked askance at the gray. " 'Tis my experience that whenever anyone says ye shouldna be afraid of something, ye *should* be afraid—very afraid. And what man of sense wouldna worrit a wee bit over leapin' on the back of so large a beast?"

"There will be no leaping today, Mr. MacCodrum."

"Ah, well, there's that at least." His attention focused on the gelding's mouth, he said, "And must ye go on callin' me Mr. MacCodrum?"

"It's proper," she informed him primly, watching him as he continued to hold the reins yet made no attempt to touch the horse.

He directed a gaze of wide-eyed innocence at her. "Och. We wouldna wish to do anything improper, now, would we?"

Realizing how priggish she sounded, Verity looked away. The breeze caught in the veil that trailed from her hat. "Having the world whisper behind your back is thoroughly unpleasant." It had taken years for the whispers to die down, leaving behind unseen scars. She lifted her head and made herself meet his gaze.

His mysterious dark eyes regarded her for a long minute. "Mr. MacCodrum it is, then," he said softly.

What was it about this man that continually surprised her? she wondered. Skilled in violence. Filled with curiosity. Blunt one moment, sensitive to the feelings of another the next. She shook her head and smiled. Who could resist his charm? "Come. You cannot avoid your riding lesson any longer."

He grinned at her and winked.

Verity laughed. "You incorrigible man. Here. Stand by the side of your saddle. Like so." She demonstrated with her own horse. "Yes. That's splendid!"

"I've only stepped two paces to my left. Ye dinna need to make it sound as if I've changed the tides."

"Hush," she told him blithely as she came around to stand beside him. "Gather your mount's reins in your left hand." She showed him how to hold the reins, and as she coaxed the leather straps between his fingers, there bloomed in her mind an image of how he'd appeared in the carriage's lamplight after he'd dispatched the last masked assassin. His hair had been a wild mane, his chest heaving, his nostrils flaring. Her breath skipped in her throat.

"You . . . you must leave a little slack in the reins," she continued, feeling his gaze on her. "You do not want to pull them too tight because the bit will cut into the horse's mouth. That looks good. Now, place your hands so." She arranged his hands on the low pommel. "Put the toe of your left boot into the stirrup. Remember, you always mount from this side. Yes, like that, and lift your body up and swing your right leg over his back."

He looked over his shoulder at her. "Is there anything else?" he asked sourly.

She grinned up at him. "You'll do well to remember that much."

Torcuil inserted the toe of one polished black boot into the stirrup and boosted himself into the saddle. She admired the grace with which he executed the move. Without being told, he slipped his other foot into its stirrup.

"I'm impressed, sir," she told him. "One would think you'd done this before."

Before he could reply, the horse began walking away.

"*Stad!* Stop!" The horse kept moving. "Stop, ye chuckle-headed beast!" Torcuil shot Verity a panicked glance. "What do I *do?*"

Quickly she mounted and rode alongside him. "Gently pull back on the reins."

His hands tightened on the leather.

"Gently," she reminded him, and watched as he carefully drew back the reins.

To her surprise, the horse danced to the side a few steps, tossing his head before it came to a halt. She eased her own mount closer beside his and leaned over to test the tension on the reins. They weren't too tight, as the animal's behavior appeared to indicate. This was one of the most docile of her father's carriage horses. Staid and calm and dull. Usually.

"You must convey to the creature that you are in control, Mr. MacCodrum, else he will not respect you."

Torcuil swung down from the saddle and, reins still in hand, came around to glare eye-to-eye with the horse. Verity was just about to suggest that he quit scowling and stroke the horse when she saw Torcuil jerk back his head and blink. An expression of profound surprise spread over his face. He pulled the glove off of his right hand. Slowly, he placed his bare palm across the horse's head, just in front of the ears. For minutes he left it there, as he gazed into the creature's large brown eyes.

Perhaps this was how he'd seen some of his people train their horses, Verity thought. Or it was a tribal ritual. A superstitious lot, the Highlanders. Why, she'd heard some of them still believed in fairies. She shook her head, gazing at Torcuil. Here was a man who needed to enter the nineteenth century if ever she saw one.

Abruptly, Torcuil stepped back, drew on his glove, and then mounted the perfectly still horse. As Verity had told him, only the toes of his boots entered the stirrups. His back was straight and regal. "Verra well. I'm holdin' the reins no too tightly, no too loosely. What now?"

He had no further trouble with the horse.

They practiced for an hour more. Verity had never seen anything like it. Torcuil was more than a natural horseman. It was as if he and the horse communed.

Finally, Verity smiled. "Shall we ride back to Dundail?"

"Aye. I think I manage well enough to avoid embarrassin' us both."

"You've done astonishingly well, Mr. MacCodrum. Are you certain your claim to never having ridden before was not a gammon?"

He shook his head. "Nay. 'Tis only that I have so fine a teacher."

They rode toward the small town side by side, and Verity covertly studied her student. He sat tall and straight in the saddle, his hips swaying with the movement of the gray.

"By what name do ye call this horse?" he asked.

"He is one of my father's carriage horses, so I usually have little to do with him, or the one I'm riding now, but I believe his name is Samson."

Torcuil repeated the name, as if testing it. He was silent a moment, then he shook his head. "Nay. His name is Wind Teaser."

"Wind Teaser? I don't recall hearing that before. I'm certain it is Samson."

"Ye may call him Samson if ye like, but his true name is Wind Teaser."

"Very well." If he wished to call the horse Wind Teaser when the creature had been trained to answer to Samson she could not stop him. She shrugged. Highlanders.

"And ye say he's a carriage horse?"

"Yes. All of Papa's teams are comprised of well-matched geldings, and all are trained to the saddle as well as pulling a coach. Each horse has been handpicked for conformation, temperament, and stamina. Fine prizes for those masked men."

"Geldings?"

"What do you call a neutered stallion where you come from?"

"Neutered?"

"Yes. Neutered." At his blank look, warmth began to creep up her neck. "You know . . ." She coughed delicately. "Emasculated."

Color drained from Torcuil's face. "*Emasculated?*"

Oh, dear. Highlanders apparently did not neuter their beasts.

"Sweet Aobh! Ye rob a creature of his sex?" Distractedly he patted his mount's neck, as if to console the gelding.

Heat moved into her face. "Well, yes. That is to say, a-a vital part is, er . . . removed." She hoped none of the villagers overheard their discussion.

It was Torcuil's turn to go red. "His *cock?*" he choked. "Ye cut off the poor beast's cock?"

"No," she denied hastily. "Not that. Only his, uh, his . . ." She cudgeled her brain for an acceptable word for the body part and failed. "The source of his, uh . . . seed."

"Och! His ballocks!" He pinched the bridge of his nose between thumb and forefinger. "Mother of us all, what barbarism. Sheer barbarism, and no mistake." He glared at her. "How can ye live with yerselves? 'Tis no wonder the magic died."

"It's done when they're quite young," she hurried to explain, uncomfortably aware that they were attracting the attention of passersby. "Shall we discuss this when we get to the sitting room?"

"Nay, we shall not," he said tightly. "I'm no certain I wish to remain in the company of such monsters."

Righteous fire flashed through her. "Monsters? Sir, I will have you know that the practice of gelding horses and other cattle, indeed, even of fowl, is common in the world." Indignation stiffened her spine. "It removes the unfortunate aggression that is so typical of the masculine gender."

He stared at her. "Unfortunate, is it?"

"Yes! You don't see women declaring wars or . . . or accosting innocent travelers, now, do you?"

"In truth," he said coldly, "I'd never seen men do it until I came here."

"Then you are a remarkably fortunate person." As if sensing her ire, Verity's horse tossed his head. She stroked a soothing palm along his neck and murmured reassurance. For all that these horses had lost their ability to breed, they were kindly treated. Her father was not one of those Corinthians who drove their beasts to injury and death.

"Ye geld horses and fowl. Do ye geld men as well?"

"No," she snapped. "We do not."

He watched the traffic in the street, and Verity was struck with the splendor of his profile. A muscle jumped in his jaw. "I suppose I should be thankful for that."

Someone should, she thought. Some fortunate woman who would bear his children. "I assure you, Mr. MacCodrum, animals have been gelded for centuries. I wonder that you are unacquainted with the practice. It has allowed farmers to improve their herds without being forced to slaughter inferior males."

They rode toward the inn and its stables. "Mayhap my father or uncles have heard of it," he said. "But we dinna practice it." He shuddered. " 'Tis too painful to think on."

"Then we'll say no more on the matter." She smiled impishly. "Except to suggest that you stay away from Turkey and China. There men *are* neutered."

He turned a wicked smile on her. "Is that no where men have several wives they keep hidden away from the sight of any other man?"

She frowned. "Yes, but I've never approved of that custom, either."

His smile curved into a grin. "Nay. I dinna think ye would."

A boy looking to be all of nine years of age rushed out of the inn stables as Torcuil swung down from the saddle. Before his boot hit the ground, the young fellow was helping Verity to alight.

"Thank you, Tim," she said. "Your gallantry is appreciated."

The young red-haired son of the innkeepers blushed. "Pleasure, Lady Verity," he mumbled shyly as he took the horses' reins in his small hands. "I'll give the beasties a good brushin' just as ye like."

"When you're done," Verity said, "come to our rooms. I have sweeties from Mrs. Glenday. Your mother told me that you may have one."

Tim's gray eyes grew large. "Thank ye, my lady!" Eagerly, he towed the geldings toward the stables, the horses plodding docilely along behind the slim child.

As she turned to walk into the inn, Verity felt Torcuil's gaze on her. When his silence continued through the common room to the base of the stairs, she suspected something was on his mind.

"Why have ye no taken a mate?" Torcuil asked as they walked up the plain wooden stairs.

The question caught her off guard. "Would you ask one of your clan's women such a thing?" she countered without turning around to see his face.

"I've offended ye." A trace of puzzlement floated through his words.

"No," she said slowly, examining her own response. "Not offended. Surprised, is all. 'Tis a somewhat intimate question for you to ask. Perhaps you should not ask it of any other ladies."

"I'm no interested in other ladies. I dinna know any other ladies, save Mrs. Candlish and Mrs. MacDougall, and they have mates."

"Husbands," she corrected as they reached the landing and went to the door of the chamber that served as their sitting room.

He cocked his head as he opened the door. "Is a husband no a mate, then?"

She entered the room and he followed, closing the door behind them.

"Yes. I suppose. But husband sounds more elegant than mate."

He shrugged as he took off his top hat and placed it on a wall peg. "Why have ye no taken a husband?"

"I haven't found the one I want yet."

Torcuil paced over to the window and looked down at the busy village street. "I overheard Mrs. Candlish tellin' her *husband* that 'twas a wonder ye'd no been snapped up by some rich lord before now."

Verity removed the pin and lifted her hat. "Mrs. Candlish would do well not to discuss her guests."

Torcuil seemed to search the street below. "'Twas a compliment to ye, I think," he muttered distractedly.

"I've been offered for several times, Mr. MacCodrum,"

she said as she noticed Mr. MacDougall's hat on the table. The surgeon-apothecary must be making his morning call to check her father's progress. "And what prompted you to interest in this subject, may I ask?"

"Naught of importance. Yer way with the lad." Torcuil strode to her father's room and cautiously opened the door. Through the crack she saw Mr. MacDougall and her father turn toward the doorway.

"Why, I was just—" Mr. MacDougall began, but did not complete his statement when he saw Torcuil raise a finger to his lips. The apothecary's eyes widened, but he complied with the unspoken request and remained quiet.

Torcuil moved silently to the door of Verity's chamber, but she intercepted him. *What's wrong?* she mouthed. He frowned, shook his head, and motioned that she should stay where she was. She nodded, and he went to her chamber door. Carefully, he opened it. Just as carefully, he scouted the interior of the room. Apparently satisfied, he continued on to his own room. The wary inspection was repeated.

He returned to her father's sickroom. "Stay with Lord Ravenshaw," he told Mr. MacDougall, who nodded.

Quickly he went to his room. When he came out a second later, he was carrying the pair of French flintlock holster pistols he'd dragged Verity out to purchase the day they'd moved to the inn. Then it had been an embarrassing show, what with Torcuil wrapped in a too-small cloak, bare-legged and barefoot. Now she was glad he'd insisted. "Go to your room and lock the door," he ordered as he checked to make certain the pans in his pistols were primed.

"What's wrong?" she repeated, her heart thudding.

"Where is Daniel? Where's Teak? They should be here guardin' yer father."

Dear God, how had she missed that? She'd been so wrapped up in Torcuil's question about a mate . . .

"Go," he said shortly. "Now. Dinna unlock yer door until I tell ye all is well."

She made a move toward her father's room, but he caught her arm. "I must be with Papa," she said.

"Nay. Yer father will be their target. Stay in yer own chamber."

She drew herself up imperiously. "I shall stay with Papa."

He snatched her reticule off of the table, then dragged her by the arm to her room and pushed her inside. "Bar yer door from inside," he ordered. Determined to be with her father, she tried to dart past Torcuil. He shut the door in her face. When she tried to force it open, the barrier remained solidly in place. She heard the jingle of keys and guessed he'd taken them from her reticule. A metallic click announced that he'd locked her in the chamber.

Verity pressed her ear to the old oak door and strained to hear something, any noise that might tell her what he was doing, but there was only silence. Remembering how soundlessly Torcuil could move, she finally forced herself to admit defeat. Muttering a dark appraisal of Torcuil's character, Verity resentfully pushed the bar into place across her door.

After assuring the marquess that Verity was safely secured in her own bedchamber, Torcuil had MacDougall bar himself and his patient inside the marquess's room. Then Torcuil glided out of the parlor into the shadowed hall. Secondhand sunlight fought its way through two small, thick-paned windows in the front of the common room, past the gloom, then up. It would be all too easy for someone without silkie sight, or unsteady on his feet, to fall over this flimsy-looking railing to the flagstones one story below.

A loaded pistol in each hand and a knife concealed in his boot, Torcuil submerged into a lifetime of training. Over the millennia, his people had maintained their warrior tradition. Silence. Swiftness. And, finally, the strike, which drew the enemy's blood.

Once, silkies had been the powerful allies of the Tuatha Dé Danaan, those people of the goddess Dana. The Tuatha Dé Danaan had failed to call them when the land had been invaded by the Milesians. Dana's people had been defeated and driven underground. Then had come the dark days. Magic had faded from the land, and the storms had come to stay.

Torcuil flowed down the stairs, pausing to listen. He sniffed the air, then wrinkled his nose against the stench of old tobacco, boiled onions, and unwashed land creepers that hung like a permanent miasma in the common room. Something else, too. Something acrid, yet sickeningly sweet. Alien, once, but now sharply familiar to him.

The scent of fear. Land folk fear.

He frowned. Where were the usual denizens of the tap room? Although there were seldom many customers during this hour, there was usually *someone* lolling on one of the wooden benches, puffing on a clay pipe or swigging from a stoup of ale, eager to exchange gossip or news. Now there was no one.

He recalled the behavior of the lad who'd taken their horses. Cheerful. Delighted with the prospect of a sweetie. Altogether too natural for him to know something was amiss. Which meant that whoever was here had not gone as far as the stables.

A muffled sound caught his attention, and Torcuil paused in his descent. His gaze sliced through the gloom. There! Ahead of him, on the far side of the room. A small movement on the floor behind the bar that separated kegs and tankards from customers. Silently, he retreated back up three stairs, to put him at a better angle to see. It didn't help much. But enough.

Three pairs of ankles and feet wriggled against their bonds of rope. Torcuil crouched, his blood surging through veins, heady warrior's wine. His every sense prickled with life.

This staircase was the only access to the rooms above. The only other way to reach the marquess was through the chambers' windows, which would require intruders to make their attempt in full view of the village high street and everyone on it. Only a fool would try that.

Torcuil's eyes pierced the gloom, but he saw no one other than those belonging to the feet behind the bar. Alert, he flowed down the steps. Bending low, he crossed the wide room, pausing behind this table and that along the way until he dashed behind the bar, pistols ready.

He was greeted by the sight of Susan Candlish, her mobcap awry, tall, able-bodied footman Daniel Leighton, and burly, barrel-chested coachman Matthew Teak, all sitting on the floor behind the bar, bound and gagged.

After a last, swift review of the room, Torcuil sat on his heels, slipped the knife from his boot, and cut through Daniel's gag. "Where are they?" he whispered as he worked at sawing through the rope that secured the footman's wrists.

"Is his lordship unharmed?" Daniel asked anxiously, his voice low. "And Lady Verity?"

Torcuil finished with the rope around Daniel's wrists and began on the one around the man's ankles. "Aye, for the moment. Now, where are they?" There was no need to explain exactly who "they" meant.

As he rubbed his reddened wrists, Daniel jerked his head in the direction of the kitchen door. "In there. They've got Mrs. Candlish and her husband."

"Are ye certain they're no in on it?"

"I'd wager against that. Mrs. Candlish was terrified, and Mr. Candlish was worried over his daughter and wife."

"How many men?" Finishing with Daniel's ankle ropes, Torcuil returned the knife to his boot, much to the consternation of Tcak and Susan.

"Three. They each had pistols. One went out the back door a minute ago."

"Do ye know why the others went into the kitchen?"

"I heard one of them say they were hungry. One was supposed to keep watch while the other two ate."

Torcuil's eyebrows drew down. "Did Lady Verity and I come in before or after you were attacked?"

"Aftcr. Thcy'd just finishcd tying us up. The mcn rushed to sit at the tables as if they was regular customers when you came through here to go upstairs."

Torcuil reached up to the bar and wrenched a knife out of a small wheel of cheese. He handed it to Daniel. "Ravenshaw and his daughter have barred themselves in their chambers. Have ye pistols, Daniel?"

The footman shook his head. "They got 'em."

"Then free these two and get ye to the shoemaker, Mr. Young. Tell him what's transpired here. Susan is to stay with his wife." He turned to Susan, whose eyes were huge above her ragged gag. "Yer brother was in the stables when we came in. I'll send him to ye at Mr. Young's place." He saw tear tracks on her cheeks and on the gag. She nodded. "Is there a back way into the kitchen?" he asked. "From that area where ye grow the herbs?"

Susan nodded again, and he gave her a cocky smile.

Without another word, Torcuil pivoted on the ball of his foot, still crouched behind the bar. He scanned the room again. There were only the four of them. He went to the door that lead into the kitchen and listened.

He heard a woman sniffling, and a man speaking in a

low, comforting voice. "Shut your gob," a different male voice commanded harshly. "Christ, I'm sick o' hearing your noise. Can't a man eat in peace?" The sniffling jerked to a stop.

"When's them toffs coming back down?" another male voice demanded querulously. "I don't like hangin' about here like this. It's dangerous."

"Shut your gob. If they don't come down before, when I've finished me supper, we'll go up 'n get 'em."

"Where's Thumb?"

"Out watchin' the common room."

Quickly Torcuil looked around again. From *where* was Thumb watching the common room? He had not been in the upstairs hall, and there were only four rooms up there, all occupied by Ravenshaw and his traveling household.

"Why don't we just go ahead 'n pop the marquess? Then the only one we'd have to worry about would be that bloody Scotsman. The three of us should be able to handle *him*."

"We'll get the girl first. That should help to keep both of the others in line. We'll take 'em out on the moors."

Once again, Verity had become a target.

Across the room, the door, which led outside to the privy, opened. Swiftly, Torcuil rolled out of sight, behind the bar. Daniel, Teak, and Susan went stock-still.

Through the door lumbered a large, bearlike man, adjusting the fall of his breeches. The curved handle of a pistol jutted carelessly out of his coat pocket. He clumped across the flagstones to the bar, where he reached over the counter and picked up a tankard, then opened the tap on a keg of ale. His beady eyes widened when the mouth of a pistol barrel attached itself to his nose.

"Quietly now," Torcuil said in a low voice as he rose to his full height, inches taller than the ursine Thumb. "Back outside." He came around the end of the bar, the pistol in his hand never losing contact which Thumb's nose. "Mr. Teak, kindly bring a couple of those ropes and a gag."

Thumb's lips parted as he quickly drew air into his lungs.

Torcuil pressed the pistol more firmly against the man's proboscis. "Ah, ah, ah. I wouldna do that were I ye. Unless, of course, I had a wish to have my head blown off."

The air evacuated Thumb's lungs in a disheartened wheeze.

Torcuil smiled. "A wise man ye are, Thumb." He slipped the pistol around to point at the base of his prisoner's skull. "Back outside. Ye're about to have another extended visit to that wee house."

Quickly, quietly, the five of them exited through the door that Thumb had entered. Several minutes later, Daniel, Teak, and Susan went to alert Mr. Young and the village to the situation at the inn, leaving Thumb bound and gagged inside the privy. Torcuil wedged several boards against the door to prevent his escape should he manage to win free of the ropes—an unlikely accomplishment, considering the zeal with which Daniel and Mr. Teak had tied them.

Next Torcuil went to the stables, where the benevolent hand of fortune provided for Tim to be raking the area. Two minutes later, the boy was running toward Mr. Young's shop, where he would be safe.

Cautiously, Torcuil made his way to the back of the inn and the kitchen door. To his surprise, it stood ajar. Had only Mrs. Candlish occupied the kitchen that would have been logical. It was the only vent in the hot room, the single clerestory window being no more than a pane of glass to let in daylight. Through the open crack, he peered inside.

Mr. Candlish sat, trussed on the floor some distance

away, but the others were close to the back door. Tears rolled down Mrs. Candlish's round, usually rosy cheeks as she served venison stew to a pair of masked men who sat at the table, their backs partially toward Torcuil. He noted the two pistols that lay in front of them.

Torcuil eased the door wider and silently slipped into the kitchen. He knew exactly when Mrs. Candlish saw him from her surprised expression. Fortunately, the masked men didn't raise their attention from their plates.

Swiftly, Torcuil moved beside them, his own pistols primed, loaded, and aimed at their thick heads. One of the men looked up. His jaw dropped. He lunged for his weapon.

"Leave it or die!" Torcuil commanded.

The man hesitated, then lowered back onto the bench, leaving the pistol untouched.

"Gentlemen, raise yer hands where I can see them. Aye, that's the way. Mrs. Candlish, please remove the pistols from the table."

"W-what should I do with 'em, sir?"

Torcuil quickly gauged the quality of the pistols. Cheap and poorly made. Probably of Scots manufacture, for they had no safeties. "Put them in that bucket of water." She followed his order, then rushed to untie her husband.

"Who're you?" the other unshaven assassin demanded, his hands up in the air.

Torcuil smiled. "I might ask ye the same question." His smile grew chill. "Only I'm in the position to get an answer."

And he did. The man's name was Alfie Noden and the men with him were his brothers, all petty thieves fallen on hard times. After some small resistance and Torcuil's sending a pistol ball exploding into the bench between Alfie's thighs, the whole story rapidly unraveled.

Minutes later, Young arrived, accompanied by what looked to be everyone on the high street at the time Daniel, Teak, and Susan had arrived to report the situation. A farmer in homespun poked Alfie in the back with his walking staff when the would-be assassin failed to show Young the proper respect as the brothers were led off toward the shed that served as the village gaol.

At the bar in the common room, Torcuil eased the cocks down on his pistols. Then he took the stairs up to the marquess's room two at a time. He rapped on the peer's chamber door and called to him. There was the sound of the inner bar being lifted, then the door swung open to reveal a glowering Ravenshaw and a harried-looking Mr. MacDougall.

"Damn it all," the marquess swore. "I vastly dislike cowering in my room whilst someone else runs off to protect me."

"Ye hardly cowered, Lord Ravenshaw," Mr. MacDougall said acidly.

"Ye engaged me to protect ye," Torcuil pointed out reasonably.

"This is all Verity's idea," Ravenshaw grumbled. "Blasted foolishness."

"They meant to kill ye. Bein' amateurs, likely they would have made a messy job of it, and hurt someone else in the process." Torcuil arched a brow. "Ye've already seen how yer daughter will fare with such men."

Ravenshaw scowled. "True, true."

Torcuil decided to help the marquess save face. "Anyone who knows ye will be certain a bodyguard was Lady Verity's idea."

"I suppose so. Who sent these devils? And why?"

"Three brothers, they are. They swore they were hired by an agent of a greater man, but who that man is, they dinna know. The agent went by the name of John Good, and wore a black cloth mask to conceal his identity. His voice was raspy, they said, so he might have been disguisin' it. Both times they met, it was in the Light Lady Inn in London. Offered 'em twenty guineas for yer life, Marquess."

"Twenty guineas? Is that all?"

"To a poor man, twenty guineas might sound like a sultan's fortune."

"He's correct, my lord," Mr. MacDougall agreed softly. "Many families live on less in a year."

Ravenshaw shook his head, and began to pace the sitting room. "The mine is at the bottom of this, I'm certain of that. But who wishes me dead? And how did they know I was here?"

Torcuil shrugged. "Everyone in this town knows ye're here. Since yer enemy also knows ye're here, we might assume that he has informers trackin' ye and Lady Verity." His eyes widened. "Verity."

He strode quickly to the door of her chamber and unlocked it. The door opened to reveal her standing there, her posture rigid with indignation, her lovely face set. "Lady Verity, I—"

"You forgot me! I've been cooped up in this room, sick with worry, and you forgot me!" She brushed by him and stalked to where her father was standing. "Are you well, Papa?" she asked, her demeanor softening. "You weren't harmed?"

"No, my dear." He smiled at her. "Like you, Mr. MacDougall and I were ordered to bar ourselves in."

"And you, Mr. MacDougall? You've survived this ordeal unscratched?"

"I have, and thank ye for inquirin', Lady Verity. Yer Mr. MacCodrum has saved the day yet again."

"My Mr. MacCodrum?" she asked, turning eyes of green flame to Torcuil. "If he were *my* Mr. MacCodrum I would not have been abandoned and forgotten."

Embarrassed, Torcuil bristled. "I dinna abandon ye. Ye'll own that I was somewhat occupied savin' yer ungrateful neck."

"Ungrateful neck?" she echoed. "*Ungrateful?*"

"Aye, ungrateful. There was only one o' me and three o' them."

The color drained from her face. "Three? You went up against three men?"

Guilt nibbled at him as his gaze took in her pale cheeks. "I did."

"And where were Daniel and Mr. Teak?" Ravenshaw demanded.

"In the common room, along with Susan Candlish, tied and gagged on the floor behind the bar so Lady Verity and I wouldna see them when we came in. Mrs. Candlish was forced to tell the real customers that there was no more ale."

Mr. MacDougall snorted. "As if anyone could believe such an obvious lie."

"They believed it enough no to grow suspicious. In the kitchen, Mr. Candlish was also bound and gagged. Mrs. Candlish was forced to cook and serve the criminals. A third man in the common room kept watch to make certain we stayed upstairs until they were ready for us."

Verity's dark gold eyebrows drew down in puzzlement. "I didn't notice anyone waiting for us."

"Did ye think he'd be sittin' out in the middle of the room, with a handbill hangin' on him, then? If he had, ye would have remembered him too well. A big, strappin' fellow, and no mistake. He was armed with a pistol, as were his brothers."

"So my footman and coach driver were no help to you," Ravenshaw observed sourly.

"Aye, but they were. They went for the constable and took Susan to safety."

Ravenshaw nodded.

Mr. MacDougall went into his patient's chamber and came out with his instrument bag. "Your father is fit to travel now, Lady Verity," he said. "Allow him to rest every night." He handed Verity a small stoppered blue bottle. "Mix a healthy pinch of this in his wine in the morning, at noon, and before he retires." He went on with his directions to Verity, obviously aware of who ruled when it came to the health and well-being of the marquess.

Torcuil escaped to the stables. Alone with the horses, Torcuil unfurled a questing thought: *Wind Teaser.*

6

The fat is in the fire.
—John Heywood

The warm mental touch that answered wasn't as clear or as complex as that of a dolphin, or as shallow and as easily distracted as that of a mudminnow. Unlike Torcuil's previous experience, it didn't shimmer at all. Instead, it lay in his mind like a patient, close breath. Again, he felt the surprised wonder he'd experienced hours ago.

You are different, came the horse's thought. *What are you?*

He went to the gray gelding and slipped his palm over the well-groomed satin neck. *I am Torcuil MacCodrum, of Clan MacCodrum.*

Torcuil felt Wind Teaser's glimmer of recognition, like the flickering wink of faery fire. *You are of the seal folk.*

That I am.

I have heard of your people. My own ancestors, Those Who Went Before, bore the Tuatha Dé Danaan upon their backs, but not the silkies. Why is that, Torcuil?

Torcuil smiled as he separated three locks of Wind Teaser's black mane. *There was no need. We move faster through the water than a horse could carry us on land. Silkies have never gone far from the sea.* His fingers expertly wove the hair into a braid.

Where is the sea now? Can you smell it?

Torcuil's fingers stilled. *No.* He closed his eyes against the constant, anxious ache that had filled him since his climb up the cliffside. *The perfume of my home no longer fills my nostrils.*

Then you have gone far from the sea. Why?

Torcuil plucked out three more locks of hair farther down the mane. *My father is ill. He has asked to see his son, Eideard.* Over, under, around, over, under, around, he braided the coarse hair.

The warm touch against his mind softened. *Only Eideard?*

He ran his hand over the broad satiny back. So far from home. *Only Eideard.*

Will you ride me tomorrow, Torcuil? I like to be outside.

I canna say for certain. Likely ye'll be expected to pull the carriage.

Wind Teaser's ears pricked up. *Where are we going?*

London.

Home? To my stable?

Aye. To yer stable.

To Wind Teaser's home. To the home of Verity and her father. But to Torcuil, another strange place. A place even more distant from the sea. There would be no rhythmic lap of endless water, no terns to send out their echoing cries. There were no sun-drenched rock islands on which to bask.

Home.

"When did you form such an affection for horses?" a

feminine voice asked from the open stable doors behind him.

Something inside Torcuil's chest lifted at the sound of that mellifluous voice, a reaction that he knew should alarm him. She was one of the contemptible land folk, a breed known to be treacherous, violent, and soulless. He wanted to hate her. Or pity her. He'd be safer if he could. But he found he could not. So he told himself what he felt, that acute awareness of her, was merely fascination for the new and different.

But he knew his reaction to her posed a danger to him.

He remained facing Wind Teaser, absently stroking the horse's neck. " 'Tis sad I am for this poor beast," he said. "Too much was taken from him." He heard her move across the stable, her half boots thudding softly against the earthen floor. She came to face him from across Wind Teaser's neck.

"I've ordered dinner for us," she said, casually brushing her fingers through the gelding's loose mane.

Torcuil nodded.

"Mrs. Candlish is so upset by what happened that her sister has taken over the cooking tonight."

Torcuil kept his gaze trained on the sections of mane his fingers absently worked. "She was sore distressed. Her mate was bound and helpless on the floor while she was forced to serve the villains a meal. She was weepin' quietly when I came in."

"She has you to thank for her safe delivery from those terrible men."

With a final pat on the horse's shoulder, Torcuil left the stall. *A fair rest to ye, Wind Teaser.*

Come back tomorrow, Torcuil of the silkies.

Aye. I will.

Verity caught up to him in a brisk stride as he walked out into the lowering twilight. "We'll be on the run until we can discover who is behind this, and that will certainly be easier to do when we are home."

"I've been told London is a foul, crowded place. The easier for yer father's enemies to disguise themselves."

"Oh, not at Ravenshaw House," she assured him. "There is a wrought-iron fence that encloses the house, the garden, and stables. Of course, the staff is all known to us. But I feel I must warn you, Papa is likely to refuse to alter his activities. He'll prove difficult about this, I'm certain of it. He's showing all the signs of building obstinacy." A small frown settled on her brow as she gazed at the ground. "We will simply have to exercise more precaution where we can. And likely you will wish to engage some assistance."

Torcuil stared at the top of her head. He wanted nothing more than to sift her golden hair through his fingers. "And how do ye suppose I'm to find Eideard when I'm glued to the side of yer father?"

"Eideard is your brother?"

"Aye," he said shortly.

"What a pretty name. Eideard." On her tongue his brother's name took on a melodic quality.

"I'm certain he would be pleased to hear ye think his name is pretty," Torcuil said dryly.

"You will simply have to be judicious in your choice of assistants," she informed him, ignoring his sarcasm. "There will, of course, be times when you must leave Papa's care to them. I'll ask Papa to engage two Bow Street Runners. They'll know London better than either you or I. I will require one to uncover the identity of my father's enemy and one to find your bother."

They reached the inn, and Torcuil held open the door for her. "Why not hire them to protect yer father as well?"

Verity looked up at him as she walked inside. She smiled, revealing her dimple. "I could never trust them as completely as I trust you, Mr. MacCodrum. No Bow Street Runner would be as excellent. They are none of them warriors, you see."

Torcuil made a dismissive noise in his throat, but his face betrayed him with a flush of warmth at her compliment.

"The Season has started," she informed him. "I've taken the liberty of sending your measurements to Papa's tailor with a list of requirements. When we reach Town, I shall arrange for a fitting."

They threaded their way through the common room, now crowded with the curious and the hungry or thirsty. The din of multiple conversations going on at once lowered abruptly to near silence as Torcuil and Verity made their way to the stairs.

"I've no doubt that you're the subject of many lively conversations this eve," Verity said as they climbed the narrow stairway. " 'Look at the hero,' they're probably saying. 'Don't I wish I was as brave as that Torcuil MacCodrum?' "

"Ha. More likely they're sayin', 'When are those troublemakers leavin' our town? It canna be too soon.' "

She laughed. It rang like an eddying wave through the two-storied room. As Torcuil glanced down, he saw several appreciative looks directed at Verity.

"Really, Mr. MacCodrum," Verity said, her voice pitched for his ears alone. "You need to have more confidence in others." They reached the landing and entered the half hall, where smoking tallow candles set in a few wall sconces gave off smelly, dim yellow light.

One corner of his mouth curled up. "Ye seem to think I have need of a great many things."

He saw her smile fade, and suddenly he wanted it back. " 'Tis only that ye always seem to be anticipatin' my needs. My need for clothing, my need for food, my need for help in findin' my brother. Ye must think me the most inept man alive."

She shook her head. "No," she said unevenly. "Never that."

Torcuil frowned as he rapped out the designated code on the door. He lowered his head to peer closely into her face. "What's the matter?"

Her smile illuminated their space in the gloomy hall. "Nothing. Nothing at all."

He bent closer. "Yer voice sounds odd. Mayhap ye've taken ill from the excitement today."

Her beautiful face belonged to a faery queen, he thought. In that moment it shone with an inner radiance that made him want to touch it.

"I'm quite well. In truth, I believe I'm feeling better than I have ever felt before."

Daniel opened the door. "Here, what's this now?"

Torcuil straightened. Without thinking, he placed his hand at the small of Verity's back and guided her into the parlor. "Have a look, Daniel. I believe Lady Verity is fallin' ill. Do ye no think her color is a wee high?"

Daniel scrutinized Verity's face. "She does look a mite flushed." He looked up at Torcuil. "A fever, do you think?"

"Aye. Best we take no chances." He fixed Verity with a stern eye. "Get ye to bed." He looked at Daniel. "Guard the door. I'm goin' for Mr. MacDougall."

"Good idea."

"No, I'd best stay guard here. You go get Mr. MacDougall."

"Right you are." Daniel started toward the door.

"Wait!" Verity cried, abruptly stopping both of them. They turned to look at her. "I have no fever. I'm not ill. Kindly calm yourselves. If I was flushed perhaps it was . . . the, uh . . . the stairs. Climbing those stairs." Torcuil and

Daniel regarded her skeptically. "I'm certain that's what it was," she insisted. "All that smoke in the common room— it's enough to give anyone the headache."

"Yer eyes were bright," Torcuil pointed out, certain her queer behavior boded the onslaught of illness. "Mrs. MacDougall told me that shinin' eyes are a sign of fever."

"Fiddlesticks." Verity waved her hand dismissively. "My eyes are always bright."

Torcuil scowled. "Nay, they are—"

"My—eyes—are—*always*—bright," she repeated through clenched teeth, scowling back at him. "A *gentleman* would agree."

Torcuil spat a string of throaty, sibilant words that she suspected were Gaelic and their meaning most ungentle- manlike.

"I think I'll just freshen up," she announced. "Dinner will be here soon." She swept into her chamber without a backward glance.

Torcuil stalked into his own room. By the sacred well of Nechtan, what a difficult female! What had caused her to send her chin up into the air like that? Och, but he rec- ognized that particular signal of displeasure. As he shrugged out of his coat and made ready for his ablutions, he thought about what had taken place before she'd marched into her bedchamber.

Perplexed, he shook his head. It must have been some- thing Daniel had said.

Verity stared at the shaft of moonlight that poured through the window of her small, simple chamber while she lay in bed, the events of the day running through her mind in a continuous circle.

She had been right. The highwaymen had been no accident of fate. Assassins were being sent to kill her father, and the only obstacle standing between her sole parent and an unknown enemy was Torcuil.

She found consolation in that thought. If anyone could keep her father safe, it was Torcuil. Torcuil MacCodrum, that stranger in a strange land.

He called himself a warrior. If anyone else she knew had made the statement, she would have felt inclined to laugh. Such an ancient term. Men of today were soldiers. They were infantry. Or cavalry. Regimental. None of which fit Torcuil. He stood alone. Powerful, swift and intelligent, he was indeed a warrior.

He was also somewhat of an innocent.

Verity found Torcuil's artless honesty more than charming. She found it enthralling. Exciting. Despite his power, his incredible good looks and his wit, despite his expertise with weapons and the fear he struck into his enemies' hearts—he needed her.

Unfortunately, he didn't seem to realize it.

Yet.

Abandoning hope of sleep, Verity left the bed and pulled a dressing gown over her chemise. She had to get out of this chamber. It was far too small. Its walls seemed to be closing in on her. Opening her door, she stepped quietly over the snoring Mr. Teak, who, for some reason, had got it into his head to start sleeping on the floor at her door. A lighter snore came from Daniel, who had stretched out on her father's threshold. Their combined noise would cause even the bravest man to tremble in fear of a monstrous beast on the attack.

A tall silhouette at the window across the parlor told her she was wrong. The bravest man was not trembling. He did, however, appear to be restless. Muslin whispered against silk as she padded across the moonlit sitting room.

He wore the blue-green silk dressing gown that had been made for him. A dressing gown and little or nothing else, she saw as she reached the window. She should have known, when he'd shown so little enthusiasm for the nightshirt Mr. Graham had sewn him at her instructions.

Torcuil's hair formed a dark fall down his back and partially over one shoulder. The black ribbons with which his warrior's braids had been dressed were difficult to see in the velvet gloom. It pleased her that he liked what she had done well enough to do it again.

"Is all this racket keeping you awake?" she asked in a light, quiet voice. "If there were other bedchambers at the inn, I would have sent Daniel and Mr. Teak there."

He continued to look out the window. "Nay. 'Tis no Daniel and Teak disturbin' me." His lilting, softly pitched baritone cast an invisible net of intimacy about them as they stood at the window, looking out on the village high street. The moon painted the austere, lime-washed stone buildings with silver and cast long, inky shadows.

"It looks like the kingdom of the frost queen," she murmured, charmed by the moon's magic, yet more aware of Torcuil's presence beside her.

"I dinna ken this frost queen."

Her eyes followed the line of his silvered profile, tracing its clean elegance into her memory. From the slight curve in his brow she discerned a small frown. "When I was a child, my nurse used to tell me fairy stories."

He turned his head to look at her. "Did she, now?"

"Yes. And the one about the frost queen was one of my favorites." Verity smiled as she recalled snuggling up on her Irish nurse's lap. Her mother had been distraught over her husband's hiring "one of those people." Verity's father, who had never learned to be ashamed of the Irish blood flowing in his veins, had brooked no argument. "She told the best stories. When things grew . . . difficult, she'd brew us a pot of tea in a kettle in her room."

"Is that why ye have such a fondness for tea?"

She looked up at him. "Tea, and its simplest rituals, have happy memories for me."

His beautiful mouth curved up slightly. "It must have. It canna be the taste ye like."

Verity chuckled. "We will have to see what we can do to help you acquire a taste for it. Unfortunately, it's almost a social requirement to drink it."

His night-shadowed eyes studied her face, but he made no reply.

"The world you come from is very different from mine, isn't it?" she asked softly.

"Aye. Verra different."

As if of their own volition, her fingers moved to one of his warrior's braids. "Is it a hard life?"

His gaze went to her fingers on his plait, then back to her face. "It can be. But 'tis also one of magic and beauty."

She smiled. "Magic and beauty. Like you, Torcuil."

He touched her hand with a whisper of his first two fingers. They moved over her wrist with the delicacy of a butterfly's wing. "Among my people, when a woman touches a man's hair, it is a sign of intimacy."

She knew she should release his braid, but her hand seemed unable to let go. "I suppose that among my people it's the same." She'd never thought of it before. But then there had never before been a man whose hair she wanted so badly to touch. Never had she so desired a man to touch her.

His fingers moved slowly up her arm. "Ye've spoken my name."

The darkness of the room enfolded them. The sound of snores faded. The rest of the world melted away. There was only the moon and the stars. Only this moment. Only this man.

"We're alone," she pointed out, finding herself curiously breathless.

"So speakin' my birth name is another . . . intimacy?" His fingers smoothed farther up her arm, warm and firm through the silk of her dressing gown.

Her eyes searched his silver-and-shadow face, and her heart clutched at the realization of how precious he had become to her.

"Ye're tremblin'."

"Aye," she whispered.

He palmed her shoulders and drew her gently toward him. Her hand tightened on his braid. Moonlight reflected from the depths of his dark eyes. Then it was gone, hidden by thick sable lashes.

His mouth was warm and supple on hers, bringing with it a tingling friction—a thrilling dizziness—a smoldering yearning. His hands slid up to frame her face. She slipped her arms up and laced her fingers through his heavy hair, eager to savor this rainbow of new sensations.

Too soon, he lifted his head. Through the layers of silk and muslin she felt the rapid, heavy beat of his heart and knew their kiss had not affected her alone.

His lips parted, and elation spiraled up in her, as heady as the first warm breeze in spring. Another kiss? Sweet words? She smiled up at him, silently encouraging.

"Go to bed, Verity." His voice was deep and low.

Disappointment drenched her as she stared at him, unable to believe that this was all he had to say after what they had just shared. In the stark bright-and-black night mask of his face, she found nothing to guide her.

"Go to bed," he repeated, more softly.

"This is what you have to say? 'Go to bed, Verity?' As if what just happened was nothing to you?" She placed her hand on his chest. Even now his heart raced as swiftly as hers. "I know better."

He took her hand and placed it at her side. "Nothing

can come of it." The solemnity with which he spoke told her he did not take the matter lightly.

"Then why did you kiss me?"

He met her gaze. "I had to know."

That crazy summer wine the kiss had sent into her blood gave her a boldness she'd never have conceived with any other man. She reached up and took hold of his side braids, dragging his face back down to hers. "Well, now you do know, Torcuil MacCodrum. And so do I. What are you planning to do about it?"

His gaze moved lingeringly over her upturned countenance. His breathing grew swift and shallow, as if he struggled in a mighty battle. Standing there in the moonlight, seconds spun into an eternity.

He dragged her into his arms and crushed her lips in a hungry, demanding, openmouthed kiss that had her fingers curling into the fabric at his shoulders. She clung to him as a desperate joy crashed through her like storm waves.

He shocked her when he thrust his tongue into her, gliding it over her teeth as if claiming territory. His tongue began to stroke against hers. Hot and wet, it kindled a growing ache, a heavy ripening.

She was conscious of the tension in Torcuil's powerful body. Against his solid chest, her breasts felt flushed and swollen. Her world narrowed to the restless movement of his hands on her back. The rhythmic rubbing of his tongue. And her awakening desire.

With a harsh sound in his throat, Torcuil broke free of her. "No more," he growled. "Never again."

Stunned by his reaction to their mystical, sensual experience, Verity's first response was hurt. Temper flared directly behind it. "Why?"

"Because nothing can come of it!" he whispered fiercely. "Now get ye to yer bed."

She stood there a moment, struggling with her despairing ire. Why was he casting aside any possibility of a future together? What gave him the right? *Who did he think he was?*

He looked away, and in that moment, the moon lit the hectic color in his high cheekbones. Closer examination revealed the pounding pulse in his neck.

He wanted her. Perhaps he even wanted her as badly as she wanted him.

Oh, yes. The signs Cousin Fanny had told her to look for were there. Dear Cousin Fanny, who worried that Verity might never find a man who could excite passion in her.

For some reason, Torcuil was resisting her. He'd told her that he wasn't wed or promised. To her mind, that eliminated any reasonable objections he might have to taking her to wife. As far as she could see, the only real obstacle might be her father, whom she could eventually bring around. His primary concern was for her welfare and happiness, and once convinced that Torcuil was essential to both, he would allow Verity her way.

She wanted to dance with delight. At last, she'd found a man who truly needed her. How fortunate that he was also the man who thrilled her with his touch.

All that remained was to help Torcuil realize that he needed her.

Verity stood up on her bare tiptoes and managed to press a pristine kiss on the bottom of Torcuil's set jaw. "You're right, of course," she told him in a low, sweet voice. As she walked back to her room, she felt his eyes on her and smiled to herself.

Just before she closed her bedchamber door, she thought she heard him mutter, "I should have listened to the broonie."

7

Past, and to come, seems best; things present, worst.
—William Shakespeare

The tall, swaying forms of brown kelp rose around him. Jewel-colored fish darted in and out of the waving forest, seemingly impervious to the current that swept through like a rhythmic breeze, gliding cool along his body. The water was rich with whale calls and the yelps and burbles of smaller creatures. Across the undersea canyon rose the mountain range that surrounded The Citadel. They were there, he knew it. His people. Joy bloomed in him as he swam out of the kelp forest, out over the lip of the canyon. In a cloud of flickering silver, a shoal of small fish swarmed up to surround him, as if in welcome. A grouper took advantage of the largesse, picking off an easy meal.

Three dolphins swimming by laughingly cried out greetings to him. *Welcome, Torcuil of the silkies. Welcome back.*

Exultantly, he answered them, spinning through the jade green water in sheer delight.

Home!

From beneath a rock ledge, an eel glowered at the world. A small cuttlefish scuttled out of Torcuil's path, and playfully he followed it for a second or two before veering off to continue across the canyon. Far below him, the ground revealed mesas and pinnacles and cliffs with sides layered by the passing ages of earth's infancy. A skate leisurely undulated its winglike pectoral fins, flying over the bottom of the canyon. Fantastical purple sponge castles clung to sturdy stone. Coral fans and branches lived everywhere. Glittering schools of fish followed the vast corridor formed by the high walls of the gorge.

He could feel the gathered presence of his clan in his mind. They were waiting for him. His heart lifted, and he shot through the silken water, eager to be back among his kindred.

Torcuil, come back. Please, come back to me. Torcuil . . . There she was, in his mind. Real and vibrant and achingly sweet. He knew there were tears glistening in her sea moss green eyes. Her slim arms reached out toward him. *Torcuil.*

He slowed, his elation evaporating. *Verity.* How could he leave her behind? She had turned to him, given him her absolute trust. When he needed a guide, when he needed encouragement, she was there, aiding him, protecting him from the sharp eyes of possible enemies. His companion-in-arms whose only weapon was her sunshine wit, her compassionate determination.

The hurt in her eyes tore at him. Her soft, full lips beckoned him to return to her. The lips that had trembled beneath his in the moonlight.

He gazed longingly at the mountain that housed The Citadel, where his clan waited.

Torcuil, came her voice, soft and sad.

He turned his yearning eyes to the canyon, to the rich, colorful life that made its home there.

This was his home.

He and his siblings and cousins had grown up among the high-spirited dolphins. He'd mastered his numbers by herding small, darting, rainbow-hued fish. In the library of The Citadel he'd learned the more advanced mathematics and the science imparted by ancient Greek and Egyptian scrolls. The mournful calls of whales had soothed him to sleep.

Water slid over his body like silk. Deep blue-green silk.

The voices of his clan rang in his brain. *You belong with us! You are a silkie. You will never be one of Them.*

Torcuil's eyes snapped open, his heart pounding harder than the surf. Dazedly, he looked down. Legs. His sheet was twisted around his hips and thighs. Gradually, his racing heart slowed as he realized he was in his bed-chamber at the Crown and Thistle.

He rammed shaking fingers through his hair. Sweet Aobh, what a nightmare! Torn between—He frowned, unwilling to continue the thought. There was no decision to make. No conflict of emotions. He wanted to go home. Torcuil slammed the tick with his fist. *Home.* It was simple.

The memory of kissing Verity wound back around to enfurl him, tangling in his chest, searing him with its passion, licking at him with a velvet smoke that sank through his skin to smolder in his blood. He'd witnessed the sweet innocence in her eyes melt into womanly desire, and it had inflamed him, sparking into a raging fire he'd been hard-pressed to control.

Even now he wanted her. Yet something, some ancient message encoded in his bones, warned him away. This would be no frolic, no mutual grope and tickle with some curious land female who wished to test the legends of silkie prowess.

This would be making love to Verity.

Love.

Therein lay the danger. Verity was of the land. The stories of silkies taking their beloved land mates to sea with them, changing them into silkies, were just that: stories. Torcuil still remembered the terrible tale his father told about one of his uncles, an uncle Torcuil had never had the chance to know. The silkie had made the mistake of falling in love with a woman of the land folk. She'd drowned when she'd tried to follow him back to his home. Distraught, he'd vanished, never to be seen by his family again.

The twain of land and sea had no lasting meeting point.

No, the broonie had been right. Torcuil must guard his heart, and see that Verity guarded hers as well. There could be no more embraces. No kisses.

No love.

The next day they started for London. Verity stayed with her father inside the carriage while Torcuil rode Samson. She had suggested to her father that another horse be obtained for the carriage during the journey. Riding was new to Torcuil, but he seemed comfortable with the gelding—amazingly comfortable with him, considering it was only the second time he'd been on a horse.

From the window of the carriage Verity offered him a few small, discreet tips on the finer points of how his feet should be placed in the stirrup irons and how to post when the horse trotted. The former he heeded. The latter he ignored. Watching him, she was forced to admit to herself that he did not need to guard against bouncing when

Samson trotted. Torcuil's body flowed with the rhythm of the horse's gait; his hips never seemed to leave the leather. Finally, she forced herself to sit back and silently observe. As fanciful as it sounded, it almost appeared as if Samson were teaching Torcuil how to ride.

None of that altered the fact that he was avoiding her.

When the tall Scotsman had spent two hours riding, she called him to the carriage. "You must accustom yourself gradually," she told him as Samson danced alongside the rumbling coach. Was this spirited creature the same beast she had chosen for Torcuil because of its docility? "Come, Mr. MacCodrum, sit with Papa and me for the remainder of the day. Tomorrow you will be able to tolerate three hours in the saddle."

Torcuil regarded her from his greater height atop the gelding's back. His fawn-colored riding coat and white cambric cravat set off his dark hair, which he'd flatly refused to so much as pull back in a queue. The brim of his black top hat cast his eyes into shadow, leaving the sun to slant across the rest of his unsmiling face. "I've tolerance enough, thank ye. 'Twould be wiser for me to spy the lay o' the land."

"Well, then, perhaps you would consider riding up with Mr. Teak and Daniel? From there you would obtain an excellent view. If you continue to ride horseback, you will become quite sore."

"How can I learn to ride if I dinna stay on the horse?"

"You ride astonishingly well for having less than three hours' experience, but you will not wish to ride at all tomorrow if you do not quit that horse now." She held her hat against a sudden, uplifting gust. "Please abandon your foolishness."

His jaw tightened as he turned his head to face the road stretching out in front of them. Sunlight glinted in obsidian eyes. "I thank ye for yer concern." With a shift in the muscles of his thighs, he urged Samson away from the coach.

"I daresay Mr. MacCodrum is in no mood for advice," her father observed.

Verity watched Torcuil ride away. She missed him. "He's being stubborn."

Her father lifted his eyebrows in mock horror. "A shocking character flaw."

Verity sat back against the velvet squabs. "Yes. Yes, it is," she replied, teased into a smile by her father's foolery. Was it only a seven-day since Torcuil had leaped out of the stormy dark to save her?

The marquess studied her face. "He's a strong young man, my dear. He's already seen how much stronger he is than the rest of us. We all have."

She sighed. "I only wanted . . ." *him with me.*

"I know." Her father smiled fondly, rocking with the tilt and sway of the carriage. "You are a kind and conscientious girl. But the lad will have his way. It seems that he, too, is conscientious."

"Yes, Papa." Conscientious and stubborn.

The day dragged on into stifling tedium. Verity sent up an unspoken prayer of thanks when, at dusk, Mr. Teak guided the horses into the yard of a roadside inn, a large, bustling establishment that catered to the coaching trade. In the yard, several coaches were in various stages of being loaded and unloaded with trunks and passengers, valises and boxes. Yardboys shouted to be heard. A dog barked. Ostlers called and whistled to horses as teams were hitched up or unhitched. Passengers clamored for attention.

Despite the apparent chaos, Daniel managed to secure rooms and a place in the coach house and stables for the carriage and horses. He and Mr. Teak went downstairs to procure the evening's meal while Verity took stock of their accommodations. The rooms were larger than those of the

Crown and Thistle, but not as well kept. She inspected the mattresses closely but found no sign of vermin. Torcuil watched with interest as she stripped off the coverings on each of the beds and deposited them outside, in the hall.

"What will be done with them?" he asked of the marquess.

Ravenshaw grunted. "I'll be surprised if they're not stolen as soon as she closes the door, but she'll insist on doing it every time."

"They're filthy," Verity said briskly. "I'll not have the disgusting things occupying space in a room for which you've paid good money. Daniel will have warned them that is my custom." She opened the trunk that contained the linens she'd brought.

As she began hauling out the bundles, Torcuil stepped in and took over.

"Should have brought a lady's maid with you," her father grumbled.

"I've yet to hire another." Verity would not brook argument on that account, not even from her father.

She pointed out the linens and blankets she needed first, and Torcuil carried them to the marquess's bed. She shook out a sheet. When he comprehended what she had in mind, he took the corners opposite her and spread them out evenly. With quick efficiency, she began tucking. Torcuil observed her for a few seconds, and began imitating her on his end of the bed.

"Then you should have brought Martha," her father persisted. "A fine thing when a peer's daughter"—he looked from Verity to Torcuil, who seemed unconcerned that he was performing women's work—"and his bodyguard must play housemaid."

"'Tis a job that must be done, and there's no shame in the doing of it. I own I did not think we would be so long away from home, Papa, or I might have brought Martha, despite her bossiness." She and Torcuil added another sheet of linen.

Her father frowned slightly. "Oh. I'd forgotten about that. The woman is a clucking hen with her orders."

Verity smiled as she and Torcuil added two of the woven wool blankets she'd had made just for traveling. They were warm, yet took less space to pack than quilts. Torcuil went back to the trunk, loaded the remaining bundles back inside, and hefted it up onto his shoulder.

Unlike their chambers at the Crown and Thistle, which opened onto the hall and onto the room that had served as a parlor, their chambers in the Jolly Prince opened only onto the hall. Torcuil followed Verity and her father into her chamber. They quickly made up the rest of the beds. During that time Torcuil said little, except to ask how Verity knew to pack enough coverings for five beds.

"I packed for six. I always take extra. Who knows when they can be laundered?"

Daniel and Mr. Teak arrived with an inn's servant in tow. Each carried a tray laden with dishes. In these rooms there was no large table where they could all gather to eat, so the footman and driver chose to take their meals in their chamber, while Verity, her father, and Torcuil supped together. The food was simply prepared, but of exceptionally good flavor. No chocolate had been available, so Torcuil was given a choice of ale or tea. He chose ale. Verity watched him quaff three generous tankards of the stuff with no ill effects. Indeed, she saw no effect at all.

"Do your clanomen drink ale regularly?" she asked.

"'Tis known to us, but we seldom drink it." He eyed the spouted brown pot in front of her. "And it holds the advantage of tastin' a great deal better than tea."

Her father threw back his head and laughed, then winced. "Spoken like a true man," he said, carefully rubbing his shoulder. He'd taken off his coat when they'd settled in their rooms. Now his sling showed plainly over his waistcoat.

"If you're finished with your meal, Papa, I would like to change your dressing and then retire." The day had been long and frustrating. Torcuil had barely spoken to her. Her father chaffed against the restrictions his mending shoulder placed on him. After long, weary hours of being ignored by one man and listening to the grumbling of the other, Verity was ready for sleep.

Save for a few rowdy souls downstairs in the common room, the quiet of the evening descended over the inn. The candle on the small table cast a circle of soft, golden light, banishing the dark to far corners.

Her father nodded, and she fetched the medicine box Mr. MacDougall had sent along. As she removed the old dressing, Torcuil studied the door.

"I thought we could move my bed in here," he said, "but now I see the bed will no fit." He shrugged. "I'll sleep on the floor."

Her father looked at Torcuil as if he'd gone mad. "Move your bed in here? Sleep on the floor? Most decidedly not!"

"This inn must be an assassin's fondest dream," Torcuil pointed out patiently. "The arrangement of our chambers makes it impossible for me to protect ye unless I stay in your room."

"You didn't stay in my room in Dundail," the marquess pointed out with rising agitation.

"Both our chambers opened onto the one we used for a sittin' room. I left my chamber door open, as did ye. We bolted all the doors leadin' out into the hall outside. There was naught else to worry about, unless ye thought yer daughter would murder ye in yer sleep?"

Verity applied fresh salve to the wound. "Papa, this looks so much better."

"I don't care if Napoleon has sent his most cunning assassins after me, I'll not have you or any other fellow sleeping with me, er, I mean, in my chamber. That is all I am going to say on the matter."

Torcuil scowled. "What's a personal guard to do but guard the person of his employer? How am I to do that if ye'll no have me near ye at night?"

The marquess examined the back of his hand. "No."

"Nighttime is when most assassins strike, ye know. They slide through the dark like sharks scentin' blood."

"You are hereby absolved of any murder committed during the hours of dark."

"Papa!" Verity exclaimed, horrified.

"No. You cannot sleep in my room," her father continued. "Not now. Not ever. What if I should seek the charms of a female companion? I'm sorry, Verity, but this must be settled now so there can be no doubt in Mr. MacCodrum's mind."

"A female companion?" Torcuil echoed, aghast. "Surely ye'd no take such a risk until it can be determined who's tryin' to kill ye? Why, what if she's an assassin herself? Och, 'twould be so verra easy for her just to drop a wee bit o' poison into yer drink, or ram a knife into yer heart when ye can least defend yerself. Females can be dangerous creatures."

"Yes," Verity said sweetly as she returned the roll of fresh linen to the medicine box. "We can."

She wished her father would occasionally seek the companionship of a woman. After all, he was yet a healthy, vital man. To her knowledge, there had been no one since her mother had fled, but her father's comment made her realize that she might not know everything going on in his life.

The marquess glanced down at the new dressing. "Thank you, my dear. You are my angel of mercy."

"Lord Ravenshaw—" Torcuil began.

"No. Absolutely not. I'm no Eastern potentate who insists on being watched and protected every minute of my life. Do give me some credit, Mr. MacCodrum. I know how to handle a pistol, and I'm a fair marksman, if I say so myself. Besides that, I'm a light sleeper."

"Have ye a pistol ye keep with ye?"

"Of course."

"No offense intended."

The marquess's bristled pride eased a little. "None taken."

Torcuil paused, his hand on the door latch, preventing Verity from leaving. "I'll say good night to ye, then, sir. I'll see Lady Verity to her chamber."

Caution warred with hope in Verity on hearing Torcuil's words.

"Good night, Mr. MacCodrum."

He opened the door and followed Verity out into the hall. Without a word, without touching her, he escorted her to the door of her chamber. He opened it and stepped inside.

Verity's heart began to race.

Without benefit of the candle she held, he checked the room for intruders. She followed him inside, disappointed at finding his purpose was only to keep her safe. He turned to go back out and nearly collided with her. In a swift movement, he stepped back.

"Good night to ye, then, Lady Verity." He started toward the door.

"Torcuil."

He stopped, but he did not turn to face her. "Aye?"

Determined, she set the medicine box on the bed and walked around to stand in front of him. She gazed up at the hard, elegant planes of his face. "Torcuil, have I offended you in some way?"

"Nay, lady. Ye've done naught."

"Then why are you behaving in this manner?"

"And what manner would that be?" he inquired politely.

"You're treating me like a stranger." Watching his guarded expression, she decided to take a gamble. "No, not even so well as that. You behave as if you've formed a disgust for me."

"I've no formed a disgust for ye," he muttered.

"Pardon? I could not hear what you said," she lied.

He looked directly at her. "I've no formed a disgust for ye." He repeated each word distinctly, grudgingly.

She gave him her most enchanting smile. "I'm so happy to hear that."

He made no reply.

"I've tried and tried to think of what I might have done to make you angry with me." She gave him a limpid, soulful look. "What was it, Torcuil?" Her mouth caressed his name. "Please tell me." She swayed slightly forward.

He reached out to steady her—or hold her at a distance, she wasn't sure. What mattered was that he was touching her. Lightly. Reluctantly. But he *was* touching her. His strong hand curved around her forearm. She closed her eyes and centered on that sweet meeting point.

He snatched his hand back. " 'Tis only that I dinna deem familiarity wise, is all."

Verity sighed inwardly. He was much too guarded. She would have to think of a way to lower his guard. She remembered how natural they'd been together when she'd given him his first riding lesson, and yearned for that easy acceptance of each other. Until then . . .

She stepped away from him. "Thank you for your help with the beds," she said softly. "Pleasant dreams."

He regarded her with his dark-eyed gaze for a moment, then inclined his head. "And to ye, lady."

After he'd gone, she struggled out of her gown, the spring chill in the chamber penetrating to her bones. Men had always courted her. Young men and old men, peers and commoners. They'd applied for her hand with tedious predictability. She'd never had a man eager to be quit of her presence before, she thought, depressed. It was a humiliating, humbling experience.

It was also a little frightening. Torcuil was the one for her, she knew it with a certainty that pierced her heart. He made her feel things she'd never felt before. He charmed her with his honesty and that streak of innocence that appeared at the least expected moments. When Torcuil was close, the clamor and demands of the rest of the world grew less audible. And when he touched her . . . Verity's breath stopped at the memory of their shared kisses. Oh, when he touched her . . . he became her world.

He wanted her, that had been as clear as the full moon last night.

Why was he resisting her so strongly now?

The next morning Verity was surprised to find she was the first visitor to her father's chamber. Torcuil usually arrived earlier than anyone.

After rapping on the door to rouse Daniel and Mr. Teak, she sent them to fetch breakfast. Then she went down the hall to Torcuil's room and knocked.

After several seconds passed with no response, she began to fret. She tried the latch but met with no success; the bar was in place. "Torcuil?" She pressed her ear to the rough, thick pine. A moan sounded from within the chamber. Alarmed, she pounded repeatedly on the door.

Relief washed through her when she heard the bar inside being lifted. Clad in his blue-green dressing gown,

Torcuil leaned heavily against the doorframe. His face was pinched and pale.

"What is it? What's the matter?" she asked in a rush, her gaze swarming over him, fearful of finding a hideous dripping wound.

He pushed away from the doorframe, and she noticed his mouth tighten. "I woke to find I can barely move."

"The inside of your legs?"

"Aye. And the backside."

She slipped in under his arm. "Here. Lean on me. Let's get you back to bed."

He scowled. "Nay." He drew away, but stumbled back against the wall.

"You're saddle sore," she told him, folding her hands primly in front of her. "There's naught for you to do but to return to your bed." She made no move to aid him, suspecting his pride was smarting as much as his legs.

He hobbled back to the bed and eased painfully down onto it, finally collapsing with a sigh. The bed was several inches too short, leaving his feet overhanging the end. "Saddle sore, ye say?" he asked after a minute of silence.

Leaving the door open for propriety's sake, Verity moved to stand beside him. "Riding requires muscles few of us otherwise use. That's why we only rode for an hour the day I gave you your first lesson. Two hours would have been ideal yesterday."

Torcuil stared at her. "Och," he groaned. "Ye tried to tell me."

Verity took no pleasure in her victory. "Lie quietly. Daniel and Mr. Teak will be here with your breakfast soon, and I—"

He struggled to get up, and she pressed her palms against his shoulders to prevent him. "Yer father is unprotected," he declared. "Stand aside."

"He's barred his door."

"I'm not at all certain such villains as we've encountered wouldna hesitate to kick down the door." He tried to get up again, his face white with the agony caused by his screaming muscles. Oh, she had some idea of what he endured.

"Kick in the door?" she asked. "That would be noisy enough to draw attention, would it not?"

He glared at her.

"Very well. *I* shall go stay with Papa until Daniel and Mr. Teak return."

"Och, that should strike terror into their black hearts," he muttered under his breath, easing down onto the mattress.

"I heard that," she informed him briskly. He said nothing, glaring at the wall. "Do I really strike terror into your heart, Torcuil?" she asked, her throat contracting. Was that why he'd avoided her? Had she grown too managing without realizing it? Too . . . terrifying?

He turned his head to look at her, and she felt his dark gaze move over her face. "Aye," he said gently. "Ye put a fright into me, and no mistake."

She lowered her eyes to focus on the toes of her practical half boots peeping out from beneath the hem of her figured muslin gown. "So many people depend upon me to keep order in their lives. If I seem overmanaging, perhaps it's because"—she raised her head and rallied a bright smile—"I am. I must be, you see. For their happiness, and . . . I've grown fond of being needed."

Before Torcuil could reply, Daniel and Mr. Teak bustled through the door bearing trays loaded with covered dishes, plates, pots, napkins, and flatware.

"Here, now, what is this? Lying abed with a lady present? Where are your manners, lad?" Mr. Teak blustered. "Lady Verity, what would your father say?"

"The door was open, Mr. Teak," she replied, knowing

the coachman for a kind, hearty soul. "And as you can plainly see, Mr. MacCodrum has made no unmannerly advances toward me."

An hour later, Verity had supervised Torcuil's swallowing every drop of his tincture of meadowsweet, everyone had finished breaking their fast, and Daniel had—to Torcuil's misery and deep embarrassment—massaged Verity's rosemary liniment into the offending muscles. The marquess stayed with Torcuil while the last of the travel arrangements were made. Two hours later, they were rumbling down the road toward London.

Torcuil rode in the carriage.

Acrid smoke lay over London like a thin, gray pall. Building after building of brick or stone bellied up to the crowded streets, their rooftops flooding the murky horizon like the choppy caps of the sea on an overcast day. The stink of horse dung, unwashed bodies, and sewage filled the air. The clangor of iron-rimmed wheels and iron-shod hooves against paving stones vied with cries of "Buy my fat chickens!" and "Hot baked wardens!" Periodically, a trumpet blast announced newspapers for sale. Land folk crammed together, flowing like krill through the streets. In carriages and in wagons, on horseback and on foot they swarmed. Young and old, male and female, dressed in a muted rainbow of various garb.

As Torcuil stared out the coach window, a tide of panic rose in him. How would he ever find Eideard in *this?* Bile burned his throat. How could his brother have brought himself to come here, where this alien smell and chaos pressed in upon one like the weight of the deep? Why would a silkie endure such eye-burning suffocation, so far from home? But Torcuil knew. Eideard had come here to learn about the land folk. He'd left the company of his kind to learn what further threat the creepers posed.

The full enormity of his older brother's sacrifice struck Torcuil with gut-wrenching force. How had Eideard survived this? he wondered. His eyes scanned the myriad faces visible to him as the carriage made its slow progress. Only the knowledge that the blood bond remained intact assured Torcuil that his brother still lived.

A woman thrust a hand clutching a mass of small red globes up to the window. "Buy my ripe cherries!" she called, striding alongside the coach. Torcuil shot Verity and her father a look to see their reaction to the intrusion, but they seemed oblivious to it.

"Uh, nay," he told the woman, feeling awkward. "Thank ye."

For the first time, she seemed to notice him. The eyes in her grubby face lighted. "Coo, ain't you a handsome one?" Her smile revealed a missing tooth. "C'mon, me lord. Buy the cherries, and I'll let you sample me other wares." The swell of her breasts above her low-cut bodice left little doubt as to the nature of her other wares. "I don't do that for just any toff, you know."

She seemed good-natured, and he felt reluctant to hurt her feelings. "I'm sensible of the honor of yer offer, madam," he told her solemnly, "and grieve that I must decline."

Her smile grew. "You're a fine gentleman, you are." She stopped. "Come to me any day, luv," she called after him. "Me name's Dolly."

Torcuil drew away from the window, unwilling to tempt others to push their goods at him. He settled back in the seat. They'd been traveling for what seemed like endless days since he'd recovered from his humiliating soreness. He'd soon returned to the saddle. Only Verity's suggestion that he might feel less distracted in the carriage

his first time in London had persuaded him to come
inside. Where London and horseback riding were concerned, he bowed to her expertise.

"Have you made a new friend, then?" she asked from
her place next to her dozing father. A peculiar tone edged
her voice.

He studied her expression. Her sweetly shaped mouth
curved neither up nor down. Her lashes obscured a clear
view of her eyes. Hadn't the past several days been excruciating enough without confusing him with trick questions?
For hour upon hour, he'd been in her company. He'd been
diverted by her wit, heard her golden laughter, and
observed the sweet curve of those lush, soft lips. Those lips
he'd tasted and burned to taste again.

It was driving him mad. He ached to hold her in his
arms. He wanted her more than he'd ever wanted a female
before.

She occupied far too many of his thoughts to be natural. She was only a land female, after all. He'd have known
if she were one of the fair folk in disguise. That queer
vibration would have slid under his skin, alerting him.

He regarded her warily. "How can he sleep through
this noise?" he asked, nodding toward her father, thinking
to turn the conversation in a direction he might hope to
control.

Her lips curved up. "He's spent many years in
London."

Torcuil determinedly focused on the slumbering peer,
whose chin rested on his chest and whose hat had slid partially to one side. "Aye," he said, thinking that years in this
pit could easily drive a man to escape into unconscious-
ness. "And until his shoulder heals entirely, he'll need
more rest."

"Yes. I shouldn't be surprised if we stay in London for
a few weeks. It's fortunate that all the partners, all except

Lord Outhwaite, that is, will be here for the sessions of Parliament. But soon he'll wish to be off to Norfolk to see Outhwaite, too. There isn't much time left before the meeting, and he is determined to do everything in his power to sway the vote."

"Are ye happy to be back in this town, then?" he asked, glancing out the window at the teaming street.

She removed her fan from her embroidered satin reticule. With a graceful motion of her hand, she opened it. "To own the truth, I much prefer country living."

That was a bit of unexpected news. "Oh? I believed ye to have some attachment to London."

The fan, an ivory and painted silk creation, gradually moved back and forth. In the stuffy interior of the carriage, a whisper of its breeze wafted across his face, bringing her female scent.

Her dimples made their appearance. "My attachment is more for my father, my cousin Fanny, and her family, who live here."

He wanted to reach out and smooth an errant tendril of her golden hair off her cheek. The memory of how silken it was to his touch, how soft her cheek, came unbidden to his mind. Determinedly, he kept his gloved hands resting on his thighs.

"Do you now see why I suggested you might have difficulty locating your brother?" she asked softly.

His gaze strayed back to the window. They had turned onto a less riotous street crowded with houses.

"We are very nearly home, Mr. MacCodrum," she said, and, unaccountably, he disliked hearing her formal use of his name. He should be glad for it, he told himself sternly. He needed as much distance from this woman as he could find.

"*Ye* are very nearly home, lady. I am only farther from my own."

Her fan drifted back and forth in front of her face, drawing his gaze to every fascinating detail of her features—the large, sea moss green eyes, the small, straight nose, and the lush, smiling mouth. He also noticed the faint smudges of purple beneath her eyes and the dullness in her usually fine skin.

She lowered her lashes. "Our home is your home."

That was precisely what he feared most. "I thank ye," he said stiffly.

The marquess gave a jerk and a snort. Blinking, he straightened in his seat, readjusting his top hat. His eyes lighted with pleasure when he looked out the window. "Home at last."

Torcuil ached with his own homesickness. He wanted to hear the crash of the waves, the hiss of the foam as it swept the shale. Sweet Aobh, how he missed the echoing cries of the terns! He seethed with the need to race through the water, feeling its cool caress along his body. He hated clomping along in the slow and ungainly manner of land creepers. He despised these suffocating layers of restrictive clothing. He'd never wanted to become involved in the conflicts and turmoil rampant among this breed. It was insane. It was degrading.

It was unavoidable.

Like it or not, he was involved. He needed them to help him find Eideard. They needed him to keep the marquess safe. It was right, this endeavor to keep the mine open. While the miners and their families might not be Ravenshaw's kinsmen, they looked to him for protection, which he clearly meant to give. His conduct was counter to everything Torcuil believed about the land folk. It was curiously silkielike. Torcuil found the comparison surprising.

The carriage rolled into a street that formed a square with three other wide streets around a gated, oval garden.

Most of the imposing buildings that fronted the avenues were built of the dusty red material Verity had told him was brick. All were large, though some more so than others. Short black metal fences formed an almost straight line in front of the mansions. Wooden posts set in the ground separated foot traffic from horses, wagons, and coaches. The carriage slowed to a stop in front of one of the largest buildings in the square.

Daniel descended from his seat on the outside of the coach to place the stepping stool on the paved ground and open the passenger door. He assisted Verity out, then the marquess. With a mischievous smile he offered Torcuil his hand and grinned when Torcuil refused it.

Confronted now with the dwelling place of the marquess and Verity, he looked up past the four rows of windows to the vast plain of roofing tiles and numerous chimney pots that he'd learned from Mrs. Candlish was a sign of vast wealth. Compared in size to The Citadel, the blacksmith's barn and livery stable in Dundail was as a droplet of water to a well. Ravenshaw House was a filled bucket.

Though they hadn't knocked, the front door swung open to admit them. As he entered behind Ravenshaw and Verity, Torcuil saw that a portly man of middle height and years was responsible for that neat trick. The fellow wore his brown hair cut short, as seemed fashionable among the land folk. The charcoal green of his coat and cream color of his trousers contrasted with the leaf green of his waistcoat.

Running footsteps clattered on the polished, pale, blue-gray flagstones. The sound echoed against the coffered ceiling twenty feet above and the Ionic columns of veined umber, ocher, and gray stone that lined the length of the walls. Flanking the black paneled double doors at the far end of the entrance hall were two tall niches. In each stood a lead statue Torcuil easily recognized as Grecian. The

Citadel held hundreds of Greek statues. Both of these were nude males. One wore a laurel wreath crown and had a cloak thrown about his shoulders and draped over an extended arm. The other figure leaned casually on a gnarled walking staff.

The overwhelming magnificence of the room made comparisons to anything Torcuil had seen in Dundail ludicrous.

A troupe of men and women stampeded into the entrance hall from an adjoining corridor to the left. As Torcuil protectively stepped in front of the marquess and Verity, he watched the others come to a halt in a line next to the man still positioned by the door. The short, plump woman standing next to him quickly patted her white, ruffled cap. A man farther down the line tugged at the bottom of his waistcoat. A young female hastily smoothed her neat apron.

"There's naught to worry about, Mr. MacCodrum," Ravenshaw said in a low voice behind him. "These people belong here."

"Aye? In what capacity?"

"Come meet them," Verity said, leading the way to stand in front of the line. "Have I not told you that this falling into line every time we return after an absence is not necessary, Mrs. Dibble?" she said gently to the short, plump woman.

" 'Tis only right and proper to welcome you and his lordship home," Mrs. Dibble said firmly. "Mr. Quenby received your letter saying you were coming back, but we expected you two days ago. Mr. Quenby sent to Mr. Fensam, telling him of the letter and that you'd not arrived yet."

The man next to Mrs. Dibble spoke up. "He suggested that you might have needed to travel more slowly than usual to accommodate his lordship's injury."

"All too true, blast it," the marquess said, resolutely stepping around Torcuil. "Been cooped up in a carriage with two mothering hens. It's enough to drive a man mad, eh, Quenby?" he asked the middle-aged man standing next to the door.

Quenby's face remained an expressionless mask. "Unquestionably, my lord."

So this was Quenby. Torcuil matched the name to the face. Verity had told him about Ravenshaw House's butler, Cecil Quenby. She'd also spoken of Ravenshaw's steward, Kenelm Fensam, and the housekeeper, Mrs. Dibble, whose mate had died in one of the land folks' many wars, as well as others who worked in this mansion, its grounds, and stables.

The marquess turned toward Torcuil. "May I make known to you Cecil Quenby, the butler of Ravenshaw House? Quenby, this is Mr. MacCodrum, my—"

"Cousin," Verity interrupted smoothly. "He has come from Scotland to stay with us a while."

All gazes swung toward Torcuil.

He barely kept his jaw from dropping in surprise. The marquess stared at his daughter for a second before he recovered his aplomb. What was that sprite scheming? Torcuil wondered.

Verity offered an apologetic smile. "I comprehend the decision was made rather unexpectedly—"

"Unquestionably," the marquess muttered under his breath.

"And so a comfortable room must be readied for Cousin Torcuil. All his trunks could not be packed in time, so please do everything you can to accommodate him and make his sojourn with us enjoyable for him." She smiled, and Torcuil recognized the amusement twinkling in her eyes.

At that moment, the first swell of baggage unloaded

from the carriage flowed through the door on the shoulders of men all wearing the same style and color: coats and breeches a light clear green, and white waistcoats. Verity thanked Mrs. Dibble and the others, then began directing where the trunks, boxes, and bags were to go.

The servants scattered back to their work, all save a short dapper fellow of approximately the marquess's years. Torcuil knew from Verity's description that this must be Ivo Newitt, Ravenshaw's valet. The man's fair hair was cut and pomaded in what Torcuil knew now was considered a stylish manner. The valet's snowy neckcloth was impeccable, as were his chocolate brown coat, his cream-colored waistcoat, and his fawn pantaloons. He'd seen slippers on a man at one of the inns where they'd stayed. In her usual efficient manner, Verity had explained that boots were acceptable footwear for many occasions these days, but that slippers were considered more elegant. He'd resigned himself to the knowledge that she'd arrange for him to wind up with a pair.

He needed to find a buyer for his gold necklace and cuff, and soon. It chaffed against his pride to be forced to remain indebted to land folk, and particularly to Verity, for his wardrobe, his pistols, and his knives. When he left, he wished to be free of any obligation to them.

"Your lordship must have suffered terribly," Newitt soothed. "Perhaps a rest is in order, and later a nice hot bath with your favorite soap will aid you in forgetting your hardships."

Ravenshaw smiled wearily. "Capital idea, Newitt, but I would rather you see to Mr.—er, my dear cousin. His own valet was . . . uh . . . unable to make the journey."

Newitt quickly smothered his obvious distress. He raked his gaze over Torcuil from head to toes. "Certainly, my lord."

Torcuil felt as if he'd come up wanting in the servant's

estimation. He found it impossible to believe that his attire could be lacking, so carefully had Verity selected each item. Stealing a surreptitious glance at what he could see of his clothing, he noticed a speck of lint on his coat, and brushed at it. A cloud of dust billowed up to envelop Newitt, who was seized by a violent sneeze.

"I ask yer pardon, Newitt," Torcuil said. "I'd no idea I'd gathered so much of the road."

"No doubt," Newitt wheezed.

"If you will excuse me," the marquess said politely, and turned to leave the entrance hall.

Torcuil was determined not to let the marquess out of his sight. "I'll come wi' ye."

"That isn't necessary, *Cousin*," Ravenshaw said with a significant glare.

"Aye, it is."

"No, it is not. See him to his room, Newitt."

"But, my lord. Your wound—"

"Aye, yer wound—"

"Is healing very nicely, thank you. Verity will see to it when she has a moment."

"I'll no be leavin' ye," Torcuil insisted stubbornly.

Verity returned to the entrance hall with a brisk step. "Gentlemen, this entry hall is an excellent conductor of sound." She smiled. "Newitt, if Papa does not mind, perhaps you will go to his chamber and make ready for him. You're quite right. We must be careful to help him to continue healing." She raised her dark gold eyebrows in question as she directed her attention to her father, who clamped his jaw tight.

"Do as she says, Newitt," he said. "I'll be up directly."

The valet vanished through the door at the end of the room.

"I wish to speak to you two," the marquess informed them as soon as Newitt was out of hearing range. "The sitting room," he said, gesturing to the left of Torcuil. "Now."

When they were all in the sitting room, he closed the door and turned to face them. "This must be settled now. First, what the devil do you mean, Verity, by introducing Mr. MacCodrum to my own household as my cousin?"

"I'd wanted to discuss it with you first, Papa, but the opportunity never presented itself. I know how you dislike having a bodyguard, so I thought you'd find a bodyguard that no one knows is a bodyguard a more palatable situation. If everyone thinks Torcuil is a relative, there will be fewer questions when he accompanies you wherever you go."

Torcuil nodded. It made sense.

The marquess regarded both of them. "No."

"No?" Verity echoed.

"That is correct. No. Torcuil is not going to accompany me wherever I go. He's not going to sleep in my room. Indeed, as of now he is not my guard at all."

Instantly, Verity voiced her strenuous objection. Torcuil scowled. What foolishness was this? The elder needed protection. To Torcuil's surprise, he found that he deeply disliked the thought of Ravenshaw coming to harm.

The marquess held up his hands, signaling silence. "I have no doubt that I am the main target of whoever is behind these last two attempts on my life. But, as a member of Parliament, I've received death threats before."

"This was no just a threat," Torcuil pointed out sharply. "Ye were shot, and they would have left ye to die."

"Listen to Torcuil, Papa," Verity pleaded. "If he'd not happened along, you'd be dead now." Torcuil heard the fear in her voice.

"Ah," Ravenshaw said, "but he did happen along. And he very adeptly dispatched the assassins. Both times. That is why, my most precious daughter, I want him to be *your* bodyguard."

8

No man is a hero to his valet.
—Anne Bigot Cornuel

"What?" Torcuil and Verity exclaimed in unison.

The marquess cut short their tumble of objections with a curt, slicing motion of his hand. "I'm not a fool; I know how to defend myself, and I will exercise caution. But I'll not have my life ruled by fear. And my greatest fear now is that whoever is behind all this may again try to strike at me through you, Verity." His gaze softened on his daughter. "That, my dear, I could not bear. You are the most precious thing in my life."

Although Torcuil had not been consulted in this change of duties, he approved of Ravenshaw's desire to do everything in his power to protect his daughter. Unfortunately, this change presented certain difficulties.

"Papa, *please*—"

"I shall consider engaging a Bow Street Runner to investigate."

"But you need protection! *You* need protection, Papa, not I," Verity insisted, tears trembling on the lower lashes of her wide eyes. "Please, *please* do this for me. You are all I have. I cannot lose you, too."

Ravenshaw took Verity's hands between his. His lips curved in a gentle smile. "Daughter, I vow to you that I shall endeavor not to allow myself to be murdered. You cannot argue the fact that I am better able to protect myself than you are to defend your own dear person." He shook his head. "The fiends have already tried to harm you, and I fear they may try again. I trust only Torcuil with your safety." The marquess lifted a hand to cup her cheek. "Allow me to render my fatherly responsibility to you, child. It will do no good to argue. I am resolved."

She implored her father with her eyes, and Torcuil was glad that he was not the one who must withstand her.

"Go now," Ravenshaw said softly. "The servants are waiting on your instructions."

She pressed her lips together and hurried from the room.

Torcuil rose to follow Verity, envisioning some of the problems this new arrangement would present him. He should say no, he thought. He should tell the marquess now that he'd never agreed to protect Verity. That he'd never agreed to spend hour after captivating hour with her. That he'd never expected—and certainly never wanted—to be with her each and every day. Only the fact that the marquess was right kept Torcuil silent.

"A word, Mr. MacCodrum, if you please."

Torcuil turned to face the marquess, not liking Verity out of his sight before he'd spoken with each member of the staff and gone through the house. "I believe yer staff should be alerted at least to the fact that ye've been threatened. 'Twill make it more difficult for strangers to get close to ye."

Ravenshaw considered Torcuil's suggestion for a moment. "Very well." The words were impatient, clipped. The elder fixed him with a stern eye. "If I had my wish, Verity's guard would be a Turkish eunuch, if you take my meaning."

"Eunuch?"

Ravenshaw enunciated each word precisely. "A neutered male."

Torcuil blinked. Sweet Aobh! He remembered too clearly Verity telling him that the Turkish gelded their men. Then he recalled her saying that her own people did not.

"I did not miss her use of your Christian name," Ravenshaw continued.

"Aye, sir. It surprised me, also, considerin' she insists on observin' the proprieties."

"She does, eh?"

"Told me so herself," Torcuil said, trying not to think of how he'd held her in his arms. Of her soft, welcoming lips. Her ripe, undeniably female body.

"She's a sensible girl," Ravenshaw conceded. Then he met Torcuil's gaze. "You are to have a care for her heart as well as her person." He raised a bushy eyebrow.

Torcuil inclined his head. "I comprehend yer concern."

"Excellent."

As Torcuil opened the door to leave the room, the marquess said softly, "I expect you to do more than comprehend it."

Verity managed to swallow her tears as she went about setting everyone on course for a return to normal. She'd conferred with Cook on the supper menu. She'd set bossy Martha to unpacking her trunks and boxes. Newitt was arranging her father's things. Daniel had undertaken to put Torcuil's few belongings away in the crimson guest chamber. Holland cloths were already being removed. She could almost hear a contented hum resounding through Ravenshaw House.

If only her father would consent to have a bodyguard. Then she, too, might know some contentment.

She saw two footmen lugging a large copper tub up the stairs, and she knew it was going to Torcuil's chamber as she had directed. Soon they would be hauling buckets of steaming water up the backstairs to fill that tub.

Torcuil MacCodrum was another robber of contentment, she thought as she watched the men cart the polished metal vessel up to the landing and disappear down the hall. She had intended him for her father's personal guard, but she had to admit, having him assigned to her fit in very nicely with her intentions. She would simply have to find another guard for her uncooperative father, though it bothered her that securing one as competent as Torcuil wouldn't be easy. Verity sighed as she made her way to her own chamber.

If only Torcuil would be more reasonable about this. He needed her, couldn't he see that? And she wanted to help him. She wanted to help him as she'd never had the faintest desire to help any man other than her father. As soon as possible, she must call on Cousin Fanny.

She refreshed herself with a sponge bath. No sooner had she finished than a light tap at the door signaled Martha's return.

The maid bustled in with a silver tray bearing a plate of small orange-scented cakes and a pot of tea. "I thought you might be needing a little pick-me-up. Like as not you've been hurrying about, taking care of everybody and everything but yourself." She set the tray on a small satinwood side table inlaid with diamonds of rosewood. "Now just come right over here and rest yourself." Martha patted the upholstered seat of the armchair.

Verity smiled and complied. If she didn't go ahead and give in, Martha would natter away at her until Verity capitulated for the sake of peace.

"There you go, now. Here's your napkin." A small drapery of fine linen was swathed over Verity's muslin-clad lap. "'Tis clear to anyone that you've not been getting enough to eat while you were gone. Why, you're nearly skin and bones." Martha poured out a cup of Verity's favorite tea.

"A gross exaggeration." Verity took a swallow of her tea, savoring its delicious warmth and familiar flavor. She had missed her special blend. Perhaps Torcuil would like this tea.

As if Martha had picked up on that thought, the thin, severe-looking maid paused in front of the open wardrobe and shot Verity a prim, sour look. "Mr. MacCodrum is a handsome man, for all that he's a Scot. I'll wager he's turned a few female heads."

Verity took a small bite of her cake. Her feelings toward Torcuil were still too new and jumbled for her to give them voice. He haunted her dreams. His kiss remained vivid in her memory, its power lingering to stir her. But the distance he'd assumed toward her hurt, despite her determination to bridge it.

She mustered a smile. "I thought I would have to borrow his sword and protect him from his admirers." Verity leaned forward and lowered her voice. "Do you know that when we stayed the night with the earl and countess of Crowles, the earl apprehended the countess as she was making her way down our hall at midnight, heading toward Cousin Torcuil's room?" Verity had wanted to punch the countess on her aristocratic nose.

"Can you imagine?" Martha shook her head as she held out a muslin gown trimmed along the hem with white-work flowering vines.

Verity nodded her agreement to wear the dress. "I've never seen so many women behave so brazenly."

"How did Mr. MacCodrum react to all this attention?" Martha asked.

"In truth, I doubt that he's aware he's handsome. The forward attentions of these women seemed only to embarrass him." A source of vast satisfaction to Verity.

"Perhaps that was because they threw themselves at him when he was in the company of respectable people. What gentleman would not be embarrassed then?"

Verity frowned. She hadn't thought about that.

Martha tried unsuccessfully to remain nonchalant. "Everyone in the house is talking about how Mr. MacCodrum saved you and his lordship from certain death. That he carried his lordship for miles. Is it so?"

Modifying the tale to omit certain details, Verity related how Torcuil had leaped out of darkness to their aid. When she'd finished, she set aside her teacup and rose to her feet. "I think perhaps I'll have a little lie-down while Cousin Torcuil takes his bath."

Martha moved the gown to arrange it over a chair. "Is it true? Is he really the son of a Scottish chief?"

"He said so. We have no reason to doubt him." Verity allowed Martha to help with the removal of her traveling gown.

"Wouldn't his lordship know?" Martha asked.

"Oh . . . uh . . . that branch of the family broke off after the rebellion of seventeen forty-five, you see. They were unjustly accused of having supported the Pretender, and the king stripped them of their lands and possessions."

"How terrible!"

"Later they regained them, but the clan refused to have anything to do with their English relatives. Indeed, they seldom left their Highland stronghold at all. Until now, that is. Cousin Torcuil has been sent to mend the rift." Guilt over her extravagant lie gnawed at Verity.

Martha pursed her lips. "How romantic."

Verity thought so, too.

Martha left and Verity, clad in her chemise and quilted dimity corset, stretched out on her bed.

She woke to a knocking on the door. Daniel called to her. "Lady Verity. Mr. MacCodrum has still not come out of his bath. He doesn't answer us when we call to him. Mr. Newitt fears the worst."

Groggily, Verity sat up and consulted her pendant watch. Dear Heavens, she'd slept two hours, longer than she'd intended. Torcuil should have been out of his bath over an hour ago!

"I'll be there in a minute, Daniel." She slid from the bed and struggled into her fresh gown. Tendrils of hair had escaped their pins, but she didn't take time to retuck them. As she hurried down the hall, she patted everything down, then forgot about it.

Newitt and Daniel stood outside Torcuil's closed door. The color was high in Newitt's cheeks.

"Are you certain he's in there?" she asked.

"Yes, Lady Verity," Newitt said. "The door is locked and we've heard water sounds inside."

"Water sounds?"

Newitt and Daniel nodded vigorously.

She leaned close to the door. Silence. She looked at Newitt and Daniel. "You're certain?"

They nodded again.

She knocked on the door. No one answered. She heard a splash from inside the room.

"Lady Verity," Newitt said, shoving a pomaded curl from in front of his left eye, "Mr. MacCodrum has locked himself in his chamber and doesn't answer my knocks,

Daniel's knocks, and now your knocks. He didn't respond when I called to him, either. I fear he may have slipped and drowned!"

Apprehension seized her. "Why do you believe Mr. MacCodrum has drowned?" She remembered the splash she'd heard.

"They'd just finished filling the tub for his bath, my lady, when he ejected me from his chamber and locked the door. That was over two hours ago! I've called to him and called to him and he won't let me in."

"Calm yourself, Newitt," she said, trying to sound soothing. "Tell me what happened."

"He *ordered* me out of his chamber." Newitt adjusted his coat with a jerk on the tails. "I was only trying to help him undress—"

"Did you ask if he wished your assistance?"

Newitt drew himself up. "Of course not. I am a valet— the valet of a *marquess,* I may add."

Verity bit down on her impatience. Newitt could be a prig at times, but he took great pride in his work, which was, her father insisted, excellent.

"Precisely what did you do before Mr. MacCodrum dismissed you?"

"Why, I attempted to unbutton his waistcoat."

From behind her, through the closed door, she heard another faint splash. "Perhaps you startled him."

"I heard," Daniel said, "that he nearly murdered a tailor in Dundail."

Newitt's eyes grew large. "Murdered?"

"An exaggeration," Verity said hastily, shooting Daniel a silencing glare. " 'Tis just as I said, likely you startled him. Tell me, why do you think he has drowned?"

"Because a while later, when I returned to make certain all was well, despite his treatment of me—I do not shirk unpleasant tasks, you know—"

"Yes, yes, you're a veritable paragon of duty," Verity agreed impatiently.

"I knocked and even called to him, but I received no answer. Not one word."

"My father's cousin is the son of a Highland chief," she informed Newitt. "Think of him as a prince. Would a prince deign to answer a servant ill-mannered enough to bang on his chamber door, demanding admittance?"

Newitt's fine-boned face reddened.

"It's not like you to conduct yourself so indecorously, Newitt."

"Well . . . I admit I felt I was poorly treated. But when I couldn't get a response from him, I grew concerned."

Verity offered him an understanding smile. "And rightly so."

"Shall we break the door down?" Daniel asked.

"I doubt that will be necessary. Daniel, please bring me my ring of keys. I'm afraid I left them on the bedside table in my chamber." The footman departed for her room.

Verity patted Newitt's rigid shoulder. "Pray go attend my father. I suspect that he feels sharing you with his cousin is an unhappy sacrifice."

Newitt brightened. "Truly? I have no wish to neglect my lord Ravenshaw."

"Of course not. Go now and reassure him." She watched Newitt hurry away.

Alone in the hall, she knocked softly on Torcuil's chamber door. "It's me, Verity," she called in a tight, low voice. "Torcuil, let me in."

Her only answer was a splash. The image of Torcuil, hunched unconscious, bobbing facedown in the tub, bloomed with terrible clarity in her mind's eye, and she hammered on the door.

Abruptly, it opened and she was jerked inside. The

door closed with a thud. Torcuil stood before her, dripping water on the Aubusson carpet.

He was nude.

Quickly she spun around, turning her back toward him. "Get dressed," she snapped.

He moved to stand close behind her. The heat of his body penetrated her clothing. "Why? Ye've seen me before." His breath against her ear sent a sensual shiver through her.

"That doesn't matter," she told him sharply, battling the sensations he was evoking in her. "Put your clothes on."

Torcuil placed his wet hands on her upper arms, drenching the cloth of her sleeves, warming her through the wet. The room was silent save for the slow, rhythmic dripping of water onto the floor.

"Ye command me as if I were no more than yer father's horses. How can it matter if I'm clothed or no?"

"It matters," she said huskily.

His fingers began a leisurely massage upon her arms. "Aye? How so? Ye dress me. Ye order me to stay. To lie. I dinna want any of this. None of this strange food, these tight clothes. 'Dinna sniff yer food, Torcuil. Dinna wear yer hair long, Torcuil. Dinna break the tailor's neck, Torcuil.' Now I'm yer father's cousin, am I? And yer father tellin' me he'd rather I was gelded!"

The motion of his strong fingers, the warmth from his body, the deep, lilting sound of his voice sent Verity's every other thought tumbling into the void. Nothing else was important. Why didn't he move a little nearer—and kiss her? Suddenly his last word penetrated her sensual fog. "Gelded?"

"Aye." His lips brushed the curve of her ear as he whispered to her, "He fears I'll mount ye."

She blinked in shock. "A gentleman wouldn't say such things to a lady." Verity swallowed dryly at the image his words conjured. A question slipped past her lips before she could stop it. "Will you?"

The breathless quality of her voice camouflaged her shocking query with a tremulous catch that he clearly read as fear. Seconds passed before he responded.

His fingers ceased their motion. "Nay," he said finally. He released her, taking his warmth with him. "I'll no plant my seed so far from home."

A lonely chill rolled through Verity. "Daniel is coming with my keys," she managed to choke out.

He moved away from her, and a soft rustle of fabric suggested he was getting dressed.

"Why did you not answer when Newitt called to you? When I called to you?"

"I was enjoyin' my bath." His clipped words warned that no further discussion on the subject would be tolerated.

Some strange urge prompted her to explain. "We thought you might be injured." As far as she could see, he had no reason he couldn't have called out, "I'm well" or at least, "Go away."

Outside in the hall, the clamor of rapid footfalls signaled someone's approach. "Are you finished dressing?" she demanded, feeling edgy and hurt and annoyed.

"I'm dressed enough."

She turned to find him stuffing his shirt into his pantaloons. "Not nearly enough," she countered, snatching up his shoes from the floor, and his waistcoat from the back of a chair.

He halted. "Why not enough? I'm covered."

"That's not enough. Like that, you look as if you've just gotten dressed."

"I have!"

"And *I* am in your room, alone with you. What do you think that will suggest?"

He glared at her and resumed tucking in his shirt. "That ye interrupted my bath?"

"Never mind. It's just highly improper, that's all." She thrust his waistcoat at him, and he took it. Quickly he jerked it on.

His fingers stopped. He stared at her. "They'd think I'd mated wi' ye?"

Blushing furiously, Verity batted his hands away and finished buttoning the waistcoat. "Put your shoes on."

He jammed his feet into his shoes and made quick work of the small buckles. "Is that what yer folk believe? That no female is to be alone with a male lest he—"

"I've taken gross liberties during our sojourn away from Town. I've been alone with you several times without a chaperon, but there was no help for it. There was no one available to accompany us. That will change now. But, as my cousin, you may be alone with me sometimes, in some places. However, your bedchamber is *not* one of those places."

Torcuil fumbled with his cravat. "It makes no sense to me. Here, cousins marry, even first cousins. Are ye sayin' that cousins may marry but not mate?"

Heat throbbed in her cheeks. "Of course they do."

A knock sounded at the door. She took over the arrangement of his cravat, her fingers flying.

"Then why—"

"Not now!" she whispered fiercely. She rushed to the window across the room and dropped into the armchair there. Hastily she smoothed her skirts and patted at her hair.

Torcuil opened the door to Newitt and her father. It was only then that she realized that his hair was still wet and unbrushed.

"Have an enjoyable bath, did you?" her father inquired with an awful pleasantness that immediately set Verity on her guard.

"Aye, sir, I did." Opening the door wider, Torcuil gestured for her father and Newitt to enter.

"Ah, daughter. I see you persuaded your cousin to allow you into his bedchamber." Pointedly, he eyed her hair, and she remembered its tousled state.

"Papa, I—"

Torcuil smoothly interrupted her. "I had finished with my bath and had dressed save for my cravat. I believed Cousin Verity would know how to arrange it properly."

"Newitt would have helped."

"But he was no longer available. Only Verity stood there when I opened the door."

Verity crossed the room to stand between her father and Torcuil.

"Why did you not answer to his knock to begin with?" her father asked with stiff politeness.

"Not to put too fine a point on it," Torcuil said, "but I sent him away in the first place. I had nothing to say to him."

The marquess's bushy eyebrows rose. "Indeed, sir? May I inquire why you sent my valet away?"

"Let's just say I sensed he dinna wish to attend me," Torcuil drawled, not deigning to even glance at Newitt, whose usually milk white skin was now flaming red.

The marquess frowned. "Is this so, Newitt?"

The valet stared down at the modest lace on his sleeve cuff. "I-I-I . . . may have . . . inadvertently . . . given that impression."

"I dinna blame the man," Torcuil said. "He has your well-bein' at heart . . . Cousin. Now, out o' the blue, he's been ordered to tend to a stranger. A man's loyalty canna be switched so easily."

Newitt nodded.

"Confound it, man, I wasn't asking him to switch his loyalty. I merely wanted him to assist you."

Newitt gazed up at Verity's father. "Truly, my lord?"

"Of course," the marquess said gruffly. "What man of any sense would willingly part with the finest valet in London?"

"True, my lord."

"What gave you such a ridiculous idea?"

"In the twenty years I've been your valet, your lordship has never before asked me to serve another."

The marquess snorted. "Won't ask you to do it again, either."

Newitt beamed.

"Damnably sorry about this, Torcuil," the marquess said. "Most embarrassing."

"Dinna give the matter another thought," Torcuil replied graciously. "Mayhap it would be well for me to obtain my own valet. Until then, if I have need of advice, I hope I may consult you or Cousin Verity?"

"Of course, of course." The marquess took the ring of keys from Newitt and sent him to finish unpacking his trunks. He handed Verity the jangling ring.

"Papa, I was just about to take our dear cousin on his tour of the house and grounds, but perhaps you'd prefer to show him, yourself? I wouldn't wish to do anything improper."

The marquess sighed. "If it's an apology you're expecting, you're doomed to disappointment. It's a father's duty to protect his daughter's virtue. And you must admit, the circumstances looked highly questionable."

She smiled. "'Tis only that Torcuil doesn't always understand our ways."

Her father eyed Torcuil sharply. "He understands enough to get you both in a very fine mess, and don't you think otherwise. He's a man."

Torcuil's mouth tightened.

"I have no wish to impugn your honor, sir," the marquess said to Torcuil, "but my first concern must be for my daughter."

"A father's natural concern," Torcuil replied frostily. "I shall endeavor not to discomfit either of us."

As Verity watched her father turn and walk down the hall, a new respect for Torcuil's quick wit took root. He'd turned her father's sharp suspicion away from them, procured Newitt's desire to return solely to her father's service, and, somehow, led the others away from the question that still niggled at her. Not for a minute was she convinced that he'd evicted Newitt because he thought the valet resented him. Torcuil was too unconcerned with the opinions of others to trouble himself over Newitt's rancor. And he certainly wasn't shy about his own nudity.

So why had he locked everyone out of his room during his unusually long bath?

9

Trust in Allah, but tie your camel.
—Arabian Proverb

The following afternoon, Verity took Torcuil to her father's tailor, who, having received the letter she'd sent from Dundail, had a proper wardrobe ready for Torcuil to try on.

"Lord Ravenshaw's cousin is truly a fine figure of a man," Mr. Wrighton observed as Torcuil stalked out of the dressing area into the parlor of the exclusive address, where Verity waited. "No padding is needed anywhere."

Torcuil was wearing evening attire at that moment. The civilized elegance of his black velvet coat, white brocade waistcoat, buff satin breeches, white stockings, and black slippers contrasted with the barbaric splendor of his sable mane and side braids. Verity had come to appreciate his long hair. To her, his wild locks personified him—beautiful and fiercely untamed.

Ignoring Torcuil's scowl, she smiled at him. "You look quite dashing, you know."

"I feel like a fool, paradin' around in one suit of clothes after another. 'Tis a waste of time and money."

Mr. Wrighton sniffed. "Everything you've tried on is of the finest quality, I do assure you," he said stiffly.

"Of course it is," Verity said soothingly. " 'Tis obvious to anyone with eyes. Even to persons with little patience for such things, is that not so, Cousin Torcuil?"

He glowered at her. "Aye."

Apparently mollified, Mr. Wrighton strolled around Torcuil, examining his handiwork with a critical eye. "Such a tall fellow," he murmured. "A perfect physique."

Torcuil regarded the tailor from beneath hooded eyes, reminding Verity of a great hawk watching a strutting pigeon. The session with Mr. Graham burning all too clear in her memory, she thought it wise not to prolong the one with Mr. Wrighton. "Only you could have created such splendid garments, Mr. Wrighton," she said. "Please have everything sent to Ravenshaw House."

As Torcuil changed back into the clothes in which he'd arrived, Verity and the tailor chatted. Until he went a step too far.

"I confess," he said. "I am a little disappointed to have missed Lord Ravenshaw."

With unhurried ease, Verity rose to her feet. She knew this self-important little man was commenting on the fact that she, an unmarried lady, interested herself in this somewhat intimate aspect of an unmarried man's life. She turned an unsmiling face on him as Torcuil again joined her in the parlor. "Good day to you," she told Mr Wrighton coolly and took satisfaction in the flicker of anxiety she saw in his eyes.

Torcuil preceded her out onto the street, turning his head as he scanned the heavy pedestrian traffic and, farther out, those on horseback and in carriages and wagons.

Finding no immediate threat, he stepped aside for her to exit the shop.

As they walked toward the spot where they'd left the marquess's carriage, she rested her palm on Torcuil's arm, looking up to see his eyes widen.

"You did not offer your arm, so I am compelled to take it," she teased.

"Offer ye my arm?"

"Yes."

His dark eyebrows drew down in puzzlement. "Why must I offer ye my arm? Ye have two perfectly good ones of yer own."

Verity sighed. This Highlander was growing to be more and more of a mystery to her. "When they are walking, a gentleman may offer a lady his arm."

"Ah." He nodded. "'Tis a way for them to touch."

Heat flooded Verity's face. "Sometimes, perhaps. But I've never heard it put quite like that."

From beneath thick, dark lashes, he threw her a skeptical glance. "Have ye ever held the arm of a man for whom ye cared naught?"

"Yes. Sometimes it is the *galant* thing for the gentleman to offer his arm. I've taken the arms of some of Papa's friends over the years. At balls and dinners I've been forced to accept them from odious men as well as pleasing ones. To refuse would give offense."

Torcuil appeared interested. "Do ye care if an odious man is offended, then?"

"Even odious men have feelings," she said gently. "Some cannot help that they are repulsive or obnoxious." She canted her head as she considered. "I think I would refuse to take the arm of an evil man."

"If ye knew he was evil."

She smiled. "Yes, there is that. It seems to me someone who is evil is apt to keep the fact hidden as well as he can."

Torcuil studied the crowded walkway ahead of them. "Not always. Evil has a voice and often it's raised in triumph."

His quiet, certain words sent a chill through her, and she lifted her eyes to study his impassive profile. So much of this man remained a mystery. He was too adept at deflecting questions about himself.

Before her thoughts could continue in that vein, they arrived at her father's gleaming black town coach, the Ravenshaw coat of arms painted in silver on the lacquered door. Mr. Teak, attired in green and silver livery, stood at the head of the lead horse. Daniel, also in the Ravenshaw livery, opened the carriage door. In minutes, the vehicle lurched as Mr. Teak directed the team of bays out into the clamorous flow of traffic.

Neither Verity nor Torcuil spoke for several minutes as they rolled toward Fanny and George Elbourn's residence. Finally Verity could stand it no longer. "Are you wondering about your brother?" she asked.

He gazed out the window of the carriage. "Aye."

"You think you should be searching for him, don't you?"

He turned to look at her, his face shuttered and unreadable. "I do."

"Papa has engaged a man who shall find your brother if anyone can. He is a Bow Street Runner and native to London. He stands to earn a handsome bonus for quickly finding Eideard."

Torcuil's eyebrows lifted in surprise at her use of his brother's name.

She smiled. "You didn't believe I'd remember."

"I dinna believe ye had reason to."

Verity pulled her India shawl more closely around her shoulders. "You are mistaken," she said softly.

He met her gaze, and a wave of yearning surged

through her. A draft created by the motion of the carriage teased at the dark curtain of his hair. Today he wore no ribbons in his side braids.

Her fingers curled into handfuls of shawl beneath the drapery of the garment. She wanted to touch him, just to feel the solid, warm strength of him. She wanted to breathe in his sea scent.

He lowered his eyes to her lips. Into her mind burst the memory of his embrace, his hungry kiss, honey sweet with the power of his longing. For a moment, he had been hers. But a moment was not long enough.

He looked away. "I am yer bodyguard only," he said tightly.

"Of course you are."

"I warn ye, dinna toy with me, Verity."

She had no intention of revealing her designs on him. "I wouldn't dream of it."

Daniel opened the door and pulled down the steps. Pleased by his excellent if unintentional timing, Verity smiled at him as he assisted her out of the coach. Torcuil emerged behind her. Without glancing at him, she knew his eyes were searching the area for possible danger to her.

She turned back to him, wanting to share her enthusiasm over this visit. "Fanny is my dearest friend and cousin."

Torcuil faintly smiled. "So ye've said. If I remember from the five times ye've told me, her husband is a lawyer and they have three children."

Verity chuckled as they walked to the door. "She is due to deliver the fourth in two months' time. Have I indeed told you this five times?"

His mouth curved upward in true amusement. "Aye. Mayhap more. 'Tis clear she's dear to ye."

"Oh, yes. Wait until you meet her."

The door opened after her first knock to reveal a tall, respectably dressed woman in her forties.

Verity cheerfully greeted Fanny's housekeeper, Mrs. Jillings.

The older woman beamed. "And good morning to you, Lady Verity, and to you, sir."

A tall young woman with ash blond tendril curls escaping from her lacy white cap lumbered into the entrance hall, burdened by her advancing pregnancy. "Verity!" she exclaimed delightedly. "I was beginning to believe you would never come home." She stretched out her arms and hugged Verity, who laughingly hugged her back.

"Has it truly been an eon since I last saw you?"

"It must be!"

Out of the corner of her eye, Verity saw Mrs. Jillings send Torcuil a sympathetic smile. Extricating herself from her cousin's embrace, she performed the introductions. As Torcuil bowed gracefully over Fanny's hand, her cousin shot Verity an approving look.

They went into the Elbourns' cozy parlor and sat down in front of a fire. A servant brought a pot of tea for the women and hot chocolate for Torcuil.

"I understand you hail from Scotland, Mr. MacCodrum, from the Highlands."

He balanced his cup in its saucer on his knee. "Aye, Mrs. Elbourn."

"This is your first visit to England, is it not?"

An odd guardedness flickered in his dark eyes. "It is."

"What do you think of London?"

He hesitated. "I dinna think I've seen enough of it to comment."

Fanny took a sip of her tea, her blue eyes alight. "Noisy? Smelly? Smoky?"

One corner of Torcuil's mouth quirked up. Slowly his

reluctant smile grew. "I canna understand why ye tolerate livin' here," he admitted.

"Oh, London has its compensations. It is the center of government and commerce. Here there is excitement, society, and—most important of all—employment. This is where important people gather, and important people have needs that must be fulfilled. In London, my husband has many clients of consequence, so I tolerate living here very well. Indeed, sir, you'll not find as many excellent shops or theaters anywhere else in Britain as you will in Town."

"Which reminds me," Verity said to Torcuil, "we must stop at the jeweler's shop on the way home. Before Papa and I went to Scotland I left my pearl bandeau there for cleaning."

"As ye wish."

Fanny set her cup aside. "You have arrived in London during the Season, Mr. MacCodrum. We shall have to see to it that you are not wanting for amusement. Do you like horses, sir?"

"I've met only one, madam, but the experience has been cordial," he said solemnly.

"Uh . . . yes, of course. I suppose the mountainous terrain of your home makes riding impractical."

Torcuil's lashes lowered. Verity sensed his guard coming back up. "Aye."

"Of course he has the use of any of our horses during his visit with us," Verity offered smoothly.

"It would be difficult to find more excellent horseflesh anywhere," Fanny assured him. "But if you would find it entertaining to visit Tattersall's while you are here, I'm certain my husband would be gratified to take you as his guest."

"Ye're verra kind to think of it."

"And then, of course, there will be the balls and the

dinners, the theater and the shopping. I'll wager you have no libraries in the Highlands such as you'll find here."

"It seems there are things about London I've yet to learn."

Fanny laughed merrily. "I pray you adore every minute of your lessons, sir. Certainly my dearest cousin will prove a marvelous teacher."

Verity felt her cheeks warm despite herself. She smiled at Fanny. How she wanted to visit with her alone for a while! With Torcuil now her personal guard instead of her father's, she feared she'd never be able to ask Fanny the questions she wouldn't dare ask anyone else.

"Will you be accepting many invitations?" Verity inquired of her cousin.

Fanny lifted the teapot and silently offered to pour Verity another cup. Verity declined the offer with a partial shake of her head.

"No. This babe is heavy, and I am too ungainly. It seems I must wait until summer to dance the ecossaise." Fanny leaned forward, assuming a conspiratorial air. "I shall rely upon your visiting me with reports of the latest *on-dits* and scandals."

Verity laughed at her cousin's mischievous air. "You shall not miss a thing, that I vow."

They chatted for a while longer. Torcuil sat in quiet dignity, responding when spoken to but offering little. Fearing to tire Fanny, Verity bade her cousin good afternoon and waited as Torcuil bowed over her hand with grave courtliness. She was unprepared for his smile as he lifted his gaze to Fanny.

"Ye carry motherhood well, Mrs. Elbourn. 'Tis rare to see a woman so radiant in her bounty."

Fanny actually blushed! Verity hadn't witnessed that in years. She shot Torcuil a speculative glance. Did he have some power over women?

As soon as Torcuil and Verity were seated inside the carriage, and instructions had been relayed to Mr. Teak to stop at Kenyon's, Torcuil began with his questions.

"What is a bandeau?"

"A woman's headdress. You'll see one when we get to Kenyon's. It's lovely, really—"

"What is Tattersall's?"

"It's a place where horses and their gear are auctioned. Why didn't you ask Fanny—"

"What is a library?"

Faintly annoyed at his interruptions, Verity explained to him the workings of a lending library.

The light of recognition sparked in his dark eyes. "Och, we have such a thing where I'm from. Enormous, it is, with thousands of books and scrolls. They're no for purchase—they belong to all of us."

Verity found that bit of news uplifting, though she suspected the "thousands" was an exaggeration. Here was a common ground. "Have you read any of the books?"

Torcuil gave her a look that told her what he thought of such an inane question. "Of course."

"Papa has an excellent library at Ravenshaw House. Please feel free to make use of it." Verity writhed with impatience over this mundane, impersonal conversation. Why had he insisted on this barrier of polite distance between them?

"I thank ye."

With an inward sigh, Verity looked out the window at the houses and shops they passed. For now, she must be content that at least he felt willing to ask her questions when they were alone together. With what she knew he had yet to learn to get him through his role as her father's cousin, there would be questions aplenty. Now, more than ever, he needed her. If only he would allow her to help him.

At Kenyon's jewelry shop, Verity and Torcuil entered to find Mr. Kenyon the elder waiting upon the duke of Marbay's demanding daughter, Lady Euphemia. She sat holding a snuffling spaniel in her lap as she looked down her hatchet nose at the exquisite earbobs and brooches displayed in several velvet- and satin-lined drawers.

Mr. Kenyon's son hurried to offer Verity and Torcuil elegant, brocade-upholstered chairs. A snap of his fingers brought an anxious mouse of a girl, who bore a tray with cups, a pot of steaming tea, and a dish of seedcakes. Torcuil advised him that they had come for the pearl bandeau as Verity and the duke's daughter accorded each other calculated nods of acknowledgment.

In the few minutes that they waited, Lady Euphemia completed her selection and departed. She swept out the door, nearly knocking down a man who was passing on the street.

Mr. Kenyon, senior, presented the newly cleaned bandeau in a drawer lined with midnight blue velvet. Twenty perfect, creamy pearls glowed in their gold floral setting.

"You have made it beautiful again, Mr. Kenyon," Verity said.

The jeweler inclined his head. "You are too kind, Lady Verity."

She lifted the ornament from the velvet and placed it on her head. As if by magic, Mr. Kenyon's son produced a looking glass, which he held for her. "If I may be so bold," he said, "my lady's incomparable beauty is the true jewel."

Out of the corner of her eye she saw Torcuil, who was turned slightly away from the two jewelers at an angle that prevented them from viewing his face. Slowly, he crossed his eyes.

Startled laughter escaped Verity. Catching herself, she managed to turn it into a cough. As obsequious as Kenyon's son acted, he didn't deserve to be laughed at.

Unlike her own father, Mr. Kenyon, senior, entrusted nothing to his grown offspring's care, leaving poor junior to make what niche he could in his effort to assist in the family business. She took a quick swallow of her tea. "Dear me," she said breathlessly, patting her chest. "That was unexpected." Very unexpected.

When she looked at Torcuil again, he was the picture of innocence as he examined the bandeau.

"I am thinking of having the stones of one of my grandmother's necklaces reset. I've never been fond of the setting, but the stones are quite lovely."

"Would those be the rubies, Lady Verity?" the elder Kenyon inquired. "The sapphires? The diamonds? My father, may his soul repose in peace, always said your grandmother had exquisite taste. She only chose his masterpieces."

Verity removed her fan from her reticule. Idly, she slipped open the ivory sticks and fanned herself with the painted silk. "I am happy to say that it is none of his masterpieces I wish changed, for I am very well satisfied with them. No, this is a necklace of lapis lazuli my grandfather bought from a gentleman returning from India."

"Lapis lazuli?"

" 'Twas a stone much prized by the ancients," Torcuil offered quietly.

Verity looked at him in surprise. "Was it?"

He nodded. "The Egyptians especially favored it. They used the stone extensively, and spread its rich blue dust over the floors of pharaoh's palace."

"I am familiar with lapis lazuli. Indeed, I have worked with the stone before, but it has been years," the jeweler admitted. "There's been no call for it."

Verity smiled. "Well. Perhaps we shall set a trend."

As soon as they got into the carriage, Verity fixed Torcuil with a mock-stern look. "A fine thing, mocking

Mr. Kenyon's compliment to me. How ungallant you are."

"I was expectin' him to fall on the ground and kiss yer toes," he drawled.

To Verity's surprise a giggle bubbled up out of her. She *never* giggled.

Torcuil's dark gaze moved over her face. "Another minute and we'd have had to step o'er the fellow when we left the shop. 'Twould ha' been an embarrassment to us all."

"Yes," she agreed, struggling to appear serious. "Most awkward." She was pleased to see the corners of his mouth twitch. "In truth, he is a very nice man whose father has trouble relinquishing even a little of the control he has over the family business. There are two more sons not even allowed to speak to the customers. They are required to stay in the back of the shop at whatever tasks they've been assigned."

"Och, poor Kenyons the younger," he said blandly.

They rode a block without further conversation before Verity could no longer stand it. "Do you not think I'm . . . attractive?" The word Mr. Kenyon, junior, had used was a bit much, but her looks had been praised far too often not to believe she was at least not homely.

Torcuil regarded her from beneath hooded eyes. "Ye know I do."

Embarrassed at her ridiculous uncertainty and, worse, her indelicate bid for his compliment, Verity turned her eyes to the scenery outside the window. "It's not as if I'm a wart," she muttered to herself.

"No a wart. More like a freckle."

She gasped with indignation.

Torcuil laughed, and the deep, masculine music of it filled the interior of the coach, surrounding Verity, tugging her spirits up, enfolding her in the magic of its spell.

"I thought I was an anemone," she reminded him.

"Aye. That, too."

Wishing to turn the conversation away from her looks, which reminded her of her brazen behavior, she smiled. "How did you learn so much about lapis lazuli?"

"I read."

"In your clan library?"

He nodded.

"Do you have a particular interest in lapis lazuli?"

"Nay."

"History?"

"Aye."

"What else?" she asked determinedly.

He cocked his head. "And why do ye wish to know?"

She had no intention of giving him the real reason. Oh, no. He was too skittish to deal with the truth yet. There would be time for that after her father was safe and his brother had gone home to their clan.

"I'm simply trying to make conversation," she replied airily.

"Why?"

"Because I grow wearied of riding through London with a silent prison guard sitting across from me."

Torcuil's brows lifted. "I'm no a prison guard. And ye're no a prisoner."

"You're right, of course." She met his gaze squarely, bracing herself against the sizzle of awareness that always brought. "You're the one behaving as if you're the prisoner."

Iron-rimmed wheels rumbled on the paving stones outside. Nearby, a cheesemonger called out a menu of his wares.

Torcuil wore a shuttered expression, leaving her no clue to his true feelings. "Things canna go back to the way they were, Verity."

"I know that."

A shaft of rare, bright sunshine slanted between the curtains. It flowed over one of his high cheekbones, the bridge of his nose, and the curled lower lashes of one eye. "Then dinna play with me," he said softly. A note of wistful regret trailed through his words, like a thread caught in a wave. "I've come to search for my brother. I've given my word to yer father I'll do my best to keep ye safe until his enemy can be found. When I've discharged those obligations, I'll leave."

Fingers of misery clenched around her heart. Defiantly, she lifted her chin. "How nice for you. In the meanwhile, is there something prohibiting you from being civil?"

"I've been civil."

Verity snapped open her fan. "If long silences and monosyllabic responses are your idea of civility, then I should dislike seeing what passes for rudeness."

"Aye," he said flatly. "Ye would, and no mistake."

Verity briskly fanned at the heat of her hurt. Then her hand faltered as, for the first time, an arrow of doubt struck her.

What if he did not need her after all?

10

Here comes the trout that must be caught with tickling.
—William Shakespeare

Quenby entered the library where Verity and Torcuil sat on opposite sides of the room, pretending to read their books. On one upraised hand, he bore the familiar small silver tray.

Verity glanced at the name on the calling card. "Where is he?" she asked.

"In the ivory drawing room, Lady Verity," Quenby intoned.

"Please tell him I'll be with him directly."

"Very good, my lady." With the measured dignity of a professional mourner, the butler left the library.

Torcuil snapped his book shut and set it down. His face might have been a mask for all the emotion it revealed.

"I suppose you've heard that Lord Sheldrake has arrived for our ride," she said stiffly.

"I have."

Annoyed at his remote air, she swept out the door, into the hall, where she paused in front of a gilt-framed looking glass. She adjusted her casquet-style bonnet of Pomona green velvet. With jaunty defiance, she flicked the dark green airy plume. A few blond tendrils whispered against her cheeks. Too bad it was the baron of Sheldrake who would appreciate them and not Torcuil, who had made a point of not noticing.

She went to the ivory drawing room, where she found her father chatting amiably with Lord Sheldrake. Oh, how pleased he must be over this outing. If Verity had announced at that moment her desire to wed the baron, her father would likely have produced the special license.

This was the first time she'd seen the baron since returning to Town. He was tall—though not nearly so tall as Torcuil—and slim. Oh, he was handsome enough, and his short brown hair was thick and promised to remain so the rest of his days. After all, he'd reached the ripe age of thirty-one and his hairline showed no sign of receding. His brown eyes were dark, but not as dark or intriguing as Torcuil's.

She smiled and strode forward in a rustle of lawn and fine-woven wool to welcome her guest, who had risen to his feet as soon as she'd appeared at the door.

"How pleasant it is to see you again, Lord Sheldrake," she said as he took her hands in his and bowed over them.

"A perfect day for a ride in the park," the baron heartily observed. "Our trip will be the maiden voyage for my new phaeton."

Verity's father scowled. "A phaeton? A bit racy, don't you think, Sheldrake? Blasted unstable, those things."

"I do assure you, sir, that this carriage is quite safe. I'd never wish to put Lady Verity at risk."

Aware of Torcuil's presence behind her, Verity smiled.

"Oh, Papa, I'm sure it will be all good fun. Now everyone will see my new bonnet." Heavens, could she sound more insipid?

"Just have a care, my dear. Don't want you falling off that thing. Long way down, you know."

"Yes, Papa."

"Sheldrake," the marquess continued. "I don't believe you've met my cousin." He performed the introduction with blessed economy. "He'll be accompanying you."

Verity and Sheldrake both stared at her father in surprise. Apparently, she thought, his concern for her safety outweighed his eagerness to see her married and settled with this man of his choosing.

When her father blandly met Sheldrake's gaze with no further word of explanation—and, indeed, as her father, he was not required to give one—the baron managed a thin smile.

"Well, then. Shall we all be on our way?" he said.

Outside, Torcuil mounted Samson. Verity was aware of his gimlet gaze on Lord Sheldrake as her suitor handed her up onto the phaeton's high seat, then climbed up beside her. A side glance revealed Torcuil's clenched fists on the low pommel of his saddle.

The baron negotiated the traffic in the few streets to Hyde Park with skill and patience. As they progressed, he asked her how she'd enjoyed the trip to Scotland. She gave him the edited version. With every word she spoke, every breath she drew, she was conscious of Torcuil riding close beside her. Without offering a word of conversation, he studied the crowds, the phaeton, and its dapper driver—though, truth to tell, Torcuil's attire was every bit as splendid, if a bit more understated than that of her father's partner. But then, she was certain, he could have been dressed in sackcloth and looked breathtaking.

Finally, they entered the park. The noise diminished

until there were only the sounds of the horses' hooves on earth and the occasional rattle, squeak, or clink from the phaeton.

"Ah! Much better, don't you think?" Sheldrake asked of Verity, the slant of his gaze cutting Torcuil out of the question.

"It is more peaceful here," she admitted.

Just then, a high phaeton careened around the wooded bend in the path up ahead, and sped toward them. The oncoming horses strained at their harness, their eyes wide with panic.

"Help!" the driver screamed, her bonnet gone, her hair in wild disarray.

As if mesmerized by the sight, Sheldrake stared at the runaway carriage, his own horses slowing to a stop.

"Get yer carriage out o' the way!" Torcuil shouted. Then he reined Samson around the phaeton and nudged the horse into a gallop, looking for all the world as if he planned to try to intercept the onrushing team and carriage.

Verity cried out against such a move. The sound of her voice must have penetrated Sheldrake's trance, for he immediately flicked the reins. Too late for them to move to safety. The other vehicle was already dangerously close.

Torcuil leaned forward in the saddle, close to Samson's neck as the gelding's flashing legs ate up the distance. Then Torcuil guided Samson into a close turn, which brought them abreast of the lead horses in the runaway team. Verity watched with her heart in her throat as he leaned over and stroked a palm down the neck of the closest animal. Then the most amazing thing happened.

The horses veered to the other side of the wide path and began to slow their pace. It seemed oddly as if the team were doing so of their own accord. Gradually, they came to a stop, some distance behind Sheldrake and

Verity, but Torcuil had not remained with the team. When they'd slowed enough to allow the driver to regain control, he'd ridden back to Sheldrake and her.

Verity knew he believed his first duty was to watch over her. As she saw the crowd gathering around the now-motionless carriage behind them, and then glanced next to her to see Torcuil's shuttered expression, she realized that only her imminent danger had prompted him to leave her side.

Danger caused by Sheldrake's inability to move his shiny new carriage a few feet to the side of the path.

"Very impressive, MacCodrum," the baron said, a dark red stain moving up his neck. "Bravo."

Torcuil regarded Sheldrake evenly, but offered no comment.

"Shouldn't we go back and make certain the driver is unharmed?" Verity asked.

Sheldrake turned in his seat to look behind them. "She's mobbed," he said hastily. "Someone will see to her if there is need." He flicked his reins and directed his team to continue ahead.

When Verity made no attempt at conversation, the baron frowned. "We'd only add to the crowd if we went back."

"I'm sure," she murmured.

A horse and rider separated from the throng and rode over to them. "You're the fellow who saved the lady in the phaeton, aren't you?" the elegantly dressed man asked Torcuil.

"I slowed her horses, aye."

"You did a great deal more than that! And I wished to thank you, sir," he said, holding out his hand. "The lady you saved is my intended." Torcuil took his hand and they shook. He glanced at Verity and smiled. "By gad, it seems you saved two ladies today."

A flurry of introductions followed, but Verity had already met the marquess of Kellaway once before. Indeed, she'd even met his father, the duke of Lyford.

"Lady Verity, a pleasure to meet you again. Good thing you have this fellow looking out for you," Kellaway said, nodding toward Torcuil.

The baron sat stiffly on the seat beside her. While she had no wish to rub his nose in his own poor judgment, she certainly had no intention of ignoring Torcuil's heroic deed.

"Yes," she agreed, smiling up at Kellaway. "Most fortunate."

"MacCodrum. MacCodrum," Kellaway muttered to himself. Then his face lighted. "MacCodrum, of course!"

Hope suffused Torcuil's face. "Have ye met my brother, then?"

"Your brother? Yes, I can see the resemblance now. Damn fine fellow, though I must tell you, my father's not happy with him now."

"Where is Eideard? Why is yer father unhappy with him?"

A shout brought Kellaway's attention back to his own party, behind them.

"Do ye know where I can find my brother?" Torcuil asked urgently, as if sensing his time was running out.

"Actually, no one seems to know where he's gone. It's as if he's vanished off the face of the earth." Another shout sounded behind them. "Really must go now. Again, you have my deepest thanks. Let me know when you find your brother—Father will definitely want to know!"

It sounded to Verity as if Eideard was in trouble with the duke. *Not* a happy position to be in.

With a wave, Kellaway turned his horse and galloped back to his intended.

When Torcuil would have followed, Verity managed to

stay him. "A duke is not a good enemy to have," she warned him softly. "It may not prove wise to catch his notice. Let me see what I can learn through my friends."

Torcuil hesitated. His gaze followed Kellaway. Abruptly, he gave her a short nod.

Sheldrake flipped the reins with barely repressed violence. Surprised, Verity turned to find the color high in his aristocratic cheeks. "Is there something the matter, Lord Sheldrake?" she asked.

His mouth flattened into a hard line, and he shot her a sidelong glance. "Don't tell me you didn't see that?"

"See what? Lord Kellaway came over to thank Cousin Torcuil for saving his betrothed's life. A gracious gesture, I thought."

Sheldrake dragged in a deep breath and let it out. His fury appeared to go with it, for he smiled, but when he turned to look at Verity, she saw the glint of cold hatred still lurking in his pale blue eyes. It sent a chill through her.

"Kellaway and I have been acquainted for years. Indeed, a few years ago we both invested in two of the same business ventures. But he has always held me in dislike, even to the point of spreading rumors. Came very near to slandering my name. And now he pretends not to know me."

"Why would he dislike you?" Why, indeed? she thought dryly.

Sheldrake shrugged slightly. "Who can say? The man is full of bizarre fancies. Clearly he was spoilt as a child." He heaved a sigh. "Not like some of us."

"Pray elaborate," she said, not certain she wanted to hear more but needing the distraction from her awareness of Torcuil's dark gaze on her.

The baron smiled. "I wouldn't wish to bore you with the details of my youth."

"No youth is boring," she coaxed.

That was all it took. Sheldrake launched into the tale of his deprived childhood, of the war between his parents. "They were always quarreling." Sheldrake's voice had taken on a singsong, nasal quality that grated against Verity's nerves. It was as if he'd told the story so often it now put him in a trance. "The least little thing would set them off."

"So you said." Several times.

"I wasn't robust enough to suit my father. He found me a disappointment."

Which he'd also told her more than once. True, Lord Sheldrake's childhood had been unhappy, and for that she felt sorry. But the man was an emotional leech bleeding her dry of sympathy. He was entirely too needy.

"My mother was a good woman. High-spirited, is all."

"Of course." If he harped on that just once more, Verity was certain she'd scream. She chanced a look at Torcuil. Solemnly, he met her gaze—then rolled his eyes. She stifled her laughter.

Sheldrake droned on. "I need a good woman, too, Lady Verity."

And she sincerely hoped he found one. Soon.

When she offered only a polite smile, he chuckled. "But enough about me. I took the liberty of having my cook pack us a luncheon." He directed the horses beneath a tree filled with the bright green of new leaves. Then he reached behind him and brought forth a wicker basket.

"I'm afraid I wasn't expecting your cousin to accompany us," he said, his voice faintly sullen.

"Oh, but surprises make for the jolliest of times," she said brightly. "I'll share my portion with him."

In minutes, a blanket stored in the back of the phaeton had been spread upon the new grass, and the contents of the basket spread over them. Verity sat between the two men. Sheldrake reclined on his side, while Torcuil sat cross-legged, his back perfectly straight.

"What a lovely idea, Lord Sheldrake," she said as she placed a slice of tongue, then spoonfuls of plum sauce on a plate. Next came helpings of spinach fancy and pickled cucumbers. She passed the baron his dish.

"I thought you'd enjoy it. Your father told me that you like fresh air."

"I do. It's one of the reasons I prefer country living."

On Torcuil's plate she placed a piece of boiled chicken, along with the vegetables. He accepted it from her with a sober inclining of his head.

"Country living?" Sheldrake echoed incredulously. "I should think you'd feel isolated and bored. Town is so much more civilized."

Sheldrake and Verity debated the plus and minuses of city living while they ate their meals. For dessert there were macaroons. When she saw Torcuil's face light over his first taste of the confection, she made a mental note to tell Cook to make them and keep them available to him.

They finished luncheon, and, as they packed everything back up, Sheldrake startled Verity by placing his hand over hers. His thumb stroked against the inside of her wrist.

His pale eyes met hers. "Please, call me Roger."

"Take yer hand off her," Torcuil ordered, the *r*'s rolling off his tongue in a warning growl.

Sheldrake's face went red. His mouth pulled down in anger. "How dare you, sir!"

Torcuil narrowed his eyes at the offending hand. Sheldrake removed it, curling his fingers into a pale fist by his side.

"I'll no have ye sullying the reputation of Lady Verity," Torcuil said.

"Sullying! You would do well to have a care over what you say to your betters."

Torcuil's smile caused Verity to worry for Sheldrake's life. "I know precisely who my betters are, Sheldrake," he said softly, "but ye dinna number among 'em. So ye'd do well to have a care over how ye behave with this lady."

"I have only the loftiest respect for Lady Verity," Sheldrake announced stiffly.

"I'm glad to hear it. Then ye'll no fondle her again."

"I merely placed my hand on hers," the baron insisted indignantly. "That could hardly be considered a fondle, MacCodrum."

No, but that stroking thumb could have, Verity thought. Still, would she have been so inclined to pull away had it been Torcuil touching her?

"It comes close enough," Torcuil said flatly. "Dinna do it again."

Sheldrake went livid. "Who do you think you are, giving me such an order?"

His eyes filled with dark wrath, Torcuil stepped closer to the baron, towering over him. "I'm her protector," he said, his voice deadly soft.

"Her father, bumpkin, is her protector!"

"He's no here now, is he? But I am."

Fearful that one of them would soon call the other out, Verity tried to intervene. "Gentlemen, please. I find this discussion most awkward and unpleasant."

"Lady Verity, your father has given me permission to pay you my addresses," Sheldrake informed her. "I had assumed that meant he trusted me enough that *I* should be considered your protector when you were out with me."

He might have had a point, had his delivery been made in a voice less likely to remind one of a spoiled, whiny child. How could her father have ever considered this man as a husband for her? Clearly, Sheldrake showed a different face to him.

"Lord Sheldrake," she said, squashing down her impatience, "what would you do if you were in Torcuil's place?"

"I say, he was a bit quick to find fault," he objected. "And a bit too strenuous."

Verity lifted an eyebrow. "Put it down to good intentions, and let's end this discussion now."

The men glared at each other for a minute, then Sheldrake nodded. "Very well."

She thought she might be pressing the matter to ask them to shake hands, especially when Torcuil still looked as if he wanted to break the baron into pieces.

When, once again, she and Lord Sheldrake sat on the phaeton and Torcuil rode Samson, Verity drew an easier breath. Save for a light, cool breeze, the day could not have been lovelier for early spring. She snuggled her hands in her swansdown muff, and turned her face up to the sun's warmth.

"I've brought you a present," Sheldrake said. He offered her an uncertain smile.

Verity smothered a sigh and tried to look pleased as he reached back into the lacquered trunk behind the seat and brought forward a silk-wrapped package.

"Oh, you shouldn't have," she said. At such an early stage of a courtship, a suitor's gifts should have been limited to a few flowers or a box of sweets. This, clearly, was neither.

"Go ahead," he urged. "Open it."

She untied the ribbons and the silk fell away. In the center of the rich fabric sat a luxurious muff made of dark sealskin.

Without knowing why, she glanced over at Torcuil. He stared at the muff, his face pale.

Lord Sheldrake had far overstepped the bounds of propriety this time. Carefully, she chose her words. "This is lovely, Lord Sheldrake. A rich gift, indeed." As she ran her hand over it, she found the fur softer than velvet. "Far too rich for me to accept."

"It will keep your dainty hands warm," Sheldrake pointed out.

"Of that I have no doubt. But I really cannot keep this."

His features took on a petulant cast. "I'll be offended if you don't."

Any vestige of sympathy she might have had toward him vanished. "Propriety will be offended if I do. As will my father. *That* is a situation much to be avoided, I assure you."

He hesitated, then nodded. "Very well, wrap it back up. I shall save the muff for a time when you can accept it."

Verity could not envision such a time. An expensive item like the muff would be an appropriate gift only to a wife, and she profoundly wished never to be his wife.

From beneath her lashes, she sneaked a glance at Torcuil, puzzled by his strange reaction to the sealskin muff. While she might have expected indignation, his shocked horror caught her off guard. His face was still pale, but rage pulled the skin over his high cheekbones taut. He looked away.

She was relieved when the baron turned the horses toward Ravenshaw House.

From experience, Verity expected that once she informed her father she could never be happy with Lord Sheldrake, he would insist she see the baron at least once or twice more to make certain it was not only an unfortunate first impression that was putting her off.

She knew whom she wanted for her husband. And she would do everything in her power to win him.

11

*The owl of Minerva spreads its wings
only with the falling of dusk.*
—Georg Wilhelm Friedrich Hegel

Dusk crept over the city as Torcuil kept his appointment with the junior Mr. Kenyon, who unlocked the door of the closed jeweler's shop to greet him.

"Good evening, Mr. Kenyon." Torcuil waited as the other man relocked the door. "I thank ye for assistin' me in this matter." A week ago, during the ride back to Ravenshaw House, Verity had related how eager this man was to prove himself. Surmising that the man would be eager to make a deal, Torcuil had specifically contacted him instead of his father.

"You're entirely welcome, I'm sure." Kenyon mopped his brow with a linen handkerchief. "You, uh, mentioned the necklace and cuff were exceptionally valuable." He placed a square of black velvet on the counter.

Torcuil reached inside his coat and withdrew the

pieces in question. As he placed them on the cloth, Kenyon's eyes widened.

Heavy gold gleamed against the plush black. Both the ornate necklace and cuff were encrusted with glittering diamonds, emeralds, sapphires, cabochon opals, and pearls. The jewelry had been selected from The Citadel for him to take with him because it was not considered exceptional, yet the gold and gems themselves would fetch a good price. Bounty from the sea.

"These have been in my family for more than a hundred years," he said.

Kenyon picked up the necklace. His thumb moved over the points on the thick gold pieces that made up the bib necklace. He held a magnifying lens up to one eye and examined the jewels.

"The cut of the stones is of a very old fashion," he murmured. He finished with the necklace and lifted the cuff. "The size of the stones . . . I see no inclusions. Amazing." Finally he completed his inspection and lowered the lens. "I must tell you, Mr. MacCodrum, I've never seen anything like this. I'm afraid we could not possibly offer you what these are worth. I cannot conceive of a store in Town that could."

Torcuil frowned, wondering what to do now. Go to another shop? He needed money. He wanted to pay the marquess back for the clothes and pistols. As much satisfaction as Verity seemed to take in helping him, he could not allow her and her father to continue to pay for everything he wore, each morsel he ate, everything he used.

Kenyon pursed his lips thoughtfully. "I know a gentleman who might be interested. A collector of antiquities."

"Could this gentleman offer their value?"

Kenyon smiled. "Oh, I believe so. He would be one of the few persons in the kingdom who could. Do you desire that I contact him?"

Torcuil indicated that he did, and the two of them struck a bargain whereby Mr. Kenyon would earn a commission in the event of a sale. Torcuil tucked the necklace and cuff back into his coat.

In the past seven days, Verity's net of friends and relatives had been able to trap only two facts concerning his brother: Eideard had frequented gaming hells up until a little over a month ago, and he had accrued a great many debts. Then he had vanished, as Kellaway had said. Torcuil's written request to Lyford for a meeting had been turned down flat. Even Ravenshaw had not been allowed to pursue the subject with the duke, but had come away from the encounter with a warning for Torcuil to stay clear of Lyford. Which left Torcuil right back where he'd been before meeting Kellaway.

"A moment more, Mr. Kenyon, if ye please," he said.

"Yes?"

"Have you seen another man who looks much like me?"

Kenyon grinned. "I think I'd remember someone who bore a striking resemblance to you. No, I'm sorry to say, I have not."

"Have ye met or heard of an Eideard MacCodrum?"

Kenyon thought a minute, then shook his head.

Disappointed, Torcuil bade Kenyon good evening and took his leave.

When he stepped back out onto the street, he discovered that the sun had set, drawing in the night. The only lantern he saw stood some distance down the street. He shook his head in wonderment. Land folk could not see in such dark, yet they did not light their places. Why would they aid the crime he'd heard about from Daniel, Mr. Teak, Newitt, and from Verity and her father? Now that he thought upon it, it seemed as if everyone in the house wished to warn him against the dangers of this town. He smiled. Even Cook had advised him against entering certain parts of London, though he had no idea where those parts should be.

"Even a strapping lad like yourself can fall prey to the villains who prowl those lanes," she'd said gravely. "You'd do well to listen to old Cook, being new to such a civilized place as you are."

He'd received her wisdom with the sobriety it deserved. She meant well, and he would not hurt her feelings.

Now he discovered there were no carriages to be hailed. Indeed, there were no carriages at all, nor even solitary riders on horseback. Glancing up and down the street, he saw there were mostly shops, which, judging from their curtained windows, had closed for the night. The hooves of a horse clattered in the narrow alley behind Kenyon's and faded into the distance.

Suddenly, London seemed more enormous and forbidding than ever before. In every direction rooftops, domes, and steeples extended as far as the eye could see, forming an unnatural horizon, dark against a darker sky.

Perhaps, if he could find his way to St. James Street, where the clubs would be open, he could hire a coach to take him to Ravenshaw House. He tried to remember the streets the hired driver had taken to get here, only to have them tangle in his memory.

Disgusted, he turned around and knocked on the jeweler's shop door. Mr. Kenyon could likely direct him.

But the shop was dark. Mr. Kenyon had left.

Cursing himself for a buffle-head, Torcuil struck out in the direction from which his coach had come. At least he knew *that* much. He strode up the street, warily eyeing the entrances to alleys and the doorways of empty shops. Here and there he saw movement. Far away, a dog barked.

Forced to estimate the distance to walk before he

turned, and in what direction to turn, Torcuil looked for a familiar landmark, but the tall, narrow buildings he passed were too similar to provide him with a guide. Gradually, the streets grew narrower and more odious.

Out of a tavern stumbled two loud drunks. The men staggered and swung wildly at each other. Abruptly one leaned over and vomited into the street. His opponent jeered at him, then wove back through the door. Here no posts had been set in the ground to separate pedestrian traffic from horses and wagons. Indeed, there was no room for such a nicety. As Torcuil continued his trek, more and more taverns spilled their boisterous clienteles into the street. Lines of laundry hung overhead. Ragged-looking females importuned men for money.

Torcuil knew the quality of his clothing set him apart as much as his stature. As he started to turn a corner, a woman slipped out of the shadows to block his path. Crude reed torches flanking the door of an inn across the street cast her in dim light.

"Fine gentleman like you needs company," she said, her words slurred, her fetid breath clouding on the chill air. "Take me with you, guv. Only cost you a shilling."

"Nay, but I thank ye for yer offer." A prickling up the back of his neck alerted him to danger. He made to walk around her.

She sidestepped to block his way. "A big handsome toff like you needs a woman. I'll show you a good time, I will." To his astonishment, she thrust down her bodice and lifted a bare breast toward him. "I could make you feel real nice."

Torcuil had seen female breasts before. His female cousins and aunts had occasionally assumed their land folk shapes—alien shapes, with no power to arouse.

But he had lived among land folk too long, covering himself as they did. The sight of the unclad breast unsettled him. Immediately on the heels of that reaction came an unbidden, unwanted thought.

The only naked breasts he wanted to see were Verity's.

"Begone!" he snarled.

The female scurried away from him, tossing vile curses at him from over her shoulder.

He stalked on, angrily trying to shut out the erotic mental image of Verity offering herself to him. Her green eyes would be hooded with passion, her lips moist and slightly parted. She'd run her slim fingers through his hair, touch his warrior's braids. Her graceful white neck would arch for his kisses. . . .

That warning prickle passed up his back again, and for the first time he noticed that he'd entered a deserted alley. Knowing his vision would be far better than any land creeper's, he ducked into the shadowed back doorway of what looked to be an empty building. He pressed back against grimy brick. The stench of urine, soot, and mildew assaulted his nose.

Minutes passed without movement. Could it have been his imagination? Torcuil counted the times that prickling had saved his life and decided he'd wait a little longer.

A man's voice called out softly. "Looks like he got away, Nat."

"You bleedin' fool! Don't say my name!"

"Sorry, Na—Sorry."

"He's here somewhere. I'd 'a' heard those expensive boots o' his walkin' away, otherwise." Nat raised his voice. "Ain't that right, toff? You're here. But you made a mistake coming to our neighborhood, see? Now you got to pay."

Torcuil wondered how many there were of them. Only the two? Three? More? More minutes of silence passed.

"You might as well come out, toff. You know you can't see in the dark. An' you don't know your way around here.

Not like we do." There was a soft thud and smothered curse. "Watch where you're goin', you bleedin' idiot!"

"Sorry, Na—Sorry. But you ran into *me*."

Cautiously, Torcuil peered around the edge of the doorway wall against which he stood. He saw two men not far from him. One sat on the ground, rubbing his head, then clambered to his feet. Torcuil tagged him as Nat.

"There's no time to quibble," Nat said in a harsh whisper Torcuil had no difficulty hearing. He doubted if someone standing at the far end of the alley would have had trouble hearing it. "That macaroni is still here, and I want those boots. If he gets away, we'll have to start all over. Now, look for him!"

"Did you see the *size* o' him? You sure you want to take on this toff?" the other fellow whispered back.

"He's rich! How many rich blokes make their way to this part of Town? Here to strike a deal with the man, I'll warrant. But this here toff won't make it to see him." Nat grinned. "You know how dangerous these streets are after dark."

"I don't know. Crossin' the man ain't smart-like."

Nat gave his cohort a shove. "Find the toff!"

"But—"

"He don't know his way around like we do, and he's not the devil; he can't see in the dark."

Torcuil smiled as he reached down for the knife concealed in his boot.

The two men moved away from him, farther down the alley. Releasing the knife, he eased silently out the other end of the alleyway and back out into the lane, pleased that the situation had been resolved without bloodshed.

A woman's voice cried out, "There he is, Benny!"

Torcuil whirled around to find the female who'd exposed herself standing across the street in front of the inn, pointing toward him. Gathered around her stood one eel-like man and two bigger, slower-looking males. The eel had her arm twisted behind her back.

"Took me goods for free, he did," she howled. "Had his disgustin' way with me and then refused to pay!"

Benny the Eel and his massive companions started toward Torcuil.

At that instant, Nat skidded out of the alley. "There he is!" he yelled. "C'mon, Harry!"

To face five opponents on their own alien ground was madness. Their kin might be only a shout away.

Torcuil bolted down the dark street.

Could he simply outrun them? If only he knew more about their stamina! He swept around a corner, into another narrow street. He thought he smelled water and headed in that direction, his boots ringing on the worn, slick paving stones.

He shot into a street that was wider than the others. Racing past houses, he decided it was time to try a new tactic. His pursuers clearly knew this territory well enough not to be entirely disabled by the dark.

Abruptly, he vaulted over a wrought-iron fence in front of a large house. He landed in a long strip of garden, sidestepping a bronze sundial with a bladelike gnomon. Quietly, he edged sideways between the side of the building and unmanicured shrubbery. Behind him, a man shrieked in pain. Apparently someone had landed on the sundial. With a burst of speed, Torcuil put the length of the rest of the property between them.

He climbed over the brick wall at the back of the property, losing his top hat in the process.

As Torcuil eased silently over the top of the wall, the scent of water again filled his nostrils, but along with that compelling smell came a stench unnatural to water. Without pausing to wonder, he dropped into the alley and took off.

His flight led them out of the residential area to a place of tiny shops and narrow, winding alleys. He heard the barracudas falling farther and farther behind.

Until Torcuil darted into a short, debris-strewn alley—with a dead end. He spun on his heels and started back. Then stopped.

The heavy panting of his pursuers echoed against the stained brick of the buildings at the entrance to the alley. A shaft of dim moonlight angled in to cast its light over wet paving stones. Into the light walked Benny and his two hulks. Quickly Torcuil stepped back against a wall, his boot striking something curiously firm in a pile of rags. A tingle skittered under his skin. But he had no time to consider it.

He knew his pursuers could not see him. He also knew that with three of them in this narrow place, they would not need to see him in order to catch him.

The time had come to stand and fight. His lips drew back in a savage smile as he slid his knife from his boot. The blade was well balanced and substantial, if not as great in length as his favored long knife. Its haft felt good in his hand.

"We . . . know . . . you're . . . back . . . there, . . . dandiprat," wheezed Benny. "Steal . . . from one o' . . . *my* . . . whores, . . . will you?"

Torcuil didn't know what he meant, nor did he care. His heart was already beating more quickly, sending the dark, dangerous warrior's elixir through him. In his callused palm, the grip of the knife was as warm and firm as a friend. His eyes pierced the black night, focusing on the three men gasping for air ten feet away from him. The reek of their sweat tainted his nostrils. Absent was the rank tang of land-creeper fear. Did they believe he feared them?

"Go get him, . . . you oafs," Benny ordered the two men with him. "I haven't got . . . all night."

The men stared at him, looked down the Stygian alley-way, then looked back at their master. "In . . . *there*?" one of them asked.

Benny gave the fellow a shove. "I've got . . . whores likely idling . . . around back at the Light. Get to it."

Each man pulled a weapon from his belt. One held a large knife. The other swung a chain. They lumbered cautiously into the alley. Three steps into the dark, the oaf on Torcuil's left stepped on a torn and rotting basket. He yelped, hopping around, shaking his foot.

Quiet footsteps sounded not far from the alley. Nat and Harry walked up to face Benny the Eel. Harry carried a lantern. The amber light of the lamp revealed the dead-end alley, stealing the only advantage left to Torcuil.

He sprang into the air, lashing out with one leg. The heel of his boot connected solidly with a jaw. The knife-wielding hulk slammed back into his comrade, who struck his head against the brick wall of a building. He slid bonelessly down to slump on the ground.

The other man rushed Torcuil, swinging his chain. Nimbly, Torcuil ducked the massive arm and rammed his head into his opponent's upper belly. Air rushed out of him, causing muscles to clench, stopping the quick recovery of air.

Now Torcuil faced Benny with his knife and Harry with his lantern. As if by sleight of hand, Nat produced a knife of his own. As one, the three men advanced on their prey.

Giving voice to the bloodcurdling battle cry of his people, he dodged Benny's thrust and kicked the lantern from Harry's hand. As Nat lunged with his knife, Torcuil nimbly danced aside, bringing up his own blade to sever the tendons in his attacker's underwrist. He shoved him into Benny. Benny's knife caught in Nat's coat. Torcuil's precisely placed foot sent Benny sprawling, dragging a bleeding, shrieking Nat with him. Harry snatched up the chain and swung it at Torcuil. As Torcuil ducked, he brought his bootheel down hard on Benny's knife hand. Benny screamed.

Harry turned to run—and ran straight into Torcuil, who slammed the heel of his hand up into Harry's jaw. The man's feet flew out from under him, and he landed flat on his back on the filthy paving, the chain skidding off into the night.

Torcuil snuffed the feeble ember in what was left of the lantern, then walked among the wounded and gathered the weapons on the ground. Then, one by one, he set about slicing the large muscle at the back of one ankle on each of his attackers. When the hulk he'd winded struggled, Torcuil slammed his head against the wall enough to knock him unconscious. Benny lost a tooth when he tried to bite him. A weeping Nat tried to crawl away. Torcuil was careful not to cut completely through the muscles, but none of these vermin would ever give chase again.

"Rejoice that I dinna kill ye," Torcuil told him afterward. He ripped the sleeve from his shirt and wrapped it firmly around Nat's wrist.

"You have," Nat wept. "Oh, God, you have."

"Ye would gladly have murdered me for my boots."

"Who . . . who *are* you?" Benny moaned, clutching his broken hand.

"A man who knows how to find ye, should ye give me cause. I've been generous this time. I'll no be so inclined again."

A glimmer passed under Torcuil's skin, and he turned to find a small, white-haired elder clad in a velvet suit walking out of the alley, carrying a small lantern lit by the stub of a candle. Torcuil's eyes widened with surprise when he saw the man's face.

"Listen to him," the broonie told Nat and Benny. "Pray

ye dinna meet the likes of him again. His sort are known as demon warriors—though, o' course, we civilized fellows know there's no such thing as demons—don't we?"

"And what are ye doin' here in this foul place?" Torcuil asked, delighted to see Seumus.

The broonie gripped his arm in a surprisingly strong hold and steered him away from the alley and the prone, wailing defeated. "Och, and isn't it a terrible town?" Seumus shook his head sadly. "So much violence."

Torcuil nodded soberly. "Aye. A man canna take an innocent walk without bein' set upon."

"And what were ye doin' out alone at this time o' night, may I ask?"

"I was doin' a wee bit of business." Torcuil related what had passed since last he'd seen Seumus. He hesitated over telling him about his feelings for Verity, then decided against it. He finished with his visit to Kenyon's and getting lost. "How long have ye been in London?"

"Two seven-days. Never did I think to see so much greed, misery, and lack of charity. 'Tis fair weighing me down with the glooms." Seumus sighed heavily.

"The poor here are in a more wretched state than those in the countryside."

"Aye, and the greater pity is that so much wealth resides here. It's as if the rich are blind. Blind, though dark, filthy warrens stand not fifty yards from their back doors."

"I know a man and his daughter who are both kind and generous, Seumus," Torcuil said, concerned about the broonie's poor spirits. "To know them would gladden yer heart." A thought occurred to him. "Where do ye live?"

"Live? Och, here and there. 'Tis difficult to achieve any privacy in a place where there's always someone breathin' down yer back."

"Why do you stay here?"

Seumus's eyes widened. "Why, never have I been needed more!" He swept out an arm to indicate the entire city. "So many await the lessons a broonie teaches. But . . ."

"Aye? But what?"

"It depresses my spirits to such gray depths. Is there no goodness here?"

"There is. Come back with me and you shall learn it firsthand." Torcuil stopped. "I have need of help. I canna keep Verity and her stubborn father safe without it. I'll no lay my faith in the skills of a mere land creeper. A Bow Street Runner, they call him, and speak of the fellow as if he's the confidant of the gods."

Seumus urged Torcuil back into motion, and they continued walking. "I've heard of them."

"What have ye heard?" Torcuil asked, guilt and hope and impatience at war inside him. "The marquess has one tryin' to find Eideard. I'd thought to seek him myself, but London is so large, and I dinna ken my way around in it, 'tis clear."

"Aye," Seumus said morosely. "I never thought to see the day when a silkie would deign to come to such a seethin' lair, much less two of them. 'Tis a sad, sad day."

"But what have ye heard of the Bow Street Runners?"

"They know their way around, and no mistake. He'll stand a better chance of findin' Eideard than you will."

Torcuil frowned. "Still, I must try." Suddenly he realized the smell of water was much closer.

"I imagine ye've smelled the water by now."

"I have, but it smells foul, like no water I've ever smelled before."

"The River Thames," Seumus announced, as they rounded a corner, and before them stretched a quay at which a few small ships were moored. Beyond that lay black, moonlit water.

For an instant, Torcuil's heart lifted at the sight of so

much water. In the next second he covered his sensitive nose. "By the sacred well of Nechtan," he swore chokingly. "What is that disgustin' smell?"

"The river. They've befouled it for centuries."

Horrified, Torcuil stared at the wide dark band. Never in his life had he come across water so polluted. Outrage roiled in his chest as he backed away, eager to be gone from this place.

When they were far enough from the river that Torcuil could breathe more normally, Seumus gave him a pitying look. "They treat their water even worse than their land, here."

"It seems they respect nothing," Torcuil muttered.

"Not all o' them. Ye said it yerself."

Torcuil didn't know why he should feel so grateful to have his accusation disproved. "So I did. But even now Ravenshaw and Verity may be in danger, with only a land creeper to keep them safe." The thought sent a bolt of alarm through him. "I need yer help if I'm to protect them and find my brother, too. Come back with me, Seumus."

Seumus considered a minute, then nodded, smiling. "I will. But how do ye propose to explain me to yer folk?"

"Would ye hate posin' as my valet overmuch? I've been told I need one, and 'twould serve our purpose of coverin' yer true identity."

Seumus cocked a cautious eyebrow at Torcuil. "And what might a valet be?"

Torcuil flushed. The broonie was no silly pixie. He stood high in the hierarchy of the fair folk. "A servant."

"Eh?" The broonie's startled expression further embarrassed Torcuil.

"A verra important servant," he said hastily. "The one who attends to a, er, gentleman's wardrobe."

"Wardrobe?" Seumus echoed blankly. "What do I know of a gentleman's wardrobe?"

"As much as I do, I'm certain. Rely upon Ivo Newitt's impeccable taste, and we'll be safe."

"Who is Ivo Newitt?"

"The marquess's valet. The fellow's feelings were hurt because he thought he was bein' fobbed off on me. Once he learned he was no bein' fobbed at all, that he still held his master's esteem, all was well."

Seumus didn't answer immediately. He pressed his lips together, then rolled out the bottom one. As he gazed up at the sky, his fingers stroked his long, white beard.

"I've no wish to insult ye, Seumus," Torcuil said. " 'Tis only that the position is open, and it seems a good opportunity—"

"Aye, aye, I can see the advantages. Ye're no offerin' me offense, lad, so dinna fash yerself." Seumus smiled. "I accept."

12

*Lord, I wonder what fool it was
that first invented kissing!*
—Jonathan Swift

Verity smiled as she refilled Fanny's cup with fragrant Kemun tea, then handed it to her cousin. The fire in the white marble-fronted fireplace crackled cheerfully. Lighted candles in girandoles cast their soft illumination over pale green painted walls, settees and armchairs upholstered in deep green brocade, polished marquetry side tables, and the delicate colors of the Savonnerie carpet.

"I'm so glad you could come," Verity said again. "I did so hate asking you to leave your house when you are so very *enceinte,* but it seems this is to be the only way I can chat with you alone." After swearing Fanny to secrecy, she'd explained the circumstances that had led to her having a bodyguard.

Fanny laughed. "Dear Verity, I'm not a fragile china

figurine. I assure you, I'm in excellent health." She grinned. "Breeding babies agrees with me."

"I thought you told me it was the making of babies that you found so agreeable," Verity teased, her face warming despite her ease with her cousin.

"That, too. Indeed, *especially* the making part." Fanny laughed again. "Your face is the color of a plum!"

"You're unkind to say so." It felt more like flame than fruit.

Fanny took a sip of her tea. "I look forward to the day when you are a matron. Then you shall be more at ease discussing the matter, for it is quite too wonderful to hide. Yet there is only you and me to indulge in the marvelous secret and yet keep our outward social dignity intact."

"I, too, look forward to that time." But that future was becoming more and more uncertain.

Fanny's eyes arched into crescents, twinkling with mischief. "Which brings us to the true reason you wished to speak with me alone. You want to know what I think of Mr. MacCodrum."

"How did you know?"

Fanny selected a small cake from the serving plate. "How could I not? Your eyes betray your affection every time you look at him."

Verity worried her bottom lip between her teeth. Had she been so indiscreet about her feelings for Torcuil that the world knew? It was too mortifying to contemplate.

"You needn't worry that you were obvious in your affections," Fanny said, placing her hand over Verity's. "You were not. I noticed because you are dear to me and I know you well. Also, because you've never been more than polite to a man before. Am I correct? Do you want Mr. MacCodrum for your own?"

Now Verity's face flamed. "Yes."

"Well, my dearest cousin, it seems to me he wants you, too."

"How can you say that?" Verity cried, frustrated with Torcuil's continuing resistance. "He's given no—"

"Your affections are clear in the way you look at him. His are every bit as evident in the way he avoids looking at you."

Verity's heart sank. "I feared as much," she moaned. "It's not that he wants me at all. He has formed a disgust for me. Likely he believes me altogether too managing, too . . . efficient."

"Only in your womanly sphere," Fanny replied crisply. "And never you believe that a man does not admire a female who can make his life more comfortable."

"I'm not at all certain he's concerned with his comfort. There's something else there, something I don't know." If only there was a way to uncover his past.

"Wear him down with kindness."

Verity sighed. "I think rather I've simply worn him down."

"If that is the case, he is not the man for you."

Verity looked at her cousin in question.

"You are a generous, thoughtful woman. It is your way. If he cannot appreciate that, then you do not want him. Could you be happy with a man with whom you must pretend to be something other than you are?"

"I—no."

"You have your answer."

As conversation turned to other subjects, Verity realized that she did have her answer. Thirty minutes later, when she saw Fanny to her carriage in the blaze of the torches carried by Daniel and another footman, she warmly embraced her cousin, who promised that both she and her husband would make inquiries regarding the whereabouts of Eideard.

Torcuil had still not returned by ten o'clock, when she retired for the evening. Anxiety gnawed at her. He'd hired a coach instead of taking her father's, which left him at the mercy of chance in finding a hackney coach when he needed one. He was unfamiliar with London. He was a babe in a very wicked forest. Oh, why hadn't he allowed at least Daniel to accompany him?

"There's nothing you can do about it," Martha said crisply as she helped Verity out of her dress. "Men will be men."

"Advice for a woman to take to heart."

"Best you do. I warrant it will save you a deal of grief."

"Pray, what makes you such an authority on the habits of men?"

Martha's tight mouth folded down at the corners. "I have experience. My Sam's no angel. Out all hours of the night gambling and womanizing."

Womanizing. The word might have been blasted on a trumpet the way it echoed in Verity's brain. *Womanizing.*

She was glad when Martha left. Verity lay in bed, watching the flames of the freshly fueled fire on her hearth. She didn't like to think that it was possible Torcuil had found the company of a diverting woman. On the other hand, she didn't want to consider that he might have been accosted by footpads. At this very moment, he could be lying injured on the wet bricks of some dark street.

Verity pounded her pillow into an unresisting lump and flopped onto her back. Life had been much easier when she hadn't truly cared about any man other than her father. She didn't want to worry about Torcuil. Right now, she didn't even want to *think* about him.

Where was he? Was he safe? Was he well?

It was well after midnight when Verity heard footsteps outside her door. She told herself to stay in bed and pretend not to notice. Instead, she scooted out of bed and dragged on her dressing gown. Quickly lighting a candle from the embers in the fireplace, she ran across the room and flung open the door.

Torcuil kept walking toward his own chamber, but she knew he must have heard her. Annoyed, she glared after him—until she noticed his hat was missing, his coat was torn at the shoulder, his breeches were smeared with dirt. She hurried to catch up with him before he shut his door.

"Torcuil, what happened?" Her eyes anxiously searched him, from his sable mane to the toes of his scuffed boots.

His dark gaze roamed over her, making her aware of her unseemly behavior. She stood, in the dark hours of the morning, at the threshold of a man's room, her hair unbound, wearing only a dressing gown over her chemise. Suddenly, she was absurdly conscious of her bare feet.

He turned away but made no move to close the door and shut her out. He strolled into his room, his fingers working at his neckcloth. "I was welcomed to London by some of the natives."

Automatically, she took a step toward him, then caught herself. "Are you . . . are you unharmed?"

"I lost m' hat, and my clothes need a wee bit of repair."

She swept aside the matter of his clothing with a gesture of one hand. "Your clothing will be attended to. Your person is of more concern. Are you unharmed?"

"Aye." He pulled off the cloth and draped it over the back of a chair.

It seemed to Verity that he focused his attention on that small act. "Will you tell me what happened?"

Negligently, he lifted one shoulder and let it drop. "'Tis naught of interest. A few scavengers thought to rob me."

"A few? How many is a few?"

His shuttered expression alarmed her. Without thinking,

she went to him. She gazed up at his candlelit face of amber and shadow. "You might have been killed," she whispered hoarsely.

The caution in his eyes softened as he gazed down into her upturned face. "Ye worrit too much." He went to the door and quietly closed it.

She followed him. "Tell me," she said softly.

Slowly, he lifted a hand to her shoulder. Its heat penetrated the cloth of her garments to touch her skin. "Ye're shiverin'." Gently, he drew her to him.

She leaned into him, absorbing his warmth and the unwavering support of his strength. The brocade of his waistcoat rasped against her cheek. He smelled of coal smoke, of sweat and mud. Through it all came that teasing, clean sea scent.

His palm smoothed over the back of her head, as if savoring the texture of her hair. It migrated to her back, riding up and down in a timeless comforting movement. Gradually, as they stood together in that island of golden light surrounded by dark silence, his hand altered pressure and range. It glided outward, dipping with her waist. It moved downward. The tips of his fingers brushed the base of her buttocks.

Flushed shock shimmered through her at his intimate touch. She lifted her head from his chest and raised her eyes. The black silk drapery of his hair framed his face. In the candle's glow, his features were sculpted planes of tawny light and Cimmerian shadow.

His fingers opened her robe. She knew she should stop him, but the voice inside her calling for her to leave was too weak. The swift beating of her heart, the quickening of her breath overpowered it. With slight movements of his forefinger and thumb, Torcuil untied the column of pink ribbon bows that secured her final garment.

He opened her chemise, folding back the fine linen to

reveal her bare breasts. Exposed to the chill night air, her nipples contracted, sending a shiver through her heated body. He reached for her, and for a moment his hand hovered over her right breast like a warm breath.

Abruptly he curled his fingers into a fist and dropped it to his side. Startled to her senses, Verity hastily closed her chemise and wrapped her dressing gown back around herself. What had happened here? she thought, dazed. He had wanted her, she had seen that clearly. He'd wanted to place his hands on her body, and, to her shame, she had wanted him to. What power did he have over her that with him, she so easily cast aside all propriety and behaved like a brazen wanton?

He spun on his heel and stalked to the fireplace. He stood there with his back to her, as if waiting for her to leave. And leave she would! She stormed toward the door, her temper rising with each footstep. He'd gone out wandering in London, likely looking for his brother despite her father's assurances that a reputable man had been put onto the job. Wasn't that just like Torcuil, the arrogant, stubborn Highlander! From the looks of him, he'd been lucky to escape with his life. Oh, she'd leave all right. Right after he paid for worrying her half to death, then toying with her, arousing her, then turning away from her.

She whirled around and marched back into his chamber, where he still stood brooding in front of the fireplace. She grabbed hold of the only braid she could reach and tugged him around to face her, taking satisfaction in his look of surprise.

"How dare you?" she demanded fiercely. "How dare you trifle with me?"

He kissed her.

Startled, she stiffened and thought to back away, but his powerful arms enfolded her. Hungrily, his mouth took charge, caressing her lips, coaxing them to part, invading her with his masterful tongue. The wild taste of him, the feel of his fingers against her scalp, the searing urgency of his body combined to ignite her own passion. Her hands curled into the loose cambric of his open shirt.

Torcuil dragged her up against him and through the cloth of his breeches she felt him against her, hard and hot. Degree by degree, he drove up the temperature of her blood. He cupped her breast, and she felt it all the way down, low into her belly. Slowly, he massaged her through the layers of linen and silk. Air grew increasingly scarce. When his thumb grazed her turgid nipple, she jerked as pleasure lashed her.

Each deft movement of his hands upon her body stoked the unfamiliar ache. With distracted triumph she felt the tension in his muscles as he slipped her chemise and dressing gown down to her waist. His lips were warm and slightly moist against her bare shoulder. Against her throat. She arched in his arms as the edge of his teeth grazed the wet tip of her breast, sending sizzling sensation through her virgin body.

He suckled her, driving that sharp, demanding pleasure deep into her womb. Buttons clicked as they struck the oak floor. She shoved the garment off his shoulders and down his arms, never breaking their wild, carnal, openmouthed kiss. She kicked the waistcoat out of her way, then pushed his shirt up, needing the feel of his flesh against hers. She pressed against him, scouring her swollen breasts against his chest, reveling in the crisp mat of masculine hair.

He picked her up and strode across his chamber. With the swipe of an arm, he cleared a stack of clothing from the top of a chest of drawers, then set her down. Immediately he stepped between her legs, dragging her chemise up her thighs with his hips, forcing her to lean back on her arms. With the tip of one finger, he lifted the skirt of her chemise a notch higher, revealing the triangle of dark golden curls that nestled between her thighs. Embarrassed, she tried to look away, but he caught her chin in his hand and turned her head back to face him. He locked gazes with her, his eyes blazing like black fire. His nostrils flared with his shallow, sharp breathing. Cupping her bare buttocks in his palms, never breaking their enmeshed gazes, he rubbed himself against her. He pressed firmly, slowly revolving his hips. She whimpered with pleasure as the hard, rounded, cloth-covered weight of him rasped softly against her swollen, sensitive bud. Her body responded with heat and moisture.

Torcuil leaned over her, supporting the weight of his torso on the columns of his arms. "Shall I no trifle with ye?" he whispered. His breath caressed her face.

She made an inarticulate pleading noise in her throat. Every fiber of her throbbed with heavy, beating need.

He lowered his face a fraction closer to hers. "Do ye want me to mate with ye?" he asked softly, his lips brushing hers.

The answer pounded in her blood. *Yes. Yes. Yes.* She'd never wanted anything more in her life. But he had asked her. He'd made her *think*. And that had opened the door to that harping, infuriating voice from deep inside her conscience. Like a phantom released from its jar, a vapor of propriety rose up. "I . . . can't. We can't. It . . . it would be . . . wrong." Her words spoke of right and wrong, but her tone, her body cried out for relief. For release. For Torcuil.

"I dinna ask ye if it was wrong," he whispered against her mouth. "I asked ye if ye want me."

He traced the tip of a forefinger down her right breast, and she watched, unable to drag her eyes away. His fingertip rode over her beaded nipple, and she shuddered with desire.

"Yes," she whispered.

"Yer answer is incomplete." He trailed his fingertip down her other breast, this time dragging his short fingernail lightly over the pink tip. A soft moan escaped her throat.

"Yes," she whispered. "I want you."

He smiled.

Stung, she glanced down at the tight bulge in the front of his breeches. "You want me, too."

His lips glided along the curve of her ear. "True, but you came to my chamber, I dinna go to yers."

"I-I . . . was worried."

"I know, sweet Anemone, but as ye've seen for yerself, I'm safe and sound. And ye've ordered me no to trifle with ye." He rotated his hips.

"Yes," she moaned. "I mean . . . no. I mean . . . What was the question?"

He tenderly kissed her mouth, and she made a small protesting sound when he lifted his head. "Ye've told me I can no trifle with ye, but, ye see, trifling is all I can do with ye."

She frowned in confusion, her mind befuddled with desire.

"I canna stay here. When I find Eideard, I must return to my own home, and I canna take a wife."

"You told me you had no wife."

"I told the truth."

"Are you a monk?"

His teeth gleamed in the candle's light. "Nay. No a monk. Never a monk. A warrior. Where I'm goin' ye canna follow, so I'll no set my seed in ye. 'Twould be wrong, more than you can know."

His words acted as cold water. The madness of passion began to evaporate, and Verity realized she was sitting half-naked on a chest of drawers in a man's room, with him standing between her legs. Hurt, furious with herself for her loss of control, she struggled to escape.

Torcuil caught her before she toppled to the floor. He steadied her but made no move to free her from her humiliating position. "Let me trifle with ye."

"No!"

He gently stroked her. "Och, sweet Verity, let me trifle with ye. I can bring ye undreamed-of pleasure yet leave ye a maiden still."

"An abhorrent suggestion," she said, but her voice trembled. "Just what benefit would *you* hope to derive from this—this trifling?"

He grinned. "I'd teach ye to trifle with me."

"Beast!" she whispered furiously.

All amusement vanished from his face. He scooped her up and deposited her upright on the floor so abruptly that she almost stumbled.

Snatching up her dressing gown, she dragged it on, then hastened from Torcuil's bedchamber. She heard the door close quietly behind her. When she reached her own room, she crawled into her bed with her chemise still wadded around her waist beneath the silk of her dressing gown.

Tears clogged her throat and scalded her eyes. Dear God, what had she done? She'd cast aside all propriety. Verity crammed her fist against her anguished mouth. She'd allowed him to touch her in the most shockingly personal way.

And his touch had brought her pleasure she'd never imagined possible.

Torcuil leaned back against the door he'd just closed and stared up at the coffered ceiling. His heart hammered. Blood throbbed in his loins. He raked shaking fingers through his hair. *Fool!* He'd known better than to touch her. Hadn't he already learned the power of his attraction for her? That night in Dundail . . . their kisses. The magnitude of his desire for her had shocked him.

Those kisses had been the blush of innocence compared to the lightning that had arced between Verity and him this night. Torcuil released an uneven breath and pushed away from the door. Sitting down on the edge of an armchair, he avoided looking at the chest of drawers. He tugged off his boots, then stood to shed his breeches. The chill of the room closed around him. Hours ago, the fire in the grate had burned down. Now only an occasional red glow flickered among the dark ashes.

His control had been strained and battered tonight. Watching her face as he touched her, hearing the small catches in her breath, seeing the swift rise and fall of her breasts had driven him with blind ferocity, inflaming him with a towering need to thrust into her, to have her surround him and accept him. And the sight of those dark golden curls, the feel of her moisture penetrating the cloth of his breeches had nearly blasted him over the edge.

Torcuil rolled onto his bed, where he lay on his back, his arms folded beneath his head. Tonight, he didn't reach for his sealskin hood in its secret place in his trunk. Instead, he squeezed his eyes shut against the throbbing demand of his body.

He could not mate with her. It would be wrong. He knew the value land folk placed upon the virginity of their maidens. There was also the consideration of her father. Torcuil knew the elder would not allow such an unforgivable transgression to pass unchallenged. Blood would be spilled. Wedding her was out of the question—he could not take her with him when he left, and he would not condemn her to live the rest of her life alone.

Torcuil's eyes moved uninterestedly over the embroidered crimson canopy above him. He doubted Verity would be as great a temptation to him after tonight. There would be no more enchanting smiles for him. No light in her eyes when she saw him enter a room.

Perhaps, in the end, her contempt for him would prove their saving shield.

The following morning, breakfast was an ordeal. Verity found it difficult to look at Torcuil without blushing. What must he think of her?

"Daniel, would you enquire when Papa is planning to break his fast?" she asked as the footman refilled her cup with tea.

"Yer father's already eaten," Torcuil said, spearing a piece of ham with his fork. His shuttered expression provided no key to his thoughts.

"Oh." She forced a smile for Daniel's sake.

"Will that be all, Lady Verity?"

Reluctantly, she dismissed the footman to attend to his other duties, leaving her alone with Torcuil in the dining room. They ate in silence for several minutes. Verity found little appetite, but, refusing to look cowed, she forced herself to choke down her usual breakfast.

"Yer father went to call on one o' his partners, then has to attend the session." Torcuil's deep, lilting voice echoed faintly in the high-ceilinged room.

Verity's gaze flew up to Torcuil's face—the first time since last night. His eyes met hers. Quickly she looked down at her plate where she fiddled with a bit of sausage. "He didn't go alone, I hope."

"He took his new bodyguard."

His new bodyguard. Verity knew nothing about that person's qualifications. Not that it mattered. When it came to her father's life, she trusted no one but Torcuil to protect it.

She frowned at her teacup. "I do wish he had taken

you instead." As soon as the words were out of her mouth, Verity realized how they must sound to Torcuil.

"I'm sure ye do."

Again her eyes went to his. Black obsidian met her gaze. "I didn't mean—"

He arched an eyebrow.

Annoyed with her misery, Verity took a fortifying breath and released it. "I believe Papa is safer with you watching out for him than he could be with even a former Bow Street Runner."

"Yer confidence is gratifying."

"One works with what one has to hand," she said stiffly. "Now, if you'll excuse me, I have calls to make this morning. If you wish to come with me, be ready in fifteen minutes." She was almost to the door when his softly spoken words reached her ears.

"I canna go just yet. My valet and some of my staff are due here shortly."

She turned. "Your valet? I thought Newitt was going to assist you."

"I prefer having my own valet."

Clearly he'd never had one before, she thought nastily. He must have engaged one last evening. "Very well. I'll arrange for his quarters."

"Thank you."

"But what is this about a staff?"

He touched his napkin unnecessarily to his lips, then neatly laid it on the table. Pushing back his chair, he rose. "When I arrived, yer father said I might hire whom I thought necessary to make this place safe."

Verity remembered her father saying something to that effect. "But he's hired a man."

"He told me that I was responsible for the safety of those in this household while I'm here. Until he tells me differently, I'm responsible."

"How many are on your staff?" she asked politely.

"I'll know when they arrive."

Verity examined her manicure. "We cannot accommodate an army."

"I'm certain there will be fewer than that."

"How reassuring." Verity regarded him down her nose—not an easy feat when he towered over her. "I'll have Mrs. Dibble arrange for them, before I leave." She headed out of the dining room, toward her bedchamber.

"If I dinna go, ye dinna go."

She halted abruptly. Slowly, she turned to face him. "I beg your pardon?"

"Ye heard me well enough."

"I will not be held a prisoner by you!"

In a few unhurried steps, he crossed the distance between them. "Until yer father's enemy is identified and apprehended, we're all prisoners."

With Torcuil standing so close to her, with his heady, personal sea scent filling her nostrils and his dangerous male potency swirling around her like an intoxicating tide, Verity decided that being enclosed with him in a carriage was not a wise idea. "When are you expecting your valet and staff?"

As if the timing had been rehearsed, Quenby arrived. "A Mr. Broonie to see Mr. MacCodrum, my lady," he intoned. "There are a man and a woman with him, sir. They await you in the north drawing room."

"Thank you, Quenby," Verity said. When the butler had left, she swept out of the dining room. "We shouldn't keep your staff waiting."

"We?" With no effort, Torcuil matched his pace to hers.

Verity looked at him in surprise. "I assumed you'd wish to introduce me to the persons you propose to bring into my home."

Torcuil set off in the direction of the north drawing room. "Ye mean ye canna tolerate the thought of there bein' something in this house ye dinna manage."

She paused, hurt. Then she tamped down the feeling and hurried to keep up with him. "Are you accusing me of being meddlesome?"

He continued at, what was for him, an easy stride, without glancing at her. "I'm no accusin' ye of anything."

"Oh! You're making a statement, are you? Well, I'll have you to know, sir, that *I* am the mistress of this house, and as such, it is my *duty* to know what or who comes through my doors."

"The mistress, is it? So that's the London name for women who insist on bein' in charge of everything?"

Verity gasped at the injustice of his comment. She slowed to a stop. He kept walking.

If she were not there to take charge of matters, who would? Ravenshaw House would still be in turmoil, and as for Torcuil MacCodrum . . . Well, likely *he* would still be parading about in an assassin's cloak.

So this was to be his reaction to last night. Belittlement. Contempt. She pressed her lips together tightly as something painful pierced her heart.

He'd told her there could be no future for them. What had made her believe otherwise? Love?

Or arrogance?

"I ask ye for help, and ye bring me a gruagach and a pixie?" Torcuil demanded, incredulous. "Seumas, what were ye thinkin'?" He faced the short, bearded, hirsute brownie and the petite, white-haired female with tilting cat's eyes.

"My, don't we think we're important?" the pixie declared with a toss of her head. "Silkies. Humph!"

The gruagach said nothing. He simply glowered at Torcuil. Not a good sign.

"How many of the fair folk do ye think are foolish enough to come to this benighted city?" Seumas asked. "There are only five of us. Six, if we're to count yer brother. At least Fearghus and Columbine here have been so good as to volunteer to help."

Torcuil eyed his would-be staff. The gruagach was dressed all in black, save his shirt and neckcloth. The pixie wore a wild-colored gown and a garish plumed hat. Torcuil didn't care for gruagachs. They were a sullen lot and carried grudges for ages. Pixies were unreliable. Flighty and emotional, they were too easily distracted. But they were all he had, other than Seumas.

"Beggin' yer pardon," he said, realizing how insulting he'd been. " 'Tis only that I'm surprised to see a gruagach and a pixie in London."

Columbine's mouth formed a pretty little pout. "Oh, we know. A big, important silkie would never think of relying on the likes of *us*."

Fearghus rumbled his agreement.

"My apologies, Columbine. I spoke in haste. I dinna mean to wound yer feelings."

"Well, you did." She looked away, her large green-gold eyes glistening with welling tears.

Torcuil felt as small as an arrow worm. He passed her his handkerchief. She accepted it with a grateful smile and dabbed at her eyes.

"I'll accept yer help and be glad for it," he said. Merciful Dana, it looked as if this was as good as it was going to get.

"There's a price," Seumas said.

Torcuil sighed inwardly. He knew there would be. The question was, could he afford to pay it? "Tell me."

"We want you to take us with you when you leave,"

Seumus said. "Fearghus and I want to go back to Scotland because we miss it. Columbine wants to go because she's never been there."

"Just to go to Scotland?" Torcuil wanted to make certain the conditions were perfectly clear.

Seumas, Fearghus, and Columbine nodded.

"And Seumas explained what must be done here?" Torcuil asked. "That we must keep the marquess and his daughter safe *and* find my brother?"

Fearghus and Columbine nodded.

"Ye must no be obvious about the tasks. Not only are we among land folk—"

"We don't call them land folk," Columbine interrupted imperiously. "*We* live on land, silkie. To us they are known as mortals." Fearghus and Seumas nodded.

Torcuil snorted. "Mortals, is it? How is that, considerin' ye dinna live forever?"

"We live a great deal longer than *they* do. Longer than your kind, too," she added smugly.

"Slow learners need more time," Torcuil countered, annoyed.

The pixie's eyes flashed dangerously. She raised a hand, her fingertips glimmering.

13

Facts are stubborn things.
—Alain René Lesage

"Halt!" Seumus snapped. "Enough, both of ye! Columbine, ye know the risk ye take in threatenin' a silkie. Yer glamours won't work on him, but his sword will work on ye. Torcuil, stop baitin' the lass. She's a pixie, and well ye know it. In pixie years, she's younger than ye, for all that ye're only a lad."

Torcuil bridled at what seemed to him the continual reference to his youth, but he held his tongue.

"Now," Seumus continued in a milder tone. "Torcuil was explainin' about our tasks."

Columbine sulkily subsided.

Torcuil ignored her. "We must be cautious to conceal our identities as fair folk from *everyone*, and no one, save Lord Ravenshaw and his daughter, Lady Verity, is to know that we are their bodyguards. Seumus will be my valet, and I'll ask Lady Verity to assign ye two to positions

on the staff that will keep ye close to her and her father."
He eyed Seumus and Fearghus. "Can ye bear to part wi'
yer beards? It will call attention to ye, but if ye wish to
keep 'em . . ."

In the blink of an eye, both the broonie and the gruagach were bare-cheeked. Torcuil said nothing about their
long hair. The cropping of their locks was a land folk
eccentricity he'd not ask fair folk to endure.

Abruptly, Seumus's hair went from long to short, from
silvery white to brown. "I'm supposed to be a man o' fashion," he announced at Fearghus's and Columbine's quizzi-
cal glances. "I've scrutinized the likes of a few tulips since
last eve. Many believe the position of valet is one of importance," he added loftily.

In the next second, Fearghus's hair went short, in the
same style as the broonie's. But where Seumus's new hair
mode exposed a round-cheeked, cherubic face, Fearghus's
accentuated his red, bulbous nose, his bushy eyebrows,
and his various warts and moles. Torcuil was touched by
the gruagach's uncustomary willingness to cooperate.

Seumus grinned. "Playin' our roles as we go about our
work will be a challenge, and no mistake."

Torcuil laughed. "Aye. A challenge for all of us, I'll
warrant."

"She's going to make me a maid, isn't she?"
Columbine asked plaintively.

He softened toward her. "It seems likely. But Lady
Verity is kind, and she's verra evenhanded. With a deal of
discretion and a bit o' magic, yer labors shouldna be oner-
ous. She'll be dependin' on ye to help her always look her
best, do ye see? Her folk place great weight on one's
appearance."

Columbine smiled delightedly.

Torcuil turned to Seumus. "Ye said there was another
of the fair folk in London."

"A faery," Fearghus said in a deep, gravelly voice.

Torcuil shot Seumus a meaningful glance as uneasiness rippled through him. A chancy lot, faeries. They could be benevolent or malevolent, but you never knew which it would be until it was too late.

"I dinna think ye wanted Neul involved," Seumus said softly, "so I neglected to mention anything to her."

"Thank ye, Seumus. But what is she doin' in London?"

"Livin' in a grand house with a beautiful garden," Columbine supplied. "But I think she finds life here dull."

Torcuil gave silent thanks for Seumus's wisdom. The last thing any of them needed to contend with was a bored faery.

Verity swept downstairs and into the columned entrance hall to find she was alone. Setting her reticule and her swansdown muff on the agate-topped console table near the front door, she paused to don her blue kidskin gloves. She was determined that today she would make her social calls and get them over with. If she didn't soon, there would be speculation as to why she'd returned to Town but had not left the house. Everything must appear ordinary.

Yesterday had been taken up with getting Mr. Broonie, Columbine—an outrageous yet curiously lovely name—and Fearghus settled. Such an odd trio. Mr. Broonie possessed such an air of mature wisdom and patience that Verity could not bring herself to address him simply as Broonie. Understanding that the trio would require the freedom to do what they must, and that they were actually under Torcuil's authority, she assigned Fearghus to her father as his personal assistant. It had been with great reluctance that she'd taken Columbine as her lady's maid. She didn't want word of her every mood or movement carried back to

Torcuil, but when she'd turned down his suggestion that she put the girl to work as her personal maid, her father had sided with him.

Verity smiled with satisfaction as she contemplated her father in the company of the dour Fearghus, who did not stand even as tall as she. Indeed, none of Torcuil's aides did, though Mr. Broonie measured only an inch or so shorter than Verity. When she'd asked Torcuil where he'd found these persons and why he trusted them, he had turned a mild look upon her and assured her he had reason to place his faith in them. More than that he would not say. Her pride had reared up to prohibit her asking more, and she had left the room in a stony silence.

The door flew open at the far end of the hall and Columbine rushed in. Her footsteps echoed against the high ceilings and polished stone floor as she ran up to Verity. Her pretty, elfin face was flushed and her bonnet had slipped askew. "Sorry, Lady Verity," she apologized breathlessly. "I couldn't find my other glove."

Verity gently straightened the girl's modest bonnet, untying the ribbons under her chin, and retying them in a more attractive bow. "Kindly do not run, Columbine. We are not in so great a hurry that you must dismiss your dignity."

Large green-gold eyes regarded her earnestly. "I didn't want to keep you waiting."

Verity smiled. For all that Columbine had little experience as a lady's maid and tended to be forgetful sometimes, she was making a valiant effort to please Verity. "I appreciate your consideration."

Picking up her muff and embroidered reticule, she turned to find Fearghus opening the door for her. Heavens, but he was a silent fellow. She hadn't even heard him enter. Her eyes widened as she saw Torcuil standing slightly behind Fearghus. He wore his garrick and his new top hat to ward off the late cold. He said something to the stern-looking little man, then stepped around him to join Verity and Columbine.

"You need not trouble yourself, Cousin," Verity said coolly. "I know you have no wish to attend these calls I intend to make. Columbine is coming with me."

Torcuil nodded his acknowledgment of Columbine, who inclined her head in answer. His gaze drifted languidly to Verity's. "Ye will go nowhere without me."

Verity stared at him in astonishment, which fired into indignation. "I believe I must have misheard you, sir," she said frostily. "It sounded as if you gave me an order."

"Ye hearing, it seems, is excellent." He gestured her toward the barouche that Mr. Teak had pulled to a stop on the street in front of Ravenshaw House.

She descended the few steps from the front door. "I vastly dislike someone giving me orders, Mr. MacCodrum," she informed him.

"Most people do, Lady Verity."

When she would have ignored his proffered assistance, he unobtrusively seized her hand and helped her into the barouche. "I am the mistress of Ravenshaw House," she reminded him through clenched teeth.

"Ye would do well to remember that." He sat across from Verity and Columbine.

They rode in strained silence for a while. Through her lashes, Verity observed Torcuil. Curse him for his arrogance and his beauty. There he sat, looking unaffected by her displeasure. His hair draped his shoulders like a black satin cloak, more elegant than the fine-quality wool capes of his dark gray garrick. His black kid gloves perfectly fit his long, tapered fingers—fingers that had been bare and warm when they had stroked her breasts, her belly, her thighs . . .

Let me trifle with you.

Verity swallowed hard against that lush, fevered memory and shifted in her seat. Would they never arrive at the Lonsleys'?

Fifteen minutes later, the baroness of Chiswell and her daughter, Miss Harriet Lonsley, received them in the Egyptian-style drawing room. Harriet looked unusually neat. Her hair was dressed to perfection and she wore a new gown of sprigged muslin that showed off her fine figure. While Harriet was attractive, Verity had never before seen her take such pains with her appearance for receiving morning calls.

"Why, Verity, dear," Harriet said as soon as Columbine had been directed to the servants' hall, and, in the drawing room, Torcuil and Verity had taken seats facing the baroness and her daughter. "Why have you never told me about your Scots cousin?" The blatantly coy tone of Harriet's question annoyed Verity.

"I've only just discovered I had a Scots cousin." She cast a sidelong glance at Torcuil, whose expression gave nothing of his thoughts away.

"I have never heard of the MacCodrums," the baroness said, eyeing Torcuil down the length of her arrow-shaped nose.

Torcuil met her basilisk stare. "Where my clan holds sway, we've no heard of Lonsleys or Chiswells."

The baroness blinked at his response, and Verity almost laughed. To her knowledge, no one had ever so flatly refused to tolerate the woman's rudeness.

" 'Tis a large world," Verity said.

"Just so, just so," Harriet hastily agreed, the twitching corners of her mouth betraying her stifled amusement. "Pray tell us, does London agree with you, Mr. MacCodrum?"

"I've no been here long enough to form a rational opinion," he replied smoothly.

Harriet gave him a smile meant to charm. "I do hope you enjoy your stay in Town. Please feel free to call upon us if we might be of assistance to you."

Verity estimated there was only five more minutes left before they could politely depart. Five interminable minutes.

"Your hair, Mr. MacCodrum, is rather long for fashion," Lady Chiswell pointed out. "I wonder that you do not cut it."

"Fashion, Lady Chiswell, can never dictate how a MacCodrum wears his hair. Tradition rules that. A verra long tradition."

Harriet leaned slightly forward. "Is there some significance to your plaits?" she asked softly.

"Aye."

"Might one ask what it is?" Harriet fluttered her eyelashes at Torcuil, and Verity stared at her. Did the female have no dignity?

"They're warrior's braids," Verity said briskly, rising from her chair. "And now, Harriet, Lady Chiswell, I regret that it's time to leave. My first day out, you see."

"Warrior's braids?" Harriet echoed breathlessly. "How very fascinating. You must tell me all about them when next we meet, Mr. MacCodrum."

The baroness quickly tugged the bellpull. A footman appeared at the door almost immediately, and she instructed him to summon Lady Verity's abigail.

As they all strolled into the entry hall, where Torcuil was brought his hat and coat and the women their pelisses, the baroness closed in on Torcuil. Verity seized the opportunity to take Harriet aside.

"Have you received callers before us this morning, Harriet dear?" she asked, wanting to know why her friend was making a cake of herself. Verity shot Lady Chiswell a glance, and was surprised to see the old dragon actually smiling—and at Torcuil!

"Why, yes," Harriet said. "You just missed Grace Halford and her sister. They visited not above twenty minutes ago."

Grace and Nancy Halford were more dependable than the sun and the moon when it came to carrying any bit of news all over London. They knew both Fanny and Lady Euphemia. It seemed obvious that Harriet had learned about Torcuil and wished to impress him. Verity winced as she imagined Harriet tearing up to her room as soon as the door closed behind the Halford sisters, to change her gown and have her hair dressed in a flurry of activity. At twenty-one years of age, Harriet worried about remaining on the shelf.

"His brother, the MacCodrum *heir,* is in London, you know," Verity confided in a low voice.

Harriet pried her gaze off Torcuil abruptly. "He is?"

"Cousin Torcuil is looking for him. His name is Eideard MacCodrum."

"Is he married?"

Verity searched her memory. The subject of his marital status had never been discussed. Like most of Torcuil's background and past. "Torcuil never mentioned Eideard's having a wife. I don't know."

"Is he as handsome as your cousin?"

"Well, I suppose Eideard is my cousin also, though I've never met him. I would imagine he'd be attractive. Looks do seem to run in families, don't you think?"

"Please find out if he's married and handsome," Harriet said bluntly, a gleam in her brown eyes.

"We're looking for Eideard. Torcuil has no idea where his brother might be staying. Do you suppose you might make inquiries of your acquaintances as to Eideard's whereabouts? For dear Cousin Torcuil's sake, you understand."

"Of course," Harriet said solicitously. "How dreadful

for them, to be separated." Harriet's brows drew down slightly. "Curious. I haven't seen or heard of a Mr. MacCodrum having attended any of the soirees or outings that have been held in Town since we arrived from the country. Surely any man of breeding who is as dashing and . . . and as pleasant-looking as Torcuil MacCodrum would have created a stir before now."

Pleasant-looking? Not for one second did Verity believe Harriet hadn't noticed that Torcuil was nothing less than strikingly beautiful. Verity shook her head. "I'm not surprised you've not met his brother. He's a complete stranger to London, poor man." She leaned closer and whispered, "Remember, he's a Highlander."

"Of course. How could I forget?" Harriet gave Verity's hand a little squeeze. "I shall make every inquiry after poor Eideard. And you won't forget to ask about . . . you know?"

"Of course not. I blush that I did not think to inquire before."

When Torcuil bowed over Harriet's hand as he said good-bye, Verity managed not to grind her teeth.

They made several more calls. At a few of the houses no one was home, so Verity left her card. At each of the others, she discovered that either Lady Euphemia or Nancy and Grace Halford had been there before them. The visits quickly fell into a routine: After enduring fifteen minutes of her hostess's flirtatious behavior toward Torcuil, Verity would privately solicit aid in looking for Eideard. Unfailingly, the reaction she received was eager concern and a promise of assistance. The pledges of cooperation, Verity thought as the barouche rumbled toward Ravenshaw House, were some small compensation for suffering through simpering smiles and coy glances directed at Torcuil, who, while not encouraging them, had done nothing to discourage them. He'd certainly not been so gracious to *her* today. Instantly, her conscience stabbed her. She'd been less than cordial to him.

On their return to Ravenshaw House, Torcuil was given an envelope that had been brought by messenger. Verity wanted to know who in Town would send Torcuil a note, but she'd have submitted to torture before asking him. Besides, they'd just called on several women who'd sent him loud silent messages. Perhaps one of the females had succumbed to a more straightforward, if less seemly, tactic to get his attention. Verity glared down at the stack of calling cards and notes that had been left for her. She found they were of less interest than Torcuil's single folded and sealed sheet of foolscap.

Mrs. Dibble, bless her, had luncheon served as soon as Verity and Torcuil changed their clothes and came downstairs. The marquess, they were informed, had arrived home and eaten earlier. Now he was closeted with his man of business.

When Verity attempted to initiate conversation into the charged, awkward silence that echoed in the dining room, Torcuil responded with short, clipped answers. He finished his meal and excused himself. "Duty requires that I leave you now."

"I thought your duty was to guard me," she said with forced lightness. "I thought that's what bodyguards did: guarded bodies. Apparently I was mistaken."

Torcuil paused at the door, and cast her an oblique glance. "That's what I'm tryin' to do, Anemone," he said softly. "I'm tryin' to guard ye from the . . . beast."

Verity flushed and looked away. She heard his boots against the polished floor as he left.

After luncheon Verity had the cards and correspondence she'd received taken to her writing table in the drawing room, where she would later go over them and the household accounts.

Now she went in search of her father. She found him in the library, at his desk. Tomes, letters, and official-looking reports covered most of the massive table's mahogany surface. The only sound in the book-lined room was the furious scratching of her father's quill pen against a sheet of foolscap bearing the Ravenshaw crest and the Alford coat of arms embossed in silver and green.

"Papa, you should be in bed. Now, you assured me you'd rest this afternoon. How will you ever heal and recover your strength if you are forever moving around?"

"I've stayed in that blasted bed as long as I'm going to," her father replied heatedly. "Damn me, but I'd fossilize if I stayed there as long as you want me to!"

She came around to his side and gave him an affectionate peck on his temple. "You are an abysmal patient." She checked to make certain the sling was properly in place and that his dressing revealed no telltale spots of red.

"You're worse than a mother hen," he grumbled half-heartedly as she laid her palm across his forehead.

Satisfied that he had no fever, she pointed to a heavy volume. "You didn't lift that, did you?"

"No. To please you, I humiliated myself by asking Fearghus to fetch it for me."

She smoothed his thick white hair back from his forehead, and he lightly batted her hands away. "Have you nothing better to do, girl, than to harass your father?"

"I have much to do."

"Then go do it."

"First I desire to know what you are doing."

He sat back in his leather chair. "I am refining my arguments for when I call on the rest of the partners. Today I spoke to Hartley Pettipher."

"Were you successful?"

"The verdict is not in yet. I was extraordinarily eloquent. Although he said he wished to consider what I had said, I believe I have succeeded to sway him to cast his vote for keeping the mine open. We shall see. That leaves only one more undecided, and, of course, Outhwaite." The marquess sighed. "I already know Isted's stand on the matter. Everyone knows. Still, I cannot believe he wants the mine closed so desperately he'd resort to assassination."

"You are in no condition to travel."

"I know that," the marquess replied testily. "But I shall be, and soon."

"Very well. When you are well enough, we'll go to Essex. You will persuade Lord Outhwaite. And the other two. I have every confidence in you."

"I'm not taking you with me, Verity. It's much too dangerous."

"You can just unset that jaw of yours, my good sir, because I *am* going. And so are Torcuil, Seumus, Fearghus, and Columbine, and perhaps we should even bring that new Bow Street Runner of yours—what's his name?"

"Boniface Kingston."

Verity lost some of her high spirits. "Has he uncovered the identity of the person behind the attempts on your life?"

"Give the fellow some time. He's only just undertaken this muddle."

"Has he learned anything regarding the whereabouts of Torcuil's brother?"

He lifted a bushy white eyebrow. "Would I not have told you—and dear Cousin Torcuil—if he'd reported such intelligence to me?"

"Yes, I suppose."

"You're worrying entirely too much about my health

and about what Kingston might have unearthed," the marquess said. "I believe it's time you began accepting those invitations I know you've received." His words were spoken pleasantly enough, but Verity did not miss the command in them.

"How could I go without you to chaperon me?" she teased cajolingly.

"Torcuil will accompany you," he told her flatly.

"Torcuil?" His name was a protest. She'd never considered him stalking to balls or parties beside her. She wondered if he had.

"That is correct." Her father favored her with a satisfied smile. "No man in his right mind would dare take undue liberties with you while he's around."

If only her father knew how she'd all but forced the most shocking liberties on Torcuil. And how willingly the dark-eyed warrior had taken them. The memory of the taste of him, the scent and the solid warmth of him haunted her every waking moment. The dizzying pleasure his touch had brought her . . . the promise of more . . .

Torcuil had undertaken to keep her unharmed. She supposed, running the tip of one finger back and forth over the polished edge of her father's desk, that harm was relative. If seeing Torcuil each day and having this turbulence in her heart could hurt so much yet still not be considered harm, she prayed that she never experienced true damage.

"Go now," her father said, waving her away. "Accept some invitations. Don't draw attention by refusing the society of your friends."

Reluctantly, she walked toward the door. "I fear having Torcuil here has already attracted the attention of every female of every house where we've called today."

"The better to obfuscate the fact that he is your bodyguard," her father muttered as he returned to his work.

Verity caught her bottom lip between her teeth. If only she could obfuscate her feelings, as well. The problem was, where Torcuil and her body were concerned, she wanted no guards. Where Torcuil and her heart were concerned, she had none.

A light knock sounded at the door. At the marquess's invitation, Quenby entered, bearing a silver salver. On it lay a folded and sealed sheet of stationery.

"This just arrived for you, sir," he said.

Verity's father thanked Quenby as he took the letter and opened it. The butler quietly let himself out of the library.

The color drained from the marquess's face.

Alarmed, Verity hurried to his side. "What is it, Papa?"

"The earl of Cowen," her father said softly, "has been found dead."

Through the library window, the pall of coal smoke lying over the city tinted the moon gray. Torcuil glanced over at Mr. Kenyon as they sat in richly upholstered armchairs in the library of Peter Asquith, the merchant prince. Now they awaited the appearance of Mr. Asquith himself.

The door opened, and into the candlelit room strode a man in his middle years, of medium height and slim build. The cut and quality of his clothes marked him as a man of wealth and discernment.

"Good evening, gentlemen," he said, offering first Kenyon, then Torcuil his hand in a forthright manner. "I appreciate your calling on me at this hour." He led them to the large desk where a black velvet cloth had been spread. He lit an Argand lamp, which glowed more brightly than a candle. "Mr. Kenyon told me he believed your necklace and bracelet to be of Persian origin, Mr. MacCodrum."

Torcuil withdrew the items in their pouch from his

coat and spread them on the velvet. "Aye. Created under the rule of Shah Abbas the First more than two centuries ago."

Asquith stared at the gold, jewel-encrusted adornments as if mesmerized by the sight. "A time of powerful rulers in the world," he murmured. He reached for the necklace, and it draped from his hand in a shimmering, sparkling fall. He examined it slowly, carefully. "Magnificent." He replaced it on the cloth and took up the cuff to repeat the process.

Torcuil imagined how these would look on Verity. The golden color of her hair would enhance the heavy gold of these baubles, he mused. The colors of the stones were vivid enough, but they could not compare to the rich brilliance of her sea moss green eyes. He wished that he could give them to her for her pleasure. Next to the understated jewelry she wore, this necklace and bracelet would appear gaudy. After consideration, he decided the Persian pieces were too opulent to suit her refined taste.

Asquith laid the bracelet down beside the necklace and named an offering figure. To Kenyon's credit, his face did not betray his sudden tension—the tension that buffeted Torcuil like the underwater impact of an exploding volcano.

He smiled dryly. " 'Tis an interestin' price, to be sure, Mr. Asquith. But not to me." Leaning over to pick up the centuries-old Persian adornments, he added, "I'll get more by pryin' out the gems and meltin' down the gold to sell separately."

Asquith stiffened. "No," he said sharply. At Torcuil's raised eyebrow, he amended his tone. "It would be a terrible waste."

Torcuil shrugged, then eased the pieces of jewelry into their pouch, aware that Asquith's intense gaze never left them. The merchant prince made another offer, which

Torcuil politely refused. From the corner of his eye, he saw the tiny beads of sweat on Kenyon's top lip.

Torcuil inclined his head. "I bid ye good night, sir." He started toward the door. Kenyon woodenly followed him.

"Wait!" Asquith sighed. "Oh, very well."

His third offer was not only interesting, it was generous, and Torcuil accepted. Kenyon dabbed at his glistening forehead and top lip with a handkerchief. After arrangements had been made for the transfer of the funds and the necklace and bracelet, Asquith himself saw them to the door and out to their carriage.

"May I inquire, sir," Torcuil said to Asquith, "if you know of a man who looks much like me?"

"You do remind me of the last gentleman from whom I purchased such an excellent antiquity. Greek, though."

"The man?" Kenyon inquired.

Asquith shook his head. "No, the items. But that fellow, also, knew the value of what he had." He frowned faintly, as if trying to recall. "He, too, was quite tall, and his hair was dark."

"Was it long?" Torcuil asked, suddenly alert. "Was it like mine?" Could the other gentleman be Eideard, who would also have been given something to sell to finance his stay among the land folk?

Asquith studied Torcuil's hair for long, excruciating seconds. "No."

Torcuil's hopes plummeted.

Again Asquith's brow drew down. "Rather, he wore his hair in a queue."

"A long queue?" Torcuil asked, too cautious to allow himself to hope again just yet.

"Why? Might he be a relative of yours?"

"My brother."

"Oh, I say. How extraordinary. But I'd hate to think I'd betrayed a confidence or . . . or . . . whatever."

"You've betrayed nothing," Torcuil assured Asquith hastily. "Indeed, he doesn't even know I'm here." He explained how he'd come to inform his brother of their father's illness.

"Well, then," Asquith said. "As I recall, his queue was rather long. I suppose that the fancywork at the sides could have been plaits."

Torcuil fixed Asquith with his full gaze, and attempted to convey the importance of his next request. "Can you tell me where I can find him?"

"My dear fellow, I do apologize. I haven't the faintest idea."

14

For fools rush in where angels fear to tread.
—Alexander Pope

Torcuil arrived back at Ravenshaw House to find the street darker than usual. While the hour was late, he'd never seen the mansion without the outside lanterns burning. The hired coach rattled away as he stood on the pavement in front of the house and looked up and down the street. Where was the private guard hired by residents of Grosvenor Square to patrol their area? All of Torcuil's senses sprang alert. Something was wrong.

With practiced skill, he forced aside his anxiety for Verity and the others so that he might concentrate on the task before him. Silently, he picked his way through the garden along the side of the mansion, then went down the steps that led into the kitchen, one level below the ground floor. Fearghus sat hunched on a stool, tending a low burning fire on the grate.

"Aye, and it's about time ye sidled home," the grua-gach rumbled.

"Where is Lady Verity?"

"All tucked up in her bed."

"Good." Torcuil strode across the room to the stairs leading to the upper levels of the house. "Columbine is with her?"

"Just outside her door, she is, guardin' our Lady Verity like a wee eagle." As if sensing Torcuil's tension, Fearghus rose to his feet.

"And Seumas? Is he watchin' over Ravenshaw?"

Fearghus shook his shaggy head. "Och, the marquess is a stubborn man. Nothing would do but that Boniface Kingston watch over him. It's because Kingston'll take orders, that's what *I* say. But Seumas is tryin' to keep an eye on Ravenshaw, nonetheless."

"We have an intruder, Fearghus," Torcuil said briskly. "Search the floor above, and I'll take the one over it."

Fearghus growled his assent. He reached into the pocket of his somber-colored coat. When he withdrew his hand, there shone the glittering, soft illumination of pixie dust.

"Snuff it out," Torcuil ordered.

"We're no all of us silkies," Fearghus grumbled. "I canna see so well in the dark."

"Snuff out the pixie dust, Fearghus, else ye'll be a beacon to the intruder."

The gruagach scowled, but stuffed the pixie dust back into his pocket. Torcuil followed him up the stairs, then continued upward until he came to the floor where Verity and her father had their bedchambers.

Just as Fearghus had said, Columbine perched on the edge of a chair outside Verity's door. In the air, by her shoulder, glowed a small glittering swirl of pixie dust.

When Torcuil spoke her name in a low voice, she

jumped, then pressed her palm over her heart, glaring at him. "You don't need to sneak up on *me*," she whispered indignantly.

"How is Verity?"

"I just checked on her. She's well."

"Ye take a foolish chance wi' the pixie dust. Snuff it."

Her bottom lip curled in a pout. "It's safe enough at this hour, Torcuil."

"Something's amiss," he told her, refusing to argue the matter. "The front of the house is dark, and I dina hear the guard callin' the time. Assume the worst."

With a flick of her slender fingers, the pixie dust vanished, leaving them in what was for Columbine utter darkness. "Now what am I supposed to do?" she whispered. "I can't see."

"Open a few of the doors to the empty chambers, and pull back the window coverings. Then stay in the shadows."

"Like some slimy mushroom?"

Torcuil clung to his patience. "Just do as I say, Columbine." He relented a fraction. "No one would ever take ye for a mushroom."

She brightened. "Truly?"

"Truly. On yer guard, now."

Grinning, she lifted her hand and flicked her fingers. Abruptly all the doors in the hall opened. A second later, moonlight poured through them, forming silver wedges on the dark floor.

Torcuil's brow drew down in a frown. "Columbine—"

"I know, I know," she said, then heaved a long-suffering sigh. "I must be careful no one sees my glamours. But I didn't open the marquess's door," she added piously.

He moved silently into Verity's bedchamber, needing to see for himself that she was safe.

He found her thrusting her arms into her dressing

gown at the same time she was trying to get her feet into her slippers. As if sensing his presence, she looked up. "What's wrong? Is Papa—?"

"Yer father is bein' guarded by his Bow Street Runner, and by Seumus, a verra capable fellow." Her lovely face looked so worried and pale. She'd already been through so much.

"I'll return soon," he said.

She nodded.

"Lock yer doors. Don't forget the one to yer dressin' room."

"It's already secured."

Reluctantly, he swung closed her bedchamber door, but waited to hear her lock it. Seconds later, the key clicked.

"Can ye no make yerself invisible?" he asked Columbine.

She shook her head, sending her curls bobbing. "Only faeries can do that. I can make myself translucent. Will that do?" She showed him.

"Nay. It wouldna do for any of the land folk to see ye that way. Be . . . careful."

He found the door to Ravenshaw's suite unguarded. Where was Kingston? Inside? Unlikely, considering how strongly the marquess felt about a bodyguard staying in his chamber. Torcuil tried the doorknob. Alarm surged through him when he found it unlocked. Cautiously, he moved into the chamber. The bed curtains had been drawn closed. As he eased the heavy velvet draperies aside to reveal the sleeping marquess, a faint sweetish smell wafted to his nose. He frowned. Laudanum?

Suddenly, the edge of a sharp blade pressed against Torcuil's throat from behind him.

"Don't move," a familiar voice warned, "and you may live long enough to hang—"

With lightning reflexes, Torcuil secured the blade and flung his assailant over his head. The man thudded onto his back with a *whoosh* of forcefully exhaled breath.

"What are ye doin' in here, Kingston?" Torcuil demanded of the disheveled man lying on the floor. Of medium height, with cropped brown hair and unremarkable brown eyes, the former Bow Street Runner was of such ordinary appearance that it would be easy to overlook him in a roomful of people or on a busy street. An advantage, Torcuil supposed, in a bodyguard. He stuck out his hand.

Kingston accepted it, levering himself up to his feet. "I say, MacCodrum, damn fine moves. Will you teach 'em to me?"

"Later. Now we've got a stranger roamin' the place." He frowned. "I dinna know Ravenshaw was takin' laudanum." Something niggled on the edge of his memory, but when he tried to capture what it was, it eluded him.

"He may now and then. Occasionally, his shoulder still troubles him."

"He claims his shoulder is well."

"Doesn't want to admit it in front of his daughter."

Probably afraid she'd rally the staff to see that he stayed in bed. Torcuil had no doubts that she'd do just that. "What are ye doin' in his chamber?"

"I might ask you the same question," Kingston replied stiffly. "I heard a noise in here and came to investigate." He straightened his waistcoat. "And I wish to remind you, MacCodrum, that I answer only to the marquess."

Torcuil regarded Kingston a moment, then handed him back his knife. "If ye allow anything to happen to Ravenshaw, ye'll answer to me, and no mistake."

Kingston's mouth tightened. "I comprehend that, as his cousin, you are much concerned for Lord Ravenshaw's safety."

"I am."

"In that case, I'll stay here with Lord Ravenshaw."

"Guard him well." Torcuil glanced down at the marquess, who lay still deep in his laudanum-aided sleep. Quietly, he closed the bed curtains.

A thorough search of the house, outbuildings, and grounds turned up nothing but a bed of trampled ivy by the side of the house, which, Seumus pointed out reasonably, might have been done by a clumsy groom or even a large dog. Torcuil agreed that was true enough, but something didn't *feel* right.

Torcuil studied the crushed vegetation. A dog might have been responsible for that. He sniffed the air. There it was, faint, but unmistakable. That acrid smell of human fear. The dark warrior's wine rushed through his veins as he lifted his gaze to the ivy that grew heavily up the sides of the house. The gardener had told him that it concealed sturdy trellises.

Torcuil's eyes moved a little farther up, and he saw what Seumus and Fearghus could not: almost one story up, a man clung to the trellis with one hand, and the drainpipe with the other. Just beyond the reach of the intruder's arm lay the sill of a window.

Ravenshaw's window.

Torcuil bolted across the ivy bed and surged up the vine-covered trellis. Grabbing the intruder's ankle, he jerked it outward. The man lost his footing, leaving him hanging, one hand clutching the pipe and the other the now-wobbling trellis. Torcuil rapidly climbed higher, gripped the man by the back of his coat, and flung him away. Unable to maintain his hold, the intruder slammed to the ground.

Fearghus and Seumus calmly waited while Torcuil leaped down, waded through the ivy bed, and grabbed the culprit by the back of his collar. Hauling him up to dangle a foot in the air, Torcuil glared at the man, eye-to-eye.

It was the Grosvenor Square guard.

Fearghus delved into his own coat pocket, then held his cupped hand aloft. Pixie dust shed a soft glow upon the guard's narrow, frightened face as he stared at Torcuil. Seumus quickly substituted a lit lantern retrieved from the kitchen.

"Don't hurt me, guv'nor!"

"Tell me what ye're doin' here," Torcuil ordered.

"I—nothing. Nothing at all. J-just checking. Thought I saw someone trying to get in. The window. That's it. I thought I saw someone trying to get in through the window."

And flounders could fly. Torcuil shook the culprit. "Go ahead," he said softly. "Lie to me. Give me the pleasure of forcin' the truth from ye." He gave his prisoner a wild-eyed, demonic smile, calculated to terrify. "I love t' hear bones crack." The *r*'s rolled off his tongue.

The guard swallowed hard. "If I do, I'll go back to prison, and this time they'll hang me for sure." His voice was barely audible.

"Perhaps. But if ye don't, ye'll die slowly. Screamin'." Even in the shades of gray available in this light, Torcuil saw the guard blanch. "Now, I ask ye once again: What are ye doin' here?"

The guard remained silent.

Torcuil broke his smallest finger.

As the man howled, Fearghus stared at Torcuil, eyes wide with shock.

Seumus nudged him. "Ye forget he's a silkie warrior," he murmured.

When information was not forthcoming, Torcuil reached for another of his prisoner's fingers.

"No!" the man cried. "I-I-I came to st-steal"—he sobbed once, long and shuddering, then forced the words out—"jewels. Oh, my finger," he moaned.

"Jewels? Only jewels? Tell me the truth, ye slimy, wee slug. Are ye here to murder the marquess of Ravenshaw?"

"Murder? No, no, I swear it," the fellow babbled. "Nobody said nothing about murderin' no marquess. Christ, man, I wasn't looking to do any harm. Not really. Just nick a few jewels. The cove what lives here's got enough to spare. That's what I was told!"

Releasing his hold on the former guard's collar, Torcuil watched him drop to the ground. The man huddled there, his every indrawn breath an anxious groan.

"Who told ye?" Torcuil asked mildly.

"Oh God, oh God, don't make me tell you. *Please,* don't make me say. He'll kill me, he will. He's got a vicious temper."

Torcuil shrugged and reached for the prisoner.

The man shrank back, hugging the ground. "No! No. John Good. John Good sent me. Said I'd be a rich man." A hiccup of hysterical laughter broke from his throat. "A dead man, more like."

"Aye, yer choice to come here was no a wise one," Torcuil agreed. "Tell me how he came to . . . send ye."

"He learned who the night guard of Grosvenor Square was and sent me a message to meet him at the Light Lady Inn. Said he had business to discuss. I'd never heard of him before. Made me an offer. Dazzled me, he did, with visions of gold and jewels, just waiting to be taken. Didn't say nothing about a marquess or no long-haired demon living here," he added sullenly.

Torcuil regarded the pathetic figure at his feet, thinking that only a fool would not have taken the trouble to learn who his victim was to be. "Have ye any proof ye came here only for jewels, no to harm the marquess or any of his family?"

The man shook his head.

"'Tis a pity." Torcuil curled his fingers into the man's

collar again, intending to search the area around the marquess's bedchamber window to see if there was any sign of entry.

Suddenly, the guard slumped, suspended from Torcuil's grip like an eleven-stone mackerel. Impatient, Torcuil shook him slightly. When that brought no response, he eased the fellow to the ground and checked his heartbeat.

Fearghus, Seumus, and Torcuil looked at each other.

"What happened?" Torcuil asked as he examined the culprit, looking for signs of life. "I dinna truly injure the wee maggot."

"Ye snapped his finger in two," Fearghus reminded him.

Torcuil dismissed that with a grunt as he checked the man's jugular vein for a pulse. "That's no enough to kill a man."

"Perhaps he died of a heart seizure or what the mortals call an apoplexy," Seumus suggested.

Torcuil glowered at the inert guard. "Now why would he do that?"

"Ye can be verra terrifyin' when ye set yer mind to it," Seumus said soothingly. "Likely he died from fright."

Indignation rose in Torcuil. "I was no attemptin' to terrify him *then*."

"He just took a breath," Fearghus announced. "I saw his chest move."

"Good," Torcuil muttered. "I canna understand why John Good would hire a burglar. Why someone to rob Ravenshaw, when before Good's hired assassins?"

"Mayhap he wants it all," Fearghus offered helpfully.

Seumus touched Torcuil's arm. "Come, lad, before ye drive yerself mad with questions ye'll no find the answers to here."

Fearghus stayed with the unconscious guard while

Seumus and Torcuil searched the area beneath the marquess's window more thoroughly.

They turned up nothing.

The guard was given over to the authorities, along with an abbreviated story of a burglary. Torcuil acted on behalf of the marquess, seeing no need to disturb him from his deep, healing sleep.

Before Torcuil returned to his own bedchamber, he stopped to release Verity from her suspense by relating what had transpired. She received the news with her usual courage, making him proud once again.

Now, in his own chamber, Torcuil prepared his weapons. It was time to pay a visit to the Light Lady Inn. He checked his pistols and secreted his knives, and when he was content with the readiness of his weapons, he donned his garrick and hat. Then he gave in to his need to satisfy himself about Verity's safety, just one more time.

Her door was locked. Pleased with her caution, he reached into the pocket of his waistcoat and brought out what he considered to be the key to the most important room in the house—Verity's bedchamber.

Carpet the color of the Aegean Sea muted his boot steps as he walked into her room. In the fireplace fronted in black-veined marble, a recently tended fire gave off warmth and golden light that dwindled out to brush against the azure draperies of the tester bed. Soft heat warmed his face and penetrated his long, multicaped garrick. His fingers eased back the damask curtain.

Verity lay on her side, her spun-gold hair strewn out across the blue satin pillow. Her eyes opened and met his.

Only the occasional crackle of the fire breached the heavy silence as Torcuil and Verity remained where they were, their gazes locked.

Slowly, she sat up, and her unbound hair tumbled onto her shoulders. "Where are you going?"

"I've some business to attend to."

Her dark gold eyebrows lowered. "You're looking for your brother, aren't you? Please don't go, Torcuil. London can be a dangerous place at night. Papa has a man looking for Eideard."

"Boniface Kingston doesna exactly inspire my confidence," Torcuil said dryly.

"Not him. Mr. Kingston's time is taken up with Papa. Another person. And I have my friends and acquaintances making inquiries regarding Eideard's location."

Torcuil regarded her for a moment. She was nothing like he'd ever expected to find among the land folk. Could a breed that produced such a caring, courageous woman be as avaricious and barbaric as his people had come to believe? He doubted it.

A corner of his mouth curved up. "I feel better havin' Fearghus with yer father."

"If only we knew who wants Papa out of the way, we could both feel better." She frowned and chewed her bottom lip. "I don't like thinking Lord Isted would wish us harm. True, he very much wants to close the mine and has done his best to persuade the other partners to his view . . ." Her eyebrows drew farther down. "He and Papa did have that quarrel"—she looked up at Torcuil—"but there was no violence. Besides, Papa and Lord Isted have dealt with each other for many years."

"Which doesna preclude murder now. Can ye think of someone else?"

She thought a minute. "No. However, I think you should know Lord Cowen was found dead. He . . . fell down the stairs."

"Aye, yer father told me."

"Oh."

Torcuil wanted to take Verity into his arms. He told himself that the less he held her, the easier it would go on both of them.

"I've found the Light Lady Inn," he said. He'd fully expected the much-vaunted Bow Street Runner to have quickly discovered the place named by the Noden brothers as the rendezvous point with John Good.

Her eyes widened. "Here in London? Where? What street?"

Her question prompted his sharp glance. "I dinna notice the name of the street," he said smoothly.

"That's where you're going now, isn't it? Just . . . Well, take Mr. Gruagach with you."

Stung, Torcuil scowled. "And why do I need Fearghus, d'ye mind tellin' me? Do ye no think I'm capable of makin' a few inquiries?"

She paced a few steps away from him, her hands clasped tightly at her waist. "I didn't say that."

"'Tis certain ye implied it."

She scowled back at him. "I implied no such thing. It's only that I wish to keep you safe. I know very well that you're handy with a sword—"

"Aye, but what I carry is a long knife."

"—and a pistol. But if you're going to the Light Lady Inn, you will very probably be in a disreputable part of town. Am I not correct?"

"Ye are."

"You'll be surrounded by strangers. There will be no one to aid you if you go alone."

"I'm goin' to spy, Anemone, no to attack."

"Oh!" She began to pace. "And won't you just make the most inconspicuous spy! Ten feet tall, hair to your knees, shoulders the width of four men—"

He resisted the smile that tugged at his lips. "Ye exaggerate."

She stopped to face him. "A little, perhaps. But still, you *are* tall and striking. Let Gruagach go in your stead."

"I canna do that," Torcuil said quietly. "The task is mine."

She took a step toward him, then seemed to catch herself. "He's less noticeable."

The fact that what she said made sense annoyed him. "He's short, hairy, and homely as a wart, and aye, ye've the right of it; he could like pass among a crowd without incitin' anyone's attention. But I'll no have him takin' the risks that are mine."

Verity tilted up her chin. "No one will talk with you," she said firmly. "They won't even come near you. You're entirely too intimidating."

A corner of his mouth curled up. "Clearly I dinna intimidate *ye*."

"I . . . well . . . yes. Yes, you do. Sometimes. But I have the good judgment to overcome it."

His smile grew as an odd pride in her warmed him. "Ye're a courageous female, and no mistake."

Her eyes flashed. "Are you funning me? I've had quite enough of—"

"*Pax,*" he exclaimed softly, lifting his hands, palms outward. "*Pax*, Anemone. 'Twas meant as praise."

"Oh."

"Mayhap ye've a point, though," he admitted.

"I'm glad you comprehend that."

It was a safe wager that Benny, Nat, and Harry frequented the Light Lady, and they would recognize him. Torcuil did not consider that a threat in itself. No, what concerned him was that they could easily sound the alarm, thereby preventing him from learning anything useful about the man Nat had mentioned. Verity was right. Fearghus could more readily glean information.

Trying not to be distracted by the way her sleeping

gown touched the curves of her body, Torcuil gave a curt nod. "I'll take Fearghus."

Her rigid posture eased slightly. "I'm much relieved. All manner of ruffians frequent such establishments. So I'm told."

"Aye, an' there're thugs, an doxies. Dinna worrit for me so, Verity. I've had dealin's with 'em before and come to no harm."

Abruptly Verity straightened. "Doxies?"

Torcuil nodded absently. "Och, aye. A brazen lot they are, too, if the one I encountered is any example."

Verity's eyes narrowed. "Encountered? You encountered a doxie? Precisely what transpired during this . . . encounter?"

Torcuil recalled the dull-eyed female who had casually bared her breasts to him. Such a creature could not begin to compare with Verity, whose vibrancy charged the very air around her. Verity, whose honest passion inflamed him as no female had ever done before. Unbidden, an arousing mental image swam into his mind: Verity, her eyes heavy-lidded with passion, her lips parted and swollen from his kisses, her lush breasts pale and warm and sensitive to his touch.

The desire Torcuil had been holding at bay lashed through him. If she knew what he struggled to control, she wouldn't be standing there in a sleeping gown that softly draped her smooth, sweet shoulders and fell over her woman's body like a white spray of seawater.

He looked away.

Out of the corner of his eye, he saw her fold her arms and assume a determined stance. "I wish to go with you."

Her announcement had the effect of icy water being dumped over him. He stared at her, incredulous. "Ye canna be serious."

"Quite serious," she snapped.

He folded his own arms over his more massive chest and stared down at her from his superior height. "Nay."

She strode to her wardrobe, flung open the doors, and snatched out a dark blue riding habit. "This should be suitable for prowling squalid areas of London."

"Ye're no goin' anywhere. Ye'll stay here where ye're safe, and that's final."

"Oh? You didn't consider me safe two hours ago." She climbed up on her bed, carrying the dress with her. With a jerk of her wrists, the bed curtains closed.

It was too much to hope that she'd seen sense and decided to go to sleep, Torcuil thought sourly. "Now what are ye about?"

Her voice issued from behind the curtains, slightly muffled by the yards of damask. "I'm changing clothes. A *gentleman* would wait outside."

A curse on gentlemen! He stalked to the door, nipping up her ring of household keys from the top of her chest of drawers as he passed. "I dinna care what a *gentleman* would do. *I'm* leavin', and I'm lockin' the door behind me. Sweet dreams!" He jerked open the bedchamber door.

Verity thrust her head out between the bed curtains. "Don't you dare! *Torcuil MacCodrum!*"

He stepped out of the room, closed the door behind him, and firmly turned the key in the lock.

Minutes later, he found Fearghus settling down for the night in the room he shared with Seumus, who was keeping watch with Columbine over the house and grounds. Grumbling, the gruagach blinked owlishly at Torcuil. "An inn, ye say? Mayhap I can interest a few mortals in a game o' chance."

"Never ye mind the cards, Fearghus," Torcuil informed him firmly. Gruagachs were notorious gamblers. It was one of their strong traits—when it wasn't one of their weak ones. "Information is what ye're seekin'. Ye want to learn anything ye can about someone the thieves and pimps that haunt the place call 'the man.' He may be the one sendin' out the assassins. Goes by the name of John Good."

"Aye, as ye will." A change of clothing appeared on Fearghus's short, stocky frame.

Torcuil studied the garments with a critical eye. They looked to him to be a step up from Nat's greasy, shabby attire and one level below Benny's cheap finery. A single nod conveyed his approval.

"Lived on the streets of this cursed pit mortals call a town," Fearghus muttered. "Ought to know what to wear."

"I ask yer pardon, Fearghus," Torcuil said, unwilling to hurt the brownie's feelings. "Yer skill at blendin' with yer surroundings is so extraordinary, 'tis easy to forget ye haven't always lived in a grand house."

Fearghus scratched his nose. "Aye. Well. No offense taken."

That settled, Torcuil led them toward the stables at the back of the property. As they walked, Fearghus shook his head.

"If it's a horse ye're thinkin' of," he said, " ye'll have to ride alone. Horses and other beasts go skittish when I'm near them."

"I know a horse who may be willin' to accommodate ye."

Several minutes later, Torcuil and Fearghus rode out of the stables, heading toward the inn. For what seemed like half the night, they made their way through London. Just as they turned into the narrow lane which led to the Light Lady, the hint of a familiar scent wafted to Torcuil on the cold night air. But it wasn't possible . . .

He halted his horse and turned in his saddle. Hanging back some distance, probably thinking the darkness and mist concealed her from his sight, Verity sat neatly upon her sidesaddle. A glance downward explained why the sound of her horse's hooves hadn't drawn his attention. Each was bound with rags.

Sacred well of Nechtan! He bit out a Gaelic oath, knowing none in English strong enough to give his temper vent. Ignoring Fearghus's questioning look, Torcuil turned his mount and rode back to Verity.

Her eyes widened when she saw she'd been discovered. She swallowed hard, but raised her chin defiantly.

"Have ye gone daft, woman?" he demanded, too furious to trust himself to say more in that moment.

She lifted her chin a fraction of an inch higher, but he didn't miss the uncertain wariness in the glance she sent him. She'd pushed at his limit, and it worried her. Good. Let her worry.

He scowled at her. "Ye belong in yer room. How did ye win free?"

"*I* say where I belong, and I'm quite weary of being locked in my room whenever you find it convenient. I came down the drainpipe and the trellis."

"I dinna confine ye to yer chamber for *convenience*." Torcuil's fingers tightened on the reins as he noticed an ivy leaf clinging to the sleeve of her spencer. "And climbin' down that trellis is a risky business. Ye show less sense than a pup." He reached over and plucked a piece of ivy from her hair, which had been wadded up beneath her plumed top hat.

"How flattering to have one's common sense compared to that of a dog," she said stiffly. "Nevertheless, I'm going with you. You can't stop me."

"Och, Anemone," he said softly, "do ye truly believe so?"

She eased backward on her saddle.

With his knee, he nudged his horse closer, willing to intimidate her, if that's what it took to win her obedience and keep her safe.

Up went her chin again, though it trembled slightly. "I promise you, if you haul me back to my chamber, I'll only climb out the window again."

"And likely break yer foolish neck."

"*My* choice."

He leaned down until they were almost nose-to-nose, the air clouding silver with their mingled breath. "I can put ye somewhere that has no window."

She scowled at him in return. "Pray, where would that be?"

"That wee room in the basement where Mrs. Dibble concocts those cordials of hers."

"Ha! I'll be out of there in a trice. Do you really believe I've grown up in this house and don't know every one of the secret passages that honeycomb the basement?"

Torcuil contemplated his pommel. If he took her back now, she'd likely only try to follow him again. She'd be totally vulnerable. If he kept her with him, she would have his protection. It seemed there was no real decision to be made.

Torcuil cast a glance at the moon. He automatically translated its position in the dark sky into the approximate hour. "Verra well. Stay with me. But I'll have yer reason for this folly of yers." He directed his mount back to where Fearghus waited.

She directed her horse alongside him. Out of the corner of his eye he watched the graceful undulation of her body as she automatically responded to the beast's gait.

"Yer reason?" Torcuil snapped.

Verity smoothed the skirt of her riding habit, then met his gaze.

"I intend," she said, "to protect you."

15

Let us make an honorable retreat.
—William Shakespeare

Verity shivered in the sharp night air, but the tremor that ran through her was not due entirely to the cold. As she stood with Torcuil and the horses in the alley opposite the Light Lady Inn, she peered through the murk, down the narrow street at the few windows where tallow candles gave off a dim, smoky glow. Outside the door of the inn, rush torches burned sullenly.

Never before had she ventured into this section of London. Until tonight, she'd taken care to stay clear of it. Now she not only lurked in the deepest shadows of a place where, in the mornings, bodies were swept up with the rest of the night's trash, but she'd even argued to get here! She heard the furtive squeaking of a rat behind her and shot a nervous glance over her shoulder. Casually, she edged closer to Torcuil.

"I canna believe ye wanted to come to this foul place,"

he said in a low voice, without taking his gaze from the tavern. Fearghus had gone inside what seemed an eternity earlier, but which was, in truth, closer to twenty minutes.

"I-I wanted to pro-protect you," Verity insisted doggedly. Was it just her imagination, or was it getting colder by the minute?

Still watching the tavern on the oddly silent lane, Torcuil unbuttoned his garrick and without so much as a by-your-leave enveloped her in it. He cradled her against his warm, solid side. "So ye've said repeatedly. What ye havena said is from *what* ye're so determined to protect me. Are ye afeared someone will cast a glamour on me, then?"

She stood awkwardly bound to his side, stiff against the marvelous contours of his body. But even the mortifying memory of her behavior in his bedchamber could not keep her indifferent to the heat and comfort he offered.

"A glamour?" she asked as she leaned against him.

"A spell," he supplied absently.

"A spell?" she echoed as she nestled a little closer. "I rather doubt there are any witches or warlocks in that tumbledown public house."

"Witches or warlocks?" He chuckled softly. "What an imagination! Did yer father ne'er teach ye that there's no a such thing as a witch or a warlock?"

"Well, of course." His glorious warmth seeped into her flesh. "But—I mean . . . who, then, could cast a glamour, if not a witch or warlock?"

"Why, a faery, of course." He frowned consideringly at the tavern. "But then, ye dinna believe in them either, do ye?"

"Of course not," she said firmly. "Any child knows that there are no fairies or witches or any other kind of magical being. They're just part of stories designed to amuse children."

He didn't reply immediately, and she thought for a minute that he'd seen something. She squinted into the night, wishing her vision in the dark were as good as his.

"Ye've still no answered the question." An eddy of silvered air issued from his lips. "From what do ye plan to protect me?"

Clearly, he wasn't going to let the matter go. "Disreputable women," she muttered grudgingly.

"Disreputable women?" he echoed, and she heard the genuine puzzlement in his voice.

Peevishly, she wondered just how far back in the Highlands he had lived. "Harlots," she snapped, her face hot despite the frosty air.

"Ah. Doxies."

"Yes."

He nodded.

Minutes passed in silence. Finally Verity could stand the suspense no longer. "Just what do you . . . uh . . . know about"—she cleared her throat—"doxies?"

The garrick shifted up, then down as he shrugged his other shoulder. "Only what Seumus told me."

She released a surreptitious sigh of relief.

"And there was that doxie who approached me a few nights ago."

Verity stiffened. "Where?"

"Here. I was standin' right there." He indicated the street a few feet away.

"The effrontery! What, uh, did she say?"

"Och, 'tis no so much what she said as what she did."

Torcuil wasn't safe anywhere! "What did she do?"

"Pulled her shirt down."

"Pulled her . . . shirt down?" How carnal could straightening one's shirt be?

"She bared her breasts to me." He continued to survey the tavern.

The only word she managed to force out emerged as a squeak. "Bared . . . ?"

"Her breasts. Aye. Wee things they were, too. Nothing to show off to strangers." He shrugged his shoulder again. "Yours are much grander."

Verity's gasp sucked in cold air so forcefully she started to cough.

Torcuil patted her back. "Easy, lass, easy. Och, ye shouldna ha' come out into this cold night air."

Eyes watering, she finally recovered her breath. Before she could retort to Torcuil's observation regarding her bosom, a furtive shadow captured their attention. It scurried down the street, staying close to the buildings. As it approached the tavern, it turned the corner and disappeared.

"That was Benny," Torcuil said. "And I'd say he has no wish to be observed."

"Who's Benny?"

"A panderer," he replied distractedly, his gaze fixed across the lane.

"A panderer. Of course. Why am I not surprised? Where there's a tart . . ." A knot formed in her chest. "Did you . . . go with her?"

"Hmm?"

"Did you go with the doxie?"

Torcuil looked down at Verity. "Go with her where?" The clouds parted, and a shaft of watery moonlight illuminated his face. His black eyebrows lifted. "Oh. Nay, I did nothing with her." The corner of his beautiful mouth nudged up. "I dinna even let her touch my hair."

Relief bubbled up in Verity. "Good."

He raised a hand to her cheek. As if he'd caught himself in an improvident act, he abruptly lowered it. "I've got to see what that worm, Benny, is about." Withdrawing a knife from his boot, he handed it to her, haft-first. "Stay here with the horses. Use this if ye must."

She nodded. Her fingers hesitated before closing around the handle of the knife.

"I'll no be long," he said, clearly reluctant to leave her alone.

"Go. I'll be safe for a minute." She gave him a smile that she hoped looked braver than she felt.

He held open his coat, and she stepped away from his warmth. With the quiet of a shadow, he moved across the brick street and vanished around the corner of the tavern.

Suddenly, the night seemed more threatening without Torcuil to hold it at bay. A drop of water fell from the corner of the eaves above and spattered on the brick next to her foot. In the alley behind her, a cat yowled. She whirled around, her gloved hand tightening on the reins of their horses. Squinting into the gloom, she could see nothing amiss. But then, she couldn't even see the cat.

As soon as Torcuil rounded the corner of the tavern, he saw the rickety stairs leading to the second story. Benny was halfway to the door at the top. Pulling the loaded pistol from his belt, Torcuil followed. Despite his quiet tread, the ancient wood of the fourth step groaned under his weight.

Benny whipped around. His eyes widened. "You!" The sight of the pistol aimed at him seemed to nail him to the spot.

Torcuil glided up the stairs, the pistol warm and balanced in his hand. "Aye, so it is. I dina wish to bother ye again, Benny, but it proved unavoidable."

The panderer's thin lips drew back over stained teeth. "Bastard! You've crippled me for life!"

Torcuil shook his head slowly. "Ye seem to move well enough. Of course, I've no seen ye runnin'."

Benny swore at him.

Torcuil's patience wore out. He crowded Benny back to the edge of the stairs. Benny looked down to the worn bricks below. Then he looked up into Torcuil's set face.

"I've no patience with a wee worm like yerself, so ye'd do well no to waste my time."

"I don't know anything," Benny quavered.

Torcuil lifted an eyebrow. "I've no asked the question, yet."

Benny made no reply, but his lips trembled.

"Who is 'the man' who comes here?"

The whites of Benny's eyes grew more pronounced. "I-I-I don't know what you mean."

"I think ye do."

"No!"

Torcuil eased a little closer, and Benny made a terrified gurgle in his throat. "Are ye afraid of him, Benny?"

The whoremonger hesitated. Torcuil wrapped one hand in the man's coat and lifted him to eye level. Benny's feet dangled high off the stairs.

"Are ye afraid of him, Benny?"

"Yes!" Benny whispered hoarsely. "God, yes!"

"Are ye afraid of me?"

Benny's face contorted, making him appear more like an eel than ever. "I hate you!" he spat.

Torcuil clucked his tongue. "That was no the answer I wished to hear."

Benny grabbed at Torcuil's wrist as he eyed the distance down to the pavement with panicked eyes. "Yes! I fear you. You scare the piss out of me! I-I've never . . . You're like no man I've ever come across. An animal—"

Torcuil's eyes narrowed. "Flattery will get ye nowhere. Do ye think I'd hesitate to make ye suffer?"

Wildly, Benny shook his head. "Please . . . no . . ."

"Ye know my question. I'll hear yer answer now . . . or never . . ."

"He'll kill me."

Torcuil's smile held no humor. It almost frightened him that he was so successful in terrifying land folk. The breed who had slaughtered his innocent cousins, he reminded himself. "*I'll* kill ye, Benny. Now, which is it to be? Answer my question and live? Or keep his secret and die? Who's to say he'll e'er find out ye told me?" He placed the barrel of the pistol against Benny's groin.

The sharp smell of human urine cut through the cold night air. Torcuil drew back his head in disgust.

"Good, John Good," Benny babbled. "That's all I know!"

"Describe Mr. Good's appearance."

"T-tall, though not nearly so tall as you. Dresses plain but quality. Always wears a black cloth mask. Meets people at the Lady. Sort of secret-like, in a back room. That's all I can tell you! I swear!"

Torcuil lowered Benny until the man's feet gained a stair, but he didn't release him. "Why do ye fear him so, little worm? Has he hurt ye?"

"No. But I've heard men talk. Heard he kills men who cross him. Kills 'em in horrible ways."

"Do ye know any man who's seen this?"

Benny shook his head wildly.

"Any who have personal knowledge of his deeds?"

"No, but that don't mean nothin'. Talks like a southern man, he does. He probably does his murdering there."

"One last question, Benny. Have ye seen a man who looks much like me?"

Benny's eyes bulged. "You mean there's another one like you?" he squealed, hysteria edging his voice.

Clearly, Benny hadn't seen Eideard. "Be on yer way now," Torcuil said. "If ye warn off John Good, I'll pay ye another wee visit."

Benny shook his head emphatically. "No! No, I won't tell anyone."

Torcuil released him and watched him scramble up the remaining stairs and into the inn's door.

Taking care not to be followed, Torcuil returned to where he'd left Verity. To his relief he found her safe and sound, standing between the horses for warmth. After reclaiming his knife from her, he opened his garrick, and she immediately stepped inside. The sharp chill from her clothing cut through his coat, waistcoat, and shirt. He shuddered in surprise.

She looked up at him. "Forgive me. I did not mean to make you cold, too." She started to move away from him.

He enfolded her in an arm and drew her back to. "Ye're freezin'."

She snuggled closer to him.

Trying hard not to think about the sweet curve of her buttocks pressed against his thigh, Torcuil scanned the street. What was taking Fearghus so long? Had he run into trouble? Desperate to do something with his hands that didn't involve Verity's beautiful body, he began to stroke Wind Teaser's forehead.

Cold, came the plaintive thought.

Aye, 'tis that indeed.

Home?

Soon. He hoped. Then caught himself. Since when had he started referring to Ravenshaw House as home?

Verity stirred against Torcuil, and he gritted his teeth. Giving her sanctuary beneath his garrick wasn't the wisest thing he'd ever done. As she warmed, her fragrance grew more noticeable, her body more pliant. As her body became more pliant, his became more rigid.

"What did you learn?" she asked.

"Eh?"

"What did you learn? A few minutes ago?" she added at his blank look.

"Oh. I learned that I was right. It is the same man the

Noden brothers told us about. His name is John Good and he wears a mask. *And* he comes from the south. Did ye no say the mine was south of London?"

"Yes. It's in Devon."

"And where does Istead live?"

Her eyebrows drew slightly down. "His seat is in Dorset. But like most of the partners, he's in London now."

"One of the miners, then?" he asked distractedly as her hip brushed close to his painfully erect manhood.

"Possibly. But why would a miner wish to do away with his only ally among the partners?"

"Good question," he said, unable to pay much attention to what she was really saying. "Here, now, I think perhaps havin' ye wrapped in my garrick is no such a good idea. If we're attacked, I'll need to move quickly."

"Oh." She sounded disappointed. "I hadn't thought of that." She moved out from under the protection of his great coat. "You're quite correct, of course."

She wouldn't have been cold if she'd stayed in her chamber where she belonged, he thought irritably, concerned about how the night air chilled her. Silently he berated himself for not simply locking her in the pantry as he'd first thought.

"It's a good thing I came along," she announced, as if she'd read his thoughts.

He grunted, feeling damnably frustrated.

"Kindly notice, you've not been accosted by any . . . any . . . harlots."

"Aye."

Apparently his answer lacked the proper enthusiasm. "Are you disappointed?" she asked, an edge in her voice.

"Of course I'm no disappointed," he said irritably. He didn't want to talk about females—any female. He especially didn't want to think about one particular managing, frustrating, confusing, thoroughly mystifying female. And he desperately didn't want to remember Verity's sweet sighs, her soft, pale breasts, and her long, slender legs. By the sacred well of Nechtan, *what was keeping Fearghus?*

"I suppose a man *likes* looking at a woman's breasts," Verity said acidly.

Torcuil turned his head to glare at her. "Aye!" he snapped. "A man *does* like lookin' at a woman's breasts." At her shocked expression, his temper ebbed. "That is to say, a particular woman's breasts." His gaze lowered to the womanly curve in the front of Verity's pelisse. Feeling awkward, he glanced away.

Verity took a step toward him. "Torcuil—"

"Dinna fear. I'll no be triflin' with ye."

"I—" She broke off at a sound behind them and turned to search the alley.

Torcuil had heard it, too. That shuffling tread of two pairs of feet. He motioned her back toward the horses, then, blade in hand, he moved to investigate the source of the sound.

Two men vainly attempted stealth as they shambled toward the entrance of the alley where Verity stood with the mounts.

"Some people never learn," Torcuil observed dryly.

The men jumped. "No!" Nat cried. "Not *you!*"

Harry backed away. He bumped into an empty wooden crate, scrabbled around it, then turned and fled.

"Ain't it bad enough Harry 'n me are starvin'?" Nat demanded in a voice reedy with fear. "Everybody hears us comin'. *Your* doing . . ." He took a step back, then another.

"Perhaps ye should think of another line o' work, then. Something that doesna require ye sneakin' up on people. Something more honest, shall we say?"

"Bugger off!" Nat snarled, taking another step back. "No one learns to fight like you can by bein' honest."

Torcuil cocked his head and calculated the distance between Nat and him. "Och, now, there ye're wrong. I'm a warrior, no some snivelin' sneak thief. I've trained all my life. But I fight only to protect my people." He thought of Verity and her father. "Or those who canna protect themselves."

"Well, ain't we the bloody noble cove?" Nat sneered as he began shambling backward.

"I wouldna throw that knife, were I ye," Torcuil warned softly.

Nat froze. "How do you know I got a knife?"

"I see it."

" 'Struth! You're bloody unnatural, you are!" He stumbled as he spun around. Frantically, he grabbed at the wall of a building for support, never pausing in his headlong retreat, following in Harry's path. "Devil!" he cried. "Devil!"

Returning his knife to its place inside his boot, Torcuil walked back to Verity, but kept his distance. She was visibly shaken, and he longed to comfort her, but he didn't trust himself to merely hold her in his arms and stroke her hair. The fire she ignited in his blood was burning too hot. That and the first wine of battle. True, a battle averted, one that had promised to be little more than a short scuffle, but his body throbbed nonetheless.

"H-how many times have you been here?" Verity asked, rubbing her upper arms with her palms.

"Only one other time."

"Those men. They knew you."

"I became lost here," Torcuil said, watching the door of the tavern. "They accosted me."

"Oh."

The tavern door opened, releasing a rowdy wave of laughter that mingled the deep guffaws of men and the higher pitched voices of women. Two men staggered out, their arms thrown around each other's shoulders. Singing with great gusto but little melody, they careened down the lane, finally vanishing into the night.

Fearghus had been gone too long, Torcuil decided after a glance at the moon. He said as much to Verity. "I've no choice but to go in after him."

The worry in her sweet face lifted his spirits. "Dinna worrit, Anemone. I'll be in and out in minutes." He gave her one of his smaller knives, one more her size, which she accepted and slid into her half boot.

Unexpectedly, she rose to her toes. She grasped his braids and lowered his face to hers, then clumsily fitted her lips to his. Reluctant to leave such sweetness, he gently took her into his arms.

A sharp yearning ripped through him. Torcuil cupped her face in his hands and tenderly kissed her trembling mouth, pouring his longing into that radiant caress. To have this woman with him always, to see her bonny smile, filled with such loving trust, was as much as any man could ever ask.

But he wasn't any man. He wasn't a man at all.

Torcuil straightened.

"Be careful," she said, her voice oddly uneven.

He nodded, reluctant to take his gaze from her upturned face. Unwilling to think of the future without her, he abruptly turned and strode across the lane. He ducked his head and entered the door of the Light Lady Inn.

The common room of the inn was crowded and smoky. A blue haze of tobacco smoke from a score or more of clay pipes hung in the air. In the wall to Torcuil's left, beyond the bar, a large soot-blackened fireplace provided heat and more smoke. To his right, across the room, a flight of wooden stairs led to the half floor where he saw the row of doors he assumed opened onto the inn's rooms to let.

The din of conversation faded into thick silence throbbing with wariness as every head in the room turned toward Torcuil. He wished he knew more about tavern customs of land folk. Was he expected to do something now? Every nerve in his body hummed with alert energy. Three men standing at a bar similar to the one in the Crown and Thistle stared at him as they waited for their tankards to be filled with ale. Only one stood even as tall as Torcuil's shoulder. He nodded to them, then kept them in his line of vision as he tried to remember what he'd observed in the Crown and Thistle. He did the only thing he could think of: He ordered a tankard for himself from a female in the common room who appeared to be standing idle.

As soon as the polite words were out of Torcuil's mouth, the masculine chuckles surrounding the young female and the angry flash in her eyes warned him that he'd erred.

The line of her mouth flattened. "I ain't a serving wench." Then she seemed to notice the quality of his attire, for she abruptly smiled. "But I can be anything *you* want," she simpered. Sidling through the crowd, she walked with a peculiar flip of her hips he'd never seen Verity use.

When the female drew close to him, she placed her hands on those hips, and that sway became even more pronounced. "A good-lookin' toff like you needs a woman what knows how to please a man."

"That's right, Mary," someone from the crowd called. "Please 'im with your French disease." A roar of masculine laughter swept through the room.

Torcuil had no idea what French disease was, but he

could tell by the female's angry look the comment hadn't pleased her.

"You shut up, Hap!" she cried. "That's a bleedin' lie!"

His expression studiously blank, the man behind the bar shoved a filled tankard at Torcuil and muttered the price. Gratefully, Torcuil gave him a coin of greater value. As he brought the ale to his lips, he scanned the area and found Fearghus waving him over from the far side of the room, where he sat at a table with three strangers. All four of them held playing cards in their hands.

Torcuil's fingers tightened on the handle of his tankard. Cards! He and Verity had been kept waiting while Fearghus played a game of chance? Seething inside, Torcuil stalked toward the gruagach. Men eased out of his way and turned back to their business, but he sensed their continued interest. He arrived at the table to find the strangers tossing down their cards in disgust while Fearghus raked a small pile of coins toward his existing collection.

"Thank ye, gentlemen," Fearghus said. " 'Tis been a pleasure." The men left the table to disperse throughout the room.

"Fearghus," Torcuil said in a low voice, "there were to be no games tonight. Verity and I have been waitin' for ye in the cold. I feared ye'd met with trouble. Verity is out there by herself now."

"Dinna fash yerself," Fearghus replied softly. "I've been waitin' for 'the man' to show himself. He's in that wee nook back to yer right. The one wi' the privacy curtain across it. He's been there by himself for a goodly time, now, and I've no been able to get closer than this to him."

"How long?"

"Since just after I arrived."

Torcuil scowled. "Is there a door out o' this place behind that curtain?"

Fearghus blinked. "I dinna know."

With forced control, Torcuil set down his tankard. "So. 'Tis possible he's no even still in that cursed nook."

"I . . . I hadna thought—"

"Why did ye no ask one o' yer cronies if there was a back door?" Torcuil cast a narrowed, sidelong glance toward Fearghus, who suddenly found his pile of coins of riveting interest.

"It dinna occur to me. There's another back door, ye see, straight back through that way." Fearghus gestured toward the door.

Torcuil studied the closed curtains. Somehow, he had to get inside there without attracting too much attention. Several pairs of eyes kept watch over that nook, he had no doubt.

" 'Ere now," Mary called, threading through the crowd. "You ain't going to believe ol' Hap, are you? Look at my skin. Clear as a babe's. I could show you a right good time."

Another woman thundered down the wooden stairs. "Mary, you stay away from him! He's a gentleman, he is, and I'll not have you usin' him ill." As she plowed between the tables and benches, Torcuil recognized her.

He grinned. "Dolly," he greeted the woman who'd been selling cherries when he'd first entered London, pleased to see a familiar, friendly face.

She beamed. "Ooo, I knowed you was a gentleman the first time I saw you."

"Have ye any cherries for me to buy?"

A man at the next table guffawed, and Dolly jabbed him with her elbow, then turned her bright smile back on Torcuil. "That's my day job, lovey. At night I . . . uh, entertain men."

Mary planted her hands on her hips, arms akimbo. "Entertains, is it? You're a whore, dearie, just like the rest of us girls. Now shove off. I saw him first."

"*I* saw him first, and he's too good for the likes of you. Breeding, you are, and planning to blame the babe on him. Well, I'll not have it. It's a filthy trick."

Mary's face went red. "Bitch!"

"Slut!"

With a loud yowl, Mary launched herself at Dolly.

The two women went at each other with screaming fury. Deciding that they would injure themselves, Torcuil finally stepped in to try to break it up.

"Piss off!" a bald man at a nearby table snarled. "Leave 'em be. We've got bets placed, see? Dolly's sure to win."

Mary tore free of Dolly's grip, leaving a handful of hair behind. "*Dolly?*" she shrilled indignantly. She swept up a tankard on the table next to her, and flung it at the bald man's head.

It struck true, then ricocheted to thunk against the back of a man at another table. With a growl, the second fellow turned around. He grabbed the bald man by the front of the shirt and drew back his fist. The bald man's drinking companions took exception, and in seconds, pandemonium spread through the common room. Fists flew, curses were shouted, tables overturned.

Torcuil stepped back, out of the way of a flying bench. He grabbed Fearghus's shoulder to get his attention.

"Get outside to Verity," Torcuil shouted as he ducked a flying fist, then picked up the owner of that fist and tossed him several feet distant.

An earthenware pitcher descended onto Fearghus's head just as he opened his mouth to reply. An expression of surprise registered on his homely features, then his eyes rolled back, and he crumpled to the floor.

A fist slammed into Torcuil's face, sending him reeling. For a second, he saw stars. He shook his head, trying to clear it, forcing the pain to the back of his mind. He grabbed the man who had thrown the punch and torpedoed him headfirst into an upended oak bench. Contact made a satisfying thud. The fellow's eyes crossed, and he slid down the unforgiving surface of heavy oak.

Torcuil scooped Fearghus up under one arm. With one fist, both shoulders and elbows, and the occasional knee, Torcuil worked his way to the curtained nook. With a quick step, he entered.

The first thing he expected to find was the door. The last thing he expected to see was John Good, mask and all, slumped over his table. A knife projected from his back.

Two fingers to Good's jugular told Torcuil the man was quite dead.

Torcuil eased Fearghus to the floor. A rapid search of the nook and its occupant turned up nothing that gave away John Good's true identity. Easing the mask up, Torcuil saw a pale face marked with regular features. An ugly puckered scar marred one cheek. He grabbed up the gruagach and moved to exit through the back door.

A bench came crashing through the curtain, tearing down the rod that held it. Instantly, Torcuil, an inert Fearghus, and the body of John Good were revealed to everyone.

A rumpled, bleeding patron pointed to Torcuil. "Look!" he shouted. "He's murdered John Good!"

Before anyone could react, the front door of the tavern banged open. In marched Verity, leading the horses. The hooves of the beasts thundered against the wooden floor as they nervously filed in, their reins fastened to the saddle of the mount in front of them.

The barkeep peered over the edge of the bar from his hiding place. "You can't bring horses in here!"

Cursing to himself, Torcuil was forced to abandon his escape route. He set Fearghus on the floor, and tapped the gruagach's cheeks. "Wake up," he commanded urgently, casting an anxious glance in Verity's direction. The taps became small slaps. "Damn ye, Fearghus, *wake up*."

A hulking bruiser ambled up to Verity and tried to take the reins of the lead horse from her.

Fearghus groaned. His eyes fluttered opened. "What—?"

"Meet me outside," Torcuil said in a rush.

Verity struggled, refusing to relinquish the reins. Laughing, the bruiser gripped Verity's chin in a meaty paw and smeared his lips over hers. She kicked his shin, but he maintained his hold on her.

Rage burst inside Torcuil's head. Blind to anything but Verity and her attacker, he cleared a swath through the brawlers, tossing bodies this way, booting them that way. Inarticulate with fury, he jerked the man away from Verity. Torcuil slammed the fellow's head down against the top of the bar. Then again. And again. And again, barely restraining himself from driving his hand into the man's body and tearing out his dripping liver.

He heard his name called, as if from a distance. Gradually it registered that the voice was Verity's.

"Torcuil, stop! Torcuil, please, you're going to kill him. Stop! Please!"

He blinked, struggling to contain the rage flaming inside him. He released the bruiser, who slid bonelessly to the floor.

"I-I heard the commotion," Verity stammered. "I was worried. But the horses—"

"Out," Torcuil said.

He didn't have to speak twice. Verity hastily began leading the horses toward the door. Torcuil took his place in front of her, prepared to protect her from interference.

Dolly stopped him at the door, grinning. Her hair was a wild mess, and the rouge on her lips had been smeared across her cheek. "You're a fine gentleman," she said. "I knew it the first time I saw you." She flung her arms around him in an embrace, then stepped back. "G'on now, afore things get ugly. I know you didn't kill John Good."

"Who did?"

She smiled sadly. "G'on, love."

If she knew the identity of the killer, she might be in danger. "Come with us, Dolly."

She shook her head. "What would you do with the likes o' me?" She cast a glance back toward the nook. "Go *now*."

"Come," he commanded, instinct warning him their time was fast running out. He thrust her out the door, in front of him.

Fearghus stumbled up as Torcuil ripped the first set of reins from a saddle. Without ceremony, he plopped the gruagach in the saddle, and Dolly right behind him. Possessively he set his hands on Verity's waist and set her up on her horse, then swung up onto his own.

By the time the tavern door opened and angry patrons poured shouting into the street, all that remained of the four escapees was the echo of their horses' hooves.

Torcuil quietly eased open the kitchen door, where they were greeted by Columbine and Seumus. In the vast fireplace, embers glowed among the ashes. Shadows crowded the towering ceiling.

Verity lit a small Argand lamp, which cast out a pool of illumination that touched the long wooden work tables, the copper pans and molds that hung along the wall, and the swept and scrubbed flagstone floor. She cast a veiled glance at Dolly. She disliked the way the woman had thrown herself at Torcuil in the tavern, but there was more here that she did not yet understand.

"Who's this?" Columbine asked, eyeing the disheveled Dolly.

Torcuil's sensual mouth curved in a half smile. "Perhaps a key to our mystery."

Dolly tossed her head. "Mayhap the only one what can keep the hangman's noose from around your pretty neck, my fine peacock."

Torcuil grinned. "Aye. That, too."

He made the introductions and explained how he'd first met Dolly. Then he, Fearghus, and Dolly related the evening's events.

Columbine's eyes widened. "Lady Verity! You did *that?*"

Verity chuckled wearily. "Yes. I, who have ever been careful to observe all the social graces, have now brought horses into a public building, been accosted by a slavering brute, and saved by a handsome prince."

Fearghus shook his head. "Ye took quite a risk."

"A terrible risk," Torcuil observed, his eyebrows drawing down over his jet eyes. "I dinna wish to think what would have happened had I already gone through that back door."

Verity didn't want to think of that either. "I was merely seeking to protect you."

Fearghus rolled his eyes.

"There's naught from which to protect me," Torcuil insisted, and in the mellow lamplight, she read the truth in his beautiful face.

"I'll not be able to go back home," Dolly said, as she looked around the large kitchen. She turned back to Torcuil. "You should have left me there."

"Ye're in danger, aren't ye?"

"I—" She broke off and dropped her gaze to her torn fingernails. Silence filled the room. "Yes."

"Who killed John Good?" he asked softly.

Dolly hesitated. Still examining her fingernails, she vented a shuddering sigh. "My life won't be worth five pence if he finds out." Then she lifted her worried gaze to meet Torcuil's calm one. "Benny did it." As if she could read Torcuil's opinion of Benny there, she smiled bitterly. "He may be a little worm, but he's a nasty little worm."

"Tell us what happened, Dolly."

She searched the faces around her, then nodded. "The door from John Good's nook opened out onto the rooms Benny rents for us girls and, you know"—she shrugged—"the customers. I was bringin' a bottle of Benny's watered-down gin to the man I was entertaining when I saw Benny enter John Good's nook." A corner of her mouth crooked up into a sarcastic half smile. "His 'audience chamber,' we all called it. Where he did business." The smile vanished. "Anyway, I guess the door wasn't closed all the way, as it came ajar as I passed it. Well, I was curious-like, so I peeked in." She swallowed hard. "I saw Benny shovin' the knife into John Good's back. I heard . . ." Dolly paused to clear her throat and, Verity suspected, to collect herself. "I heard that gasp, all bubbly-like an' rattley." She shuddered. "I knew Benny'd kill me, too, if he knew what I'd seen, so I hurried back to my little room."

She turned wide eyes to Torcuil. "I don't mind telling you that I've been scared Benny saw me. Benny's a mean 'un. More 'n one girl of his bears his scars." Absently, she rubbed her palm over the sleeve of the coat Fearghus had shrugged off and placed over her shoulders not long after they'd left the Light Lady.

"Do ye know why Benny murdered John Good, Dolly?" Torcuil asked.

She shook her head. "No, but I'd wager it was for money. Money is what Benny loves best."

"What can ye tell us about John Good?"

"Not much, I'm afraid. He'd stay at the Light Lady, then leave for a while, then return. Then leave again. I heard he came from the south." She frowned. "No, it was the west. It was the southwest."

"Where in the southwest?"

"Just the southwest, is all I know. Once Mary sneaked a look through the peephole in his room when he was takin' off that mask o' his. She saw a terrible scar." She shrugged. "That's all I know about him. Kept mostly to himself."

"Do ye know if he had any visitors from the south?"

"No. The only people I saw him talking with were the ones who came to him at the inn and spoke to him in his little curtained throne room, where you found him."

"So our questions remain," Seumus said. "Who is John Good, and why was he trying to have the marquess murdered?"

"And a burglar," Columbine added. "Why did he engage a burglar? What sense does that make?"

"All right, Dolly," Torcuil said. "Where's the ring?"

"Ring?"

Torcuil lifted an eyebrow. "The ring ye took off Good."

Dolly's eyes widened. "How did you—?"

"The pale place on his finger," he explained as she withdrew the silver band from her bodice and handed it to him.

He inspected it. "There's writing inside. Verity, move the lamp closer."

Her shoulder brushed his arm, sending a frisson of awareness through her. The kiss they'd shared before he entered the inn loomed up in her mind. As she held the lamp nearer to him, her hand trembled slightly. Even the strong smell of burning colza seed oil could not diminish the memory.

"'To Richard from Alice, with all my love,'" he read. "He wore this a long time. See how the inscribing is faint in some places?"

"A wedding band, I'd say," Verity murmured. "Some men wear them. I've always thought it a lovely sentiment."

"So our John Good may really be Richard," Torcuil said.

Verity nodded. Poor Alice. Who would tell her that her husband was dead? Would she simply be left to worry and to wait for his return?

Torcuil tucked the ring into his waistcoat. He flipped a coin to Dolly, who caught it with a grin. It disappeared into her commodious bosom.

"Ye canna go back to the Light Lady, Dolly, that seems clear."

Dolly nodded. She'd already appeared weary and bedraggled, but now she was homeless, too.

"If ye had the choice, where would ye go, now, and what would ye do?"

"Well, my first choice would be to wed with you and settle down in some lovely rose-covered castle, but"—she threw a knowing glance at Verity—"I can see that's out. My next choice would be to move to Kennington, where my sisters live with their families, and maybe open my own chop house. But I've never believed in miracles or magic."

"Mayhap they're one in the same," Torcuil said with a wink. "But for tonight, at least, ye'll stay here."

He looked at Verity for her assent, which he seemed altogether too certain of obtaining, she thought petulantly. But as little as she liked having under her roof this voluptuous woman who seemed much too intimate with Torcuil, Verity knew it was the right thing to do. Grudgingly, she mustered all the grace at her command, and plastered on a pleasant smile.

"You are welcome, Dolly," she said.

As she lighted the way to Dolly's quarters for the night, it seemed to Verity that they hadn't made much progress in the search for her father's intended murderer. Still, Torcuil had accomplished more than the Bow Street Runners.

And the ring he'd taken from John Good might provide them with valuable information.

If Alice was still around to give them answers.

16

Such sweet compulsion doth in music lie.
—John Milton

The sun had not yet risen when Torcuil and Seumus escorted Dolly to the address of a costermonger she knew. The fellow agreed to rent his wagon and his assistance to Dolly, accompanying her to Kennington. The several gold coins Torcuil had given her to finance her chop house were tucked safely into her bodice.

Torcuil helped her up onto the wagon bench seat. The only illumination there on the brick street was the lantern that hung by a bent nail on the side of the old wagon.

"I've never known anyone like you afore, Torcuil MacCodrum," Dolly declared, misty-eyed. "You're a special man, you are." She gave him an uneven smile. "If ever there was a one to make me believe in magic and the like, it's you, luv."

He felt the warmth of embarrassment creep up his

neck. "I'm honored that ye feel so, Dolly. Mayhap I'll see yer chop house one day."

"You bring your lady with you when you come. I doubt she'll let you leave her behind, anyway."

Torcuil thought of what it would be like to walk into a public place and truly be able to claim Verity as his own lady. He smiled up at Dolly. "Good fortune, my friend."

Tearfully, she hugged him, then quickly released him, ducking her head and dabbing at her eyes. "Let's go," she said to her acquaintance, her voice cracking. With a flick of the reins, the burly fellow signaled the two horses into motion. The rumble of the iron-rimmed wheels slowly faded into the distance.

Seumus patted Torcuil's arm. "It's a fine thing ye've done, laddie. She'll be safe enough from Benny and his ilk." The broonie winked. "I've added a bit o' my own magic to yer generosity."

Torcuil chuckled. "Thank ye, Seumus." He dug John Good's ring out of his pocket. "Here, take this. It should take ye where ye need go."

Seumus accepted the tiny circlet of silver, fingering it. "Aye, ye're right in that. I'll find out all I can."

He closed his fist around the ring, smiled—and winked out of sight.

Dawn came too early for Verity. She wanted nothing more than to burrow under the wonderfully warm bedcovers and sleep the day away. It didn't help matters when Columbine arrived, looking annoyingly fresh and lively.

Today, Verity decided, she would stay in and attend to her correspondence and household matters. The sight she saw in the looking glass, with those purplish circles under her eyes, quickly confirmed her decision.

At breakfast, her father looked from Verity to a

bruised-eyed Torcuil. "I know these attempts on my life go hard on you, but I assure you, I'm in excellent hands. Mr. Kingston is most alert."

As are Seumus and Fearghus, Verity thought, having noticed that at least one of them was with her father at all times. Boniface Kingston might be a nice enough sort of fellow, but after hearing the grandiose tales of Bow Street Runner success, Verity found him somewhat disappointing.

"Are ye feelin' well this morn?" Torcuil asked her father.

The marquess looked faintly surprised. "Why, yes. Thank you."

"Yer arm is healin'?"

"Amazingly well. Those comfrey poultices MacDougall ordered are working wonders, aren't they, my dear?" The marquess directed his question to Verity, who smiled.

"Indeed. I've already written down the receipt and stocked the leaves for my own medicine chest, for future."

Kingston shot Torcuil a conspiratorial look, then continued with his breakfast.

The marquess's answers would have contented Torcuil, had it not been for that niggling bit of memory that eluded him.

The discussion around the table turned back to the events of the night before. The marquess had already expressed his sentiments regarding Verity's accompanying Torcuil and Fearghus to the Light Lady. His wrath had come down on Torcuil's head, who had stoically taken the censure. When Verity had tried to speak up, to accept the blame for her actions, her father had ignored her, and finally Seumus had signaled her into mutinous silence. Torcuil and her father had already agreed that she was Torcuil's responsibility. How irritating males were!

"You've not forgotten our discussion, Daughter?" her father asked her now. "It is my wish that you divert yourself from all this unpleasantness. Attend some of the parties to which you've been invited. You don't wish to cause talk, do you?" he added slyly.

She straightened in her chair. "Certainly not."

"I may even attend a ball or two," he said. "I've been invited, you know."

"Yes, Papa, but do you believe it wise? I mean, your wound isn't fully healed yet."

I'm quite capable of an occasional dance. I imagine our dear cousin is chomping at the bit for a quadrille or two."

Torcuil met the implied question with a blank look.

"*Not* to mention the attempt on your life," she persisted, her anxiety mounting. She shot a glance at Torcuil, wondering why he made no protest over her father's entering a crowd.

"I have no intention of hiding like a scared rabbit," the marquess retorted. "Am I not entitled to a bit of entertainment once in a while? I'm proposing to go to a ball, not wade into a gaming hell. My shoulder is healing well. I'm feeling fit. Not exactly as if I have a foot in the grave, y'know."

"No, of course not, Papa. No one would ever imply that. I simply don't understand your desire to attend a ball. I thought you hated them."

Her father's face grew a rosy hue. "I never did! Well, not *hated* exactly. It's only that many of them tend to be—"

"'Deadly dull'?" she asked, quoting his exact words. "'Tedious to an extreme'? 'Flattery, flummery, and fustian'?"

The marquess shifted in his chair. "I've been to a few exhilarating dances."

"Did you have a particular ball in mind?" she inquired

sweetly, suspicion nibbling at her. She was all for her father's finally rejoining society. He'd never really been part of it since her mother had run off. Despite that woman's death in Italy over two years ago, he'd shown no interest in returning to the fold of the *ton*. And now was not a wise time to correct that omission.

"The Faradays' gathering, next Thursday," he answered promptly.

"I shall, of course, respond immediately. But, may I inquire—any particular reason why?"

"I suppose you're old enough to know. There is a ravishing creature who has taken London by storm. She's a diamond of the first water, even though she's slightly more mature than a girl. I wish an introduction. Lady Faraday will make one."

"And does this ravishing creature have a name?" she inquired, delighted. Finally! It was time Papa took an interest in a woman.

Her father smiled. "She's chosen to go by only one name, and an odd one at that. An original, I suppose, like her."

"Which is . . . ?"

"Neul."

Fearghus dropped his fork. It chimed against the polished marble and echoed through the room. He sent Torcuil a significant glance. Torcuil's shuttered expression revealed nothing of his thoughts. Kingston continued eating, apparently unaware of the uneasy silence growing in the room.

But Verity knew something was wrong. Very wrong.

"Don't worry, Mr. Gruagach," she said, hastily covering Fearghus's error. "There is a clean fork on the sideboard."

He shook his head, ruffling his featherlike hair. "Nay, I was finished with it. That is, thank ye, Lady Verity."

"My pleasure." She turned to Torcuil. "I see that you're done eating. Excellent."

His fork, with its slice of ham, hesitated midair before it continued to his lips. Defiantly, he chewed.

She grabbed his hand and tugged. "Come. This is the day we've both been waiting for."

He swallowed. "It is?" he drawled. "May I know what we've been waiting for?" He excused himself to the marquess and stood.

"Why, what you've been clamoring for! Today you get your first dance lesson."

Just before noon, Verity opened the towering door into the grand saloon, aware of Torcuil standing behind her. She stepped into the vast, elegant chamber and swept out an arm. "Enter, please."

Although she knew Torcuil had already seen the room on his initial tour, she also knew it never failed to impress the viewer. In the center of the ceiling, fifty feet above them, was a coffered dome from which enormous chandeliers of glittering Irish crystal were suspended. The walls, chairs, and sofas were covered in pale blue damask silk. Since breakfast that morning, Verity had instructed Daniel and his fellow footmen to move the furniture to the perimeter of the room and to roll up the carpets, as if a ball were being planned. One of the long walls was punctuated by large, gilt-framed mirrors that flanked a great fireplace and its columned alabaster surround. The expanse of the opposite wall was broken by a bank of tall windows, through which the watery sunshine of winter shone. Not far from the fireplace stood a pianoforte.

His jaw set, Torcuil followed her into the saloon. Behind him filed a sullen Columbine, a sour Fearghus, and a mildly interested Mr. Broonie. Last, but certainly not least, came her father, who seemed almost jovial. She took that as a positive sign that he was well along the road to recovery. A few seconds later Fanny arrived.

"I came as quickly as I could," she told Verity breathlessly. She swept into the room and embraced her uncle, then her cousin. "Did I hear Daniel correctly, Verity? You're giving dancing lessons?"

Torcuil glowered at Verity. "Excellent. If ye've entrusted Daniel with the intelligence, it'll soon be known in every household in the city that ye've taken poor Torcuil MacCodrum under yer wee flutterin' wing. I'll be seen as a pathetic flounder."

The marquess chuckled.

"Don't be such an old bear, Torcuil," Verity said, undaunted by his admittedly intimidating disapproval. "Daniel isn't like that at all."

Fanny laughed as she went to the pianoforte. "Of course he is. Daniel is an outrageous gossip, but he's so good-natured, no one does anything about it. And he's completely loyal when it comes to the important things."

Torcuil pulled the bench out for her. "I see. My dignity is no important enough for his silence." He offered his support while she lowered herself to the padded bench.

"While I do not approve of such unbecoming behavior," the marquess said, "Daniel gossips only about little things. I've seen him come to blows over what he deemed a slight to the house of Alford. Salt of the earth, that fellow."

Verity smiled up at Torcuil. "By tomorrow, you'll dance so marvelously that everyone will believe he was mistaken. You have a natural grace that will aid you."

His only answer was a guttural noise in his throat.

"We're waiting for two more persons. A country dance must have at least three couples. For our purposes we'll have four, since four couples are needed for the quadrille."

The saloon door opened to admit two young maids in mobcaps and white aprons over practical green dresses. The taller of the two smiled shyly. "You asked for us, my lady?"

Verity waved them over. "I certainly did, Kate. Come, we're in desperate need of dance partners for these two poor gentlemen. You and Dorcas must help me teach them the quadrille and the Sir Roger de Coverley."

Blushing and giggling, Kate and Dorcas hurried over. Verity arranged Dorcas alongside Mr. Gruagach and Kate paired with Seumus. She instructed Columbine to stand to the marquess's right, then stepped to her own place next to Torcuil.

"Pretend that I've drawn a large diamond shape on the floor, in the center, here. Each couple is standing at a point of that diamond." She asked them to take note of where they each stood in relation to the others. Verity explained the first figure they would execute, then she walked them through it, step by step. Mr. Gruagach trod on Dorcas's toe. Although she assured him it was of no matter, the shaggy little man grew flustered. Finally, with brisk cheer, Verity told him there was always much toe-treading involved with learning a new dance, and then she moved them on to the next figure. After that she walked them through the dance they'd learned so far.

Pleased with her students, who were trying, despite their initial reluctance, she said, "Very good! Now let's dance to music."

She looked over at Fanny, whose smile indicated she was enjoying herself. "Maestro, please," Verity said in a comically pretentious voice. "Music for the quadrille."

With a flourish, Fanny struck the first chord, then moved into a lively tune that was popular at assemblies and balls.

Standing beside Verity, Torcuil went still. She felt his

tension in his uplifted hand, where her palm rested, and raised her gaze to find him staring intently at Fanny. Slowly, he cocked his head.

"Is there something amiss?" she asked quietly.

When he didn't reply, she signaled for Fanny to quit playing.

Torcuil's response was immediate. "Nay, dinna stop!"

Aware that he now had the attention of her father, her cousin, household servants, and his own assistants, an innate protectiveness toward this sometimes oddly innocent man rose in her. She leaned closer and spoke so softly she hoped no one else could hear. "Torcuil, tell me what has disturbed you."

His unusually dark eyes met hers, and his eyebrows rose in question. "Music?"

The single, low-spoken word sounded unfamiliar to his tongue.

Verity did not allow herself to ponder his peculiar behavior. Above all else, she wanted to shield him from the curiosity, or, worse, the censure, of others. "Unless you wish to excite the interest of everyone else here over this matter," she whispered, "behave as if you have heard Fanny playing the piano all your life."

He glanced wistfully in Fanny's direction, then brought his gaze back to Verity. For a second, he seemed to study what he saw in her eyes. *Trust me,* she thought. *Please trust me.* Torcuil hesitated, then nodded once, his beautiful face solemn. Heady exultation rushed through her.

"Shall we call a conference?" her father inquired dryly. "Perhaps we may be of assistance to whatever problem you might have."

"No problem," Verity chirped. She gave him her brightest smile. "Maestro," she called to Fanny. "Start again, if you please." She blessed her cousin's understanding temperament when Fanny's fingers rolled expertly across the keyboard.

Torcuil frowned with concentration as they went through the figures of the dance, as if trying to shut out the music.

" 'Tis easier when you move to the tempo of the music," she murmured.

"I dinna wish to be distracted."

The marquess laughed. "Oh, this brings back memories," he declared. "I'd forgotten the pleasure to be had in dancing."

Columbine began to skip as she linked arms with the marquess and swung around, in their turn. "What fun!"

"Smoothly, Columbine," Verity's father advised. "You are a flower petal floating on a lake."

Promptly, the girl altered her gait until she flowed gracefully. Her sunshine yellow gown flowed out behind her as they promenaded arm in arm around the other couples.

"Superb!"

She glowed with pleasure as they returned to their place, and Fearghus and Dorcas began.

The afternoon passed quickly as they practiced the quadrille, then moved on to the Sir Roger de Coverley, usually the dance that closed an evening's festivities. Frowns finally vanished, and there was much good humor and laughter. Even Fanny took her turn when Verity offered to spell her at the piano. Verity slowed the tempo of the music enough to allow her cousin the gaiety of dancing without a struggle to keep up. Torcuil handled Fanny gently and accorded her every consideration—a fact that did not escape Verity's notice. The thoughtfulness he showed her dear friend touched her.

Suddenly an image flashed into her mind. Torcuil, naked, mud-spattered, storm-drenched, drawing his long knife across a man's throat in a quick, expert stroke. Verity struck the wrong key. She looked up in time to see Fanny cross her eyes at her. Verity sent her cousin a distracted smile. How was it that a man so skilled in meting out death would even think to assist a woman heavy with child into her chair? Or to twirl her more slowly than his more nimble partners? Violence and tenderness. How could they both be part of the same man?

A burst of laughter brought Verity's attention back to the dancers and the music, and she found herself quickly tugged into their jollity.

Her father seemed more carefree than she'd seen him in years. She couldn't remember the last time he'd danced. Well . . . yes, she could. It had been shortly before Juliana Alford had absconded with Verity's dance master.

After that, he had never really reentered society. Alone, Verity had weathered the avid, quickly averted glances and the whispers. With unspoken defiance, she'd refused to be shut away by the disdain of others. She'd managed to conceal from the world the deep hurt caused by her mother's defection.

As Verity observed her father and Torcuil goodnaturedly heckling each other, a spark of contentment caught in the tinder of her hope, filling her with the glow of happiness. Life among her family didn't seem so terrible for Torcuil. He could be happy here.

She must make him see that.

The lessons continued a little longer before Fanny had to return home and Verity's father left to keep an appointment. Fearghus insisted upon accompanying him. After that, everyone else returned to their household tasks. Everyone except Verity and Torcuil.

After the last echo of footsteps faded from the grand saloon, they stood in silence that seemed to grow heavier by the second. Finally, Verity cleared her throat.

"You did very well," she said. "No one will believe you haven't been dancing for years. At least, dancing the quadrille and the Sir Roger de Coverley." She smiled. "I told you your natural grace would come to your aid."

Torcuil walked to the piano. "I own Roger Sheldrake will know the difference."

"Why should you care about Lord Sheldrake?"

Turning his head slightly, Torcuil sent her a veiled look.

A tiny thrill of delight shimmered through her. Torcuil was jealous! She had been right all along; he did care. "I doubt if Lord Sheldrake has ever saved anyone's life."

Torcuil looked away. Carefully, he stroked his long-fingered hand over the polished wood surface of the piano. "Ye told me ye'd show me more . . . music."

Verity studied his face, consumed with a powerful yearning to know more about this compelling man, this strange prince. She wanted to hear about his childhood, about the things he did as a boy. What kind of life must he have endured to only now be discovering music? Her heart expanded as she longed to heal the stark deficits in his life.

She patted the bench next to her, inviting him to sit. He eyed the bench, but remained standing.

"I promise, you're perfectly safe from me," she assured him, only half teasing. "I'll endeavor not to compromise your virtue."

His mouth curved slightly upward. "So ye say." He lithely sat beside her.

"This is a pianoforte," she explained, aware of his greater size and warmth, and his personal scent. She struggled to concentrate. "Have you never seen one?"

Slowly, he shook his head.

She couldn't help noticing the distance he tried to keep between them. Because of his size, only an inch could be managed, and that with him nearly teetering off the edge of the bench, but the inch might have been a foot for the effort he put into its maintenance.

Deciding to ignore that for now, she said, "A pianoforte is a relatively new instrument, but there are many with which we can make music. The music, you see, comes when we follow the notes that make up a melody." She picked up the sheet music in front of them. "Each of these little dots here is a note." She pointed to one. "An A sharp." She indicated another. "Here's a B. A composer wrote down everything one needs to know to play his work. Tempo. Emphasis. Key. Anyone who can read music and knows how to play an instrument will be able to play the melody he invented."

"You 'read' music, and you 'play' it?"

In moments like these, despite Torcuil's strength and skill in violence, Verity thought him quite adorable. "Here, let me show you."

She paged through her music book until she found "Greensleeves," and sent her fingers over the keyboard, coaxing forth the wistful, sweetly sad melody. As she played, she sensed Torcuil's absorption in the music. She darted a glance to her side. He sat perfectly straight, his head slightly cocked, his eyes closed. And then he started swaying. Only a little. His torso moved in time to the music.

Experimentally, she began to sing. His eyes snapped open, and he stared at her. The words of the song died on her lips. She ducked her head and focused on playing the piano.

"Why did ye stop?" he demanded.

She looked at him, surprised. "I thought—it seemed—the way you looked at me, I assumed that you didn't like my singing."

"Singing. I've heard that word before." He frowned.

"At the time, I dinna know what it meant. But I like the music ye make with yer mouth. 'Tis lovely."

"Oh."

"Sing more." It was a royal command more than a request, but he didn't seem to notice. His attention riveted to her lips.

Suddenly self-conscious, she moistened them with the tip of her tongue. His eyes followed the movement. Quickly, she dropped her gaze to the music in the book and started again. Miraculously, her fingers cooperated, and they found the proper keys without fail. Against the high ceiling of the grand saloon, her soprano voice rang like a bell, echoing faintly until the last note faded. She couldn't bring herself to look at him. What if he hadn't liked what he'd heard? *So?* a small voice within her demanded. *It's only singing. It's not as if he's weighing the value of your soul. Or your heart.*

Torcuil sat there without saying anything, a tall, immovable presence. As she breathed in, she caught that faint sea scent. His broad shoulder brushed against her shawl.

"Again, please," he said softly.

She dared a glance at him. Dear God, Torcuil was beautiful. She drew in a schooled, level breath. "Very well. But you must sing with me."

His eyebrows rose. "Me?" Color tinted his high cheekbones. "I dinna know the right words."

The uncertainty she heard in his tone brought her protectiveness rushing forward. She smiled. "But you would if you read them." She indicated her music book. "See? I've written them down. That's how I learned them."

He leaned a little forward as he regarded the book. "Och, and so ye have, ye clever female."

Her spirits lifted a little higher with his praise. She poised her fingers over the keys. "Shall we try it together?"

He nodded, never taking his eyes from the neat script.

Striking the opening chord, she began to sing. A beat late, he joined her. He sang softly at first, as if he didn't want anyone to hear him, but she sent him an encouraging smile and nod, and gradually the tentativeness in his voice evaporated, revealing a resonant baritone with the rich warmth of golden honey on a summer's day. It melted around each note, flavoring the song with an almost touchable sensuality, leading the listener to believe that Greensleeves was a fool.

When the final notes of their duet faded, Torcuil grinned at her. Delight danced in his eyes, and as she admired the curl and thickness of his lashes, she found herself swept into his joy. Wanting to hold onto it as long as possible, she reached for her music book.

"Would you like to sing another song?" she asked as she rifled through the pages.

"Aye, I would." He leaned closer to see the titles as she flipped the pages. " 'Tis odd how the music lingers in yer mind, spinnin' around and around." He glanced up, and their gazes collided—and held.

"How . . . how about a rousing ballad?" she asked half-heartedly, unable to look away from the intensity she saw in his dark eyes.

He looked away. "I dinna ken 'a ballad,' " he muttered.

"In this case," she said, furiously searching the book for the single ballad she'd liked well enough to copy, "it's a song about a battle."

Torcuil's head snapped around. "A battle?"

Verity chuckled with relief. She should have known that would interest him. "Ah! Here it is. 'The Field of Bannockburn.' I'll play the tune first, and then we can sing it, agreed?"

"Aye."

"I think you should especially like this, as it's about Scotland."

He nodded absently, apparently impatient to get on with the music.

First she played the melody, then they sang it, leaning together to see the words chosen by Robert Burns.

> *The Fraser bold his brave clan led,*
> *While wide their thistle banners spread—*
> *They boldly fell and boldly bled*
> *Upon the Field of Bannockburn.*

Their voices rose to mingle in the air, his strong and daring, hers clear and ethereal. Two verses into the song, she converted to harmony. He looked surprised, but kept singing. Enchanted with the beauty of their sound, Verity kept to the harmony.

After the last energetic chorus, they looked at each other and burst into breathless laughter. Verity's heart felt as if it had taken flight. This, *this* was what she'd wanted to recapture with Torcuil. The miracle of his wonder. And the trust that allowed her to share in it.

" 'Tis a bonny noise we make," Torcuil announced a few minutes later, when they'd recovered.

Intoxicated by the happiness of recovering that trust, she leaned close to him. "Would you like me to show you a new dance? A"—she looked either way, as if making certain she wasn't being overheard, though they were the only ones in the enormous saloon— "forbidden dance?"

His eyes widened. "Forbidden?"

She nodded.

"Why is it forbidden?"

"Tut, tut, tut. Do you want to learn or don't you?"

A slow smile spread across his lips. "Do ye wish to teach me?"

The fox! She shook her head. "That's not my question. Do you, or do you not, want me to teach you the dance?"

"I dinna see how ye can. The others have all gone."

Casually, she turned the pages of her music book, to the very last one. "For this dance, we need only two people."

He quirked up a single dark eyebrow. "And why is the dance forbidden?"

"Because it's scandalous," she whispered conspiratorially.

He grinned, revealing strong white teeth. "Ah. Then, by all means, teach me this wicked dance."

"Very well," she said merrily. "Since you insist. First, I'll play the music, so you may get the feel and tempo. With this dance, the tempo is especially important."

She played the waltz tune once all the way through, and then again for good measure. Then she rose from the bench and walked out to the middle of the vast floor. Torcuil came to stand beside her, as he'd learned to do with the other dances. Verity turned to face him.

He stood unmoving. The impressive proportions of the room suddenly diminished into nothing as her senses filled with him, with his height and breadth, with the sheer masculine perfection of him. His glossy dark hair, with his ever-present warrior's braids, hung in front of his wide shoulders, like satin drapes. The cut of his dark gray coat showed his broad shoulders to advantage, but then, she was certain anything he wore would do that, with such a physique. His pearl gray pantaloons hugged his long, muscular legs. The air around him vibrated with a male competency that she'd never experienced with any other man.

It called to the female in her. Not the dutiful daughter. Not the efficient hostess, or the expert chatelaine. The deep-down, unmannerly, unvarnished *female*. Being this close to him, this close and alone, brought her an awareness of not only him, but of herself. Her breasts felt slightly heavier. That shadowy nether region between her thighs only he had touched now responded to his potent presence with a faint throbbing.

Verity held her right hand up, slightly to her side, and hoped he didn't notice the tiny tremor. "You clasp this hand with yours." She darted the tip of her tongue across suddenly dry lips. "Yes. No, you keep it up. Like so. Ex . . . actly . . ."

Her heartbeat increased even more as the warm energy of his body passed through his palm and fingers, into hers. An instant of panic seized her. He was standing dangerously close. Even now, she could feel his spell closing around her, that powerful spell that muted her logic and filled her with his scent, his compelling sensuality and that imperative, arcing pleasure his merest touch brought her.

Let me trifle with ye.

A quiver ran through her.

He'd told her not to toy with him. He'd said he intended to leave. He'd never lied to her.

Only unhappiness could come from pursuing Torcuil MacCodrum. So why was she tempting fate? Tempting her heart?

He would never be hers.

From the dark recesses of her mind, a small voice filled with wicked laughter taunted her: *It's only a dance.* Only a partial truth, but it was what she wanted to hear, so she seized on it. It *was* only a dance. A dance with Torcuil.

Unable to bring herself to meet his gaze, she placed her hand on his shoulder. The mohair of his coat was smooth under her palm. "Now, you place your hand on my back. A little higher. There, that's right." She stared at the lapel of his coat, conscious of the slight weight that settled against her. "Remember the music? Let it flow in your mind." She hummed a couple of bars. "*One,* two, three . . . *one,* two, three . . ."

Still reluctant to lift her gaze to his, she showed him

how to move his feet, and the initial attempts brought some bumping of toes, but he caught on quickly.

They glided over the polished wood floor in perfect time to the music playing only in their heads. Around and around they went, circling the floor as if their feet were laying down an ancient spell. Suddenly Torcuil swept her into an unexpected, exuberant twirl, then out again, with such even grace and timing that she didn't miss a beat to his impromptu movement.

They flashed by mirrors, catching glimpses of a man and a woman bound together by a rhythm only they could hear. Entranced. Intense. Moving in another world. Magic, she thought. If ever there were magic, this was it.

Her hand moved slightly against his shoulder. As she fell more deeply into the spell cast by their silent music, the movement grew into a caress. His arm tightened slightly, drawing her closer to him. As they danced, her breasts brushed his chest now, and then again, sending sparks shooting through her body until she feared her knees would fail her. As he slowly whirled with her, she encountered bold evidence that she was not the only one affected by their music, their movement—their moment together.

As if by mutual accord, they came to a gradual stop, but neither attempted to move away. Slowly, she lifted her head, and her eyes met his. The intensity she saw in the depths of those black eyes caused her breath to catch in her throat.

Her brain cried for her to run, to hide, to forget Torcuil MacCodrum. He could bring her only the pain of loss. The memory of him would haunt her the rest of her lonely life.

Her heart called out to unfurl her wings and soar to him.

For better or for worse, Verity followed her heart.

He searched her face. "Verity," he whispered liltingly, the *r* rolling softly off his tongue, making the word something unique and lovely. Only Torcuil had ever spoken her name as if it were a sacred charm against the dark of the world.

"Torcuil," she answered, savoring the strong, uncompromising sound of the word. His name fit him well.

He bent his head and kissed her. His lips skimmed across hers, lightly, like a soft breath, piercing her with sweet longing. She rose to her toes, slipping her hands up his chest to rest against his shoulders. Then she closed her eyes and gave herself over to heady sensation. The firm, coaxing warmth of his lips. The sea scent that was his alone. The even pressure of his large, long-fingered hands as he caressed her upper arms.

He nibbled and persuaded until she parted her lips for him. His tongue carried out a lush exploration, skimming across her teeth and along her cheeks. Then it began to woo her tongue with flicks and strokes, evoking in her new, stirring sensations. Breathlessly, she responded. Her fingers stole up to lace through his hair as she leaned into him, straining to taste and feel all that he evoked in her.

His hands moved restlessly across her ribs, their heat branding her flesh through the muslin of her gown. She felt flushed. The ground seemed to spin away from her feet.

"Torcuil, please . . . trifle with me," she murmured.

He went still. In the immense room, only their labored breathing could be heard.

"Torcuil—"

"Nay. A kiss. A kiss is all I'll share with ye."

She stared at him, feeling betrayed. "But you said—"

"I know what I said," he grated. "You were right, then, and I was wrong."

"Why?" she asked, her throat closing on the single

word. What had made him change his mind? Did he think less of her now?

He dropped his hands to his sides. "Because ye deserve more than that, Verity. Ye deserve far more than I can give ye. I'll no take advantage of yer innocence or yer goodness."

She looped her fingers at her waist to keep them still. To keep them from reaching out to touch him. "Perhaps I'm not so innocent, nor so good as you think."

A sad smile lifted the corners of his lips. "But ye are. And I know it. It's a husband ye want, sweet Anemone, and it's a husband I can never be to you."

She frowned down at her fingers. Then she raised her gaze to his. "It's you I want, Torcuil."

He shook his head, but yearning was stark in his face.

She swallowed hard. "Just one night together."

He looked away.

"Must I beg?" she whispered raggedly.

" 'Tis no light thing ye ask. Afterward, ye would never feel the same. No about yerself. No about me." He dragged in a long breath and huffed it out. "And I'd have to leave ye like that. Once, in the heat of our touchin', I thought I could no bear it if I dinna have more of ye. Now I see the folly in it. The danger. I'd no have ye despise me, Verity. When I leave, I want yer memory of me to be fond."

"You always speak of leaving," she accused chokingly. "Yet you will not tell me *why* you must go."

At his sides, his hands bunched into fists, then opened straight. "I've made a promise to my father—"

"Come back after you've kept it!"

"Ye would no want me if ye knew what I really was."

She gripped his arms. "I don't care what you've done in the past. I don't care what your family has done. You are Torcuil! More than that does not matter."

Verity reached for his warrior's braids, and he moved his head so that they eluded her fingers. Burning with determination, she leaped to her toes and grasped the plaits in her fists. He made not further resistance, and she dragged his head down to hers. She kissed him with all the passion of her desire, her frustration—and her love.

Torcuil answered in kind, dragging her into his arms, ravishing her mouth as if she were sustenance to a starving man. Abruptly, he pulled away, and took a step back.

"Think on it," he said, his lilting voice rough with emotion. "If ye still wish me to trifle with ye, ask me again—"

She parted her lips to speak the words.

"—later," he continued savagely. "After ye've taken the time to consider. And consider well, Verity. Ye're askin' me to strip ye of yer innocence. Once ye've experienced physical pleasure, ye'll no wish to settle for less again."

Without another word, he strode from the room, leaving her alone with the echo of a closing door.

17

In the country of the blind, the one-eyed man is king.
—Desiderius Erasmus

Torcuil stalked into his bedchamber. For a moment, he stood staring unseeingly at the doorknob. Turbulent emotion surged through him.

He glared at his hand, spreading wide his fingers. He hated living as a man!

Even before that thought faded, his conscience rebelled at the lie. With a sigh, he dropped his hand to his side.

When had that changed? When had he stopped despising the life he'd been forced to live upon this land? It had been better, before. Better when he burned with discontent.

Easier, that rejection of land folk and everything they stood for. He looked out the tall window, onto the winter garden, finding beauty there, despite the nakedness of the thorny rosebushes.

Safer.

He went to the trunk he kept at the foot of the bed. Unlocking it, he went directly to the false bottom. From it, he pulled his hood. Soft, and as fine as silk, it had the glossy black color of his own hair. His mouth curved in a humorless smile. Indeed, it *was* his own hair. His silkie hair. And without this hood, he could not return to his silkie form. He must remember, he told himself fiercely. *This* was what he truly was. He swam with whales and dolphins, basked in the sun on rock islands. By the sacred well of Nechtan, he lived beneath the sea!

Would Verity continue to gaze at him with her heart in her eyes if she knew he'd spent most of his life in the guise of . . . a seal? Oh, he could well imagine her reaction.

His fingers stroked absently through the dark fur. He missed his mother and his father. He longed to hear Anndra's young voice. Torcuil wanted to see his uncles and his coddling aunts. What were his cousins doing this minute? If only Eideard had never left. Everything would have remained as it should.

But then, Torcuil would never have met Verity Alford.

Why did his people believe magic had fled the land? True, the magi had vanished with the Tuatha Dé Danaan, and the Milesians after them, but there was magic here still. It might be more subtle now. Often elusive. Yet it remained. In music. In the dancing that presented a more awkward version of the elegant glide silkies took for granted each day of their lives as they swirled through the deep.

Magic could grow in the hearts of land folk. Not all of them, perhaps, but enough that they composed songs celebrating its glory, mourning its loss, as the one Verity and he had sung together to the faithless "Greensleeves." Verity's people held more in common with silkies than Torcuil wanted to believe.

The realization left him shaken. He must not think of

the similarities between their two peoples, not until he returned home with Eideard. Then, when Torcuil had returned to the sea, he might give himself over to his memories.

Reluctantly, he returned the hood to its hiding place.

A knot clenched in his chest at the thought of leaving Verity. Each day she grew more important to him. Thoughts of her, of her smile, of her generous, managing ways occupied him far more than he'd ever imagined possible. For all that she was the accomplished mistress of a great household, adored daughter of a man of consequence, he'd caught glimpses of her vulnerability. Her mother had abandoned her, and he saw that it had scarred Verity with doubts. In addition to that, according to the customs of her people, she was fair prey for that tube worm, Roger Sheldrake.

In the world of land folk, it seemed a grown female was naught without a husband—a husband whose power over his wife was so extreme that he held her very life in the palm of his hand. True, the arrangement could work nicely. Torcuil had observed Fanny and her husband, George, together. Their affection and mutual respect was evident for anyone with eyes. But Torcuil had also seen Cook's assistant arrive in the kitchen each morning with a new bruise laid down by her brutal mate.

Torcuil had given his father a promise—a promise that affected the welfare of his people. Eideard must be found. With the chief ailing, the heir must return to the clan.

But . . . Torcuil was not the heir.

Verity needed him. She needed his protection against the harsh ways of the world. Against the destruction of her bright benevolence. Against the tyranny that would come with marriage to Sheldrake.

She needed him to nourish the magic in her.

*   *   *

George Elbourn handed the bank draft across the gleaming mahogany desk to Torcuil. It represented the sum of what Verity had spent on Torcuil's clothes, the pistols she'd purchased at his request, and sundry other small items, although Fanny's husband hadn't been made privy to that information. Nor did he know the funds came from the proceeds of the sale of an antique gold necklace and cuff. He knew only that he'd been retained by Torcuil as a man of business, and that the account he'd set up at the bank in Torcuil's name held a very great deal of money. Torcuil had impressed upon him that he was to speak to no one of their arrangement.

"Thank you, Mr. Elbourn. Ye've been most helpful." An understatement, considering Torcuil knew nothing about banks, bank drafts, or accounts. But who better to turn to for such matters than Fanny's attorney husband?

George inclined his head. "A pleasure, I assure you. And, please. Do call me George. Fanny has taken to calling you Torcuil. I presume you have no objection to that?"

Torcuil smiled. "None at all . . . George."

He liked Fanny and her husband. They were good, honest folk who tried to do their best by others. Odd. Lately he'd found more land folk who would do honor to any breed. True, he'd run into some honorless bottom feeders, but what race did not have its weak kinsmen?

From George's offices, Torcuil went to Ravenshaw House, where he inquired after the marquess's whereabouts.

"In the library, sir," Quenby answered with his usual lack of exuberance. "Lord Isted is with him at the moment."

"His partner?"

Quenby hesitated, as if not certain whether he should divulge such information. "Yes, sir."

Apprehension trickled through Torcuil. "Who is with Ravenshaw?"

"With, sir? As I have said, Lord Isted—"

"Is Kingston in the library with your master?"

"No, sir."

The apprehension swelled. "Mr. Gruagach? Mr. Broonie?"

"No, sir."

Apprehension crystallized into alarm. Abruptly, Torcuil strode toward the library. Then he broke into an all-out run. Wide-eyed servants scrambled out of his way as he tore through the halls. Finally, he skidded to a stop outside the closed library door.

He heard voices from inside raised in anger. Without knocking, he opened the door and stepped inside. The two men in the room didn't notice him. Silently, he stepped next to the window. The sunlight would make it difficult for Isted to see him.

The marquess was at his desk, but he'd risen to a standing position, facing a taller man of approximately the same age who remained seated across the desk from the marquess.

"By heavens, Isted," the marquess bellowed, "you can't throw all those men out of work! Besides, the mine has untapped veins of copper. A wealth of copper."

"You can't be certain of that," Isted said coolly. "You're asking us to invest more money in an uncertain venture. You expect us to take additional risk."

"This is an *investment*. There is always risk involved in such ventures. That's why we generally reap such a high return. The less the risk, the lower the return."

"And just what kind of return would we get on copper?" Isted demanded. "Can you guarantee the market for copper will continue? That the partners won't be left with just an expensive hole in the ground?"

"Of course not."

"I believe you're being swayed by your concern for the miners. Admirable, perhaps, but very poor business."

"*I'm* not the only one who sees the potential for Coristock."

Isted lifted his eyebrows. "But are there *enough* of you to swing the vote? May I remind you, your staunch ally, Cowen, is dead. His heir has decided the risk is too great. Like the rest of us, he'd rather close the mine and sell. Your little sample tests failed to impress him. He saw the sense in my arguments."

"Bit of a ghoul, aren't you? Cowen barely cold in his grave, and you're badgering his son to close a mine? How old is the boy? Seventeen? Eighteen? I imagine he was putty in your hands." The marquess snorted. "Nothing to be proud of, certainly."

Isted rose to his feet. "Bid the mine good-bye, my dear marquess. You need one more vote in your favor if you hope to win, and we both know you won't get it."

Verity's father straightened. "There's Outhwaite."

Isted loosed a bark of laughter. "That spineless creature. He intends to abstain, he told me so himself."

"I take it, then, you've already been to Norfolk to see him."

The taller man nodded slowly, triumph clear on his face. "I have."

The marquess was silent a minute. "Perhaps I can be more eloquent than you."

"Perhaps. And perhaps cows can fly. Accept the inevitable, Ravenshaw. You will lose on this vote, but if we close the mine you certainly won't continue to lose money." Isted picked up his hat and his walking cane.

Torcuil tensed, ready to defend the marquess if his partner resorted to violence.

"A pity about the miners, of course," Isted continued.

"They will simply have to find employment elsewhere." He turned toward the door, and as he did, he saw Torcuil standing quietly near the window.

Isted raked his gaze over Torcuil, then delicately arched an eyebrow and spoke to the marquess. "Spies, Ravenshaw?"

The marquess's smile lacked any trace of humor. "Cowen did die rather mysteriously."

Isted's thin lips curved in a smile. "Yes, he did, didn't he?" He walked out of the library.

"What did he want?" Torcuil asked after making certain Quenby arrived to lead Isted away.

The marquess sighed and wandered to the window, his hands clasped behind his back. "To gloat, most likely."

"Will ye lose the vote, then?" Torcuil asked.

"Yes, unless I can convince Outhwaite to cast his vote with me. The problem is, 'tis much easier to frighten men than to inspire them into taking a chance."

Torcuil nodded slowly. Isn't that what had happened to his own people? The heinous deeds of a handful of land folk had caused the silkies to pull back from having contact with them after centuries of living side by side in harmony. But what of men like the marquess? Or women like Verity? He wished he knew if there were many more like them.

Then he remembered his purpose for seeking out Verity's father. He withdrew the folded bank draft from his waistcoat pocket.

"I've come to pay ye back for all that ye've spent on me," he said, holding out the draft to the marquess.

Ravenshaw frowned. "That's not necessary."

"Aye," Torcuil said quietly. "It is."

He made no move to take the draft. "I owe you my life, and that of my daughter. It has been my pleasure to equip you with whatever you've needed."

"Please consider this a matter of honor. My honor. Or

at the verra least, my pride." Torcuil continued to hold out the bank draft with its weighty amount.

The marquess hesitated, then nodded. He accepted the draft. "Very well. I suppose I can understand your sentiments, as ill-conceived as they are." He glanced at the amount written. "Good lord, have I spent *this* much on you?"

Torcuil caught the twinkle of humor in the older man's eyes and grinned. "I'm worth every penny of it.

"I've spoken with that wee frogfish of a tailor," he continued. "In future I'll attend to the matter of clothing on my own. With your permission, I'll consult Lady Verity when necessary."

"Ha! Just try to purchase as much as a waistcoat without her help. She will have her say. My daughter is certain our lives would be poor things without her to smooth the way."

Torcuil forced a smile. "Aye." He feared Verity was right.

A glimmer rippled under Torcuil's skin as he stood at the washstand, shaving, dressed save for his coat. Seconds later, Seumus winked into view, looking none the worse for his journey from Devonshire.

"I found our Alice," he said as if he'd walked across the hall instead of flashing across more than a hundred miles. In the blink of an eye, his velvet suit vanished, replaced by the more modest one he wore as Torcuil's valet.

"Welcome back, Seumus," Torcuil said with a grin. "What took ye so long?"

"Och, and aren't we the cheerful one this dreary morn." But Seumus smiled. "I believe ye may be able to use what I learned."

"Tell on. I hope ye'll no take offense if I finish shavin',"

Torcuil said. "That sand shark, Sheldrake, will be here soon, and I dinna wish to have Verity keepin' him company alone." He scraped the blade through the soap lather, over his chin.

"Do ye truly believe he'd harm her?" Seumus asked, herding Torcuil over to a chair. "Sit."

Torcuil sat and relinquished the razor to Seumus. "'Tis doubtful. All the same, I dinna wish to take chances."

Seumus chuckled as he bent to his task. "If ye were to ask me my opinion—"

"Which I'm not—"

"—ye dinna want another potential mate alone with her. It's a wise man who cuts his competition from the field. And that baron seems determined to claim Lady Verity."

Torcuil glared up at Seumus. "She doesna like him."

"Has she told ye this herself?"

"She doesna have to tell me. I can see it for myself."

"Indeed?" Seumus delicately slipped the sharp razor through the soap lather, up the underside of Torcuil's chin. "How, I'd like to know, when ye'll no allow them even close enough to touch?"

"It's no proper for him to be touchin' her," Torcuil said flatly.

Seumus swished the razor through the water in the porcelain basin. "And have ye always been proper with her?" he asked softly.

Torcuil felt the telltale heat of a crimson blush flood his face.

Seumus sighed. "I thought as much." He set the razor on the washstand, finished with his task. "Do ye care for her, Torcuil?"

"Aye." The single, hoarse word stood as both a confession and a statement of his plight.

"I dinna need to ask if she cares for ye, for it's there for everyone to see. She loves ye, lad, and no mistake. Have a care for her heart."

Torcuil nodded, miserable with the battle that raged constantly inside him these days.

As if he sensed Torcuil's conflict, Seumus handed him a damp towel with which to wipe his face. "Now, do ye wish to hear my news?"

"I was wonderin' when ye'd finally get around to the tellin' of it." Torcuil removed the soap residue and tossed the towel on the washstand.

Scowling at Torcuil's neckcloth, Seumus climbed up on the chair and began untying it. "Alice Dare is the wife of Richard Dare."

"Did her Richard have a scar on his face?"

Seumus began expertly retying the neckcloth. "He did. It came of an accident years ago in a mine just west of Coristock. He was a miner, ye see. Anyway, as I was sayin', the timbers of the mine were rotted and needed to be replaced. The marquess was one of the several mine owners, but Dare held him responsible for the cave-in."

"Only Ravenshaw?" That seemed decidedly strange.

"Aye. Because when Dare recovered sufficiently to confront the only owner who lived nearby, he was told that Ravenshaw had refused to put any money into new timbering." Seumus finished retying the neckcloth and climbed down from the chair.

"And do ye know the name of the partner who spoke with Dare?"

Seumus met Torcuil's gaze. "Sheldrake."

"The bottom feeder." Thoughtfully, Torcuil strolled to the wardrobe and removed his coat from its pegs. "I canna imagine Ravenshaw putting men's lives in danger like that," he said. "Did Alice know what her husband was doin' in London?"

"Do ye mean hirin' assassins? Nay. But she did say that

her husband claimed to be workin' for an important man. She told me that this important fellow must have been the one to provide the coach tickets, for they had no money to buy 'em themselves."

"And did she happen to know the identity of this verra important man?"

"Nay. 'Tis sore straits that she's in, too. Four bairns and no man." Seumus cocked his head and peered up at Torcuil with a smile. "Asked me to stay for supper, she did, though they barely had a crust between 'em."

"And will she be rewarded for possessin' a good heart, Broonie?"

The smile widened into a full grin. "That she will. Indeed, the machinery is already in motion for her to inherit a house and a modest stipend from a relative she dinna know she had." Seumus sighed happily. "Och, I dearly love it when I find someone with a kind and generous spirit."

Torcuil paused at the door. "And do ye often find them, Seumus? Among the land folk, that is." Suddenly he needed to know.

Seumus considered a moment. "Aye, more than ye think. Often 'tis life in the city that makes people cruel and hard. I dinna think people were ever meant to live so close together. But even in London I've found good mortals. And so, my fine silkie, have ye."

Torcuil was still thinking about what Seumus had said minutes later, when he rapidly took the stairs down and strode through the halls, on his way to the ivory drawing room. Verity's voice coming from the library brought him up short in his tracks.

"I know, Papa," she said. "But I don't wish to wed a man I cannot even *like*. And I have tried, you know. Even you must admit that."

"Blast it, Daughter," came the marquess's gruff voice,

"I only want to see you married and settled. And you did say . . ." His words grew lower and impossible to hear.

Conscious of his transgression, but wanting to hear, Torcuil stepped a little closer outside the door.

"I know, but Lord Sheldrake goes beyond that, Papa. He's like a leech. He feeds on sympathy. And he has sucked me dry of every drop. I cannot marry him. I can barely tolerate him."

The marquess sighed. "Very well. But you must tell him."

"Yes, Papa."

Quickly Torcuil continued down the corridor, elated despite himself. Verity had seen the baron for what he was—a lamprey! After today, Torcuil doubted if Sheldrake would come schooling around her again, and the thought delighted him.

He emerged into the vast entry hall just as Quenby admitted Sheldrake on the far side. Kingston was also there, standing slightly behind the butler. As Torcuil watched, unnoticed yet, Sheldrake handed Quenby his gloves, walking stick, and top hat. Then he lifted his gaze above the butler's head.

Torcuil felt certain that the look that passed between the baron and the bodyguard held unspoken meaning. These two men knew each other.

Then Sheldrake's eyes turned toward Torcuil. "Good morning, MacCodrum," he said coolly. "I see we are once again blessed with your company."

Torcuil's lips sketched a smile. "Thank ye, Sheldrake. 'Tis gratifyin' to be appreciated."

The door he'd just entered opened and Verity swept in, looking as lovely and as golden as ever, Torcuil thought. As she passed him, her skirts brushed against his trousers. Her scent teased his senses, exciting him. He hastened to tamp the rising heat in his blood.

"Good morning, gentlemen," she said, walking across the entry hall to the door that led to the ivory drawing room. "Mr. Kingston, my father has need of you. Cousin Torcuil, Mr. Gruagach has a question I believe you might help him with, if you'd be so good? Lord Sheldrake, please attend me."

Sheldrake turned and flashed Torcuil a smirk of triumph as he followed Verity into the drawing room.

To Kingston's clear puzzlement, Torcuil cheerfully hummed the waltz as he went in search of Fearghus.

The sun was nearly on the horizon of rooftops before Torcuil found the chance to speak with the marquess alone.

"When ye hired Kingston," he asked as the two of them sat in the library, "did ye know his history?"

"History? If you mean credentials, yes, I inquired before I engaged his services. Why do you ask?"

" 'Tis no a strange question, is it? Kingston has failed to impress me as bein' a particularly efficient bodyguard."

"Ah, Torcuil, I fear that you will find most other bodyguards lacking. Your standards are unusually high. Many of the Runners are naught but former criminals themselves."

"And Kingston?"

"A former Runner, but if he was ever a criminal, he's kept the secret well."

"Has he also kept secret that he's acquainted with Sheldrake?"

"No, why should he? Sheldrake recommended him to me, but Kingston has also done work for Pettipher. I'd rather have a man who comes well recommended than to simply take my chances with just any man."

"And ye trust Sheldrake and Pettipher?"

"Certainly! Would I have allowed Sheldrake to pay court to Verity if I didn't trust him? Oh, he's a trifle fussy for my taste, and he's not as courageous as I'd like him to be, but I believe him to be honest. And the same goes for Pettipher."

Och, well, now he had the answer to whether or not the baron and Kingston knew each other, Torcuil thought dryly a few minutes later as he left the library. Now all he had to do was discover who was trying to murder the marquess.

And find Eideard.

18

The art of living is more like wrestling than dancing.
—Marcus Aurelius

Verity glowed with satisfaction as Daniel helped her to alight from the carriage in front of the stately house. This was the Season residence of Lord and Lady Faraday. She'd taken particular care with her appearance, settling on a pearl-trimmed gown of sea green sarcenet, long, dark green lace mitts, and a pair of green silk moiré slippers. On her head, she wore the pearl bandeau she and Torcuil had retrieved from Kenyon's. An ivory shawl draped her forearms.

Her gaze went to Torcuil, who stood, silent, beside her. Tonight his glossy hair caught the light of the blazing lamps at the front of the mansion. After he'd finished one of his long, private baths, he had allowed her to brush it, an intimacy she always deeply enjoyed. Tonight, she'd entwined only a thin black ribbon through each of his sable warrior's braids. The cut of his midnight blue coat revealed an impeccably arranged stock that was as pristine white as his shirt. His black velvet waistcoat had been embroidered with golden sea serpents. Well-cut oyster gray breeches hugged his muscular thighs, just as his white silk stockings clung to his calves. Black slippers covered his feet. Under his arm he carried a black chapeau bras, which, he'd made clear, he considered a ridiculous ornament.

On the other side of Torcuil stood her elegantly clad father, who, over Torcuil and Mr. Kingston's objections, had refused to bring his bodyguard. Verity secretly believed her father cherished the hope of spending time in the company of the fabulous Neul and saw a bodyguard as an unwanted hindrance.

On a visit to Verity's cousin, Fanny had confessed to having actually glimpsed Neul. *Stunning* was the word Verity's cousin had used in describing this Season's belle. She'd gone on to relate that it was said Neul was so beautiful that she inflamed men by simply walking into a room. No one knew where she'd come from or anything about her antecedents. The gentlemen, it seemed, did not much care. She reigned as queen at any event she chose to attend.

Verity would have preferred to see her father interested in a nice sensible woman, but she'd take what she could get. At least he was inclined toward sociability again. Now she sneaked a glance up at Torcuil. When she'd managed to gently put an end to Lord Sheldrake's addresses, she had also escaped his earlier suggestion that he escort her to this ball. The baron paled into insignificance beside Torcuil. Frankly, she doubted any man in the realm could hope to compare favorably with the Highland prince. He was tall and handsome and charming and brave and—he wanted her.

Oh, yes. She'd seen the raw yearning in his eyes, felt it

in his every movement when they'd danced yesterday evening. He wanted her as much as she wanted him. And that realization had sent her soaring with elation. There was hope for them! Whether or not he accepted that, she blazed with certainty.

He was homesick. Only a blind woman would have missed that far-off, longing look that came over him at times. Although he never spoke of his parents, Verity believed they must be good people to have taught their son such honorable ways.

She loved Torcuil. Last night it had been apparent that he was struggling against his feelings for her. Strong feelings. Perhaps even love. Verity's heart beat faster at the thought.

Much of yester eve had been spent tossing restlessly in her bed, but in the deep of night she'd come up with a plan. It was quite simple, really. First she would bring him to admit that he cared for her. Then she would offer her help in solving whatever problem it was that made him believe they could not wed. He needed her; she'd help him to see that.

And tonight was the ideal start for her plan.

The three of them entered the impressive residence and waited patiently to be announced. Not that many present could probably hear the servant's loud voice, she thought. Such gatherings were accompanied by a crush of guests and the dull roar of myriad simultaneous conversations, with music from the ensemble thrown in. The advantage of this particular ball was that the hostess, Lady Faraday, always kept the crowds from spilling over into the area where the dances were being conducted. And Torcuil liked to dance.

Finally, the footman bellowed their titles and names, and the three of them entered the earl of Faraday's grand saloon. The edges of the lofty ceiling were trimmed with gold medallions, and the walls were covered with panels japanned in black lacquer and gold. Red-tasseled crystal chandeliers and sconces provided illumination from beeswax candles that filled the air with the scent of honey. A large fireplace was located in the center of one long wall. Its white marble mantel was supported on each end by a white marble peacock. In the opposite wall, red velvet curtains trimmed with black bobbin fringe draped the tall windows.

In the candlelight, jewels and military medals sparkled. Gorgeous gowns in a pastel rainbow of satins, silks, and muslins adorned the ladies in the vast, tightly packed room. Civilian men wore suits of rich fabrics in more subdued colors, while the uniforms of the officers stood out in even more brilliant hues.

Almost as soon as they stepped into the room, Verity's father was swept away by his comrades, who exclaimed over his long absence from society. Lady Faraday made her way through the crowd to personally welcome Verity. In her gruff, good-natured way, the countess demanded that Torcuil be introduced to her at once. As Verity complied, Torcuil bowed over Lady Faraday's hand and murmured that she smelled good.

The richly gowned countess stared at him in surprise, and Verity quickly searched her mind for a plausible excuse she could offer for Torcuil's unorthodox comment. Before she could come to his defense, Lady Faraday burst out laughing, a deep-throated, boisterous sound.

"By God, I like a man who says what he thinks." She grinned and slapped Torcuil on the arm with her fan. "Especially if he likes my sweet water. No wonder all the ladies are so impressed with you." With the tip of her fan, she indicated his hair. "Your cousin is a true original, Lady Verity."

Verity smiled, and her gaze drifted from Lady Faraday to Torcuil. "Yes, he is."

"Well, run along, you two. Drink, eat, dance, and be merry." The older woman fixed an eye on Torcuil. "I expect a dance with you, young man," she said with mock severity.

He inclined his head, his sensual mouth curving into a charming smile. "I'd deem it an honor, Lady Faraday."

Verity placed her hand on his proffered arm as they entered the crush. "So you're popular with the ladies, eh?" she teased, disliking the jealousy that wriggled through her.

Torcuil made no comment. His eyes swept the crowd. He stood head and shoulders above them. His mane of jet hair and his warrior's braids set him doubly apart from other men. His remarkable beauty sent feminine heads turning, as did his broad, masculine shoulders. He moved with a predator's grace, silent and purposeful. Like sheep before a wolf, people moved to make way for him.

"I'm worried about Papa," Verity confided. "I wish he'd allowed Mr. Kingston to accompany him. Or even Mr. Gruagach."

"Too many people here," Torcuil muttered. Then he added, " 'Twas indeed foolish of him."

"Where is he now?" she asked.

"With the same men who welcomed him when we arrived. Are ye acquainted with them?"

"Yes. They are members of his club. While he avoided most of society, he has continued to visit White's. We can't very well hover over him, Torcuil. I don't wish to imagine his reaction if he found us spying on him."

Torcuil nodded grudgingly. "Aye. He'd have an apoplexy, and no mistake."

Verity worried her bottom lip. "Perhaps he wouldn't mind an occasional visit from us."

"I think he'd know what we were doin', Verity. Yer father's no a thick man."

"Yes, but I don't think he'd be *too* annoyed."

He gave her his smile, and she found herself completely enchanted. "Aye, well," he said, "I canna believe he'd hold it against us, if we're discreet."

Out of the corner of her eye, she saw someone plant himself in their path. She turned her head and her heart sank. Roger Sheldrake held two cups of claret punch in his hands.

"Good evening, Lady Verity. MacCodrum," he added, the word clipped and tight. He turned back to Verity. "I've taken the liberty of securing you a cup of punch."

"Oh. Uh, thank you, Lord Sheldrake." She hated claret punch, but she accepted the filled cup anyway, glancing down into the milky pink liquid, then quickly away as her stomach gave a queasy lurch.

"My cousin and I were just on our way to speak with her father," Torcuil said bluntly.

Sheldrake's lips curled up in a cool smile. "Ah, well, perhaps I might accompany you? I'm delighted your father has chosen to return to the fold, Lady Verity. I wish to add my own welcome to what I'm certain will be a heartfelt reception."

Verity didn't want Sheldrake's company, and she hadn't expected him to be so tenacious, but she had no wish to hurt his feelings, and perhaps he was just behaving like a gentleman. It was entirely possible that he wanted to show her father there were no hard feelings. Yes, doubtless that was the baron's reasoning.

She didn't need to see Torcuil to know his opinion. He'd never tried to conceal his dislike of Sheldrake.

She summoned the grace to sound convincing. "I'm sure Papa will welcome your good wishes."

The baron's thin smile warmed a degree or two. Before

he could speak another word, Torcuil led Verity in the direction of her father, effectively forcing Sheldrake to stay or follow. Before they'd taken more than five steps, they were stopped by another man, one Verity had never seen before.

The fellow stood taller than the baron, but much shorter than Torcuil. He wore his blond, pomaded hair *à la Titus,* and his clothes were scrupulously stylish. "I say, Sheldrake, old man, do me the honor of introducing me to this radiant goddess, will you?"

Torcuil's gaze moved over the man's hair, and his nostrils twitched, as if he'd smelled something foul. Beneath her hand she felt a slight tensing in his arm. Nervously, she shifted her weight from one foot to the other as she wondered how he would react to what he might perceive as an intruder. How many weapons had he secreted about his person, anyway? Then she remembered what he was capable of without any weapon. At that moment, the thought brought her none of its usual comfort.

Sheldrake turned a baleful look on the newcomer. Grudgingly, he performed the introductions, and Verity met the new earl of Taunton, Harold Rapley. She'd heard of him during the course of her social calls. The death of the old earl and the investiture of the new one had set many a mama speculating, for Harold had yet to choose a wife.

They chatted for a few minutes, Harold lacing his conversation with lavish if predictable flattery to Verity. Just as she sensed Torcuil getting restive, Harold smiled at him.

"MacCodrum is a Scots name, is it not?"

Beneath his thick, black lashes, Torcuil cast Verity an oblique glance. "Aye."

"Is that the way hair is worn there?" From what Verity could tell, the question was spoken with innocent curiosity.

Sheldrake lowered his cup of punch. "You've been to Scotland, Taunton. Have you ever seen anyone—any *man*—wearing his hair in such a fashion?"

"No, but I didn't travel all over. Just sailed along the coast to Edinburgh. All I can say is that I saw no one there with hair like Mr. MacCodrum's."

Torcuil brushed Sheldrake with a deceptively lazy look before he turned to Taunton. "I've no been to Edinburgh, so I canna say what they do there. In my clan, 'tis the right of only a proven warrior to wear the side braids. Of those entitled to wear the warrior's braids, only the best may wear the third braid, in the back."

"How charming." Sarcasm dripped from Lord Sheldrake's every syllable.

The earl ignored the jibe, directing his question to Torcuil. "Are you entitled, sir?"

"Aye." He grinned. "My valet advised against it."

The earl laughed. "A veritable fashion tyrant, eh? I have one, myself."

"When I take a mate, she'll make the braid."

"Clever man. Best way around it. A wife's prerogative, and all that."

Verity sneaked a glance at the smooth back of Torcuil's hair.

"Do your clan's, uh, warriors always wear their hair in such a manner?" Taunton inquired.

"Often we do not."

When was that? Verity wondered. Except for that first day, when he'd washed his hair, she'd never seen him without his braids. Her eyes followed the thick fall of sable silk down his back. She'd wager it had never been cut.

"One of those times might best have been tonight," Sheldrake said, then took a sip of his punch.

Verity lifted her chin. "*I* like it." He wasn't being very gentlemanly after all.

Torcuil surveyed Sheldrake in a leisurely manner, then looked away with the distinct air of having seen nothing of even the slightest interest. Sheldrake flushed.

"A pleasure to meet you, sir," Torcuil said to the earl. Taunton made a pleasant reply, and Torcuil led Verity in the direction of an extravagantly decorated table laden with cut crystal punch bowls and cups.

"Hold on, now," Sheldrake demanded, impatiently shouldering his way to face Torcuil. "How dare you simply walk off like that?"

Torcuil regarded the baron from beneath hooded eyes. "Easily."

Sheldrake blinked. "What?"

"Ye asked me how I dared. And I told ye—easily."

His face dark with fury, Sheldrake turned to Verity. "I thought it was understood that we would meet here."

She stared at him in surprise. "Why would you possibly think that?" How could her father have ever considered that she would consent to be this man's wife? Verity snapped open her fan and fluttered it impatiently.

Color mounted in Sheldrake's face. "I didn't think you really meant . . . I assumed . . ."

She'd been gentle, but she'd made her feelings quite clear. And now he insinuated that she'd put them both through what she considered a horrid ordeal but did not know her own mind well enough to be taken seriously? Or, worse, that she was a jilt? Such effrontery! "You assumed incorrectly, sir," she informed him icily.

He attempted to collect his composure. "May I at least inquire if you did come with someone?"

"She came with me," Torcuil said softly. Only a fool would have missed the warning in his voice.

Sheldrake was arrogant and needy, but he wasn't a fool. He turned on his heel and shoved his way through the crowd.

Verity snapped her fan closed. "The toad," she muttered.

"He was angry with me, but tried to take it out on ye instead. 'Twas easier for him to feel superior when he thought I was no but a bodyguard."

"And are you? More than a bodyguard?" She wanted so badly to hear him say he cared for her that her breath stopped while she waited for his answer.

He sent her a guarded glance. "I've always been more than just a bodyguard."

Disappointment sank inside her. He'd chosen to misinterpret her meaning.

At least Sheldrake wouldn't bother her again. "I thought we were going to check on Papa," Verity said.

"He is here."

Sure enough, when Verity looked, she found her father standing at the far end of the table, talking with a different group of his friends.

Torcuil removed the cup of claret punch from her hand and set it on the table. "Perhaps there is something here you would prefer?"

"Lemonade, please."

He ladled the sweet-tart liquid into a cup for her, and she accepted it with thanks. Despite the early spring chill outside, it was warm in the saloon.

At that moment, three of her acquaintances arrived, their fans fluttering, their eyes only for Torcuil, even as they greeted her. Reluctantly, she performed introductions to this trio of unwed doves. They proceeded to hang on his every word—the few he uttered. They sighed over his brogue. They gushed on about his romantic hair. Their avid eyes ate up his exceptional good looks and his manly physique. So annoyed with this unseemly display was Verity that she didn't notice when Harriet Lonsley arrived to stand beside her.

Harriet leaned toward her. "I have news," she announced softly.

Verity turned to find Harriet gazing at Torcuil, who was gallantly replying to a coy comment from an insipid miss. "News?"

Harriet met Verity's eyes and nodded. "Yes." She grinned. "You've had any female who's even glimpsed the magnificent Mr. MacCodrum scrambling to find his brother."

Verity smiled. "Yes. Mr. MacCodrum *is* rather magnificent, isn't he?"

"An understatement, Verity. I've never seen another man who can equal him. We're all quite green that he's already taken."

Verity flushed. "How did you know?"

Harriet chuckled. "How could we not? He never leaves your side. He takes every opportunity to touch you, though," she added in a rush, "he's never obvious about it. And I've never seen your eyes shine so brightly as when you're looking at him."

He never leaves my side because he's my bodyguard, Verity thought wryly. As to his touching her, she'd be happier if he touched her a great deal more.

"His eyes are so very dark," Harriet continued consideringly. "Do you ever have difficulty guessing what's going on in his mind?"

"Of course. He's a male."

Harriet nodded sagely. "Yes, their thought processes do seem alien to ours."

And his are more alien than most, Verity thought. Aloud, she asked Harriet what she'd discovered about Eideard.

Harriet released a heavy sigh. "He's left London."

Verity's heart skipped a beat. "Left?" If he was no longer in London, would Torcuil leave, too? Dread formed a stone in her chest. "Where did he go?"

"That, I could not discover." Harriet sighed again. "I should have known it was too much to hope for."

Distracted by the other woman's dejection, Verity asked, "What was too much to hope for? That you might learn Eideard's new location?"

"No. That I might find Eideard MacCodrum. Since I cannot have your Mr. MacCodrum, I'd hoped to find a MacCodrum male for my very own. The heir, too, you said. That would have been sufficient to gratify my mother, and more than sufficient to gratify me." She gave Verity a woebegone look. "Oh, I just know I'll end having to marry that odious Lord Videau. Mama sees that he's a viscount and that he has eleven thousand a year. What she doesn't see is those nasty little leers of his when her back is turned. He's so *old*. Forty-six years old."

Verity only half listened to Harriet's catalog of complaints. If Torcuil knew his brother had left London, would he leave, too? If he was to keep his promise to his father, she didn't see any way around it for him. Her father had a new bodyguard, and she couldn't keep Torcuil here with the excuse that she needed his protection. Not when it was obvious she didn't.

Still, she needed more time to make Torcuil see that he needed her . . . and that she loved him. Once she accomplished that, she felt certain his problem—whatever it was—would fall into perspective, and they could wed.

How bad could his obstacle to their union be? she asked herself for what seemed like the thousandth time. Once again, she enumerated the reasons in her mind, having given up on getting an answer from Torcuil. Silently, she supplied the answers herself. He'd told her that he wasn't married. Indeed, he'd said he wasn't even betrothed. She knew he wasn't penniless. Was he concerned over the difference in their stations? Well, as the son of a clan chief, he might be considered a prince, by some. She'd explain that if he ever gave her the chance. If he ever *listened*. He was bound to accept such reasoning. Heaven knew, he possessed the arrogance of a prince.

Her eyes narrowed as another, less easily surmounted, reason moved up her list. What if Torcuil's parents hated the English? She'd heard there were still a few such persons left. She tapped her fan against her lace-covered palm. Hmm. Not as easily solved. Torcuil would likely place great value on his father's wishes. As touchy as this might prove, she refused to give up. They might not change their minds about the English in general, but she'd find a way to weasel her way into their hearts.

First, however, she needed time with Torcuil. Time enough for him to *see*. That she loved him. That he needed her.

She might have that time if Torcuil didn't know his brother had vacated Town.

Verity leaned toward Harriet. "Thank you for your news," she said in a low voice. "I'd appreciate it if you said nothing. Allow me to break the news to my dear cousin when the moment is right."

"Of course."

"How did you learn that Eideard MacCodrum has quit London? Where was he staying while he was here?"

Harriet flicked open her fan. "By the oddest coincidence. I'd asked everyone of whom I could think. Then along came a friend of my elder brother, who stayed the night with us before going on to meet his regiment in Portugal." She employed her fan, sending the small curls on her forehead dancing with each leisurely flutter. "He stopped at a coaching inn outside London, on his way to our house. He said he saw a quite tall Scotsman with long dark hair—and braids. He got into a coach heading out of London."

"Did he know where?"

Harriet shook her head.

"Well, thank you so very much for the information. You've gleaned intelligence a Bow Street Runner could not."

Harriet blushed with pleasure, and a smile lighted her face, reminding Verity how pretty she was. It would not do at all for her to wed the wizened, lecherous old Videau. Harriet was too much of a romantic to survive such an alliance. What she needed was a fashionable peer not more than ten or twelve years older than herself. A green lad would never do. But the fellow must also have a respectable income and pedigree, more to please her dear mama, that dragon, than Harriet. And Verity knew just the fellow.

Waving to Torcuil, who was now surrounded by a bevy of twittering admirers, Verity ignored his panicked look and steered Harriet toward Lord Taunton, who had separated himself from Sheldrake and now made his way toward the door of the saloon.

"What are you doing, Verity?" Harriet asked laughingly.

"Playing cupid. As to the matter of matrimony with the vexing viscount of Videau—have you been introduced to Lord Taunton yet?"

"You know I haven't. Heavens, it was just the other day that we were talking about that—"

"Ah, so we were."

She arrived in front of Taunton, Harriet in tow. "Oh, Lord Taunton, you weren't leaving yet, were you?"

"Well, I—" He noticed Harriet, who blushed a vivid pink. "No," he concluded firmly. "No, I was not."

Excellent. A gentleman. "I'm so pleased to hear it. After all, the musicians are just tuning up for another set, and I thought you looked like a man who enjoys dancing. You do enjoy dancing, don't you?"

"Well, I—"

"Of course you do. I noticed your grace and agility the moment you joined us. Not like Mr. Morris." There was no Mr. Morris. "Now don't mistake me. Mr. Morris is a most congenial fellow, but his sense of rhythm is just a bit off. As dear as he is"—Verity leaned slightly toward Taunton with a conspiratorial air and lowered her voice— "he can't dance. There. I've said it. He can't dance, and he has trod upon Miss Lonsley's tiny foot. Imagine! Oh, but I am *so* sorry, Harriet, dear, have you and Lord Taunton been properly introduced?" She knew very well they had not, but rolled right on and made the introductions she'd planned to make all along.

"Do I hear a country dance starting?" Verity asked, and, as if by previous arrangement, the musicians at the far end of the saloon introduced the melody of a popular country dance. "Lord Taunton, you *will* help dear Harriet overcome her terrible experience with Mr. Morris, won't you? Restore her faith in British manhood?"

The earl's blue eyes twinkled. "I'd deem it a privilege, Lady Verity." He bowed to a red-faced Harriet, clicking the heels of his patent-leather slippers. He held out his arm to her. "Please do me the honor of allowing me to dance with you, Miss Lonsley—for England!"

Harriet giggled and placed her palm on his arm. With a wink at Verity, Taunton led Harriet away to join the dancers.

Feeling quite pleased with herself, Verity turned around, ready to undertake the task of extricating Torcuil from his admirers, those husband-hungry hussies. Towering over those around him, Torcuil sent her a silent plea. It delighted her that none of the females clustered around him, some of them exceptionally lovely, had managed to entrance him.

She eased through the flock of deceptively delicate-looking muslin- and silk-clad hunters, and saw more than one pair of eyes flashing resentment at her supposed intrusion. What none of them understood was, Torcuil was *hers*.

"I've come to claim my dance," she said when she finally reached him.

Without a word, he offered his arm, and she placed her hand on it. According the other ladies a nod here and there and a smooth, pleasant word, Torcuil led her past her father and his friends, toward the section of the chamber where the dancers had gathered.

"Your admirers were hoping you'd ask one or twelve of them to dance with you."

From under thick, dark lashes, Torcuil cast Verity a tempestuous glance. "I dinna wish to dance with any of them."

Verity could barely contain her delight. "Likely, if you'd asked one to dance, you would have broken the hearts of all the rest."

He made a rude noise in his throat.

Verity grinned, then quickly tempered her mouth to a smile. "Do you mind awfully dancing with me?"

Torcuil cocked an eyebrow at her. "Ye know verra well I want to dance with ye." His marvelous lips sketched a smile. "I've no heard a waltz bein' played."

She felt the heat of a blush rise in her cheeks. "No, you haven't."

"Shall I speak to the music makers?" A wicked light danced in his black eyes.

"Musicians," she corrected absently. "And speaking to them is the prerogative of the hostess. I very much doubt she'll request a waltz."

"Oh."

She smiled. "I told you it was a scandalous dance."

"Aye, that ye did, but I dinna ken why it would be

considered so wicked. If ye left off the kiss at the end, that is."

Verity opened her fan and moved it in front of her face, hoping to obfuscate her heated blush. She wondered who might have heard.

"What is this about a kiss?" demanded the imperious voice of Lady Euphemia Beauvais. From around Verity's side stalked the daughter of the duke of Marbay, and with her came the gossipy Halford sisters, Grace and Nancy.

His expression neutral, Torcuil inclined his head to acknowledge the arrival of women he'd met during the course of Verity's numerous social calls and the many guests received at Ravenshaw House. "Lady Euphemia. Miss Halford. Miss Nancy." He neglected to say that it was a pleasure to see them, which almost made Verity smile. Torcuil didn't lie.

Lady Euphemia, who was no older than Verity's eighteen years, seemed to assume it her right, by nature of her rank, to speak for the trio. "Mr. MacCodrum." She directed a curt nod in his direction, but beneath the affected droop of her eyelids, her gaze raked avidly over Torcuil before she turned to Verity.

Angered by the other woman's hungry perusal, Verity drew herself up to her full height—a height that topped Euphemia's by a couple of inches. "Good evening, Lady Euphemia," she said coolly. Her eyes flicked over the Halford sisters, and she grudgingly recognized them with a nod.

"You asked us to tell you if we heard anything about Eideard MacCodrum," Euphemia said.

Verity remembered. She hadn't really expected them to make an effort. Perhaps they'd held the same hope Harriet had cherished. Or maybe they'd simply been curious. Either way, it surprised her.

"Have you found him?" Torcuil asked. Verity heard the tension in his deep baritone.

"No," Euphemia said. "Amazing as it is, we found nothing at all." She looked to the sisters, who nodded their agreement. "Are you quite certain your brother came to London, Mr. MacCodrum? Usually, my—our—sources for information are exceptional."

"I was told London. Usually my sources of information are exceptional also. I thank you, ladies, for looking."

Euphemia waved away his thanks. "Think nothing of it. It amused us. Now what was this about a kiss?"

Torcuil's dark eyes gave nothing away. "Lady Verity and I were only sayin' that there is such an aversion to dancing the waltz, ye'd think it ended with a kiss."

"Well! The dance is almost an embrace," Euphemia said stoutly.

"It *is* an embrace," Nancy Halford piped.

Grace nodded emphatically. "Indeed it is."

"No a verra close one," Torcuil observed. When nailed by all four gazes, he added hastily, "So I hear."

"The man and the woman are facing each other," Euphemia declared, opening her fan. "Closely, indecently," she elaborated in a low, thrilled voice. "Why, they're practically *rubbing* against each other!" She rapidly whacked her fan back and forth, sending a gale to cool her fevered face. She shot Torcuil a furtive glance. "Oh, I feel so faint."

Instantly, the Halford sisters sprang to her aid, clucking over her, herding her out to the balcony and fresh air despite her struggles and outraged glares. Torcuil made no move to help.

Verity simply looked at him, smothering her laughter.

"I ken what ye're goin' to say," Torcuil said.

"Oh? Pray, tell me my words."

"A gentleman would have helped Lady Euphemia." He glowered. "She's no lady, I'm thinkin'. 'Twas no but a ploy. The haughty hake has likely never felt faint in her life. Look at her! In fine health she is, fightin' off her two minions. If wastin' time on malingerers is what a gentle man does, I suppose I'm no a gentleman." The stormy cast to his face told Verity he was expecting an argument.

"A gentleman would probably know what Euphemia was up to, and conduct himself in a chivalrous fashion anyway," she said gently.

"Aye, and he'd be a hypocrite, bowin' and flutterin' all over her, when what anyone with a grain o' sense would want to do is—"

"Tut, tut, tut," Verity cautioned hastily. "This is neither the time nor place to discuss her shortcomings." A smile crept out to claim her lips. "Her *many* shortcomings."

He laughed, and the deep, masculine sound of it tripped ripples of happiness within Verity, and she laughed with him. If her love for him shone in her eyes for everyone to see, she didn't care. When she looked at Torcuil, she forgot the press of people around them. This was their special time together. No household duties could interrupt. The moon had risen, but they were not kept apart by the walls of their separate chambers. Tonight they were together. Tonight the magic would return.

They joined the dancers assembling for a quadrille, and Torcuil held out his hand to her. Without hesitation, without breaking her gaze from his, she accepted it. His palm was warm against hers.

Now they were close enough to the ensemble to hear their music without the filter of countless voices. The blending and counterpoint of the viola pompasa, violins, flute, and oboe afforded a different, more complex rendition of the same melodies Fanny had played alone on the pianoforte.

His dark eyes took on a faraway look, as if he'd been transported to a different place. Home? she wondered. It saddened her to be excluded from his memories, and she turned her head, unable to bear the reminder that he kept her away from the life he clearly missed.

She felt his touch on her chin and realized he'd laid his fingertip on it. Slowly, he coaxed her face back to him. His beautiful mouth gradually curved, silently reassuring her. She lifted her eyes to meet his dark gaze. Dark as the stormy night he'd leapt to her rescue. Dark, perhaps, as his well-cloaked past.

A polite cough reminded her that they were not alone. She dropped her gaze to the toes of her green moiré slippers and smiled despite her embarrassment, feeling suddenly shy. To her surprise, Torcuil laced his fingers through hers and gave her hand a light squeeze.

The musicians began to play, and the dancers swung into motion. The tempo was brisk and the melody uplifting. Among the participants there were smiles and laughter. Verity marveled that Torcuil, after only a few simple lessons, moved as if he'd been dancing the quadrille for years. She took pleasure from his delight in the music, the movement, and the good-natured company of the other dancers.

When the dance came to an end, they returned to the beverages table, where her father still talked with his friends.

"You were the prettiest girl out there," the marquess declared. "Don't you agree, Torcuil?"

Torcuil grinned as he handed Verity a cup of lemonade. "Aye, sir. The prettiest, and that's a fact."

"Yes it is," the marquess agreed. "And you cut a dashing figure, Cousin. Caught the eye of many a lady, I'll warrant." He arched his eyebrows in unspoken query.

Abruptly Torcuil sobered. "Ye're too kind."

"You could fair see their fingers itching to get into that mane of yours," one of the marquess's cronies chortled. "May have set a fashion."

The marquess studied Torcuil for a long minute, as if he were trying to decipher his reaction. Before he could speak, a hush rippled over the crowd. Attention seemed to focus on the door.

"What—?" the marquess began.

"Didn't you hear the footman?" an eager-looking dandy next to him asked. "Neul has arrived."

The doorway into the saloon received almost every male guest's rapt attention. Every male guest except Torcuil, it seemed. While he appeared to anticipate this Neul person's arrival, he did so with considerably less delight than the rest, though his expression revealed nothing of what passed through his mind. Verity fretted as she waited for the mystery lady to make her grand entrance.

A slim woman of about Verity's height strolled through the door and paused. Her gilded silver hair was a mass of ringlet curls pulled to the back of her head, where a golden silver froth topped a curly fall to the middle of her back. Her gown of silver tissue caught the light, and the bejeweled shawl of gossamer draped negligently behind her and over her forearms twinkled in the multitude of candles.

Suddenly she went still, as if she heard something and tried to locate the source. Verity listened, but the only thing audible to her was the occasional shuffling of feet, and a cough, here and there, throughout the room. Then Neul proceeded into the crush and was immediately swamped by admirers.

The marquess eyed the mob. "I had no idea so many could abandon their dignity so easily," he muttered.

"Are you certain it's not a riot?" Verity asked. She'd never seen anything like it. "How will you ever meet her in *that?*" With a wave of her hand, she indicated the milling pack that surrounded London's latest toast.

Verity's father sized up the scene. "I don't suppose

that I will. Not tonight, at least." He concealed his disappointment well, but Verity sensed it there under his calm. She hated to see his enthusiasm for the evening wither away and was wracking her brain to think of a solution when he turned to her and asked for the honor of the next dance.

She smiled and opened her mouth to reply when she saw a figure furtively duck out of the sea of Neul's admirers. Once free of them, she quickly glanced around. Spotting the marquess, Verity, and Torcuil, she hurried over to them. Her large, slanting gold eyes and her lush, ripe-berry smile took in Torcuil and Verity, but it was directed toward the marquess. She addressed herself to him.

"I do hope that you'll forgive my lack of propriety, sir, but will you save me from this horde? A dance. A refreshment. A stroll on the balcony. Please, I place myself at your mercy."

It was as if a shimmering bit of manna had fallen from the heavens, straight on top of his head. He rallied admirably. Taking her elegant hand, he bowed over it, introducing himself.

"Charmed," she murmured. "I am Neul."

The marquess smiled. "Pray, who could not know that? May I make known to you my daughter and—"

Neul sent Verity and Torcuil an apologetic smile. "Please forgive me, but I fear the hounds may give chase if we stay within sight. Any second now they'll notice I'm gone. There were simply so many of them that it was easy to lose myself for a minute. I'm not certain such an evasion would work a second time."

Sure enough, a murmur rippled through the crowd that had surrounded her. The men began to look about, as if searching for something—or someone.

"Best we make our escape now," the marquess said

and led Neul away, threading their way toward the end of the saloon, where an old-fashioned minuet was being played.

Torcuil watched them leave, his face an unreadable mask. Verity watched her father and the unusual woman vanish into the crush with growing unease.

"You know her, don't you, Torcuil? And you don't like her."

He shook his head. "I dinna know her. I only know of her."

"But you don't like her." It was a statement asking for reassurance.

"As I dinna know her, nor even much about her, how can I dislike her?"

"Then what is it? 'Tis clear to see that she makes you uncomfortable."

"She's verra powerful. That's all I can tell ye."

Verity's eyes widened with alarm, and she touched Torcuil's arm. "Is she a danger to Papa?"

Torcuil's eyebrows slanted down as he considered. "I've already asked myself that. I dinna know. If ye want my best guess, I'd say she's taken wi' yer father." He began guiding her toward the dancers. "He's a good-lookin' man for his years, ye ken."

"True."

"A more mature man appeals to some females."

She nodded consideringly. "Also true." She wanted to believe Neul had singled out her father for those reasons. Still, men of every age and description had sought after her. Verity said as much.

"Perhaps there's the answer," Torcuil replied as he eased them into place on the edge of the dancing area.

"Do you mean to say, she might want Papa above all the others because he *did not* move to beg her favor?" She thought on it a minute. "If she is mobbed by men as a matter of course, the man who has pride or wit enough not to join the herd might prove quite attractive. A challenge, perhaps. How contrary people can be."

The corners of Torcuil's lips twitched slightly upward. "Aye."

"I sense a slur, sir," Verity admonished absently, content, for the moment, simply to drink in his virile presence as she stood beside him, watching her father and Neul move through the figures of the dance with stately dignity. Their expressions declared that they enjoyed each other's company.

It had been so long—too long—since her father had danced. And Verity couldn't remember him ever revealing such delight in a woman's company. To her mother he'd shown courtesy and respect, but Verity could see more clearly than ever that there had never been any love between them. An arrangement it had begun, and an arrangement it had remained. Until her mother had broken and run. She'd been able to taste love only by becoming an outcast.

Verity traced Torcuil's clear-cut profile with her gaze. Was he an outcast? Was his brother? Her fingertips pressed against the beveled edges of her fan's ivory sticks. She wanted time to allow Torcuil to accept his need for her, but did that give her the right to conceal information about his brother? Their father might be dying even now. Would Torcuil ever forgive her if he arrived home too late? Would she?

What if she lost him forever?

She looked at him studying her father and Neul. Despite her father's insistence that his bodyguard not accompany him, Torcuil still kept watch over him, even as he did over Verity.

"Torcuil," she said softly, to gain his attention.

"Hmm?" His eyes never stopped searching the crowd around them.

Verity cleared her throat, hoping to remove the tightness.

He looked at her. "What is it, Anemone?"

She swallowed. "Your brother has left London."

19

Love is the crocodile on the river of desire.
—Bhartrihari

Verity lay in her bed, staring up at the canopy. Moonlight poured through the long windows. A small fire burned on the grate. How long had it been since they'd returned home from the ball? Hours? It seemed more like an eternity.

As soon as she'd told Torcuil the news of his brother, he'd stalked straight to Harriet and questioned her. Unfortunately, there was nothing more Harriet could tell him. After that he'd grown quiet and preoccupied. With a sinking heart, Verity had been certain he was planning to leave London. Finally, she'd pleaded the headache and her father had insisted that she and Torcuil return home without him. Torcuil had refused to budge until he had sent for Mr. Gruagach, who arrived with amazing speed, arrayed in handsome evening attire. She and Torcuil had left her father and Neul gazing deeply into each other's eyes.

Now she thought of Torcuil leaving, and it sent

Verity's heart into a panicked flutter. She leaped up and began to pace the floor of her bedchamber. He couldn't leave. He just *couldn't*. She hadn't finished convincing him that he needed her. What if he left, then thought he didn't need her enough to return?

She considered all the things she didn't know about him. Of all the experiences they had not shared. There had been naught but a reluctant wooing, yet she felt closer to Torcuil than she'd ever felt to any man. They shared a give-and-take in which her part was as important as his.

Oh, if only there had been a waltz tonight! Perhaps, if they might have prolonged the magic . . .

Verity stopped her pacing in the middle of the chamber. Her bare toes dug into the pile of the carpet. He was the man she wanted. Not Roger Sheldrake, or any of those other men her father had thought appropriate over the past two years. No, she wanted Torcuil MacCodrum of Clan MacCodrum, and she wanted to be with him for the rest of their lives.

At this very moment, he might be packing to leave— and here she stood like a cow-hearted ninnyhammer, doing nothing about it. She tried to think what to do to convince him to stay. Or at least, not to leave until she'd had time to make him see that he needed her. She covered her face with her hands. Think. *Think!* Desperately, she cast about for something to get his attention, something that might delay him. Their future happiness depended on her.

What would dear, wise Fanny do in a situation like this? If her George felt duty-bound to leave, would she pace the floor and cover her face? Suddenly, Verity lifted her head. A bubble of terrified laughter escaped her throat.

She knew exactly what Fanny would do.

* * *

Dark plants swayed around him as he swam through the forest of kelp, emerging onto the grassy plain above the canyon. Joy animated him, sending him into swirls, glorying in the cool slide of water over his body. At last, he was returning home!

He entered the vast canyon, admiring the delicate, multihued anemones, the vivid sponge castles. In the distance, he heard the mournful call of a whale. A glittering shoal of small fish moved like a cloud before him, as if guiding his way to The Citadel.

In his mind he felt the presence of the assembled clan, waiting to welcome him home. His heart filled with happiness. Finally, he would rejoin his kindred.

Torcuil, come back. Please, come back to me. Torcuil . . . There she was, in his mind.

Real and vibrant and achingly sweet. Tears glistened in her beautiful green eyes. Her slim arms reached out to him. *Torcuil.*

He slowed, his joy dissolving. Then he tried to swim on.

Torcuil cried out, the wrenching pain in his heart growing as he moved away from where he'd left her. Where once the wondrous warmth of her shared company had filled him, only aching emptiness remained.

How could this be? She was no sorceress to cast a glamour over him. She had no power to stir a love potion or chant a charm. The elements were not hers to summon. Yet she possessed an undeniable magic. And she'd cast her sparkling net over his heart. Without her, joy could be only momentary, happiness only an illusion.

He gazed longingly at the mountain that housed The Citadel, where his clan waited.

Torcuil, came her voice, soft and sad.

He turned yearning eyes to the canyon, to the rich, colorful life that made its home there.

This was his home, too.

He and his brothers and cousins had grown up among the high-spirited dolphins and the indulgent whales.

Water slid over his body like silk. Deep, blue-green silk.

Suddenly the under-seascape altered, changing form and color. An enormous expanse of bright, clear blue, feathered with sweeps of white stretched endlessly above. Beneath his feet, land—green, craggy, with studded stone—rolling out in hills and dips as far as his eyes could see.

He began walking. He heard her soft voice in his mind again, and he broke into a run, making his way back to Verity. Verity, who was his, and his alone.

The indignant, disappointed voices of his clan rang in his brain. *You belong with us! You are a silkie.*

He saw her in the distance, standing on the crest of a hill, her golden hair unfurled in the fresh breeze, the skirts of her white gown rippling.

Torcuil. She held out her slim arms toward him.

The grief of his people washed through him like an echo. *You will never be one of Them. Never. Never . . .*

"Verity!" The cry was still on his lips as Torcuil sat bolt upright in his bed. His chest heaved as he struggled to drag in enough air. Wildly, he looked around him. He was still in his bedchamber at Ravenshaw House. He raked a shaking hand through his hair.

The meaning of his dream frightened him.

Only the glow of her candle pierced the dark of the hall. Verity took a deep breath, hoping to calm her racing heartbeat. The attempt proved futile. Quietly, she opened Torcuil's bedchamber door.

A warm fire in the fireplace cast its net of golden light across the middle of the room, consigning the rest to shadow. Her fingers eased somewhat around the candlestick, and when she saw his trunk at the foot of the bed, she inhaled a shaky breath of relief. He had not gone yet.

"What are ye doing here?"

She jumped at the sound of the deep, gruff voice that issued from the stygian cavern of the tester bed. Nervously, she clutched her dressing gown more tightly around her. Gathering her courage, she walked to the bed and set her candle on the table beside it. Dancing light from its small flame slipped over the man, shifting bright and soft, light and dark.

Close enough to touch, Torcuil lay on his side, his head propped against a fist. His slightly tousled mane fell in front and in back of his broad, naked shoulders. The crimson satin quilts had fallen down just below his waist. Bare to her gaze was his deep chest, and a goodly portion of hard, flat belly—fair skin dusted with sable hair. Long and sleekly muscled, he reminded her of a panther she'd once seen in a country neighbor's park. Only *that* beast had been safely caged.

"Go back to yer chamber, Verity."

She moistened lips gone arid. "I came—you said—" She dragged in another breath. "I want you to trifle with me."

"Nay." The single word was short and harsh.

Indignation rose in her, and she wanted to argue with him. She wanted to remind him what he'd told her after their waltz in her father's grand saloon. But she sensed in him a readiness for argument. So she moved to avoid it.

Verity opened her dressing gown and allowed it to slide off her shoulders. It sighed down her bare body to pool at her feet like a rose-tinted shadow.

"Trifle with me," she said again, her voice surprisingly low and husky.

Torcuil remained where he lay, but his gaze moved over her like a hot brand. Slowly, without taking his eyes from hers, he sat up and threw back the bedcovers. With feral grace he swung long legs over the edge of the bed.

Her mouth went dry. He stood before her, tall and sleek and powerful. She'd seen him naked before. She knew he possessed the masculine beauty and symmetry of a Greek statue, but that's where the similarity ended. Unlike the carved stone, Torcuil pulsed with life. She'd touched his skin and remembered its warmth. She'd heard his heart beating within his chest. She'd felt his breath on her cheek.

Now, she was starkly reminded that Torcuil MacCodrum was pure male.

He prowled around her in a leisurely circle. His eyes kindled as he raked his gaze over her face, her breasts and hips, over her blond triangle of curls, over her legs and buttocks.

"Ye've come to me on a bad night," he said, his voice low. "I'm no feelin' particularly loverlike."

She turned her head, watching him, feeling like a rabbit to his panther. "What . . . what do you feel like?"

He smiled, and firelight gleamed briefly on his teeth.

She cleared her throat. "I said—"

"I heard what ye said." He lifted a lock of bright hair from her shoulder. His fingers brushed her skin, sending a thrill of heat through her. "I know what I told ye."

He breathed in the scent of her hair, then stepped closer. His thigh glanced hers. The peppering of his crisp hair against her skin created an instant's friction that caused her stomach to clench with desire.

A flare of temper abolished her tangled nerves. She stood naked in his bedchamber. She knew men who would commit crimes to have her thus. Was this the best he could do? Seek to intimidate her? Verity tossed her head, effectively releasing the lock of hair from his fingers.

"I don't think you remember at all," she informed him crisply. "But I do. Quite clearly. I recall the first time you said it." She slid her glaze slowly up his chest, pausing on his lips, before she met his eyes. "You had me on the chest of drawers." Her voice went huskier at the memory.

Pinpoints of candlelight reflected in his black eyes. One hand cupped her jaw, tilting her head up. Though she could feel the power in his fingers, his touch was gentle. He moved nearer, and the room narrowed to his smooth shoulders, to his masculine, columnar neck. To the wild beauty of his face.

His lips eased across hers, incorporating a universe of sensation into the subtle caress. She rushed to experience it all, but found him deftly tempering her brash eagerness. Gradually, she tarried for the moment. To her surprise, she found more pleasure in it.

The tip of his tongue stroked a corner of her mouth, then went on to glide along the seam of her lips. She parted them for him. He drew her still closer to him. She felt the heat of his body. Shaping her palm to the side of his neck, she accidentally brushed the lobe of his ear.

He tensed, and she looked at him in question. Then, as realization arrived, a smile claimed her: his earlobes were sensitive. Before she could explore her discovery, he stroked his thumb over her nipple. It was as if he'd plucked harp strings spun of nerves, strung tautly between her breasts and that secret nether region between her thighs. She gasped.

Stepping behind her, he brought their bodies into full contact. Glorying in the feel of his flesh against hers, she pressed closer. He nuzzled her neck and spread kisses up her jaw and along the edge of her ear. As he plied her with his lips, his tongue, and his teeth, her body grew languid and heavy, yet more and more restless as a curious tension coiled within her.

He skimmed his palms over her breasts, and she exhaled a shuddering breath. With seductive strokes and teasing touches, he stoked the throbbing low in her belly into breathless need. Her hands traveled up and down his arms, feeling the muscles rippling beneath his skin.

"Is this why ye came to me, fair Verity?" His lips moved against the shell of her ear, his voice soft and deep. "Is this what ye wanted?" His hands spread over her hips and buttocks, drawing her back into his groin. The heavy evidence of his desire pressed against her flesh.

Her brain seemed fogged, and she struggled to find the words. "I . . . came for *you*, Torcuil. I want . . . you."

He turned her around in his arms, and stared down into her face. Dazed, she couldn't fathom what he sought, so she gazed back at him, waiting, telling herself that this man with the narrowed black eyes and unsmiling, sensual mouth was her Torcuil, her courageous, wonder-filled warrior.

She lifted her hands and smoothed the tips of her fingers over the lids of his obsidian eyes, along the line of his beautiful mouth. He covered her hands with his and pressed a long, haunted kiss to her fingers.

"I also came to tell you—" She broke off when he jerked his head up.

"Ye were sayin' . . ." he prompted.

She gathered her courage. "I also came to tell you that you need me."

His handsome face moved into the devil's own smile. "So, I need ye, do I?"

She nodded, uncertain of his reaction to her announcement, then gasped as he took the tip of her breast into his mouth. He laved and suckled and nipped, forging a spear of blind, hammering demand that drove straight to the core of her. Then he moved to her other breast and began again. Vaguely, she fretted about this awesome power he wielded over her. The power that she'd chosen to give him.

She shivered and leaned into him for support as molten, carnal sensations coursed through her. Without conscious command, her hips began to move.

He eased his thigh between hers. Then he drove his hands through her hair, scattering pins that chimed faintly as they struck the floor. The pads of his fingers pressed against her scalp as he took her mouth in a hot, demanding, openmouthed kiss.

Blindly, she pressed herself against his leg, and friction sent sparks flying through her. His tongue rubbed against hers. She moved against him again. His breathing grew labored. Verity stroked herself against him again and again, her short shallow breaths mingling with the sharp delirium that drove her.

"Aye, that's right, Anemone," he said, his voice oddly rough. "Take yer pleasure. Does it feel good to ye?"

"Yes," she whispered. "Oh, yes."

But how could that be? She felt desperate, and unfocused, and ready to shatter. How could it feel so very . . . very . . . *good?*

His fingertip unerringly located a spot that sent her fingers curling into his bare shoulders. Her moisture intensified his precisely applied pressure, sending Verity arcing away from him, strangling on her moan.

Torcuil swung her up into his arms. He placed her on the bed. Framed between her thighs were his broad, bare shoulders, the dark crown of his head. His tongue flickered on her sensitive blossom of flesh, dashing away all thoughts, enslaving her to sheer sensation. From far away, she heard small, breathy cries. Dimly she realized they were hers.

Energy vibrated from Torcuil into her from each place where they touched, detonating tremors of delight that grew increasingly more intense. She reached. She needed . . .

Suddenly, a storm of pleasure crashed through her. Torcuil held her as it gradually ebbed, leaving ripples, then glimmers, then naught but a contented haze.

She wiggled her toes. "You've made my toes warm," she murmured.

Against her cheek, his mouth curved up. "Och, and I did more than warm yer wee toes, I'm hopin'."

She smiled. "Oh, yes. Much more."

He rolled to his back, and with one arm, drew her snugly to his side. Hesitantly, feeling curiously shy considering what she'd just experienced with this man, she ran her hand over his ribs. He watched her without comment, his expression solemn. She moved her hand across his ridged, taught belly, fascinated when his muscles jerked reflexively.

"Why did your muscles jump like that?" she asked.

Even in the firelight, she could see the color heighten in his elegant cheekbones. "Likely it's defensive. 'Tis a vulnerable area, do ye see? A hard blow or a blade to that spot can easily kill a man. Not an easy death, either."

"Oh." She didn't want to talk about blows or death. Her gaze moved lower. "But—!" She turned wide eyes up to his. "You're still—that is to say—you didn't . . . ?"

He shook his head. "I didn't."

She caught her bottom lip between her teeth, thinking that such swelling must be an agony. Wasn't that just like Torcuil to hide his pain?

"Is there something I can do to"—she cleared her throat—"help?"

"Well, ye can stop starin', for one thing."

She dragged her gaze away from his massive arousal. "It looks painful."

"For ye or for me?"

"Why, for you, of course. It hasn't come near me."

"Nay, it has not," he agreed sourly.

"But don't you need for me—"

His eyes flashed with anger. "I dinna *need* anything from ye."

Verity felt as if she'd been struck a mortal blow.

Numbly, she stared at him as the raw wound on her soul gushed forth her hopes and dreams of their future together. Unable to speak, she slipped off the bed and walked carefully toward the door, feeling as if she were going to splinter into myriad shards. She paused to pick up her dressing gown from the floor.

"Remember," he snarled. "Ye came to *me.*"

Verity swallowed against the anguish swelling in her throat. What had she done to cause such fury? Fumbling blindly, she drew on the dressing gown.

She managed to quietly let herself out of Torcuil's chamber, closing the door firmly behind her.

Torcuil sat naked on the floor in front of the cold fireplace, worrying his lush sealskin hood between his fingers. Normally, holding it gave him a measure of comfort. Tonight he found none. After what he'd done, he doubted he'd find comfort of any sort ever again.

He'd committed an unspeakable sin.

He'd fallen in love with a land woman.

How could such a thing happen? They were separate breeds. They had naught in common. Her people were young and quarrelsome. His were ancient and cautious. Her folk thrived on the land, his in the sea.

He was only the second silkie in a generation to venture among the land folk—and a fine mess he'd made of it, too. He hadn't found his brother. Instead he'd spent his time following a trail left by assassins, a thief, and a whoremonger.

And falling deeply in love with a generous, sensitive woman. Aye, his father would certainly be proud of *that*, he thought wretchedly. Rather, his sire's lack of enthusiasm over his second son would be justified and confirmed.

Worse than anything he'd done, Torcuil had hurt Verity. Furious at being forced to face the truth he'd worked so hard to deny all along, he'd lashed out at her.

She was right. He did need her.

And that knowledge shook him to the depths of his soul.

He couldn't live in London. Maintaining his man form required periodic immersions in water, natural water, in his seal persona. He'd had hopes for the Thames until he witnessed its hopeless pollution. His long baths had helped extend that period, but he could not continue much longer without reversing The Change for a night.

A mere century ago, land folk had burned unfortunates suspected of practicing magic.

Verity had told him that she didn't believe in faeries. By the sacred well of Nechtan, if she didn't believe in something as obviously real as faeries, could Torcuil believe she'd willingly accept a silkie into her life?

Land folk made clear distinctions between themselves and other species. They rated all others as inferior to themselves. To call one of Verity's people a dog or a cat—both beloved pets—was to issue insult. A horse or a cow was even worse. All but man were seen as lower forms of life. Less intelligent. More expendable.

Torcuil carefully returned his hood to its hiding place. Then he pulled on a pair of stockings, breeches, and a shirt. He could guess what Verity's reaction would be to any revelation he might make regarding his true nature. The thought of it twisted him into knots. He hoped that someday he would feel confident of a more positive reception to his news. But until then, he couldn't live with the knowledge that he'd hurt her. He would go to her and ask her forgiveness.

Hot tears spilled down Verity's cheeks as she hurried along the dark hall, her bare feet drumming against polished wood and Abusson carpets. She gained the sanctuary of her bedchamber in a rush. Leaning back against the door, she rolled her head from side to side, wanting to deny all that had taken place in Torcuil's room.

She'd failed. She had gone to Torcuil hoping to make him see that he needed her. Instead, he had shown her that he didn't need her at all. Instead, he'd awakened her body to the intoxicating world of passion. And he'd been right—never again would she be satisfied with less. She'd offered up her innocence, and he'd flung it in her face.

Verity bowed her head and give in to her grief. Harsh, animal sobs tore up from her chest as she finally accepted the bleak truth. She loved Torcuil MacCodrum with all her heart, and he would leave her without a backward glance.

He'd obliged her when she'd thrown herself at him. How could it be more than that, when he knew so much, and she so little? She had pressed Torcuil, despite his warning. Bonelessly, Verity slid to the floor, hugging herself in solitary misery.

Dear Lord, she had gone to his bedchamber *naked*. What contempt he must have for her. The thought of his disgust shredded through her pride to tear at her heart.

She needed him, it seemed. She needed his wonder, his arrogance, his kisses, and his love. Now she had nothing. How could she have been so wrong? Tears drenched her arms. She'd truly believed that he harbored feelings for her. A tortured sound raked past her lips as she recalled the anger in Torcuil's face when he'd told her that he needed nothing from her.

Nothing.

Wearily, she hauled herself to her feet. Without thinking, she followed the only light in the room. The path of moonlight led her to the window. As she gazed up at the bright silver orb nestled in its black sky, she couldn't remember ever feeling so alone. Not even when her mother had deserted and her father had retreated into his work. It had been the need of the staff for harmony in the house that had given Verity purpose. The need of the staff. The irony of that thought brought a hiccuping sob. Her need as well.

The door to her chamber quietly opened. Sunk in her unhappiness, she almost hoped it was an assassin.

Large, familiar hands gently turned her from the window. She looked away, unwilling for Torcuil to see her tearstained face, but a fingertip coaxed her back. Her eyes met his.

"Sweet Aobh," he breathed roughly, regret keen in his voice. " 'Twas I who did this to ye."

She dropped her gaze. "I did it to myself."

"Verity, I beg yer forgiveness," he said softly.

She tried to pull free of his hold, and he released her. Placing a distance of several paces between them, she stopped. Drawing the tattered remains of her pride around her, she drew herself up to her full height. "You're forgiven. Now, please go."

He stood there looking at her, his hands by his sides. Moonlight limned him in silver, casting much of him in silhouette darkness. She saw his throat work.

"Ye frightened me, Anemone," he said hoarsely.

She stared at him. "I frightened you? Coming to you like a . . . a . . . *doxie*—"

"Don't!"

"Worse than a doxie. You only saw *her* b-b-breasts. I forced to you see—"

In two short steps he crossed the span between them and took her arms in his hands. "Verity, don't do this. 'Twas a gift, what ye gave me. A priceless gift. And it . . . well—" He released a harsh breath and drew another before he met her gaze—"it terrified me."

Her short bark of laughter broke into a sob, and she blinked rapidly up at the ceiling. "Oh, come now."

"Have I ever lied to ye?"

She swallowed. "I don't know, Torcuil. Once I thought you would never lie. But then, what is there to lie *about*? You've never really told me anything."

"I've wanted to. Och, Anemone, so many times I've wanted to confide in ye. But—"

She hung on his word.

"I canna do that. For many reasons."

Verity tilted up her chin in challenge. "Name one."

He nodded. "Verra well. Here's one reason: ye'd ne'er believe me."

"Ridiculous. Name another."

Torcuil looked down at his hands, still clasping her upper arms. "Ye'd be afraid of me. Or disgusted. But ye'd have no wish to abide with me."

Her eyes traced the beloved lines of his face. She saw unhappiness there. "Are you a cannibal?" she asked with feigned lightness.

He frowned. "Nay, o' course not."

"Have you slain your father? Married your mother?"

Torcuil drew his head back, clearly repelled. "By the sacred well of Nechtan, Verity, I'm no monster."

Her smile surprised her, and with it came a lightening of her heart. "There. You have said it, yourself. You're not a monster. And, you see, I'm only afraid of, or disgusted, by . . . monsters." Her eyes searched his face, looking for some sympathetic spark. "I could never believe you were a monster, Torcuil. If you'll let me, I'd like to help. Whatever it is that concerns you so, we can face it together."

Hesitantly, as if he feared she might resist, Torcuil drew her to him. Seeing his uncertainty, she allowed him to cradle her against his body. She rested her cheek against his chest, wondering if, after all this, he would still break her heart.

"The decision is no just mine to make, Anemone. I can only ask for yer patience. But come what may, I want ye to believe this: ye're dear to me. And . . . well . . . I have lied to ye, ye see."

Surprised, she lifted her head to look at him.

He solemnly met her gaze. "I do need ye, Verity. I want ye, and . . . I love ye."

"Oh, Torcuil." Her throat closed on his name.

He kissed her. His lips moved over hers in an act of contrition, a tender pledge. She accepted, even knowing there was much yet to be settled between them.

"Are you sure," she said, torn between laughter and tears, "that you're not only saying this to keep me from returning to your chamber?"

He touched his forehead to hers and groaned. "If ye only knew how hard it was no to just lay ye down and have my wicked way wi' ye, ye'd no be talkin' so lightly of it."

"You have no idea how difficult it was for me to take off my dressing gown in front of you," she admitted shyly.

He chuckled raggedly. "I thought my heart had stopped for good when that gown fell off and ye stood there, as fair as a pearl, bare and perfect." He groaned again. "I can see ye still, so clearly in my mind, Anemone. 'Tis no a good subject for discussion."

She looked down at his long-fingered hands. "I'd never dreamed there could be such pleasure between a man and a woman."

He cleared his throat. "Verity . . ."

"But you took no release for yourself."

"Enough."

A sense of power grew in her, and she couldn't help teasing him a little more. "Are you certain, Torcuil? I could help. Just tell me what to do."

He nibbled behind her ear, then slanted his mouth across hers in a long, leisurely, thorough kiss. When he released her, Verity was breathless and dizzy.

"There's no but one way I wish to take my release," he told her, "and that's by plantin' myself deep inside ye."

"Oh."

"Aye. 'Oh.' If the time comes when I can take it, I swear, ye'll be the first to know."

She nodded.

"Good night, sweet Anemone."

"Good night," she replied faintly, still a little dizzy.

He closed the door silently behind him. Verity stumbled to her bed and fell in.

That Torcuil MacCodrum certainly knew how to apologize.

Torcuil made his way back toward his room, amazed at how much better he felt knowing Verity had forgiven him. More, knowing she understood how important she was to him. For the first time, he wondered if there might be hope for them. He wasn't a cannibal. He had *not* murdered his father or married his mother. Mayhap not all land folk had such a disgust for those unlike them. Indeed, along the coasts of Scotland and Ireland, land folk had once revered silkies. His mouth tightened.

Before they'd started to kill them for the sake of a few fish. As if any silkie would be heartless enough to steal some struggling fisherman's catch. No. There were seals, and then there were silkies. Two very different creatures.

Deep in thought, Torcuil almost ran into Seumus.

"I dinna mean to startle ye, lad, but there's been a development."

"Aye?"

Seumus nodded. "There's a lass in the kitchen. Claims her name is Mary, and that ye met her at the Light Lady. Says she has a bit of information for ye."

"Mary?" Torcuil searched his memory. Lately, there had been so many new names to remember. "Does she look like a doxie, Seumus?"

"She appears a wee down on her luck, aye, that she does. Bold and sassy as ye please, though."

Torcuil started toward the back stairs. "Did she come alone?"

"No, she came with Dolly." Seumus hurried to keep pace with Torcuil. "She's afeared, Torcuil, but she'll no talk to anyone but ye. And I think ye should know, she's already insulted Fearghus twice."

"By the sacred well—! Best we get to her before he tricks her into speaking one of his incantations. Columbine said the last fellow who insulted Fearghus wound up as a crow."

"Aye, he did," Seumus agreed. "But he deserved his fate, and no mistake."

When they arrived in the kitchen, they found Mary and Fearghus squared off, with Columbine and Dolly doing their best to keep the situation from exploding.

"Here, now, everyone calm down. Fearghus, I expect better o' ye. Ye're a gentleman now."

"Aye, well, she's no a lady!" Fearghus declared.

"You little wart!" Mary cried, and flung herself in his direction.

Dolly jerked on her arm. "Siddown," she commanded. Mary lowered herself onto a stool next to Dolly. "Ye've no cause to behave like this," Dolly continued. "Dressed like ye are, and considering the hour, no one would have let you into any decent house. Look like a tart, you do. And you about to be a mum." Dolly clucked her disapproval. "Sit up proper, now. Slouching's not good for the babe."

Sure enough, Mary was breeding. Sitting down, her belly took on more distinctive proportions than when she was standing. Dolly had been right all along.

"Good eve to ye, Mary. Dolly, are ye well?"

She beamed. "Fine as a new fiddle. Me chop house is well, too. Well enough to take on a bit more help, and Mary, here, has a mind to get out of her present line o' work. Wants to be respectable-like."

Torcuil smiled. "Good news, indeed. For both o' ye. How may I help ye, then?"

"It's us what wants to help you, dearie." Dolly nudged Mary with her elbow. "Go ahead and tell him, Mary. Don't be shy. We're among friends, here."

With a last dark look at Fearghus, Mary turned her attention to Torcuil. "Benny's left the inn. He's taken quarters not far from St. James Street."

Torcuil leaned back against the work table. "How do ye know this, Mary?"

"He don't think much of his girls. Believes we live in fear of him." She shrugged. "Which we pretty much do. So he talks in front of us, sometimes."

"What did Benny say?" Torcuil prompted.

"Said his money had come in, and he was going to be a toff."

"Anything else?"

She thought a minute. "He did say something about his trip to Devon—"

Torcuil straightened. "When did he go to Devon?"

"Few weeks ago. Came back smug as a cat filled with cream." Mary made a face. "Nasty bugger."

"What did you hear him say about his trip?"

"That his new business partner was not going to get rid o' Benny as easy as he thought."

"Did he mention the name of this business partner?"

Slowly she shook her head, as if she were still searching her memory. "No," she said finally.

"Nothing about John Good?"

"Nothing."

"Verra well." Torcuil walked over to where Dolly and Mary stood. He pressed a coin into Mary's palm and thanked her. When he tried to give Dolly money, too, she shook her head.

"Oh, no. I'll not be taking more from you, Torcuil MacCodrum. You've given me near all that I own, already." She smiled. "You've given me a better life, you have, and I won't forget that." She plucked the coin from Mary's hand, ignoring Mary's small cry of protest. "It's a husband Mary'll be needing, and soon. This bit of gold will be her dowry." She gave Mary a stern look. " 'Tis more'n many women ever have."

After Dolly and Mary left, escorted by Dolly's hired jack-of-all-trades, who had been waiting in their wagon outside, Torcuil returned to his chamber. As he stripped off his clothes, he considered what Mary had told him, trying to fit the pieces of the puzzle into place.

That Benny had been hired by a "new business partner" to murder John Good—or, rather, Richard Dare—he doubted not at all. The assassins the man had engaged had all failed, which made him a poor agent. And Torcuil had never believed that Dare was the real enemy. That had been borne out by Alice Dare. Ravenshaw had not recognized the name. Indeed, he'd only been to Devon twice, neither time coming into contact with any of the miners.

Torcuil discounted the idea that the marquess's enemy had given up, which meant that a new agent would soon be at work. Or that someone was already in place, set to strike when the command was given.

That thought sent a chill through Torcuil, yet the idea made the most sense. Time was running out. The marquess had already called on all but one partner. If this last man could be swayed to the marquess's point of view, the vote would go in Ravenshaw's favor, and Coristock would be kept open.

As he settled back among the bedcovers, Torcuil knew that tomorrow he must again take up the search for Eideard.

And somewhere, soon, he must find a body of undefiled water and undergo The Change.

20

Fire is the test of gold, adversity of strong men.
—Seneca

The marquess spent the following four evenings in the company of Neul, at various balls, suppers, and musicales. Then, as scheduled, he departed for Outhwaite's estate in Norfolk. Ravenshaw, Verity, Kingston, and Torcuil rode in the first coach, Seumus, Fearghus, and Columbine in the second. Each of their mounted escort went armed.

None of Torcuil's inquiries had turned up information regarding the direction Eideard had taken when he'd left London. That he had been at a coaching inn on a main route out of town was all that Torcuil knew. Perhaps the gods would smile and the road to Norwich would be the right one.

They followed the turnpike, heading toward Norwich, the town closest to their destination. Their first night on the road was spent at an inn, where they discovered that Neul and her small entourage of servants were also guests.

The marquess had taken the meeting as a stroke of good fortune and was further delighted when he learned that she, too, was traveling to Norwich. Torcuil considered the whole thing suspicious, and certainly no coincidence, as Neul would have them believe. Over a merry dinner, the marquess and Neul agreed that she should travel with the Ravenshaw party.

From all appearances, she adored the marquess, and the marquess, for his part, behaved as if he were smitten. Neul's affection seemed to extend to Verity, as well. She frequently solicited Verity's opinion and even offered the loan of a shawl that she said would be perfect with a gown Verity wore.

At every stop, Torcuil asked if anyone had seen a tall, dark-haired Scot. His efforts proved fruitless.

The night before they arrived at their hotel in Norwich, where they would stay during the marquess's discussion with Lord Outhwaite, Torcuil saw Verity to her chamber. As usual, with witnesses all around, he was forced to content himself with meaningful gazes and a chaste, if lingering, kiss on her hand.

As he walked back to his own bedchamber, down the dimly lighted hallway, Torcuil felt restless and ill-tempered. Kisses were no longer enough. He wanted more. He needed more. Much more. He would make a better husband for Verity than that bottom feeder, Sheldrake.

The idea stunned him into stopping midstride. Marry Verity? For the first time, he didn't automatically thrust the idea away as impossible. Instead, he turned it over in his mind, considering, as he let himself into his chamber.

Neul sat in the dark.

"What are ye doin' here?" he demanded as he closed the door.

She flicked her fingers, and a flame appeared on the

wicks of myriad candles around the room. "I keep forgetting silkies see in the dark."

Torcuil stood where he was, silently studying her, wondering at her real purpose for this visit. She had never before acknowledged that she knew he was a silkie, though he'd have thought it strange if she didn't know.

"You don't like me very much, do you?" she asked, gracefully rising to her feet.

"I dinna know ye well enough to dislike ye." His gaze followed her as she strolled around the small, plain chamber.

"Very well. You don't *trust* me, then." She moved an index finger, and the room tripled in size.

Torcuil frowned. "What game are ye playin' with Ravenshaw, Neul?" he asked bluntly.

Her eyes widened, and he could have sworn he saw hurt in their depths. He shook his head. Ridiculous. Faeries didn't feel hurt or remorse, or many of the other emotions others suffered—did they?

She glanced down at the pine table beside the bed. Instantly, it was transformed into an elegant rosewood side table. "What do you know of faeries, Torcuil?"

"Only what I've heard," he answered cautiously.

"We are the most powerful of the fair folk."

He watched her from beneath hooded eyes. "Aye. So I've been told."

"The other fair folk fear us," she said, turning to face him.

Torcuil made no reply.

She smiled. "Perhaps I should say, other fair folk, save the silkies. More often they are merely wary. Are you wary, Torcuil?"

"A powerful stranger has taken a sudden, pointed interest in two people I admire," he said, his voice low and deep. "A powerful stranger who is rumored to be temperamental, unpredictable, and careless with the lives of mortals. Aye, I'm wary."

Neul touched the washstand. It altered into beautifully carved ebony with a ewer and basin of faceted Irish crystal. "A sudden interest. Yes." She turned to face him from the middle of the room. "The first time I saw Philip I felt as if I'd been struck by lightning." She smiled softly at the memory. "He looked so handsome, standing there with you and Verity, with his marvelous thick, white hair. His fine gray eyes. He stood apart from all those cattle, those men who had fawned on me, touched me." She shivered. "It diminished their dignity. It diminished my dignity. I felt as if I couldn't *breathe*."

Torcuil had experienced that feeling several times since his arrival in London, and he nodded his understanding. Too many people in too little space. He didn't see how land folk tolerated it. Then he remembered Verity telling him she preferred country living. Perhaps not all land folk enjoyed a crush.

"He danced so well," Neul continued. "I do like dancing, don't you? He told me things—interesting things. Did you know that their government has parties? And that Philip is a member of something called the House of Lords?" Her eyes looked off into the distance. "He made me feel special." She shook her head, and silvery blond ringlets danced. "Not like some prize to be won away from the next man, or a rare creature to be put in a glass cage. Philip made me feel as if I were . . . cherished. Protected." A wobbly chuckle escaped her lips. "*Me*, cherished—and protected of all things!" She sighed. "I quite adore it. I quite adore *him*."

"And when ye tire of him?" Torcuil asked softly. "What happens then? He's been hurt once, Neul, by his wife."

"What makes you think I'll hurt this wonderful man?"

"He's more than yer 'wonderful man,' Neul. He's a *good* man. He has courage and a sense of justice—"

"Spoken like a true silkie. Self-righteous as ever."

Torcuil scowled. "Self-righteous, is it?"

She waved her fingertips over the squat, lumpy bed, and a second later, a gorgeously draped tester bed stood in its place. "That's right. Silkies have a reputation among the fair folk, did you know that?"

Self-righteous? Is that what he was? Judgmental? Had he judged land folk too harshly? Held them to impossible standards? Perhaps expecting their young breed to conform to the standards of peoples far older than they was unjust. Like children, perhaps they needed time to mature. And like children, sometimes they needed guidance. But who was there to guide them when all the more ancient races had pulled away?

"I know of only one silkie who isn't self-righteous," Neul said, tapping her slippered toe on the worn floorboards. Suddenly she and Torcuil were standing on green-veined marble tiles.

He barely noticed. "What is the name of this silkie ye know?"

She looked up. Her eyes met his. "Eideard MacCodrum, of Clan MacCodrum."

Torcuil took a step toward her before he stopped himself. "Eideard! Where is he?"

"That I cannot say. But he stayed with me while he was in London." She sadly shook her head. "Poor boy. His stay in London was quite tumultuous. Such an innocent! Not fortunate enough to have Verity's subtle protection and guidance, as you've had."

Torcuil knew it was true. Verity had protected him against ridicule and awkward situations. She had guided him into her society with a deft hand. He smiled dryly as that word came to him. Guided. He, a son of one of the most ancient races, had been as lost as a child before she, a daughter of rambunctious youth, had come to his aid.

"I have strong feelings for Philip," Neul said solemnly. "What I feel may even be love. I've never been in love before. I know only that I can't stay away from him. I want to be with him. I want to hear him laugh. The sound of his voice, it . . . makes me happy." She looked up at him, asking Torcuil with her eyes to understand.

He did understand. He almost smiled.

She moved across the marble floor to lay a slim hand on his arm. "I suspect Philip is in danger of some kind. I've asked him, but he won't speak of it."

"How did you know?"

"The armed outriders. The armed coachmen. I saw them come into the inn. Philip doesn't strike me as a man to worry unnecessarily."

"He is in danger. So is Verity."

"Who—?"

A knock on the door interrupted Neul.

"Torcuil?" came Verity's voice, soft and close to the door.

He looked around the fabulous room. This was no coaching inn bedchamber. Neul waved him toward the door. Carefully, he opened it a crack, hoping Verity wouldn't see the countless candles and the sumptuous size and trappings of the ensorcelled room.

"Ye should be all tucked up in yer bed by now, Verity," he said. "It's no safe for ye to wander about by yerself." He stuck his head out of the door and scowled down the hall. "Where's Columbine?"

"Asleep. Even she is exhausted."

He glanced back into his room and saw with relief that it had been returned to its original state. Neul had vanished. Then he looked up and down the corridor. When he found no one to witness an indiscretion, he hurried Verity inside. He was surprised to find her attired in her night chemise and dressing gown.

"I've been having a nightmare, Torcuil," she told him in a small voice. "Please hold me."

Concerned at this uncustomary insecurity, Torcuil sat down on the side of the bed and cradled her in his lap, against his chest.

Her arms wrapped around his torso and clung to him as if she feared the consequences of letting go. "I've been having the same horrid dream for the past two nights. I fear something terrible is going to happen."

Torcuil stroked her unbound hair, wanting to comfort her. "Have ye ever had a dream come true before?" he asked, ruling urgency from his voice.

"No."

He released a silent breath of relief. "Then 'tis doubtful this dream shall come to pass."

She worried her bottom lip between her teeth. "But what if it does?"

He kissed the top of her head. "Then ye'll have more to worrit about than what actually happens."

She turned her face up to him, anxiety etching every sweet feature. His heart twisted at the sight of it.

"What do you mean?" she asked.

He smiled to allay her fear. What would it be like to hold her in his arms whenever she woke in the night? To banish her fears with tender patience and, afterward, with passion? "Och, pay me no mind, Anemone. Tell me about this fearsome dream. Perhaps the tellin' of it will make it less monstrous."

She cleared her throat. "It may sound silly."

"Nay, dear heart. I'll take it for what it is—a dream."

"Very well. We enter Lord Outhwaite's house—"

"Have ye ever been there?"

"No. But in my dream it's an enormous, old brick

house. The sky is dark. Papa is in the library with Lord
Outhwaite. Then they come out and announce to us that
Lord Outhwaite will cast his vote for keeping the mine
open. Suddenly all the candles blow out, as if by the
breath of some terrible demon." She shivered. "And then,
when we manage to again light the candles, we find Papa
dead." She turned her face into Torcuil's waistcoat. "I
know this is foolish of me," she said, her words muffled.

"Dinna fash yerself, Anemone. 'Tis a terrible dream, to
be sure." He felt a tremor go through her and stroked her
back more vigorously. "Ye know I'll do everything in my
power to keep yer father safe."

She nodded, her face buried against his chest. "I don't
think I can ever get back to sleep. I wish I had a tiny bit of
brandy. That's what Papa uses when he can't sleep."

Suddenly, an incongruous memory rushed into his
mind. The memory that had been eluding him for so long.
The scent of brandy mingled with the heavy, sweet smell
of laudanum. "Didna Mr. MacDougall say yer father
would be better off without the laudanum?"

Verity raised her head. Her eyebrows drew down
slightly in clear puzzlement at this jump in topic. "Yes."

"So he's no been takin' the stuff?"

"No, of course not. He's followed Mr. MacDougall's
instructions most scrupulously."

"That ye know of."

"Well, yes," she conceded.

If the marquess hadn't taken laudanum, then someone
had slipped it into his drink. Laudanum, Torcuil knew
from having talked with Mr. MacDougall, could produce a
very sound sleep. To one of the land folk, whose sense of
smell was not acute and who refused to sniff their food or
drink, the odor of the opium would likely have been
masked by the brandy.

Verity nestled closer, and Torcuil struggled with his

body's rampant reaction to her soft bottom pressing against the crux of his groin.

A few minutes later, Verity finally fell asleep, and he carried her back to her chamber, where he tucked her into her bed.

Likely her dream was just a nightmare, he told himself firmly.

But another part of him worried that it might be a portent.

The following morning, as they gathered around the tables in their private dining area, Ravenshaw announced only he and Kingston would ride over to Outhwaite's estate. The outcry was immediate and loud, Torcuil's protest the most strenuous, his alarm ignited by all that he knew. But it was Neul who enticed the marquess's cooperation.

"Philip, my darling, that is quite selfish of you," she announced airily as she spread marmalade on a wedge of toast.

After facing down everyone else's direct protest, this reasoning seemed to catch him off his guard.

"Eh? Selfish?"

Having garnered his full attention, she proceeded to nip off a tiny bit of the sweetened toast, lifting her full upper lip slightly to reveal to him the merest edge of her straight, white teeth. His gaze glued to the sight.

She smiled as she swallowed the tiny morsel. "You know how much I love to visit these country estates."

"I do?"

Neul leaned toward him and smoothed her hand over his shoulder, as if brushing out a wrinkle in his impeccably fitted coat. "I thought I'd told you. I delight in touring such places. And this would be the first house on the sea that I've visited. But more than that"—her eyes met his directly—"I wish to watch you conduct your important business."

"Important business, you say? Yes. Er, uh . . . quite. It *is* important." His face flushed with pleasure, the marquess cleared his throat. "But I should think you'd find it deadly dull, my sweet. You can't very well be present while Outhwaite and I debate, you know."

"Of course. Two men deciding the fate of thousands—"

"Actually, only hundreds—"

"—of lives. I could wander through this residence, imagining you doing manly things."

"Manly things?"

She slowly nodded. "Sometimes I believe you forget how powerful you are, beloved. But Outhwaite never shall, after today. Perhaps it is greedy of me, but I wish to be with you to savor your success while it is fresh."

He gave her a pointed, skeptical look.

Neul flushed. "Oh, very well. I just want to be with you. Is that so terrible?"

"No. But you seem very certain that I shall succeed. Isted did not."

She shrugged her slim shoulders. "Isted is motivated only by self-interest. You are moved by far more worthy reasons. Your honor and mercy will elevate you to an eloquence Lord Outhwaite will be unable to resist."

Torcuil shot Neul a suspicious glance. Did she intend to interfere with the decisions of mortals? His uncles had told him that faeries often delighted in such tampering.

The marquess sighed in resignation. "Very well, my dear Neul. You may all accompany me."

Against all propriety, Neul lifted the marquess's hand and pressed into his palm a lingering kiss. Ravenshaw smiled, blushing like an awkward stripling. Verity suddenly found her meal fascinating, but Torcuil saw the upward curve of her sweet lips. Seumus, Columbine,

Fearghus, and Kingston grinned, while Daniel and Teak stared in surprise.

Soon after the meal, as everyone was preparing to depart for Outhwaite's estate, Torcuil sought to single out the marquess, to ask if he had taken laudanum the night of the attempted burglary. With so much commotion going on in preparation of departure, his efforts proved futile. He did not, however, fail to notice that Kingston was sticking to Ravenshaw as never before. Strangely, the impression Torcuil came away with was that the bodyguard seemed more interested in keeping his employer and Torcuil separated than in staying with the marquess for any reasons of protection.

Torcuil did manage a few minutes alone with Neul.

"What is it, dear Torcuil?" She looked up at him. "Must silkies be so tall? I vow, it quite puts a kink in my neck trying to see your face."

"Ye dinna plan to use yer faery magic to influence Outhwaite's decision, do ye?" he asked, ignoring what he saw as a preposterous complaint. Of course silkies were tall. They were supposed to be. " 'Twould no be right, Neul, and well ye know it."

She toyed with her fan. "I had thought of it. After all, imposing the outcome of this meeting would be so easy. And I would do anything to make Philip happy." Her mouth curved up at one corner. "But I find I am loath to tamper in this matter that is so important to him." She chuckled. "I've never before suffered the restrictions mortals and silkies impose on themselves—their peculiar definitions of right and wrong. Faeries have their own ethics, which have little to do with other races." Neul's pale eyebrows drew down in a frown that reflected her perplexity. "No, I shall not tamper. It seems to me it would be . . . disrespectful . . . of Philip." Her expression cleared. "So I shall amuse myself as I told him—touring the house. Verity is excellent company. She's fretful over this, so perhaps I can help to distract her."

Torcuil found some of his reserve toward the faery dissolve. Mayhap she truly cared about Verity and her father after all. "I thank ye, Neul."

She tapped his arm with her fan. "Keep him safe, silkie."

As the coaches rumbled down the gravel carriage sweep, Torcuil was relieved to see Outhwaite's house was made of stone, not brick, nor did it look very old. It was, however, enormous. It dwarfed Ravenshaw House, though Daniel, apparently unimpressed, pointed out that the marquess's London residence was not one of his larger houses.

The host, who had never taken a mate, came out to greet them as everyone climbed out of the carriages. To Torcuil's surprise, Outhwaite didn't look like a spineless creature at all, despite Isted's description of him. The man who stood a little taller than the marquess was stocky, and looked to be in his middle years. His eyebrows were extraordinarily bushy.

"Damn me, Ravenshaw, did you bring all of London to my doorstep?" he demanded gruffly. Despite his words, it was clear that he was not displeased.

The marquess performed the introductions, and then everyone entered the house. The interior of the place proved to be considerably less magnificent than Ravenshaw House, yet still grand, leaving one with an impression of lustrous dark wood, crystal chandeliers, and striped silk upholstery.

Though Torcuil tried, he could not manage to get the marquess alone to ask his question about the laudanum. Once again, Kingston moved to unobtrusively cut the marquess away from him, and Torcuil decided the answer to his question no longer mattered. His suspicions about the former Bow Street Runner were sufficient to warrant additional precautions.

Quietly, he arranged for Seumas, Fearghus, Columbine, and Neul to surround Verity with their protection. So when Kingston tried to shut him out of the library, where Outhwaite and the marquess arranged themselves for their discussion, Torcuil struck the door with the butt of his hand so hard, the door cracked a surprised Boniface Kingston in the face.

Ravenshaw looked up from his notes in surprise when he saw Torcuil stride into the room. "My daughter—"

"Is safe," Torcuil said flatly, refusing to be denied. He didn't know what Kingston was up to, but he'd not stake the marquess's life on it. The former Bow Street Runner was behaving too strangely. And Torcuil's suspicion that Kingston had drugged the marquess was too strong to ignore.

"What is this, Ravenshaw?" Outhwaite asked, clearly surprised to see the two men ranged beside the marquess. "Don't tell me you have bodyguards?" He barked a laugh. "What are they protecting you from? *Me?*"

With a daggered glance toward Torcuil, whom he must feel had drawn attention to the fact, the marquess reluctantly explained. He told of the assassination attempts, as well as the danger to Verity. As he spoke, their host's face grew darker. By the time Ravenshaw had concluded his account, Outhwaite had calmed. He politely invited the marquess to say what he'd come to say.

Ravenshaw spoke so eloquently that Torcuil found it difficult not to be distracted by the marquess's arguments for converting Coristock to a copper mine. When Kingston tried to get next to the marquess, Torcuil prevented it. The anger he saw in the Runner's eyes warned him that he had an enemy.

The two peers debated the merits of risking further investment into the mine. The clock on the table indicated that they had been closeted for two hours when the discussion wound down.

Tense silence filled the room as they awaited Outhwaite's decision. Several minutes passed before their host spoke.

"I had decided to abstain from the vote," he said, slowly at first. "I felt emotions had run too high over something in which I had little interest. I didn't wish to be pulled into a lot of bickering." His eyes met those of the marquess. "I will tell you that I had distinct reservations about agreeing to your coming here. That ass, Isted, had already paid me a visit that left a decidedly bad taste in my mouth. But I wanted to be fair."

He rose to his feet. "Damn me, I *am* going to vote! Threatening a man's life—and worse, that of his daughter—is not to be tolerated! From what you say, I wouldn't be surprised to learn that Cowen was murdered over his opposition to closing the mine." He struck the mahogany table with his fist. "It's one thing to abstain when you don't wish to be bothered. It's quite another to abstain from cowardice." He thrust his open hand toward the marquess. "As of this moment, sir, you have my support. I will vote to invest the additional monies in Coristock to keep it open."

Torcuil heard the faint click of a key in a lock, and saw that Kingston had incarcerated them in the room. He also saw the cocked pistol in the man's hand, aimed at Ravenshaw.

Instinctively, Torcuil threw himself at the marquess just as Kingston's pistol flashed, its noise deafening in the paneled room. Pain exploded in Torcuil's side. His momentum carried him and the marquess to the carpeted floor. The landing drove stars before his eyes.

"Down!" he shouted at Outhwaite, who dove for the floor.

Torcuil rolled and came to his feet, his own pistol drawn. His first shot missed Kingston when the other man dodged away.

Kingston aimed a second loaded pistol at Outhwaite, but ducked behind a display case of sea shells when Torcuil drew a second pistol of his own. He fired through the glass and wood case, and was rewarded with Kingston's cry.

With one bleeding, unsteady arm, Kingston tried to aim around the side of the shattered case. Torcuil whipped the knife from his boot and sent it flying, straight into Kingston's upper arm. Kingston's pistol discharged as it struck the floor. The ball burrowed into the carpet a foot from Outhwaite's nose.

Drawing the knife from his other boot, Torcuil launched himself at Kingston. They crashed to the floor, knocking over a tall cabinet, scattering books in all directions.

Suddenly the library door slammed open, revealing Neul standing in the hall. Behind her crowded the others, their eyes wide with disbelief.

Instantly, Torcuil returned his attention to Kingston. "Who sent ye?" he ground out, the dark wine of his warrior's blood surging through him, mingling with his pain.

White-faced and panting, Kingston glared at him. "Bastard. You just had to interfere, didn't you? Curse you, you've ruined everything."

As Neul and Verity rushed to the marquess, and Seumus assisted Outhwaite, Torcuil gathered his feet under him and hauled Kingston up along with him as he stood.

He slammed Kingston against a wall and held him there. "Och, well, I'm sorry I've spoilt yer plans. Now, ye'll tell me what I want to know."

Kingston told him what he could do in the coarsest of terms.

Torcuil bared his teeth with a savage, humorless smile. "Aye, well, that's not an option ye'll have, is it now?" He notched Kingston's earlobe with the tip of his blade.

Behind him, he heard Neul order Columbine to take Verity from the room. Verity protested sharply, but her father joined with Neul in having his daughter removed from the library. Torcuil was glad for it.

Kingston's ear bled freely. Torcuil considered it for a moment, then took stock of the culprit's other, more extreme wounds. He pressed his thumb into the deep slash in Kingston's upper arm.

Kingston screamed.

"Who sent ye?" Torcuil asked again, his voice soft and deadly. "Yer last chance to answer while ye still possess all yer extremities."

Kingston's eyes grew wide as he whimpered with pain. "What . . . what do you mean—extremities?"

"Och, now, I should think that's obvious. Fingers. Hands. Yer manly bits."

Kingston squeezed his eyes shut. "Oh, God," he moaned. "He's not worth it. Nothing's worth it."

Torcuil lowered his blade, setting it against Kingston's groin with just enough pressure to convince the assassin of its location. "Tell me," he invited.

"Sheldrake," Kingston sobbed. "Sheldrake hired me. I was to move only if the men Dare hired failed to kill Ravenshaw. He proved incompetent, and Sheldrake had him killed—a lesson to me."

"Sheldrake, that foul toad!" came Verity's indignant voice at the doorway.

The marquess stepped up beside Torcuil. "Why would Sheldrake want me dead?"

"He wants the mine," Kingston wailed. "Please, don't cut me," he begged Torcuil.

"Why?" the marquess inquired.

"Be-be-because he wanted to buy it cheap. Once it's closed for a whi-while, the miners will be willing to work for next to nothing. He knew there was copper there, and he knew he could make an enormous pr-prof-f-fit. And he needs the money. He's in debt up to his arse."

"And Cowen?" the marquess asked.

"I broke his neck, then pushed him down the stairs, so it looked like an accident."

"Also for Sheldrake?"

"Yes!"

"What were ye plannin' to do here?"

Hatred burned in every line of Kingston's face. "I was going to kill Ravenshaw and Outhwaite, and escape through the window. *You* got in the way."

"Aye," Torcuil said, his voice soft with restraint. "And the burglar, as long as ye're makin' a clean breast of it. Why did Dare send a burglar?"

Suddenly the strength seemed to leak out of the assassin. "'Twas to throw you off. I was to have done Ravenshaw then and blamed it on the thief," he said wearily.

"Was that why ye drugged his brandy? So there'd be no struggle when you killed him and it would look as if the burglar killed him in his sleep?"

Kingston nodded. "You're bloody troublesome, MacCodrum."

Torcuil yanked Kingston away from the wall. "Have ye a place t' put him until yer authorities can deal with him?" he asked Outhwaite.

The partner instructed his own men, who had just

arrived, where to lock him. Servants bearing pistols bore
the bleeding man away.

"You saved Philip," Neul told Torcuil in a low voice,
pitched only for his ears. "You have my eternal gratitude.
For your gift of Philip's life, I give one to you in return. I
am breaking a promise I gave, a pledge that I would tell no
one."

He waited, somehow knowing what she was going to
say before the words were uttered.

"I know where your brother is."

21

A man's character is his fate.
—Heraclitus

Torcuil dismounted from Wind Teaser in front of the manor house on the coast of Essex. Impatient with the slow progress of the carriages, he had ridden on ahead of Verity, her father, Neul, and the others.

Torcuil wanted time alone with his brother. When he broke the news that he was not going back to their people, his older brother was certain to express his outrage. The fewer witnesses the better.

The house was half the size of Ravenshaw House and much older. It appeared well cared for, but it made no claim to splendor.

Taking the two steps in one stride, he knocked on the front door. Immediately it opened. The servant's eyes grew large.

"Aye, I see ye recognize my kinship with Eideard MacCodrum," Torcuil observed, not waiting for an invitation into the house. "Take me to my brother at once."

"I—that is to say, sir—"

A tall, dark-haired man stood at the far portal of the entry hall. "Thank you, Tims. That will be all for now."

Quickly Tims bowed and left.

The brothers regarded each other for a long moment.

"Hello, Little Brother," Eideard said solemnly.

Torcuil grinned. "Och, little, is it? I'm as big as ye any day, ye great prawn!"

Finally, Eideard's handsome face broke into a happy grin, and he laughed. They roughly embraced each other, both speaking at once. At last they drew apart.

"What are ye doin' with yer hair in a pigtail?" Torcuil asked. "It looks silly."

"Silly? Look at ye, ye insolent pup! Yer warrior's braids have ribbons in 'em!"

Laughing, Eideard held out his arm, indicating the corridor behind him. "Come. Ye've traveled a long way. Rest yerself and talk with me." He looked around. "Where are yer things?"

"On their way. I dinna wish to wait for the carriages."

Eideard's dark eyes widened. "Oh ho! Carriages, eh? Aren't we grand?" He led Torcuil into a cozy drawing room and offered him something to drink.

"Chocolate, if ye have it."

Eideard went to the embroidered bellpull and gave it a tug. Minutes later the servant Torcuil had rattled entered, and Eideard asked him to fetch a large pot of chocolate.

"And your guest, sir?" the man inquired.

"Enough for the two of us, please, Tims," Eideard said soberly.

"Very good, sir." Tims hastily withdrew.

"Do ye no like tea?" Torcuil asked.

"Nasty stuff. How do they drink it?"

Eideard asked about their mother, about Anndra, about their aunts, uncles, and cousins. He wanted to know if there had been any more raids by fishermen. Torcuil had no chance to ask his own questions, but he didn't miss Eideard's failure to inquire after their father. Likely he'd concluded that their father had sent Torcuil to fetch him back. Still, it seemed odd that the heir and favorite did not even ask. Aware of the carriages on the way, Torcuil knew it was time to talk of important matters.

"Father is ailin', Eideard. I thought he was near dyin' when I left, but I've no felt any break in the blood bond."

Instantly, the elder brother sobered. "Nor I."

" 'Tis time for ye to return to the clan and take yer place as Father's heir. He's asked for ye."

"Torcuil—"

"I won't be goin' with ye," Torcuil blurted. "I'm in love with a land woman, and I wish to take her as my mate."

There. He'd said it. Now let Eideard rage and get it over with before the others arrived.

Eideard's eyes widened. The color drained from his face. "Ye canna, Torcuil," he said, his voice low and strained. "Ye canna stay. Ye *must* return to the clan!"

"I expected yer objection, Brother." In truth, he'd expected a more violent reaction. Anger, not this unsettling, quiet horror.

He continued, determined to lay out his case, as if by doing so he could keep Fate from denying him. "I dinna come to my decision lightly. I know what I relinquish, and I know 'tis no small thing. But she's worth it." Suddenly it was important that Eideard understand. "She's like no one I've ever met." Torcuil leaned forward in his brocade upholstered chair, willing his brother to comprehend what Verity meant to him. "It's no that she's lovely, though she is, as lovely as any faery. Nay, I care for her because she's generous and spirited and charmin' and wise. She's taught me things—wonderful things." He laughed, his heart soaring as he recalled moments spent with Verity. "Things I'd never have suspected land folk possessed!"

Torcuil placed his hand on his brother's still arm. "Eideard, I love her. I dinna want to live without her."

In the distance, he heard the light clink of the tack and the rattle of iron-rimmed wheels on the gravel drive.

A soft knock sounded at the drawing room door. It opened, and Torcuil expected Tims to enter with their chocolate. Instead, a well-dressed young woman stepped inside. She was pretty, with hair the color of copper and skin like the cream Verity poured in his tea whenever chocolate wasn't available. Torcuil rose to his feet, as did his brother.

"Eideard?" she said softly, as if inquiring whether or not she should come in.

Eideard held out his hand to her, and, with a shy smile, she walked across the room to take it. Her eyes shone as she looked at him.

Cold dread trickled into the pit of Torcuil's stomach as he turned his gaze to his brother's face. What he saw there could not be denied. This woman was dear to him.

"Ye're the heir, Eideard," Torcuil said. "Ye must return. Father—"

"*Nay!*" Eideard's single harsh word drove into Torcuil's chest like a blade.

As the two brothers stared at each other, the dread in Torcuil gradually transformed into anger. Then rage.

"Ye *will* return home, Eideard."

Eideard dragged in a deep breath and huffed it out, seeming to recapture his composure in the process. Then he shook his head. "I canna go back. Darling," he said to the woman, his tone gentling, "I wish to present my brother, Torcuil."

Torcuil managed a curt nod. He didn't trust himself to speak.

The woman smiled. "I'm so happy to finally make your acquaintance. Eideard has spoken so often of you."

"Torcuil," Eideard said softly. "I'd like ye to meet Richenda. My wife."

Wife. The word seemed to echo through the room.

Volcanic rage exploded in Torcuil. *"Wife?"*

"Best ye leave now, Richenda," Eideard murmured to her. "My brother and I have much to discuss."

She nodded. As she turned to leave, sunshine pouring through the windows behind her silhouetted the outline of her body. The slight roundness, earlier concealed by the construction of her dress, could not be mistaken. Realization struck a blow to Torcuil's gut.

"Ye bastard," he snarled as soon as she was gone. "Ye've gone and gotten her with child!"

" 'Tis natural between a man and his wife," Eideard said stonily.

"Dinna go an' get all high and mighty wi' *me*. Ye're the bloody heir to a silkie clan!" Torcuil roared, raging against the trap he felt closing around him. "Ye're the favorite of our father. The coddled prince! 'Tis yer place, yer born *duty* t' lead our people."

Eideard glared at him. "Nay, Torcuil. Now it's your duty."

The injustice of it all fed Torcuil's fury. Eideard had been the favored son, the all-important heir, while Torcuil had received their parents' distracted crumbs of affection. Left to find his own place in the clan, Torcuil had practiced and worked and risked his life again and again over the years, hoping to win notice and perhaps even approval from his parents, but all he'd won was the status of the clan's finest warrior. Although he'd never expected to discover anything good during his quest on land, he'd found the treasure of a lifetime—someone who wanted *him,* a woman who had been so determined to make him hers, she had laid siege to his heart until she'd won it.

And now Eideard expected him to go back to shoulder *his* responsibilities of leading the clan. Eideard, who had enjoyed the benefits of being the chief's favored son and had now cast aside his obligations to his parents, his brothers, his aunts, uncles, and cousins, and mated with a land woman.

Torcuil remembered the fiery torture of his struggles to resist making love to Verity and cursed himself for a fool. Like Eideard, he should have taken what he wanted with no thought to his clan.

But he could not.

"Is this why ye hid?" Torcuil demanded. "Half of London looked for ye but none could find ye. Were ye goin' about, trying to learn the ways of land folk as ye were supposed to be doin', I'd have found ye easily enough."

"I did at first," Eideard said. "I moved among the land folk as a Scottish laird, and learned to savor their pleasures . . . and their vices. In gamblin' hells, I increased the money I got from the sale of the ancient necklace and lived high—high enough to frequent the homes of important men. I learned much about their politics—and their attitudes toward other living things. I liked the feel of velvet and satin, the smell of French perfume, the taste of chocolate. And then I met Lady Richenda, the loveliest, most fragile female I'd ever seen."

"And ye mounted her," Torcuil surmised darkly.

"Aye, I dinna deny myself. But I dinna expect to fall in love with her. Like yer Verity, she taught me things. Her gentle, shy ways made me wish to protect her."

"And what of yer people, Eideard? What of them? These are dangerous times, and they need guidance."

"Which ye can give them as well as I."

Tims entered the drawing room, carrying a heavy silver tray loaded with two cups and a silver pot from which wafted the aroma of chocolate.

"Other guests have arrived, sir," he informed Eideard, who gave him a short nod of acknowledgment. Silently, the servant withdrew.

Torcuil ignored his brother's offer of a filled cup. "Have ye even told her what ye are?"

"I have."

"Before or after ye wed wi' her?"

Eideard scowled. "Before."

"And did she still choose to take ye as her mate, or was it a matter of necessity?"

Eideard set down his cup with a heavy thud. "Ye go too far, Brother."

Torcuil lifted an eyebrow. "Necessity, was it? How did her father feel about that?"

"It was *not* necessity," Eideard informed him stiffly. "Richenda didna start breedin' until we'd been wed several months. But . . ."

"Aye?"

"We eloped. Her father didna ken we'd wed until the matter was accomplished. Then he couldna find us to do anything about it, because a faery gave us sanctuary." He shrugged. He didn't need to tell Torcuil that if a faery did not wish something found, then found it would not be. "We stayed in her house, just outside of London."

"Neul," Torcuil said, sick with anger and regret. "Ye stayed with Neul."

"Aye. The duke's men could no find us." Eideard picked up his cup and took a swallow of chocolate.

"No one could find ye," Torcuil observed dully. An odd memory slipped into his thoughts. "Do ye know a marquess of Kellaway? He told me he wanted to know when I found ye."

Eideard set down his cup. "I imagine he does. Simon is Richenda's brother."

"He dinna seem verra upset with ye."

"Of course not. He knows I adore his sister."

Torcuil regarded his brother from beneath hooded eyes. This favored son had been spoiled, but had never been so devoid of morals. "What happened to ye, Eideard? Ye're no the man I knew."

Eideard looked away. "I was seldom a man when ye knew me."

"Ye are who ye are, no matter the outer form."

"Well, I like *this* outer form."

White-hot fury surged through Torcuil, and he swung his fist, landing a blow squarely on his brother's jaw. Eideard staggered backward and slammed into the wall. Looking dazed, he slid to the floor.

"I'll never forgive ye for this, Eideard," Torcuil ground out. "Never."

Even as he threw open the door and stormed out into the hall, Torcuil's rage cooled as shock at what he'd done jolted him. Sweet Aobh, he'd struck his own brother.

His world shattered around him, demolishing his hopes. The future he'd wanted with Verity had splintered into razor-sharp shards that lacerated his heart as he realized that he couldn't abandon his people in their time of need.

Torcuil had witnessed the teeming masses of land folk in London. He knew London was just one of many such centers. Someday, in the not too distant future, their ever-increasing numbers would demand more space, need more sources of food. And there would be nowhere to turn to but the seas.

Now more than ever, Clan MacCodrum needed a leader familiar with the ways of land folk. Torcuil was not the son his father wanted, but he was the only one left who might have a chance of saving their people from extinction.

He must return home. He must deliver the news of Eideard's decision to their ailing father.

He must face a lifetime without Verity.

At that last despairing thought, his throat tightened with turbulent emotion, just as Verity, Ravenshaw, Neul, and Seumus walked into the entry hall.

Verity's heart quickened with happiness the instant she saw Torcuil striding toward them. In the next instant, she realized something was terribly wrong. She'd never seen that wild, furious expression on him before. It brought to mind a panther trapped in a hunter's net, panicked and desperate to be free.

He nodded curtly as he passed them, and continued out of the house, his stride hastening, his long legs carrying him swiftly away. Stunned, she watched him vanish around the corner of the manor house, not going to the carriage or even to his horse, but rather toward the gardens and, beyond that, the sea she had seen in the distance from the carriage.

She started after him, but Seumus's gentle hand on her arm stayed her. "Best ye give him a wee bit of time alone," he said.

"What's the matter?" she demanded. "What's happened?" She searched the faces of her father, of Seumus and Neul. Her father appeared as perplexed as she was, so she turned back to Seumus and Neul. "Why is Torcuil upset?"

"That is for him to tell ye, if he chooses," Seumus replied, his expression somber, his eyes sad.

Neul cast a glance at the marquess, then turned her gaze full on Verity, who couldn't remember ever seeing the older woman look so serious.

"I have something to show you . . . and your father," she said quietly. "Please come with me."

Verity turned her head toward the direction Torcuil had gone. "But Torcuil—"

"Come," Neul coaxed softly. "There is something you must see."

"What is all this about, Neul?" the marquess demanded. "First Torcuil's in a rage such as I've never seen, and now you're being mysterious. I, too, would appreciate some answers."

"Patience, my love."

She led them to a secluded part of the gardens, where tall, old hedges and bowers removed them from the view of others, then she urged them to sit on the stone benches.

Her gaze met the marquess's. "Do you love me?" she asked.

Verity stared at Neul, and then her father. Anyone could see they felt great affection for each other, but she had no idea it had developed into love.

A crimson stain flooded the marquess's face. "I have said it, have I not?" he countered gruffly.

A tender smile curved Neul's lips. "Yes, my love. Please remember that." Then, she turned away and held out her arms, her fingers working.

With a soft pop of air, Roger Sheldrake appeared on the garden path in front of her.

Verity and her father shot up from the bench, exclaiming at once. Seumus remained calmly seated.

Attired as if he were taking a stroll in the park, Sheldrake looked around frantically. "Where am I?"

The marquess vaulted across the short distance between him and the baron. "Villain!" He seized Sheldrake by his stock and began shaking him.

Seumus gently but firmly pulled the enraged marquess off Sheldrake.

"Will I never be rid of you?" the baron demanded, straightening his stock. "Now that you're dead, you insist on plaguing me in my dreams as well?"

"Are you dreaming?" Neul asked.

"I must be," Sheldrake snapped. "I was just leaving my house in the carriage—" He scowled. "But what are *you* doing here?" he demanded of Seumus.

"I'm not dead, Sheldrake," the marquess said flatly. "Your attempt to have me assassinated failed."

Sheldrake's eyes widened. "Who—? How—? Where's your bodyguard?"

"You mean your hired killer? He's in the hands of the authorities, as you shall soon be!"

"No, he's not," Neul said calmly.

"Who is not?" the marquess and Sheldrake asked.

"The bodyguard. He's not in the hands of the authorities."

"Why is he not?" the marquess thundered.

"Because I did this to him."

She flicked her fingers again, and, where Sheldrake had stood, there remained only a pile of clothing. Until, upon closer inspection, they saw the toad. He struggled out of a leg of the pantaloons, his warty green and brown skin stark against the buff color of the fine wool.

It glared up at Neul. "Ribbit."

"Farewell, Lord Sheldrake," Neul said pleasantly. With the tip of one slipper, she nudged him out of the clothes, which she then caused to disappear.

"Dear God," the marquess muttered, staring at the toad, who sat there a minute longer before hopping away into the bed of Sweet Williams. "Dear God."

"How did you do that?" Verity asked, wrestling with the tiny doubt that argued what she'd just witnessed was not merely clever trickery.

Neul smiled. "Quite easily, I assure you."

"Where is Sheldrake?" the marquess asked.

"Neul pointed to the flower bed. "There."

"Was that real?" Verity struggled with what she'd seen with her own eyes. "Is Lord Sheldrake truly a toad?"

Neul regarded the direction in which Sheldrake had hopped. "Haven't you always thought so?"

"Yes, but—"

The marquess seemed to study the older woman, his face slightly pale. "What *are* you, Neul?"

She took a deep breath and quickly released it. "A faery." She swallowed, but maintained a composed demeanor.

"Ridiculous," the marquess announced. He hesitated. "A faery?"

Neul and Seumus nodded.

"Are you a faery, too?" Verity asked Seumus.

"Nay," he answered.

Verity saw Neul's eyes glisten with moisture as she looked at Verity's father. Seumus strolled away, his hands in his pockets. Verity took Neul's hand and gave her an encouraging little squeeze. After all, she understood what it was to love someone who considered himself different from you.

"And Torcuil?" she inquired softly, afraid of hearing the answer, yet needing to know.

"His kind are not called faeries," Neul said gently.

Verity turned on her heel and ran across the lawn in the direction she'd last seen Torcuil walking.

She sped through a formal garden, between hedges and flower beds. A painful stitch caught in her side. Her bonnet flew off. At last she came to a large bower lushly covered with a vining plant she did not recognize. It bloomed in profusion, studding the bower with fragrant white flowers. In the deep shade of this perfumed haven, she found Torcuil.

He sat on a long granite bench, his booted feet planted wide on the new spring grass, his elbows leaning on his knees, his head bowed. Listlessly, he twirled a white flower between the fingers of one hand.

Her mind whirled, her heart trembled, she wanted to hear Torcuil deny her fears.

"Neul just showed us the most amazing trick," she told him, her words rushed and breathless. "She turned Lord Sheldrake into a toad, and she said—"

"I have to return home," Torcuil said, his voice flat.

She froze. He hadn't denied anything, hadn't commented on the wildness of her tale, but all she could think of was that he was leaving. "I'll come with you."

He lifted his head and looked up at her. "Ye canna come where I must go."

Verity sank to her knees in front of him. She grasped his strong upper arms. "I will go wherever you go."

Torcuil shook his head. "Nay. Ye canna go, Anemone." He traced her cheek with the flower, and through the vine-filtered sunlight, she saw the misery in his beautiful face. "Ye'd no survive."

Desperation tightened her fingers on his arms. "I will," she insisted. "I'm much stronger than I look, you know."

"Ye'd drown," he said, his voice dull and lifeless.

She frowned in confusion. "Drown? Where is this home of yours?"

"Beneath the sea."

A hysterical bubble threatened to burst inside her. He was teasing. It was poorly done, but he didn't mean what he was saying. He couldn't. But she found no evidence in his expression to indicate that what he said was anything but the truth.

At the bottom of the sea? Impossible! She didn't believe anyone but fish could live beneath the sea. But then . . . she hadn't believed in faeries, either.

"Are you"— her voice cracked—"a water faery?"

He hesitated, his dark eyes searching her face. "Nay. No a water faery. I'm . . ." He dragged in a raw breath and harshly released it. "I'm a silkie."

Verity moistened her suddenly dry lips. "What is a silkie?" If he would only tell her, she would try to believe. She *would* believe—her future depended upon it.

He rose slowly to his feet, drawing her up, too. Then he began to undress.

"What . . . what are you doing?" she asked.

"Showing you."

She held her silence while he finished undressing. When he finally stood nude, he reached into an inner pocket of his coat and removed a folded piece of richly furred sealskin.

She followed him out to the long sand flats, to the edge of the water.

He turned his head, but his eyes didn't meet hers. "Stay here."

Torcuil waded farther out, and when the water came to his waist, he opened the sealskin, and she saw that it was, in fact, a simple hood. He slipped it on his head and dove into the water.

Verity waited for him to come back up, but she had no idea what to expect. Minutes passed with no sign of him. No one could stay under water that long—not and survive!

"Torcuil!" Heedless of her gown and slippers, she ran into the water, slogging forward as she went deeper. "Torcuil!" She found the place where she thought he had been standing when he'd dived. With her hands she tried to feel around, hoping to find him, fearful of encountering his lifeless body. "Torcuil, please! Come back to me." Her body convulsed with silent sobs.

Then, some distance from her, a sleek sable head

broke the water. She tried to hold herself still, her breathing shallow and uneven, as dark eyes watched her.

It couldn't be, she thought. He couldn't be . . . She choked down wild laughter. It was only coincidence. Of course, that was it—coincidence. But something inside her told her it wasn't so.

The seal disappeared under the water. Verity stared at the spot where he had been.

Dear Lord.

A seal.

The man she loved could turn into a seal. He lived under the sea. *And he was leaving her.*

Torcuil rose up out of the water in front of her, tall and beautifully human once again. Water runneled down his face. His heavy, wet hair clung to his neck and shoulders.

"A silkie," she murmured shakily.

"Aye," he said.

"Not a Highlander."

One edge of his mouth curled up. "No a Highlander."

"Well." She searched for words to more articulately express her surprise and confusion, and tearing anguish. But she could only think of one thing to say. "Don't go," she whispered hoarsely.

His throat worked. "I canna stay, Anemone," he said, his voice low and rough. "To do so might condemn my clan to extinction."

"Will you come back?"

He looked away. "Dinna do this, dear heart. 'Tis already more than I can bear to leave ye once."

"Do you love me, Torcuil?"

She saw the torment plain in his face. "How can ye ask? I love ye more than I've ever loved anyone in my life." He lifted a dripping hand to smooth her hair. "More than I'll love anyone ever again."

"Then love me now," she whispered raggedly, reaching

up and gently taking hold of his warrior's braids. "Love me now, for the rest of our lives."

"Now, when ye know 'tis the end?"

"Especially now. How else will I be able to go on?"

He framed her face with gentle hands, the hands she had seen wielding a sword and pistols with ruthless skill. Then he lowered his face to hers and tenderly claimed her lips. Softly at first, feathering across her mouth like a sigh, tempting her with ethereal promise.

She wouldn't think of his leaving, she thought fiercely. Time was eternal. This moment could last forever, encapsulated in infinity. Twining her arms around his neck, she willed it to be so.

His lips moved across her cheek in a trail of lingering kisses to her jaw. "Ah, my sweet Anemone," he breathed against the curve of her ear. "Ye hold my heart in the palm of yer hand."

Her throat tightened with unshed tears. "As you have always held mine," she told him chokingly.

As if she were no heavier than a leaf, Torcuil lifted her in his arms. He carried her out of the water and across the sand flat, back into their sheltered corner of the garden. In the bower, he spread his coat upon the generously proportioned bench. Then he folded his waistcoat and set it at one end.

A pillow, she thought incongruously. He'd made a pillow for her head.

He reached out and plucked a velvety white flower from the bower's vine. This he tucked behind her ear.

Tears spilled over her lashes, onto her cheeks. She clung to him in silent desperation, her cheek pressed to his bare chest, listening to the hammering of his heart.

He cupped her chin in his palm and gently lifted her face toward his. With the fingers of his other hand, he lightly brushed away her tears, then kissed the salty trails upward, to brush a soft caress against each of her eyelids.

Stepping behind her, his fingers went to work at the hooks, ties, and buttons of her sodden gown. Then he removed her corset, her chemise and petticoat. As her garments came off, the sun warmed her skin. A crisp whiff of breeze glided over her, and she marveled at the sensuous freedom. Was this how silkies felt?

He again drew her into his embrace. She ran her hand over his upper arms, enjoying the graceful undulation of smooth skin over long, strong sinew. Nimbly, he removed the pins from her hair, seeming to enjoy the tumble he liberated. His fingers laced through it, careful not to dislodge the flower.

She smiled up at him, her heart expanding as she drank in the sight of his beloved, beautiful face, framed by the dark fall of his hair, his warrior's braids entwined with the black ribbons she'd plaited through them this morning.

He slanted his lips over hers, teasing, tasting, enticing. His tongue stroked against hers, filling her with a restive aching. His hands sleeked over her bare back. Against her, she felt his growing arousal. Its rigid size sent a curl of anxiety through her, until she recalled the wonders Fanny had confided to her. Then she forgot everything when he stroked his fingertips over her breast, coming near, but never touching, her nipple. His hand moved to her other breast, where his fingertips trailed over the pale, delicate skin, circling the hard, aching nipple, until she thought she'd go mad.

Then, lowering his head, he took one distended bud into his mouth. He suckled, he nipped, then suckled more, sending the sweet, spicy wine of desire pounding through her veins. The heavy, throbbing ache within her grew more demanding. Instinctively, her fingers curled around him. His sharply indrawn breath hissed through his clenched teeth.

Instantly, she released him, shoving her hand behind her back. "I-I-I'm sorry," she apologized, her eyes large with worry that she'd harmed him. "I didn't mean to hurt you."

He leaned his forehead against hers. "Nay, Anemone. Ye dinna hurt me. 'Tis only that yer touch felt so verra *good.*"

Good? "Shall I . . . shall I touch you . . . again?"

"Aye," he whispered. "Touch me again."

Emboldened by his response, she touched him again, sliding her hand over his pulsing, voluptuous arousal. He arched his head back, the muscles in his neck erect with tension. As her hand moved, his breathing grew shallower, his chest rapidly rising and falling. And then she felt it, the humming, glittering energy she'd felt once before, pouring into her through her point of contact with him.

Abruptly, he caught her wrist and moved her hand away. He lifted her in his arms and lay her on the wide, long bench, her head pillowed on his waistcoat. Kneeling beside her on the grass, he swept his hands lightly over her body, as if memorizing each curve, swell, and dip of it.

The tingling hum of energy thrilled her every nerve. He seemed to know where to touch her, how to touch her. He employed fingers, tongue, and teeth, leading her higher and higher. His breath sighed warm against her sensitized skin, sending her the short remaining distance into trembling need.

"Torcuil," she pleaded, unsure of what she truly needed.

He joined her on the bench, rising above her, his body supported by the columns of his arms. She laced her fingers through his hair, and he brought his mouth to hers in a desperate joining. His touch infused her with the radiant, tingling shimmer that rippled through her, bringing with it pleasure that penetrated every fiber of her.

Torcuil thrust into Verity. Dazedly, she wondered that her body could accommodate him so easily. So joyfully. With each deep stroke, the shimmering increased in intensity, yet still a hunger burned inside her. She rose to meet him, shimmering, expectant, not knowing what she reached for, only aware that there was something else, something more . . .

The shimmer and the pleasure coalesced into a blinding sun of sensation, sending her arcing up off the bench, her fingers curling into his back. He captured her scream of startled rapture with his kiss. Then a tremor passed through Torcuil, and his body went taut, his head thrown back, his eyes squeezed shut. He clenched his jaws closed, locking the sound in his throat down to a growl.

Oh, Fanny had been so right, Verity thought dazedly.

Torcuil lowered himself to the narrow ledge on the bench, lying on his side. He gathered her into his arms, and she fit back to his chest, resting her head on his well-muscled arm. He gently smoothed her hair back behind her ear. "I'll love ye for the rest of my life," he said, his voice low and hoarse. "Ye are my own true mate."

She lifted her head. "Torcuil—"

"I want ye to remember that, Anemone."

The ragged urgency in his voice prompted her to nod, her chest tight with reawakening grief. "I will," she promised chokingly, unable to say more. She could not turn far enough to see his face, so she lifted her hand for him to take. It touched his cheek, and she felt the wet of tears.

She awoke to find herself alone in the bower, the garden shadows growing long. Without raising her head, she saw the tops of Torcuil's boots, with his chamois breeches and shirt folded neatly on top.

Beside her on the pillow of his waistcoat lay two black velvet ribbons.

22

Can there be a love which does not make demands on its object?
—Confucius

It was a quiet party that arrived back in London. After Neul's revelation to the marquess of her true nature, he had ceased courting her. Neul had called upon them a few times after their return to Ravenshaw House, and if Verity's heart had not already been so badly damaged, it would have broken as she watched brave Neul struggling to recapture what she and the marquess had shared before that day in the garden. But it took two people for love to prosper, and the marquess had pulled away.

Verity no longer went out to visit her friends and acquaintances. After a few had called on her, she'd informed Quenby that she was not at home to anyone. She felt disinclined to share in chatter about fashions, dances, and who had recently become engaged or wed. The man she had hoped to wed was gone. Now her life stretched out before her, long and gray and lonely.

She wept the morning she received notice that Fanny had delivered her baby, and Verity knew hers were selfish tears. She would never bear the children of the man she loved. As she sat in her darkened room, she felt sick with shame that she could not be more pleased for Fanny and George and their new baby boy. She sent her congratulations and went deeper into her depression.

Three weeks after the birth of Master Elbourn, the door to Verity's room swung open to reveal Columbine standing at the portal holding a tray bearing tea and toast. Her pretty young face set in stubborn lines, she marched into the bedchamber. Setting the tray on the bedside table, she arranged a wedge of toast on a plate and poured a cup of tea. These she held out to Verity, who lay on the tester bed.

"Here," Columbine said briskly. "Drink this tea and eat this toast. I'm not leaving until you do."

Verity would have shaken her head if it had not been so much of an effort. "Just put it on the table, Columbine."

Columbine's white-blond eyebrows drew down in a scowl. "You can't go on like this. You're not eating enough to keep a butterfly alive. And look at this room! You keep it so dark in here only a mushroom would prosper." She continued to hold out the tea and the toast.

With a resigned sigh, Verity took them. There would be no more solitude until she did as the girl bid, that was clear. She took a bite of buttered toast.

"All of it. You've got to eat every bite of the toast," Columbine said sternly, indicating the additional wedges on the tray. "You've lost so much weight, your gowns look like sacks on you. When you bother to put one on, that is. You do realize, don't you, that dressing gowns were not meant to be worn all day long, every day?" She boosted herself up to sit on the edge of the high bed. With obvious satisfaction, she watched Verity take another bite.

Verity swallowed. The stuff might have been sawdust for all the pleasure it brought her.

"Your father is pining, too," Columbine informed her. "Seumus is trying to coax him into taking a stroll in the garden."

Taking a sip of tea to wash the bread down her arid throat, Verity accepted that news with no surprise. Her father loved Neul, anyone could see that.

"Two more of your servants have quit." Columbine watched Verity take the last bite of the wedge, then slipped off her perch and picked up the plate. She loaded on two more half slices and handed it back.

Verity tried to muster enough concern to worry over the loss of Ravenshaw House staff. She'd wondered why Columbine, Seumus, and Fearghus had stayed on after Torcuil had left, but not enough to ask.

"Who quit this time?" she inquired, her voice faintly husky with disuse.

"An under footman and one of the maids. Said they couldn't stand working in a tomb."

Leaning back against the carved oak headboard, Verity choked down another piece of toast and wished the queasiness in her stomach would go away. In the several weeks since their return, she had taken no interest in running the household, and the harmony in which she'd once taken such pride had fallen into shambles. Only a handful of her staff remained, and now even that had been reduced. Verity found she simply did not care.

Columbine seemed to study her for a moment, pressing her lips together, rolling them inward a little. "He wanted to stay, you know," she said quietly.

Verity instinctively knew who "he" was. She swallowed hard against the lump of grief that gathered in her throat.

"He told his brother he wanted to stay and marry you."

"I know." Torcuil's brother had confessed to her what had passed between them.

"Torcuil wouldn't want you to do this to yourself," Columbine insisted.

Verity's stomach churned. "I know."

"I imagine he's pining for you, too," Columbine muttered.

Suddenly, Verity's stomach gave a threatening roll. She scrambled to the floor and dragged the chamber pot out from under the bed. Huddled miserably over the china receptacle, she retched up the little she had eaten.

Instantly, Columbine was at her side, smoothing Verity's hair back from her face until it was over. Then she rose and went to the washstand, where she moistened a cloth. She returned and handed it to Verity, who gratefully took it to wipe her mouth.

"This is the third time," Columbine said. "I'm sending for Mrs. Elbourn."

"Oh, no, don't," Verity replied weakly. She had no doubt that Fanny would come, if Columbine sent her a note relating Verity's illness. "It's only that my stomach is shrinking."

But Columbine refused to accept that the vomiting was not indicative of something more serious. "Then I will call a healer."

"No."

Columbine stood, arms akimbo, and studied Verity, who sat wilted on the floor. "Very well. Then *you* shall go to see Mrs. Elbourn."

Despite Verity's protests, Columbine bullied her into putting on a gown—a gown that hung loosely on her.

"I can't go out of the house looking like this," Verity whined as Columbine herded her down the stairs and through the entrance hall.

"Perhaps you should have thought of the consequences when you went into your decline," Columbine answered primly, nodding at Quenby, who opened the front door for them.

Mr. Teak sat waiting atop the carriage, in the street. Columbine ruthlessly hurried Verity forward. Daniel leaped down from his place and opened the door for them, handing them in with solemn concern.

As the coach rumbled into motion, Verity admitted to herself that she wanted to see Fanny anyway. Her cousin was too dear to her not to make the effort to personally felicitate her on having another healthy child. And, despite herself, Verity wanted to see the baby.

"We must stop at Kenyon's," she said. "I have purchases to make."

As soon as she entered the shop, she knew it had been a mistake. Memories of her visit with Torcuil, of his silly crossing his eyes, flooded her. Blinking back the tears, she managed to make her purchase of gifts for the new baby and Fanny and reach the coach before her grief overwhelmed her. Would there ever come a day when she would no longer spend the hours weeping?

When Verity and Columbine arrived at the Elbourns' house, they were greeted by Mrs. Jillings, who escorted them into the nursery, where Fanny sat by a sunny window, cradling her son in her arms. When she saw Verity, her face lighted. As her gaze moved over her, Fanny's expression changed to concern.

Verity pretended not to notice, managing a smile for her beloved cousin. "Do let me see little Jeremy."

"Would you like to hold him?"

With a sense of reverence, Verity took the infant into her arms. "Oh, Fanny, he's beautiful." The weight of the child in her arms brought the tightness of loss to her chest; she would never have children. "I own, he is very small," she said softly, fascinated by his tiny fingers, by his small mouth and button nose. Wide blue eyes regarded her.

Fanny chuckled. "They all start out that way."

"She's been sick," Columbine told Fanny bluntly.

"I can see," Fanny said, her sympathetic gaze taking stock of Verity. "I know you've been grieving over Torcuil's departure, Verity, but I didn't realize it had affected you to this extreme. I wish you had let me come to see you."

Shame filled Verity, but before Verity could answer, Columbine said, "No, I mean truly sick. She eats little enough, but she loses it each morning."

Fanny frowned slightly. "How long has this been going on?"

"It's only that I haven't felt hungry of late," Verity told her. "Likely my stomach is shrinking. It will take a while to get used to eating properly again."

"Two pieces of toast is not 'eating properly,'" Columbine informed Verity. To Fanny, she answered, "Three. This was the third morning."

Fanny took a slumbering Jeremy from Verity and placed him in his cradle. Immediately, a young woman Verity had not noticed was in the room came forward to take over the care of the babe.

As Fanny led Verity and Columbine out of the nursery, she said in a low voice, "Columbine, I wish to speak with my cousin alone for a few minutes. Would you please go downstairs and ask Mrs. Jillings to bring tea for the three of us to the drawing room? We will meet you there."

"Perhaps you can talk some sense into her," Columbine said. She headed toward the staircase.

Fanny guided Verity into her bedchamber and quietly closed the door behind them. Then she turned to her cousin. "Verity, did you have congress with Torcuil?"

A hot tide of embarrassment swept up Verity's face. "Yes."

"Have you . . . had your monthly courses?"

"I-I don't remember." Time had melted into a meaningless, empty misery. Now, as she tried to think back, she realized that she had not. "No."

Fanny touched her cheek. "Verity, dear," she said gently. "I believe you are with child."

Slowly, the full meaning of what Fanny was saying dawned on Verity. With child. Torcuil's child. She felt as if the sun had suddenly risen in her heart. For the first time in many weeks, she truly smiled. She grabbed Fanny's hand and held it between her own. "Torcuil's child." Tears of joy rolled down her cheeks. "Our child."

As the months passed, the scandal was discussed in every drawing room and club, whispered about at countless balls and dinners and musicales. The verdict was always the same: Like mother, like daughter.

Verity's father never raged, never condemned her. Perhaps it was because she bloomed with such life. The babe she carried gave her new purpose. She moved about the house with much of her old energy.

"It's time we left London, Daughter," he told her one morning at breakfast. "There's nothing for us here."

Verity's gaze moved over her father's dear face. He'd lost weight, and while he attended to his business affairs and even occasionally visited his club, he was only going through the motions. "There is Neul."

Her father looked out the window. "There was Neul. But my blasted fear and pride drove her away. The damage is done." After a minute, he turned to her. "What do you say to my opening the house in Ireland?"

Verity went to her father, and kissed him on the cheek. "It's a wonderful idea, Papa."

So while her father tied up loose ends in his business concerns, Verity prepared to move and arranged for the closing of Ravenshaw House except for a maintaining staff. Then she wrote Neul a letter. Lastly, she called on Fanny to bid her good-bye. The cousins wept until George promised to take the family to Ireland for a visit after Verity delivered her baby.

On their last night at Ravenshaw House, Neul appeared at the door. The marquess hesitated, as if he expected to be rebuffed, then asked her to join him in the drawing room. An hour later they emerged, exchanging loving glances, their faces wreathed in smiles. Verity's father announced that Neul had consented to be his wife.

Verity exclaimed, and felicitated, and congratulated, and poured the wine to celebrate the occasion. Later, when she lay in bed alone, she wept for Torcuil, for the husband she would never have.

The wind smelled of rain to come, but Verity continued toward the cliffs. She lifted her face to the moist sea air. Walking was less graceful these days, she thought with a smile, as she lumbered to her customary spot. Soon she would hold her child in her arms.

The terns wheeled above her, their mournful cries echoed against the tall cliffs and rocks. All around her, the tall emerald grass swayed. She'd found a measure of contentment on this remote Irish estate. She took shameless pleasure in Neul's mothering, and she enjoyed the twinkling humor and good sense of the Irish country folk. But this spot was her favorite. Here, more clearly than anywhere, she could conjure the memories of Torcuil.

As the sky darkened and the wind strengthened, Verity

knew she should go back to the house, but something held her there as she watched the storm roll in.

Rain burst from the low, ominous clouds, driving down to pelt against her. Below, waves battered the cliffs.

Salty tears mingled with the wet of rain as she recalled that she'd first met Torcuil in a storm like this. He'd leaped from the night, beautiful and dangerous, his hair flying around him like a dark flag.

As she gazed out over the sea, she noticed a tall figure climbing the stone-carved steps that led from the narrow, beleaguered beach. To Verity's astonishment, he was naked. His long sable hair streamed on the wind. With a familiar grace, he made his way toward the top.

Before he drew close enough for her to see his face, she knew who he was. "Torcuil!" she cried, but the storm tore his name away and she knew he could not hear her.

Yet he looked up. His eyes widened, and his solemn mouth curved in a joyous smile.

Torcuil raced to the top of the steps. He swept her into his arms, whirling her through the fine gray mist, away from the cliffs. Wet grass licked at her skirts, at his long legs. She felt the strength and warmth of his arms around her, as she'd never thought to again.

"Dinna weep, Anemone," he said, his deep, lilting voice dearer to her than any other.

She laughed through her tears, drinking in every treasured detail of his beautiful face. She reached up to touch his forehead, his cheeks, his nose, his lips. Her fingers went to his warrior's braids, now adorned with nuggets of gold and bits of red coral.

"It's you," she said, her voice unsteady. "It's really you."

"Aye." His voice was husky with emotion. "I've been searchin' for ye for months. I thought I'd never find ye."

Her face crumpled. "I thought I'd never see you again," she sobbed.

He brushed back her windblown hair. "I couldna live without ye, Verity." He took her mouth in a kiss that told her of his desperation and fear, and of his love. When he finally lifted his head, he looked down at the swell of her that separated them, and in his dark eyes she saw wonder bloom.

"So that's what it was," he said, his words filled with the hush of awe. He raised his eyes to her's. "I felt the glamour."

"Glamour?" she hiccuped.

He laughed and kissed her again. "Aye, the glamour. The fair folk feel it when one of their own is near." He carefully stroked her belly, and she felt a curious tingle pass from his hand to their child within her. As if in recognition, the babe moved. A smaller, fainter tingle issued from her womb.

"'Tis a silkie child ye bear," he said softly. "Will ye be able to love him?"

She nodded, emotion high in her throat. "With all my heart, as I love his father." A thought occurred to her, and she caught her bottom lip between her teeth. "Torcuil, when it's time, will he—or she—be born as a . . . seal?"

He touched her cheek. "Nay. Only were ye to be a silkie in seal guise would he be delivered so. But, a silkie he *will* be. And he'll need to spend some time in his seal form."

Verity swallowed. It would take some getting used to, that ability to change form, but it would be a small price to pay for this precious child. "Have there been many such unions? Between silkies and, uh, people?"

Torcuil laughed. "Dear heart, silkies are people, too. But fruitful unions have been few." He took her rain-drenched hand and pressed a kiss into her palm. "Perhaps the love must be great before a child can come of it."

Her lips trembled with the force of her emotion. "Yes," she whispered.

For the first time, Torcuil seemed to notice the driving storm around them. "Ye should no be outside in this. Let's go see yer father." He eased his arm around her waist and started toward the great, rambling country house, visible in the near distance. "I've come to take ye for my mate."

She lumbered beside him, following her belly. "I think you already have."

He grinned. "Aye. And 'tis a beautiful sight ye are."

Abruptly, Verity stopped. "Are you staying?" she demanded. "Because if you're not—" Her throat closed and she shook her head.

"I'm stayin', dear heart. My father recovered well enough. Our argument shook the caverns when I told him I intended to wed a land woman. Then Eideard returned to make his explanation." He shrugged, but she knew the time could not have been easy for him. "My youngest brother is now my father's heir. Eideard and I will serve as councilors. Should something happen to my father, Mother will act as regent until Anndra comes of age."

Torcuil swept Verity up into his arms and continued toward the old mansion. "I went to Ravenshaw House, but it was closed. Fanny and her husband had gone to attend an elder in the country, but no one could tell me where. I scoured England searchin' for ye. When they finally returned, she told me ye'd come here."

"Will you have to visit your people often?" she asked. Would she be left behind, again and again?

"Once in a while. But my people can come to me as often as I go to them." He stopped and, despite the rain, searched her face. "I swear, I'll be a good husband to ye, Verity. Will ye be my wife?"

Verity smiled up at him. They were truly going to make their life together. She laughed from the happiness she couldn't keep bottled up inside her. "I'll be your wife, but only if you answer my question correctly. Do you need me?"

"More than my life's blood," he said, and kissed her with such tenderness she knew her need for him was every bit as great.

As Torcuil strode through the storm, with her in his arms, Verity's heart sang. This man had brought her wonder, and she had brought him love.

Together they had magic.

Epilogue

It takes all sorts to make a world.
—Seventeenth-Century Proverb

The moon rising high above the Scottish coast drenched the ancient castle on the cliffs in pale silver. The windows of the great hall shined golden with the glittering light of pixie dust, and, within, the ethereal strains of "Greensleeves" followed the more sprightly melody of "The Faeries' Reel."

Verity welcomed the tall, attractive silkies, who entered the hall in a steady stream. They bore gifts of golden chalices and platters from sunken galleons and nautilus shells filled with pearls.

Seawater ran down their long dark hair and their graceful, nude bodies, so she escorted them into the rooms where giggling pixie children helped with the baths and a handful of good-natured faery matrons cast their magic to dry them. From there, Torcuil's clansmen knew their way to the chamber where Verity kept the fabulous gowns and suits she'd had made for them. Laughing and chatting, both males and females of the clan donned their garments in the same large room, unconcerned with the proprieties of land folk. Once attired, they hurried to the great hall.

When Verity and Torcuil had taken up residence in the long-deserted castle of Dunmuir shortly after their wedding, Torcuil had wanted his clan to meet her. More than that, he had wanted them to embrace her, so he'd insisted that he and Verity give a ball for Clan MacCodrum, hoping the music and the dancing would please his kin as much as it had him, thereby creating a favorable impression. The silkies had seen through Torcuil's machinations, but they had taken Verity to their hearts anyway. And they had been thoroughly enchanted with dancing and music. Now, any excuse would do for a ball, so Verity kept sumptuous clothes ready for them. It presented quite a sight, these tall, graceful people, clad in their marvelous gowns or breeches and coats, dancing barefoot. They had spurned the constriction of stockings and shoes, just as they rejected undergarments as utterly useless.

Eideard and Richenda had moved into the mansion they'd built less than a day's ride north of them. They, too, were here tonight, though they'd left their two young daughters at home asleep.

This evening's celebration was in honor of Seumus's natal anniversary. Which year it represented, no one knew, for broonies lived very long lives, and Seumus had ceased counting decades ago.

When finally it appeared as if all the MacCodrums had entered the great hall, Verity went to the bathing room. "Thank you so much for helping," she told her assistants. A cherubic pixie child clung to her leg, drenching the cloth-of-silver skirt of her gown. Verity picked him up. "Where is your mother, little acorn?" she asked. With one chubby hand, the small pixie pointed in the direction of the ballroom.

With a flick of her fingers, a faery matron smilingly dried the child and Verity's gown. "Columbine is in the great hall," she said. "Come, we don't want to miss Seumus cutting his cake."

The custom of presenting a tall, fantastical cake with gossamer icing had started with a modest cake on the refreshment table at the first ball. Fearghus had tried to cut the thing and had wound up with cake all over the floor, the table, and himself. The fair folk had found it hugely amusing, and so with each ball the cake had grown more and more elaborate, and someone special was chosen to cut it while everyone watched. Verity had never understood what they all found so funny, but neither did Richenda. Perhaps it was strictly a fair folk thing, some peculiar quirk in humor.

As Verity, the young pixies, and the older faery ladies hurried through the Gothic stone halls, Torcuil reached out from behind a stone column and caught Verity's arm, twirling her into his embrace. Columbine's youngest giggled and flew out of her arms into those of a faery, who winked at the silkie and his wife, then hurried on.

"I havena had two minutes with ye all night," Torcuil murmured, teasing her lips with light kisses. "Have I told ye how lovely ye look tonight?"

"Yes," she answered breathlessly, struggling to distract her rising desire. "But your family—"

"Knows that I'm mad with love for ye." He backed toward the stairs that led to their bedchamber, tugging her gently along with him. He wore a wickedly sensual smile, and she read the promise in his eyes.

"You're playing unfairly," she objected softly.

"Aye." He gave her one more, thorough kiss, then relented with a long-suffering sigh. "Shall we go together to wish a good night to yer son?"

"Of course," she murmured, still clinging to him. Then she blinked. "Why is he *my* son of a sudden? What mischief has little Lachlann done?"

"More than most two-year-olds can manage," Torcuil assured her with a proud smile. He took her hand and they walked through the wide, arched corridors of aged stone toward their son's nursery.

As they wound their way through the castle, her husband's hand warm around hers, Verity reflected on the things that had changed in two years. She had a new sister who might one day be able to turn wicked men into toads, but it was too early to tell if she was more faery than mortal.

Torcuil had been working with George Elbourn—a man upon whose discretion they could depend—to make Clan MacCodrum a landowner, a financier, an importer, a shipbuilder—oh, the list seemed endless, and the treasury of the clan was still barely scratched. Someday in the not-too-distant future, Clan MacCodrum would be a power to be reckoned with, and they would wield their might to keep themselves safe from extermination. Land folk wouldn't know the MacCodrums were anything but tall, comely Scots with an eccentric refusal to cut their luxurious dark hair.

Seumus and Fearghus had returned to Scotland with Torcuil and Verity, while Columbine had fallen in love with a handsome faery in Ireland, where they now made their home among his kindred.

Between kisses and caresses, it took longer than usual to reach the nursery, where, as Verity had suspected, they found the marquess and Neul reading faery stories to Lachlann.

"Aye, I thought as much," Torcuil said, as he and Verity reached their son's bed. "Spoilin' the wee lad again, eh?"

"We only just got here," the marquess objected, relinquishing the child to his father. "Your parents have been monopolizing our grandson most of the evening."

Torcuil stroked Lachlann's unshorn blond hair, his beautiful face filled with tender affection. "It's disturbed them that his hair is this golden color. A seal with golden fur might prove a target for land folk hunters. But they're comin' to terms with their concerns."

It worried Verity, too, but Torcuil was daily teaching their son caution. The true nature of silkies and other fair folk must remain a secret if they planned to safely move into the spheres of land folk and eventually into their chambers of power.

Nestled safely in his father's arms, Lachlann turned his head to see his mother, and his dark eyes crinkled with delight. Verity leaned forward and nuzzled his sweet little cheek, breathing in that faint, fresh scent of sea air from his skin. So very much like his father, she thought, her heart expanding.

She looked up to meet Torcuil's gaze and experienced a renewal of her love. His loyalty and his courage had set them on a path that would determine the future of Clan MacCodrum. This child in their arms, and the ones to follow, would inherit a much richer world, one filled with music and magic, but also with challenges as yet unknown.

As their father had done, they would have to learn to master the storms that raged in the seas and in their hearts. Like Verity, they must seize the wonder.

She prayed they would all rise to the tasks before them, and she knew that she and Torcuil would do everything they could to see their children through. But not even a faery could predict the outcome of this vast undertaking.

Only the future would tell.